Twilight Forever Rising

LENA MEYDAN

TRANSLATED BY ANDREW BROMFIELD

TOR®
fantasy

A TOM DOHERTY ASSOCIATES BOOK
NEW YORK

This is a work of fiction. All of the characters, organizations, and events portrayed in this novel are either products of the author's imagination or are used fictitiously.

TWILIGHT FOREVER RISING

Copyright © 2005 by Elena Bichkova

English translation copyright © 2010 by Elena Bichkova

Originally published as Кровные братья by Alfa-Book in Moscow, Russia

A Tor Book
Published by Tom Doherty Associates, LLC
175 Fifth Avenue
New York, NY 10010

www.tor-forge.com

Tor® is a registered trademark of Tom Doherty Associates, LLC.

ISBN 978-0-7653-6552-1

Tor books may be purchased for educational, business, or promotional use. For information on bulk purchases, please contact Macmillan Corporate and Premium Sales Department at 1-800-221-7945, extension 5442, or write specialmarkets@macmillan.com.

First Edition: October 2010
First Mass Market Edition: October 2014

Printed in the United States of America

0 9 8 7 6 5 4 3 2 1

Acknowledgments

I would like to thank my agent, Robert Gottlieb, Trident Media Group, LLC, for his faith in this book, and perseverance. Olga Gottlieb for her support and invaluable help in adapting the book and in the communications. The translator, Andrew Bromfield, for his wonderful translation that has preserved the lyricism and melody of the original language. Stacy Hague-Hill for her excellent work in editing the text, as well as to the Tor publishing house for their professionalism and for helping the book to find its readership.

PROLOGUE

September 12, 1977

The city had been drowning in rain for two days. The raindrops trickled across the battered asphalt surface of the road and tapped on the roof of the blue Bentley. One of the car's windows was lowered; there was a lighted cigarette glowing on the driver's side, and quiet singing came from the radio. The car was parked in a side street, concealed from the eyes of anyone walking past by the thick curtain of rain and the late-evening gloom.

But who would be out walking in this weather, in this place, at this hour? Taking a stroll after sunset in a district with no streetlamps, where human vermin roam the streets, could cost you your wallet and your health in the bargain. Although even the local specialists in easy pickings were in no hurry to come out tonight and were still lurking in their dens.

There were several dark forms—large garbage bins—standing near the car. One of them had been tipped over, and its contents were scattered across the asphalt.

"Very picturesque." The man sitting at the wheel chuckled and contemptuously shook the ash off his cigarette onto the wet surface of the road. "A perfect match for the local scenery and the philosophy of that new youth movement. What is it they call themselves? Punks? A garbage dump is just the right place for that kind of trend."

In Vladislav Volfger's opinion, human beings just kept getting crazier as time went by. Always thinking up something new, trying to organize their days so they could escape from themselves for a while and feel completely independent. Free of everything that interfered with their lives. Free of laws, society, rules, politics, morality, the opinions of others. Always struggling to break away from the foul morass of life and soar above it. If they failed, they became garbage themselves. They set themselves against everything in a desperate attempt to feel the thrill of really living, only to die sooner or later anyway. That was how it had always been, that was how it would always be. An implacable law. Death came for everyone. Well . . . almost everyone.

There were occasional exceptions.

A scraggy rain-soaked cat was fishing scraps of food out from under the lid of one of the bins. Volfger had been sitting still for about five minutes already, watching the animal. It could sense his presence. In fact, it had almost run off immediately, but hunger had proved stronger than its sense of self-preservation. And anyway, the man hadn't made any attempt to attack, so after hesitating for a moment, the cat had begun its meal. But it remained on the alert, eating hurriedly, and it was obvious from every movement that it wanted to get out of there as quickly as possible.

The wail of a police siren sounded faintly through the shroud of rain and died away in the distance a few seconds later.

The police were rarely seen in this part of the city, which was a maze of crooked alleys, courtyards, and dead ends. Cops didn't like places like this. There were too many problems to deal with— and who needed that? Especially on their pay. They were much better off patrolling the brightly lit central boulevards of the capital—wander into a swamp like this and you just got stuck, with a whole heap of useless reports to write before you could escape.

Twenty-three thirty-eight.

The radio and the rain sang along together. Joe Dassin was telling the whole world what would happen to him "if not for you." A good song.

The cigarette burned all the way down, and Volfger tossed it into the darkness outside the window.

Chris had wanted to come with him. He'd been planning to. And "if not for her," he would definitely have come. But Flora had driven up in her poisonous red Jaguar and walked into the hall of the mansion with her rapid stride cramped by her long narrow skirt and enveloped everyone in the fragrance of Chanel No. 5. His pupil's face had assumed a quite indescribable expression of amorous idiocy, painstakingly concealed.

"Mentor, are you sure you don't need any company?"

"Quite sure. You can go. She won't wait for long."

"I can put off the date."

"No, you can't. She's already got the collar on you. All she has to do now is fasten on the lead."

Chris had smiled. He didn't appear frightened by the idea of playing the part of a beautiful Dahanavar's devoted dog. He was willing to pursue his destiny to the end.

"Go on, go. She's waiting."

Flora was standing in front of a painting by Monet, examining it with cool interest. When she heard footsteps, she turned around with a smile and held out her hand to be kissed.

"My compliments, my Lady. You are quite astonishingly beautiful today. As always, indeed."

"Good evening, irresistible Chris," Flora said, smiling even more enchantingly, and a cunning glint appeared in her topaz blue eyes. "Are you willing to be my escort tonight?"

It would have been stupid to refuse and choose a boring meeting and his old teacher over a woman like that.

TWENTY-THREE forty-five.

Volfger looked at his watch again and allowed himself a small display of feelings. He frowned in annoyance.

The person he was waiting for was late, and this was as strange as the place chosen for the meeting. The other party was famous for his punctuality.

Could something have happened? There was no point in running through all the possibilities. Diplomatic relations were too unstable nowadays. New alliances were constantly forged and just as quickly falling apart. It was impossible to second-guess everyone. They all tried to win the best arrangement for their own side and make things as painful as possible for their rivals. That was the way it always was. The petty infighting had been going on for years. But this time, something serious seemed to be happening.

Joe Dassin had finished his song a long time ago, and now the speakers were relaying some mawkish tune. The Mentor ruthlessly switched off the radio and started listening to the rain. In his opinion, it sounded far less irritating than modern music.

Volfger and the cat heard the footsteps at the precise same moment. The little animal raised its head from its food, pricking up its ears. Deciding not to take any risks, it jumped nimbly down off the garbage bin and disappeared into the basement window of one of the scruffy buildings.

The Mentor strained his eyes, trying to make out the figure that had emerged from a side entrance. But the rain blurred his view. All he could see was a vague silhouette standing at the far end of the short street. But one thing he was certain of—it was one of the brothers. So the meeting was going to happen after all. Excellent.

Volfger frowned in exasperation when he realized that the late arrival was not going to approach the car. He just gestured with one hand for Volfger to follow him, then turned away and disappeared around the corner without looking back.

The Mentor hadn't been expecting that sort of impudence: *I wonder who that young whelp is? Some novice who doesn't know the rules, or . . . Can this business really be so serious that the other party is afraid of his own shadow? Who could he be worried about? Amir? Or are Miklosh's soldiers trying to arrange another night of blood?*

Volfger pensively drummed his fingers on the steering wheel. All right. Today he would make an exception and play according to the rules of the person who had invited him to meet. He took the keys out of the ignition, dropped them in his pocket, picked up his raincoat off the seat beside him, and stepped out of the car. As if to spite him, the rain started falling more heavily, making his upturned collar useless. After glancing around one last time at the empty little street, Volfger set out to follow his kinsman.

He never reached the corner where the other man had disappeared. The humans appeared so suddenly, they seemed to spring up out of nowhere. Seven of them. Tough young guys with guns in their hands.

For a brief moment, Volfger felt disappointed. Had they no respect at all for him, if they could arrange a farce like this? And even use humans? Any idiot could have seen that this was a trap. And a senseless one. A pitiful bungled job. Could the Nachterret possibly have set this up? Without Miklosh's permission? He would never have allowed any nonsense like this. Before he made a move, he always made certain it couldn't fail.

The Mentor didn't wait for the strangers to tell him what they wanted. He had no intention of holding protracted negotiations in the torrential rain, let alone of meeting any of their demands. Volfger curled his lips scornfully and snapped the thumb and middle finger of his left hand. The seven humans collapsed onto the wet, pitted asphalt. Into the puddles and the garbage from the overturned bins.

He didn't look at them. Men who had died from instantaneous heart failure didn't represent any danger. But the person who had beckoned him into the trap and disappeared into the alley could still cause problems.

The minutes kept passing, but Chris's teacher still didn't move. He was waiting. Listening to the rustling of the rain that had completely soaked his hair and was flowing down his face and pouring inside his collar. A quarter of an hour went by before the Mentor allowed himself to relax. Apparently, whoever set the trap had realized it had backfired and got out while the going was good. He wondered who it was.

Volfger walked across to the nearest body and nudged the pistol clutched in its hand with the toe of his shoe. What had they expected to achieve with that? People really were going crazy. It was strange . . . these young guys didn't look like hired killers. They weren't that professional. The job had been bungled too badly for the experienced hit men that Miklosh hired. He leaned down over the dead man.

He could bring him back to life and make him tell the truth.

A fine stream of necromantic magic flowed into the human body. Concentrating to his utmost, Volfger filled up the dead cells with his own energy. He had to take care not to damage the brain accidentally, otherwise it would be impossible to get articulate answers to all his questions. A mindless zombie was no use to him.

As he worked, he intuitively monitored the situation, listening carefully all the time. He heard the rustling of the rain and the quiet wheeze as air was drawn into the lungs of the reanimated man. Everything was calm. There was no danger, but there was still something vaguely bothering the Mentor. Keeping him on his guard.

Before the thought could even take shape in his mind, the Mentor acted, throwing himself forward and to the left and simultaneously summoning the Veil of Night.

But he was too late.

The back of his head was scorched by a sudden frost, and he collapsed to his knees. The cold ran along his nerves, jamming the synapses and neurons. It fettered his muscles, paralyzed his body, sheared away his will. The unknown attacker had deprived him of the ability to use magic, catching him out like a stupid young pup. They had lured him into the open, waited until he felt safe, and struck from behind. It was the only way to defeat him. Not one of the elders could have coped with the Mentor face-to-face. And even now, the sorcerer could tell that the strength of the Medusa Kiss used by his enemy had been multiplied ten or even twenty times over. Not just one blood brother, but several had put their power into the paralyzing spell. And by no means the weakest of the brothers, either. . . .

The sound of a car approaching. A door slamming. Footsteps walking through puddles.

"Pick up the body. Mr. Volfger Vladislav has a long journey ahead of him. Someone drive the Bentley away. Preferably to a place where no one will ever find it. . . ."

The Mentor felt totally humiliated. And he had only his own poor judgment to blame. When you live too long, you start believing in your own invulnerability, and then sooner or later, you make a mistake.

A few minutes later, there was not a trace left of what had happened in the dark street. The bodies had all been cleared away, and the cars had driven off.

Nothing but darkness and rain.

The hungry cat emerged cautiously from its hiding place and looked around. Seeing that the danger had passed, it went back to the garbage bin.

The Telepath

I can stand brute force, but brute reason is quite unbearable. There is something unfair about its use. It is hitting below the intellect.

—Oscar Wilde, *The Picture of Dorian Gray*

September 11, 2004
Darel Dahanavar

"Well, do you like her?" I heard Chris whisper behind my back, but I didn't answer, just cleared my throat.

She was standing under a streetlamp, leaning against the railings of the bridge with her long hair fluttering in the wind. The girl I had been following for a week.

"Then what's the problem?" my omnipresent friend asked again. "Go across to her and let's get going."

"I'm not sure."

"Nonsense. Go on, I'll wait."

There was something strange about this girl. Something unusual. I couldn't understand what exactly it was that disturbed me so much whenever I was near her. It was as if she gave off a fresh, cool breeze. Like the air streaming off a glacier. And it wasn't even a matter of how pure her blood was, although I could tell it wasn't polluted with drugs or nicotine or disease.

"Group one," Chris murmured. "Rhesus positive."

Seeing the expression of annoyance on my face, he laughed. "Take no notice. Just thinking aloud."

He turned and walked away along the dark, windy street.

The girl with a golden halo that looked like sunlight raised her head, following the flight of a white moth, and I glimpsed her gentle smile.

But it disappeared the moment she saw me standing beside her.

"Hi. Not disturbing you, am I?"

This girl I didn't know shook her head and lowered her eyes, and her lips quivered again in that half-smile that made my heart contract so sweetly.

"Darel," I said in a quiet voice, realizing that I was already unobtrusively *clouding her awareness*. Just a tiny bit, so that she would feel she could trust me.

"Loraine."

I had heard her voice before. Clear and gentle, as mellow as this autumn night. She had spoken only three words then— "Botanic Lane, please"—and the yellow taxi had whisked her away just when I had made up my mind to approach her. But she wouldn't escape so easily today.

"Do you like walking at night?"

"Yes." A single light, carefree word, a flutter of long eyelashes, and then again, more quietly: "Yes, I like it."

She was already starting to get used to me. Going through the stage of *recognition*. For her, it ought to feel like meeting someone she knew, and more than that—someone she liked very much.

"It's a nice way to pass the time."

We were already walking side by side from one streetlamp to the next, with our shadows running on ahead of us, growing shorter and longer by turns. She kept glancing at me curiously, too shy to keep her eyes on my face for long, but more at ease now. More natural. And I didn't have to look at the girl. I could *see* her with my inner vision: the breeze from the glacier, the cool, steady current of air. And the light. The diffuse light of a sunny autumn day.

I knew the way her eyelashes were fluttering, the way the lobe of her little ear turned pink when the wind touched it, blowing the golden curls of hair onto her cheeks; I knew her blue eyes were reflecting the cold light of the streetlamps, the black river, perhaps even my face in profile.

"Shall we go in?"

I glanced across at the brightly lit windows of a bar, and of course, I heard a quiet "Yes" in reply.

It was warm inside; there was soft music playing and a bluish haze of cigarette smoke drifting in the air. I saw Bert at a table at the far side of the room. I didn't know his girl, but she smiled, raising her glass, and I got the feeling I'd met her somewhere before.

Bert nodded coldly in reply to my silent greeting and turned away. I hadn't expected anything else.

Loraine noticed this expressive exchange of glances, but she didn't say anything, although her eyes flashed with curiosity. I ordered whiskey for myself and light French wine in a tall glass for her. Loraine smiled at my choice. "How did you know I like Aligoté?"

I thought the color of the wine was like her hair. But I didn't answer, I just raised my glass.

When she turned her head, I saw the line of her exposed neck and a slim vein pulsing rapidly under the thin skin. . . . My lips felt hot and I raised my glass to my mouth so that the touch of the cold glass would quench the unbearable fever.

The girl looked out the window. On the opposite side of the street was a gigantic billboard with a huge black-and-white photo in the Gothic style. I read momentary regret in Loraine's feelings as she thought that she would never get to the opening night of the season that was plastered over all the billboards just then.

I nodded at the poster. "Would you like to go to that opera?"

She gave me a rather scornful look. "The tickets are all sold out."

"On a personal pass. A good friend of mine always has a couple to spare."

"Is he the director of the theater?"

"No, he's singing the lead."

Loraine smiled suspiciously and declared in an officious voice: "Hemran Vance is singing the lead in the *Phantom*."

But the girl hadn't caught me out in a lie. I really did know the famous rock singer, the idol of the entire younger generation. When I told her I did, her eyes turned round in amazement. I was scorched by the brightness of her elation.

"Really! You know him! Hemran himself?" Any number of exclamation marks could have been inserted into this impulsive outburst. "How long have you been acquainted?"

"Quite a long time. I can introduce you if you like."

"Of course!" she exclaimed loudly, then looked around, embarrassed. Bert was looking down into his glass. His girl was smiling and checking out the barman. No one was taking any notice of us.

I found myself liking Hemran more than ever. He'd never know what a good turn he had done me.

"In that case, I invite you to the theater."

She smiled again with that self-confident eighteen-year-old girl's smile.

"So you really could introduce me to him?"

"Yes, tomorrow, after the opening night." I got up and put some money on the bar counter.

She hadn't been expecting me to go so soon. I saw a glint of surprise in her eyes, but it faded immediately.

"I'll be waiting for you in the foyer, tomorrow evening at nine."

Gentle lights glimmered in the misty depths of her eyes. Like the final rays of the setting sun. I watched this miracle for a few moments, then turned away quickly and walked out.

The stars were going out one by one. Cool air was streaming off the river as it awoke to the day. The darkness of the night was slowly receding across the transparent sky toward the west, retreating in the face of the rising sun. . . .

Of course, Chris hadn't waited for me. But I made it in time. As always. The first bright rays shot over the horizon just as I closed the door behind me.

THE opera house was built in the century before last. A massive building of gray stone, copiously decorated with columns, statues, and bas-reliefs. Monumental, cold, and majestic. Lit with gentle golden spotlights.

Marble Apollo in his flowing tunic could hardly hold back his four-in-hand of rampant horses straining to leap down off the slope of the roof. Muses, nymphs, satyrs, and maenads posed in a frozen dance around the sun god, as if they were about to throw themselves under the wheels of his chariot.

Seagulls sat on the shoulders of the stone dancers and the heads of the horses. When the entire flock rose into the air, their piercing cries drowned out the noise of the city.

There was a breath of freshness blowing from the direction of the river. The broad black ribbon glinted in the light of the streetlamps, reflecting an inverted bridge and the buildings on the embankment. The quivering forms seemed to be floating over the shallow waves. The sluice gates were closed, and three pleasure boats were waiting in the lock for the water to rise to the right level. I could hear music playing, the hubbub of people out on the town, the cries of seagulls.

There were people inside the opera house; I could feel them even through the stone walls. A gathering of small warm lights. A buzzing swarm with high voices like the screeches of the river birds soaring above its low, monotonous song. Loraine's *note* was a pure, resonant G.

I saw her slender figure beside one of the columns in the foyer, her golden hair tumbling across her shoulders as she looked around impatiently, trying to spot me in the crowd. I saw her twirl her rolled-up program in her hands and mechanically tuck a rebellious lock of hair behind her ear, already sensing my intent gaze but still not aware that I was watching her.

A group of skinny, long-legged teenagers was hovering about not far away. Edgy, defiant, and insecure all at the same time. They "creaked" like wagon wheels that needed grease, or their inner screeching rose to an almost unbearable crescendo. I shuddered inside and damped down my sensitivity.

"Hi."

Loraine gave a gentle start and turned around. Now I could see her glowing face with the slightly embarrassed expression, the faint shadows under her eyes, the bright flush on her cheeks.

"Good evening." She was excited; she had been looking forward to this meeting. And now she saw me in the bright light of a thousand electric lamps. My pale face, my eyes, the red rose in my hands. She blushed and turned her eyes away.

In the box I sat slightly behind her, moving my chair back so that I could see the line of her neck with those golden tresses cascading onto it, the snow white lace of her blouse . . . and the stage.

I had surprised the girl yet again.

Loraine had expected me to try to sit as close as possible. She didn't know that now, as my gaze caressed her tanned, unprotected neck, I was much closer to her than ever. Loraine turned her head to look at me, and those warm little lights were trembling in her blue eyes. The rose I brought had started slowly opening on her knees, responding to the warmth of her body.

The lights went out. The first chords of the overture sounded. Dangerously close, I heard the loud, ecstatic beating of a human heart.

I leaned forward and supported myself on the back of her chair, and Loraine started when she felt me breathing so close. I heard her trembling intake of breath, almost inaudible through the music. Without realizing what she was doing, obeying my secret desire, she leaned her head over slightly toward her shoulder, and there, so close to my lips, was the velvet skin of her neck.

Very slowly, very carefully, I moved aside the cascade of golden hair to reveal even more of that defenseless hollow between her shoulder and her collarbone. Again I heard words that were not spoken: *So what's the problem, kiss her!* A hot flame seared my lips, the music froze on a single note, the girl stopped breathing, the dancers hung motionless in the air, the world came to a standstill . . .

But I squeezed my hand into a tight fist until it hurt. Until my nails cut into my skin. The pain blunted my passion, and the fire receded. Again I could see, hear, and feel beyond my own desires.

I pulled away from the girl, the orchestra started playing again, and shaking off my dangerous web of enchantment, Loraine looked around and asked me:

"Do you like it?"

"Yes."

In the darkness of the hall, her eyes sparkled; golden light, almost like sunlight, glinted deep inside, where only I could see. I had completely forgotten that such things existed. But in some places they still did.

"But you're not even listening!"

"Yes, I am."

She shook her head and touched her lips with the scarlet flower. My feverish hunger became almost unbearable again.

"You're not listening. You're looking at me as if, as if . . ."

She couldn't find the words she wanted and turned back toward the stage.

There was no way she could have found them.

* * *

As usual, Hemran did not disappoint his fans. He was magnificent in the role of a bloodthirsty phantom with a heart full of torment. The rock singer's low, powerful, husky voice wove itself into the mighty strains of the organ, and I felt a chilly shiver run down my back when I heard those words of passionate despair: "I have set my life to music." Bach's composition set my heart pounding. The musical phrases held too much truth and pain, too many vivid living images.

I had to close my eyes and clench my fists again, because I was overwhelmed by a torrent of human feelings. Exultation, spellbound delight, dazed shock, sadness, superficial skepticism—"We've heard better than this"—but still, underneath, the same exultant admiration. And right there beside me, almost blinding me, Loraine's vivid astonishment. The girl was enthralled by the magic of the music and Hemran's voice. It was a shame that she didn't understand the Italian in which the phantom sang his aria.

I leaned close to the British singer's young fan and started translating in a whisper:

I am a madman! My eyes are opened now. There is no peace,
Only the passion within me is all-powerful.
My dream was as dangerous as the blade of a sword;
I have set my life to music,
I am a madman.

She listened carefully for a few seconds, then shook her head once and whispered furiously:

"No! Don't! It's not as good like that! I don't understand, but I can feel what he's saying!"

I moved back to my old position. It was true.

A long, lingering note from the organ drowned the singer's voice. The final words dissolved in a trembling F minor. For a moment the audience sat there in silence, spellbound, then it exploded into applause.

The girl turned toward me, her face glowing with delight. Her eyes were sparkling.

"Incredible! Absolutely fantastic!"

"Loraine."

She raised her dark eyebrows inquiringly.

"I'm sorry, I have to go out for a short while."

She started getting up to follow, keeping her eyes fixed on me in disappointment and surprise, but I touched her shoulder gently and made her sit back down.

"No, stay here. Wait for me. I'll be back soon. . . ."

I came back when the interval was almost over. My heart was calm again, almost cool. The embers of the recent conflagration were glowing peacefully somewhere in the depths of my soul.

Loraine didn't turn around when I walked into the box; she carried on absentmindedly tapping her program on the railing and gazing into the auditorium.

She was offended because I'd left her on her own in a theater she'd never been in before and she hadn't had a chance to look around.

"I'm sorry. I was delayed."

A slight shrug of the shoulders, setting the golden cascade of hair trembling, a brief, indifferent sigh. But my heart remained calm.

"Would you like an ice cream? Vanilla with nuts and maple syrup."

She glanced at me out of the corner of her eye and raised her eyebrows in surprise when she saw the perspiring cardboard cup with the plastic spoon in my hand. She laughed and took my offering.

"You must be telepathic. How did you guess I was absolutely dying for an ice cream?"

Just as she was about to start on her treat, she glanced at my face and said in an anxious voice:

"Darel, is that . . . blood?"

I touched my lips and looked at my fingers. On one of them there was a small scarlet drop of blood.

"I must have bit my lip."

"Do you want my handkerchief?"

She reached for her pocket, but I stopped her.

"No. Thank you. I have one. Eat your ice cream."

IN the final scene, when the human Phantom dies to the somber strains of the dark, heavy music, Loraine sat there cowering in her chair, deafening me with her pity for this imaginary character.

The curtain came down in total silence. And then there was more applause. Vance, hot, sweaty, and happy, with his silk shirt open across his chest, came out to take his bow, accepted the bouquets of flowers wrapped in crisp cellophane, and smiled at his colleagues onstage. But Loraine suddenly felt this wasn't the real thing any longer. She preferred the solitary, dangerous Phantom to this Brit reveling in the spotlight. She even began to doubt that she wanted to meet the singer.

"You should never touch your idols," I said in a low voice, "the gilt comes off on your fingers."[1]

"What?" Loraine asked, looking around at me from halfway between her chair and the door.

"Do you still want to see Vance close up?"

"Yes, of course." The momentary doubts were forgotten. *It's Vance, after all,* she thought.

---

1 Darel is quoting, slightly inaccurately, a phrase from Gustave Flaubert's novel *Madame Bovary*.

* * *

Unlike the glittering stage and the magnificent auditorium, the working premises of the opera house were cold, gray, and gloomy. Ceilings that were too high, with the remnants of old moldings, heavy chairs that creaked, drafts and all the noises that always go with an old building that isn't lived in. Swamped by the backstage bustle, audible only to my superacute hearing, were the singing of the wind in the attic, the cracking of the wooden panels as they dried out, the scrabbling of the rats in the heaps of old stage props in the basement. Rustling, whispering, sighing. The remains of old emotions, echoes of ancient passions. I think Chris would have seen genuine phantoms here, inhabitants of the world beyond who had not found peace.

I could only hear voices speaking scraps of monologues and sense the feelings. Sometimes distant and gray, as if they were covered in dust, sometimes exploding into bright, burning pain.

People had lived through other people's feelings here for too long, suffered too convincingly, loved and hated—every evening on the stage, every day in the rehearsal hall and the dressing rooms. Some of the more sensitive actors had probably seen phantoms here—sad, graceful little ballerinas with shoulders blue from the cold and slim legs; the black, hunchbacked figure of an old tragedian flitting across the end of a dark corridor.

But nobody was interested in mysterious sounds right now. The opera house was buzzing with live voices.

Vance was sitting in his changing room, in the company of some actor friends, a pair of attractive female admirers, and several bottles of wine. The narrow, brightly lit room was crammed with baskets of flowers. Their scents hung in the air, mingling with the smells of human sweat and theatrical makeup. The aroma of the white lilies was especially stifling.

Hemran was not playing to his audience anymore, but he still looked impressive, as he always did. His long, dark wavy hair hung down to the collar of his white shirt in casual style, and he had a silver chain as thick as a finger around his neck, with an amulet of some kind dangling from it.

His black leather trousers were slightly worn, and a drawing made in lipstick was drying on his right knee—a heart with a strand of barbed wire running through it. His face was like a peasant's or casual laborer's, with broad cheekbones and a heavy chin. Dark green, elusive eyes.

Vance preferred to look down into his glass rather than at the person he was talking to. But if you managed to glance into his eyes, you could see the human strength shimmering brightly in them. Inner genius. That was how I thought of that light.

The only reason the Faryartos hadn't taken him yet was that he wasn't handsome. And our bohemian community accepted only physically perfect human beings into its House.

Loraine stayed behind me, feeling a little shy but looking around curiously at the surroundings.

I was greeted with exclamations of friendly delight. They gave me a place beside Vance and handed me a glass of wine. Loraine squatted beside me on the edge of the chair, gazing delightedly at her idol.

On closer examination, the Brit looked tired. Absolutely whacked, exhausted. He had dark circles under his eyes and hollow cheeks. His heavy peasant hands lay wearily on the armrests of his chair as if they had just let go of the handle of a plow. Hemran had plowed the furrow of his opera honestly, and now he was resting. He wasn't buoyed up by the seething nervous energy that so many performers have after a show. The fatigue hit him just as soon as the curtain came down. He wanted to sleep, but tradition required him to sit with his friends and drink to a successful opening night.

"Well, how was it?" the rock singer inquired vaguely, scrutinizing the toe of his boot. The question was addressed to me. He knew I'd been at the performance.

"Great. I liked it. Only in the last act did you overact a bit."

"Ha!" said a young guy sitting opposite me, sticking out his lower lip contemptuously. His hair was dyed black, and he was dressed entirely in black leather. "The opinion of a dilettante."

Vance ignored this remark and looked at me intently. "How about the audience?"

"Absolutely ecstatic. Especially in the third act."

The deep crease in the singer's forehead relaxed, and he smiled.

"Rubbish," the skeptic declared. "You saw the audience reaction for yourself."

"Darel is an empath," Vance explained patiently. "He doesn't just see, he feels as well."

I felt Loraine's quick, thoughtful glance on me.

"And exactly what form does this hypersensitivity take?" The young guy in black leather looked at me suspiciously. "Can you sense the reaction of the entire audience?"

Kenzo laughed. I didn't know his real name, only his alias. He was the theater's leading man for almost all romantic hero roles. Not that he had any particular talent, but his regular, sculptural features were always pleasing to the eye.

"What, don't you believe him, Lord Vampire?" he asked mockingly. He took a bottle of champagne out of the ice bucket and drank from it, trying not to drop water on his trousers.

I thought I must have misheard.

"What did you call him?"

"Lord Vampire," repeated Ell, the bass guitarist with Vance's band. He reached out and took the bottle from his friend. "He's a Goth."

One of the girls, a blonde in a blue dress that was too tight for her, giggled. The other one, whose hair was unnaturally black, gazed adoringly at the "Lord," hanging on his every word.

There were many strange individuals among my friends, including some characters with highly exotic personality disorders. But I had never associated with Goths before. I stared at this new specimen of humanity with a curiosity matched only by Loraine's. I wondered how serious his interest in otherworldly forces really was.

The Lord Vampire thought he had shocked me, and now he waited with smug satisfaction for questions.

"Are you actually a vampire? A real one?"

"In our world nothing is real or permanent," he replied, relishing the attention everyone was giving him. "Everything is relative and temporary. Yes, I am a vampire."

Beside me, Loraine smiled skeptically, but she didn't make any comments. I looked intently at Vance's Goth friend. Black hair, almost certainly dyed, dark clothes, pale skin without a tan. Boundless delight in the dramatic image that he had invented for himself. And yes, of course yes, magnificent false fangs, which he demonstrated for me in a broad smile. A superb example of the art of dentistry.

"Incredible," I said thoughtfully. Convinced that he was more original than I, the Lord Vampire was flattered by my astonishment. "So you drink blood, then?"

"Naturally," he admitted casually. "Now and again it's necessary."

"And where do you get it?"

"Out of a can of tomato juice," said Kenzo. "The color and consistency are almost identical, and imagination supplies the missing taste and smell."

The "vampire" flashed his eyes at him angrily. Loraine and the blonde in the blue dress both snorted with laughter at the same moment. And I suddenly saw a vivid picture from the Goth's memory. A dark kitchen, lighted candles, red curtains on the windows. The Lord in a long-waisted burgundy dressing gown walking up to a black refrigerator, opening the door, and taking out a jar of thick red liquid. Filling a crystal goblet with an expression of impervious majesty on his face. Going into a room where a girl wearing a black negligee is lying on red silk cushions on the bed. She is wearing dark cherry red lipstick with black eye shadow, and her short hair is also as black as night. She slowly reaches out her hand, and the "vampire" hands her a goblet of tomato juice representing blood.

I bit my lower lip to stop myself laughing. It was better for this young guy to play at being a vampire than to become a real one. One of the Nachterret, for instance.

"I like Gothic, too," Loraine said unexpectedly, and blushed when everyone looked at her. "I mean Gothic music. Hemran, I heard your album *Nemesis,* it's all about that."

"I play all kinds of music," Vance replied condescendingly.

"This is Loraine," I put in. "A great fan of yours. Give her your autograph."

Hemran pulled out the drawer of the table beside him and rummaged noisily through its contents. "I had a gift edition CD in here somewhere. . . . Ah, there it is."

He took out a square flat box and a felt-tip pen, pulled out the paper insert from under the lid of the box, and signed it with a flourish below his photograph. He held it out to the girl.

"Here."

"To Loraine, who likes Gothic as much as I do," she read, and gave a deep sigh.

"Thank you! I never thought I would ever get to talk to Hemran Vance in person!" She blushed even more deeply.

"Don't mention it. Come again, I'll be glad to see you," he replied with a smile. He was pleased. Words of approval and the adoration of an attractive young fan were just the kind of support he needed. Creativity can be capricious; it requires constant stimulation.

We sat there for another fifteen minutes or so, listening to the musicians' small talk, then said good-bye and left. Loraine could have spent the entire night in the theater, but I was beginning to feel hungry.

IT was cold outside. And windy. The sky was covered by low clouds, and every now and then they released a sprinkling of drizzle.

We walked to the metro through the back streets and court-yards. It was quiet, and the only people we saw were a couple of melancholy dog owners who had to accompany their four-legged friends on urgent sorties. The humans took no notice of us, but the animals were alarmed.

A huge Alsatian raised the fur on the scruff of its neck and growled—but there was more fear than menace in its voice. A shaggy lapdog squealed and dashed to the far end of a court-yard, then started barking hysterically.

"Dogs don't like you," Loraine remarked. "I wonder why?"

"Probably because cats do," I joked. Although it wasn't true. Cats were afraid of me as well.

The girl smiled and let her mind wander, her attention skip-ping from one thing to another: *My friends will be surprised . . . Vance's personal autograph . . . Darel's a nice guy, even if he is a bit weird. But at least he's not like that Goth. . . .*

"I think it's stupid." She voiced her most recent thought as she looked at the brightly lit window of the building we were walk-ing past. "Thinking that you're a vampire."

"You think so?"

"You can play at being someone else. But being certain that you're a vampire is just weird. Don't you think so?"

"Pretense and reality are very close." I stepped across a puddle reflecting the glowing orb of a streetlamp and held out my hand to help her jump over the water. "You'd be surprised if you knew how many people want to be something that they really aren't. They find it easier to be someone else than to be themselves. It's a way of escaping from reality and their own shortcomings."

Loraine gave me a suspicious glance. "You wouldn't happen to be a psychologist, by any chance?"

"You heard already, I'm an empath."

"And you're happy with everything about yourself?"

"What makes you think that?"

"You look very pleased with yourself, kind of nonchalant. And you give off the same kind of feeling. A man who has everything in perfect order." She smiled. "No, I mean it, you're very . . ."

Loraine pondered, trying to find the right words. "Untroubled, I think that's it."

"Everyone has problems," I replied rather sharply. Talking about myself was beginning to wear thin. But that didn't bother Loraine.

"And what problems do you have?"

"I don't get out enough."

She laughed in surprise. "This is what you call not getting out enough?"

I glimpsed something unpleasant in her soul. The suspicion that I was lying and, even worse, trying to make myself seem special.

"I already said that lots of people would like to be what they're not. What they show is not what they really feel. But I sense their genuine feelings. Have you any idea how rarely I come across someone whose inner and outer emotions coincide?"

Loraine frowned. "You feel that because you're an empath?"

There was still a hint of doubt in her voice.

"Yes, being with you is easy for me. You say what you feel. I don't get that feeling of constant dichotomy, like when someone smiles at you when what he really feels is profound loathing."

Loraine lowered her head and looked down at her feet, considering. She accepted my explanation. And I admired her profile.

"But lots of people realize when someone's lying to them or being hypocritical. You don't have to have any special abilities for that."

"They realize. But they don't *feel* it the way I do."

The girl nodded. She wasn't offended or startled by my confession of uniqueness.

"And where do you work? I mean, is your job somehow connected with your abilities?"

"I'm a consultant with a . . . firm." It wasn't even a lie. Just a simplification.

"I see." Loraine couldn't possibly have any idea whom I advised about what, but she felt it would be rude to keep asking.

After that, we walked for five minutes without saying anything. The silence wasn't the oppressive kind, with two people trying desperately to think of ways to keep a flagging conversation going. I looked at her beautiful pensive face and relished the calmness that she radiated. It wasn't only my magical influence that was making her like me more and more.

We came out onto the avenue, where there was a strong, gusty wind. Patches of black sky were visible through breaks in the clouds, but we couldn't see the stars since they were outshone by the bright lights of the advertisements. Cars went rushing past along the road, fine drops of water flying off their smooth, polished sides.

I offered to take Loraine home in a taxi. But she refused, saying the metro was more convenient for her. We exchanged telephone numbers. I waited for her to go down into the subway and then walked along beside the highway, studying the people hurrying toward me. Faces that were tired, preoccupied, sullen, happy, indifferent, interested . . . I liked to wander around the city, among the humans. Not with any purpose in mind. To pick someone out of the crowd without looking and read his thoughts, see the world colored with his feelings. For one person the night was black, hostile, and cold, for another it was mystical and romantic, and for another it was best used for sleep or sex.

I walked up a narrow stairway onto a railway bridge. Leaned on the railing, watching the occasional car zoom past below me. A suburban train rattled by behind me, enveloping me in a wave of heat. The iron railings shook, transmitting the vibration to my hands.

I realized I already missed the feeling I had when Loraine was there. Warm and carefree. Cheerful. I saw the world illuminated by the sun, so real in her memories. For some reason, none of my human friends had images in their minds of leaves dappled with sunlight, long shafts of light reaching between the trunks of trees, the black shadows of buildings. No one, except her.

I closed my eyes, picturing it all more realistically, and suddenly, through the clattering of another train, the murmuring of voices, and the howling of the wind in the piers of the bridge, I heard a distant *call*. A desolate, desperate howl.

Darel! Darel, help! Help!

Turning toward the direction from which the *call* had come, I said in my mind:

I hear you. Who's calling me?

Artur . . . Archie. I'm at the Chameleon.

I'll be there . . . I glanced at my watch. *In fifteen minutes. Wait.*

I'm waiting, the voice sobbed.

I was there in seven and a half minutes. I knew the street well. It had several nightclubs and bars with dubious reputations. Soldiers from the military academy around the corner often came to this street to take a break from the tedium of the army. I used to come here myself perhaps once every two weeks to eat—there were about thirty similar spots in the city, and I visited them regularly.

I could sense Archie's presence from his shrill flashes of panic and fear.

I'd seen him at Constance's place—a young guy who'd been turning up there occasionally for the last three months. Tall, skinny, awkward, nervous. When he ran into me in the corridor, he stared at me in awe and stepped aside to make way. He had the look of a naughty puppy who was expecting a slap; he always wanted to do everything right, though he had absolutely no idea what "right" actually meant. And hidden away in the depths of his soul was the rage of despair.

I wondered what my younger brother had done. I didn't need to wonder why he hadn't asked Constance for help. The hot-tempered Irishwoman tended to hand out severe punishments even for the smallest mistakes. But I had a reputation in the House as being liberal and lenient.

As always, the club was noisy and dark and smoky. Girls, decent and not so decent, jostled in the doorway. A group of brash young guys made lazy conversation as they watched from a distance with avid greed. Mostly they were interested in the not-so-decent girls and the cheap drinks you could buy with a guest flyer. There were some young ladies wandering about whose profession could be read easily enough in their faces. . . . Food, nothing but food.

By established tradition, one of the female security guards latched on to me. She checked my pockets twice and, as usual, didn't find anything taboo. She remembered my face and was genuinely convinced I was a pervert who came to the club for some shady gratification. I found her prudish arrogance and spiteful "I know all about you" amusing.

Chris never went to clubs like this. He was irritated by the crowd, the rudeness of the security guards, and the music. In fact, though, we had come here together once: he had looked around the small dance hall with an inscrutable expression, walked into the bar, and then walked out without saying a word.

ARCHIE was waiting for me. He was squatting with his back against the wall in the men's restroom, looking at the tiled floor. His tangled hair was hanging down over his face, the leather jacket intended to bulk out his skinny figure had slipped off his shoulders, his bent knees stuck out at a sharp angle, and his jeans were torn across one of them. Either a fashion statement or the result of a fight. No one was taking any notice of the young guy in distress. They didn't want to know.

Hanging just below the ceiling were three TVs. One of them was sluggishly running through the scenes of an old porn movie. In the opposite corner two guys were smoking hastily, passing a joint back and forth. In one of the cubicles something was beating against the wall at regular intervals, and water was running in a broken tank.

Guys came in and went out, leaving behind a field of quivering, confused emotion that I tried to cut myself off from completely.

"Hi."

Archie lifted his head and saw me, and the profound despair on his face was replaced by desperate hope. He jumped to his feet, staggering because his legs were numb after sitting in the same pose for so long. He grabbed hold of my sleeve.

"Darel. It's great that you came."

The guys with the joint glanced at us curiously, but I put up a light *screen,* and the smokers lost all interest in us. For a while, we ceased to exist for humans.

"What happened?"

He let go of my sleeve, clenched his fists, and sniffed.

"I killed her. A woman. In the Labyrinth. I didn't mean to. It just happened. By accident. She jerked and I . . ."

He was having difficulty speaking, as if he had to force out the words. And he looked at me bitterly, expecting to hear justified reproaches and insults.

"Are you sure?"

"Of course! Yes, I'm sure."

This was ugly. And bad timing. A human being killed in a public place by one of the Dahanavar would affect the delicate political balance among our Houses. I could just imagine Amir's smug face. "Esteemed mormolikas, you talk about being humane, but you yourselves slaughter mortals in brothels. Ah, it wasn't a brothel? A nightclub?"

My feelings as I imagined these words must have shown on my face, or the echo must have reached Archie. He sniffed again.

"I know! I shouldn't have done it. I didn't mean to. It happened by accident! Constance will realize straightaway that I killed her. We're not supposed to. We don't have any right to kill. And the police . . . They'll find the body and . . . My fingerprints are all over the place. On her handbag and her necklace. She had this wide, shiny thing round her neck. . . . And my phone number, I gave her my card. Idiot! What an idiot I am."

He punched his fist against his forehead in his despair. I grabbed his arm before he could do himself any more serious damage.

"Where did it happen?"

"In the Labyrinth. I told you. They'll arrest me now, won't they? They'll put me in jail. Listen, I can't go to jail. I just can't."

"Calm down!"

He shuddered and stopped talking, frightened by my yell.

"First, let's go and take a look."

"I'm not going. No! No, I can't go back there."

"You're going."

And, of course, Archie went.

I glanced briefly at my companion, trying to *feel* him. It's more difficult with kinsmen than with humans. As if each of us is surrounded by a dark, thick curtain concealing our thoughts and feelings. If he wants to, a brother can part it slightly in order to communicate mentally or tighten it to make his mental defenses impenetrable.

But I could disperse a *shield* no matter how secure it was (which was why I was valued in my own family), only this time there was no need to demonstrate my abilities. Either Archie didn't yet know how to defend himself against telepathic attack or he was too upset. Even when I just barely *touched* him, I felt his fear. And I couldn't tell what he was most afraid of—Constance's anger (our Dahanavar Ladies are terrible in their fury), the police (for some reason, this fear was very strong), or the unpredictable consequences of breaking the Oath taken in ancient times by several families: the Dahanavar, the Cadavercitan, the Nosoforos, the Ligamentia, the Faryartos, and the Upieschi were not supposed to take the lives of mortals.

Dahanavars like myself had no right to cause humans any harm, either physical or psychological. Out of ethical considerations and for the good name of the family. The Cadavercitan and Upieschi were humane for purely practical reasons—kill today and tomorrow you'll have nothing to eat. The Ligamentia took the Oath for reasons of their own that are almost impossible to explain. The Faryartos were simply too beautiful and as extreme aesthetes abhorred the spectacle of death.

As for the Vricolakos—the only principle they upheld was the rule of circumstance and natural necessity. They could quite easily release a human alive, as long as he didn't start to annoy them somehow, in the same way gorged tigers sometimes do. But it wouldn't bother them for a moment if their victim happened to die.

The other two Houses couldn't give a damn for the Oath, for humans, or for us, either.

The Asiman could have based a case for their indifference to the lives of others on scientific necessity. If they had wanted to, that is. But they never tried to justify themselves to anyone. They couldn't care less about that. And the Nachterret were regarded as degenerates. While it was sometimes possible to reach an agreement with the Asiman about something, the "saviors of the night," as the Nachterret called themselves, perpetrated such gross atrocities that even Chris, who had seen so much, could talk about them only in Old French, because modern languages have lost more than half their expletives.

I knew almost nothing about the other families. They had disappeared, vanished at some point during the centuries gone by. Besides, nowadays nobody was much concerned about their ethical principles.

WE walked out into the corridor. The party was winding down. The main lights had been switched off, and the few people who were still there were all wasted, dazed, and spaced.

In the main hall, they were still playing syrupy tunes to young girls glumly strutting their stuff for first-year military students. As usual, the neon flashes from the ceiling set all my teeth aching.

The music on the second dance floor had a heavier beat. Girls wearing short silver skirts and skimpy tops were gyrating professionally in four cages set around the spacious room. In the center was a stage, and on Fridays they held vulgar competitions like "Win a sound system for the most erotic pose" or "Feel like a transvestite."

Running between the two dance floors was the Labyrinth. A dark corridor with niches that weren't lit provided secluded places for couples who came to the club. Standing to the right of the entrance was a security guard in a black suit with a big white badge on his chest. On the left there was a brand-new vending machine offering condoms and chewing gum. Pitiful flashes of emotions came surging out of the darkness, as if a crowd of drowsy reptiles had crawled in there to warm themselves.

I automatically shook my head and glanced at my companion, who was chewing on his lower lip.

"In there?"

"Yes."

"I'll go take a look."

But before I could, a torrent of incandescent fear, so powerful that it paralyzed my receptors for a moment, came flooding out of the Labyrinth. Then there was a loud howl and a teenager dashed into the hall, fastening up his jeans on the way.

"She's in there!" he howled. "In there! Dead! Covered in blood!"

Then the senseless panic began. Running, screaming; general pandemonium.

"That's it," Archie said in the calm, fated voice of a man who has resolved to commit suicide. "I'm finished."

"Not yet, you aren't."

I took him by the elbow, overcame his slight resistance, and led him to the corner as far away as possible from the entrance to the Labyrinth.

"I know who could help you."

My hopeless young kinsman squinted at two young girls hovering nearby and asked in a trembling voice:

"Who?"

"A necromancer, of course. Now keep quiet for a while."

Archie froze, not sure whether he should take my remark about a necromancer seriously. I focused, listened, and *called* in my mind:

Chris . . . Chris!

An entire minute of waiting, until finally:

Darel?

Chris, I need your help. Urgently.

Where are you?

The Chameleon Club.

On my way.

Archie looked into my eyes devotedly, shuddered, and asked: "Well? What?"

"We wait."

"Will he definitely come?"

"He promised. Now relax and explain why you're so afraid of the police."

Archie wasn't able to relax. He couldn't take his eyes off the dark opening of the Labyrinth, where the woman he had mutilated was lying, and he kept sighing nervously. In his memory I *saw* the girl, her bloody neck twisted unnaturally.

"They have something on me in their files. I was released on bail, and if they hang a murder on me as well . . ."

"Well, so what?"

"Dar, you don't understand? It's been too long since you were human. It's all the same to you! No one knows your address or remembers your face, except for others like you. But I . . . My parents will simply die if they find out their son's a murderer."

I took hold of his shoulders and turned him toward me, then looked into his face.

"And what will happen to them if they find out their son's a vampire? I presume they don't know about that?"

Archie bit his lip. I got the feeling he was about ready to burst into tears.

"How do you manage to hide it, boy? It's just not possible."

"My father goes away on business trips, he's away from home for a long time. I tell my mother I work nights. I know things can't go on like that for long, but . . . Darel, I love them, they're not to blame for anything! I can't abandon them."

"Oh, sure." I pushed the boy away, and he pressed himself

back against the wall again, looking at me with red eyes full of misery. "What I can't understand is why Constance turned you in the first place."

"I'm great with computers, a born hacker, I can break into any system. Constance says that could be very useful."

"Is that why the police are interested in you?"

"Yes. I got caught once. I managed to wriggle out of it. But this time . . . This time I don't know what's going to happen."

"How old are you?"

"Twenty."

"How long have you been in the family?"

"Four months."

"You stupid young fool. Does Constance know you're still seeing your human family?"

"I haven't told her, but she probably has some idea. She told me I have to forget my old life, my friends, my parents, but I can't. Don't tell her. She won't understand. And you . . . I know you can read feelings. Do you understand me?"

What desperately painful yearning. And all the mistakes he was going to make, trying to combine two incompatible lives.

"I understand you."

I understand how it is now, but it won't last long. In a few years you'll feel the strength inside you and lose your sympathy for mortals, you'll start to get annoyed by their clumsiness, their senseless scurrying about, their habits and weaknesses. The smell of human food will be unbearable, and the smell of their blood will be sweet and alluring. Then you'll become a worthy member of the family and Constance will stop getting angry with you.

"Darel." Archie touched my arm, interrupting my disagreeable reflections, and indicated a tall figure approaching us.

Everyone had heard of the legendary Chris, the most powerful sorcerer of the House of Cadavercitan. My Dahanavar brother gazed at this historical celebrity with an avid curiosity that overcame even his fear about his own fate. His thoughts amused me: *About twenty-eight . . . maybe thirty? Tall. But they say in the old times he used to be short. How long has he lived? Eight centuries? Ten. Yes, I can see he's old. It's not a modern face. Like something out of a picture. . . . But he's built. The girls must go crazy for him. He's French, isn't he? That's right. . . . And he's got black hair, too. Too long. And his eyes are a weird kind of green. Or is that because he's a necromancer?*

Recalling the Cadavercitan's specialty, Archie involuntarily took a step back. I laughed to myself and stepped forward to meet the sorcerer.

"Chris. I'm glad to see you. You got here in the nick of time."

"I know." My friend looked around, scanning the space in his own manner. He could already sense the familiar smell of death.

Archie sighed and gazed at me imploringly.

"You're his last hope," I said to the Cadavercitan, nodding toward the boy. "Do something, or he'll end up in big trouble."

Chris gave the hacker an indifferent look. Archie cringed under his gaze and didn't dare try to make any excuses.

"Chris, for my sake."

The Cadavercitan studied the petrified Archie for a few moments, then turned away and said in the same haughty tone of voice:

"Only for your sake, Darel. By the way, there are two police cars outside, with officers geared up for action, so you should be thinking up a plausible alibi for yourselves."

"Can we get to the body now?"

Chris shook his head; his gaze became blank, and his eyes turned dark as his pupils expanded. There was a sharp, fresh smell of aniseed in the air, completely out of place in the smoky Chameleon. Something started moving in Chris's fingers. He squeezed the round lump, which seemed to be alive, as hard as he could, whispering an incantation over it, then quickly bit his own wrist and allowed a few drops of blood to fall into the pulsating sphere.

"What did you do?" My curiosity was ill timed.

"You'll see in a moment," said Chris, gesturing for us to move farther away.

A moment later the corridor was filled with men in uniform, who pushed back the curious onlookers with calm efficiency. The most important witness—the teenage boy—was excitedly telling a somber-faced officer, obviously not for the first time, where and how he had found the body. The bleak-faced assistant director of the club was halfheartedly trying to explain the purpose of the Labyrinth and looking around anxiously. A doctor approached the opening.

At that moment, Chris raised his hand. Just after that, something incredible happened. With my inner sight I *saw* the girl, who only a few moments earlier had been lying in a dark cubbyhole in an unnatural pose with her neck twisted, jump up and take a few steps.

Then there she was standing in the entrance, beside the representatives of authority. Alive. What's more, there wasn't a drop of blood anywhere on her throat or face.

"What's wrong?" she asked an astounded police officer. "Come on, I said, what's wrong?"

"I'm sorry, young lady," the policeman began his unpleasant explanation. "We were informed that you—"

"But she was dead!" The young man could feel his status shifting from principal witness to general laughingstock. "I tell you, she was covered in blood, and she wasn't breathing!"

"Have you all lost your minds?" I didn't know what the woman was like when she was alive, but after she died she was definitely cantankerous. "What is this, some kind of idiotic joke? So I'm dead, am I?"

She turned to the doctor, who was smiling rather scathingly, and grabbed hold of his hand, screeching, "Touch me. Am I a corpse?"

Archie watched everything intently and giggled, glancing in delighted admiration at the director of the drama. Chris gave him a sideways look, winked almost imperceptibly, and then turned his attention back to the stage. The girl demanded that the doctor take her pulse, and he made a feeble attempt to fight her off.

"Calm down, young lady," one of the impassive police officers advised the "victim." "There's been a misunderstanding. The young man was mistaken."

"So I'm crazy now, am I?" the boy started up. "I saw her lying there with her neck broken. Right there! Like this!" He tried to demonstrate exactly how the dead woman had been lying, but they grabbed him by the scruff of the neck and put him back on his feet.

"I'll break your neck for you, you miserable junkie!" the dead beauty screeched furiously, and went for him.

The police officer turned crimson as the doctor turned away and started searching for something in his briefcase. More people joined the crowd, and the security guards tried in vain to push back the curious onlookers surrounding the pale assistant director, who had already realized that he would have to bear the full brunt of the entire scandal. And just at that moment, Chris opened his hand with a faint smile. The pulsating sphere twitched one last time and vanished in a puff of smoke.

Halfway through the sentence "I won't allow anyone to . . ." the girl suddenly turned pale, clutched at her heart, and, with a look of excruciating pain as the light in her eyes faded rapidly, collapsed on the floor.

The crowd froze. The total silence was broken by a woman's shrill sob, and a wave of amplified human emotions swept over me. The doctor instantly stopped grinning and dashed over to the girl. His assistant was already hastily pushing his way through the crowd to reach her. They started working on her, checking her pulse, applying cardiac massage and mouth-to-mouth resuscitation, but the motionless body failed to react.

"Pointless," said Chris, wiping his hand on a snow-white handkerchief. "She's dead."

"She's dead," the panting doctor repeated like an echo. "Cardiac arrest."

He looked in annoyance at the young boy who had started the whole mess. "You seem to be clairvoyant. She really is dead now."

"They'll decide that she had a weak heart," said Chris. "Let's go, there's nothing left for us to do here."

Archie and I followed him to the exit. Nobody stopped us. The police were satisfied that the whole thing amounted to no more than an ordinary incident, the management was glad the club wouldn't be closed, the crowd was busy digesting what it had seen. Of course, no one would stick their nose into the Labyrinth for a while, but the tragic event would gradually be forgotten, and everything would be the same as it was before.

"Thank you, Chris," Archie said in a surprisingly serious, calm voice. "You saved me. I owe you. If I can ever do anything to help you . . ."

The Cadavercitan glanced at him derisively, and the young Dahanavar stopped in confusion.

"It's hardly likely that I shall ever require your help, boy. That was primitive magic. It was no effort for me. Go, and next time be more careful."

Archie nodded, shook my hand furtively, and disappeared into one of the dark side streets at a fast walk, almost a run.

"It's a fine night," said Chris, looking up at the thin layer of light cloud covering the sky.

"So that was primitive magic?"

I looked at his wrist. The wound hadn't closed yet, and its edges were bleeding slightly.

"Absolutely primitive, Dar." My friend watched as the police cars drove away from the club.

"But you . . . what did you do, put her soul back into her body?"

The Cadavercitan looked at me in amused surprise.

"Oh, come on. Of course not. I'm not Lord God Almighty, to go breathing a soul into a dead body. It was simply a walking, talking puppet. I set the mechanism going for a few minutes and then stopped it again."

"And could you have made her live longer?"

"Yes, I can make zombies, they'll live for as long as necessary. But that's distasteful work. And trivial. It doesn't give me any satisfaction."

I decided I'd rather not know what kind of work did give the Cadavercitan satisfaction.

2

THE COUNCIL

It is always a silly thing to give advice, but to give good
advice is absolutely fatal.

—Oscar Wilde, "The Portrait of Mr. W. H."

September 14
Darel Dahanavar

Constance already knew everything—the instantaneous mental
communication between a teacher and the pupil she has turned
never fails. The enraged Fury with the bright red hair was attacking poor Archie mercilessly: "Cretin! Brainless imbecile!
Bungling fool!"

I sat in a chair and stretched out my legs, waiting to see what
would come next. The Irishwoman's low, slightly gruff voice had
a faint accent and was pleasant to listen to, and the black leather
suit with the short, tight skirt and her fiery red mane made her
look most exotic. At the same time, she looked very much in
place in Felicia's mansion. White columns, statues, marble walls
and floors, red-figure vases, and, smack in the middle of all this
antique magnificence, a hot-tempered, ginger-headed *dir dale*—I
think that's what the Irish used to call the vampirelike supernatural creatures who resembled us.

"What did I teach you? Can't you even remember elementary
rules, you idiot?"

"But Constance . . ." Archie sobbed, standing to attention in
front of her. "It happened by accident. I didn't mean to do it."

"Just look at him! He didn't *mean* to do it. We'll be feeding on rats soon, thanks to boneheads like you. But you couldn't even catch a rat."

Picturing Archie in the role of a rat catcher, I couldn't help smiling. Constance immediately turned on me.

"And which way were you looking?"

"Ease up, will you? This doesn't concern me."

"It does concern you, and it concerns me, too. The killing of a mortal concerns all of us. On the day when we're going to accuse the Asiman of treating humans with unjustifiable cruelty, my own pupil kills one of them!"

"Calm down." I took poor mortified Archie by the sleeve and sat him down on a chair. "The incident is closed. Chris did a magnificent—"

"Don't you understand?" Constance hovered over me, blocking out the light with her superb body. "How many times do I have to say it? Outsiders should never be involved in the private affairs of the House."

I jumped to my feet, forcing her to step back sharply.

"Make up your mind, my dear. What's most important to you, our reputation or preventing outsiders from interfering?"

That quieted her down a bit as she realized it made no sense to attack me. She nodded to tell Archie to leave, and he cut and ran. We heard him stomping up the stairs.

"I don't trust the Cadavercitan," Constance said. "I know he's loyal to us. But I simply can't put my confidence in a Master of Death."

"You just don't understand his magic."

"And you do?"

"No, but I can feel it."

"And by the way, about your special gift . . ."

She didn't finish what she was saying. We heard the sound of light footsteps, and Felicia walked into the atrium. Felicia, the beautiful Greek.

No doubt it was because she had always been the First Elder of our House that female Dahanavars were sometimes referred to as mormolikas. In ancient Greece, that was the name for girls who ensnared youths with their beauty and drank their young blood in the night.

Felicia of Alexandria was not tall. Her height of one meter and sixty-five centimeters was the same as that of the Venus de Milo. She had a classically proportioned figure, too, with wide-set, light-colored eyes and ash gray hair, and the bridge of her nose was straight. I think if any sculptor who knew his Hellenic art saw her in her pearl gray tunic, he would be bound to ask her to disrobe so that he could capture her perfect body in marble.

One day I thought about this too loudly. Our First Lady smiled demurely in my direction and glanced at a statue of Aphrodite by Praxiteles, drawing my attention to the remarkable resemblance between the living goddess and the marble one.

"Darel," Felicia said, looking up at me and rousing me from my reminiscences, "you're to accompany me to the council at the Regenant's mansion today."

"Can I take my car?"

"Do whatever you think necessary," our Lady replied.

Since the engine under the hood of my Pontiac could hardly be heard, there was nothing to prevent the song the speakers were playing from meandering lazily through the dark interior of the car like a slow-flowing river.

The midnight sun shone so brightly,
When I danced with you for the first time.
It has lit up my love,
And I believed your promises,
Like a child

A beautiful song. Most of my brothers might despise the human race, but not one of them was capable of creating music that conveyed intense feeling. I hummed along with the familiar melody. Dancing under any kind of sun, even the midnight variety, was an impossible dream now. From the moment I first saw Flora, I was no longer a child of the sun.

Well, look at that. In less than a minute, my reflective mood had taken a turn into depression. Could Constance be right? Was I starting to get old?

I turned off the CD player and put my foot down on the gas.

I was moving pretty fast, but I wasn't afraid of coming off the road. At that hour it was already deserted, and there aren't that many suicidal drivers in the world who really like to drive like the wind.

For a few minutes, there was nothing but wind and speed. The clear night sang all around, enveloping me in an autumn melody that urged me on to even greater recklessness.

Faster. And even faster.

When I saw the sign indicating my turn off the highway onto the road lined with private houses, I took my foot off the gas and became an exemplary driver.

On the road to the Regenant's mansion, I overtook only one car—a long black Rolls-Royce. I sensed my brothers behind the tinted windows, and once I was in front, I allowed myself a minor breach of the proprieties and read the passenger's thoughts. Currency exchange rates, falling oil prices, the sale of land for the construction of a new housing development. No doubt about it, these were the thoughts of the highly respected Upieschi.

Ten minutes later, my Pontiac pulled up in front of a pair of tall wrought-iron gates. There were only a few security guards. All humans, of course. Two broad-shouldered guys in suits came over to the car. I lowered the window and smiled.

"Good evening, gentlemen. I'm here for the meeting."

"Your name?"

"Darel Ericson."

One of them checked the papers he was holding, found my name in the list of guests, and nodded.

"Your ID, please."

I held out my driver's license. The security guards studied the photograph and checked it against the politely smiling original.

"All in order. Do you know the way?"

"Yes."

"Then good night to you, Mr. Ericson."

I nodded, flashed him another smile, and drove the Pontiac through the park toward the mansion. The young guy had been very courteous, from which I could draw only one conclusion: The House of Nachterret had not yet arrived. After they met Miklosh, human beings stopped being polite.

The avenue I was driving along was brightly lit, and the late-nineteenth-century-style lamps looked like immense glowworms. I couldn't help remembering.

When I was a child of eight, I got lost in a forest. It was dark. I was cold and afraid, and I didn't even have enough strength left to cry. But hundreds of bright little stars started twinkling in among the fir trees. The bright green specks of light drifted about haphazardly in the night, transforming it from a sullen old woman into a joyful young girl. They made me forget my fear and wait for that beautiful moment when the first rays of the sun shone through the trees. They helped me find my way.

Years later, when the night was already an old, familiar friend, I went back to that forest of my childhood. And there were bright glowworms. But now, every night I had to leave long before the blaze of dawn lit up the eastern sky.

THE Regenant's mansion was built in the Empire style. I drove the car to the left wing and parked it beside Felicia's black Jaguar.

There was a Ford Mustang there as well, but I didn't know whom it belonged to.

Constance was leaning casually against the Jaguar. She glanced at me with an annoyed look on her face. I didn't try to *read* her. The Irishwoman's chaotic thoughts and feelings could easily have given me a headache.

"Where's Felicia?"

"She's waiting for you inside."

Our First Lady was waiting in the vestibule beside a gigantic aquarium. In the constant stream of water flowing behind the glass, two huge sturgeon were swimming about lazily, barely moving their fins and occasionally touching each other with their pointed noses. The bony plates covering their long bodies looked smooth, but their skin seemed as tough and coarse as sandpaper. They gazed around intently through the black-slit pupils of yellow eyes that weren't like fish eyes at all. I could quite happily have spent a few minutes watching them through that transparent wall.

Felicia heard our footsteps as we approached. She turned around with a smile.

"Good night, Darel."

"Good night, Lady."

The Council Hall hadn't changed at all.

A round table of polished wood. High-backed chairs that were beautiful rather than comfortable. Scarlet-and-gold drapes, carpets and tapestries with images of ancient animals, paintings of classical subjects from ancient times set in heavy frames. Too much gold-and-scarlet brocade, too many unicorns. It all dazzled my eyes, and that blunted my sensitivity a bit.

We had turned up early. The Regenant's tall throne was empty. Felicia wanted to have a look around and give me time to concentrate. But, as I expected, the Dahanavar were not the only ones to use that strategy.

First of all, I saw Amir from the House of Asiman with two bodyguards. Amir was sitting in an armchair, looking as if these luxurious surroundings were his own private property and he found anyone else's presence tiresome and irritating. The yellowish skin of his lean face reflected glimmers of color from his flame red robe, making his hollow cheeks seem hot and flushed with fever. The thin, tightly compressed lips of an ascetic. A long nose, with nostrils ready to flare in anger at the slightest provocation. Behind hooded eyelids, the almond-shaped eyes blazed with a boundless craving for power, wealth, homage, and adoration. A craving that parched him even more powerfully than the fiery magic of his House. On the forefinger of his right hand, the chief warlock of the Asiman wore a ring with a ruby that attracted the eye with its glitter. His bodyguards gazed around indifferently.

Amir replied politely enough to Constance's greeting, but he ignored me. That was all right. My self-esteem wasn't going to be dented by his arrogance.

Alexander, head of the House of Faryartos, was also there. When he saw us, he came over to greet his Dahanavar allies. He looked as if he were thirty-eight years old. A tall, handsome man with the thoroughbred face of an aristocrat; long, wavy shoulder-length chestnut hair; and striking dark purple eyes. Dressed in casual, artistically elegant style: a cravat instead of a tie, a velvet jacket, a shirt with lace cuffs. A platinum signet ring with a translucent alexandrite on his little finger. His manner was relaxed and confident, yet I could sense caution in him.

"Felicia, glad to see you. Good evening, Darel."

Our First Lady replied with an elegant courtesy, expressing her affectionate goodwill for the entire Faryartos family and Alexander in particular. Not being gifted with that kind of diplomatic talent, I simply nodded.

Alexander gallantly led the smiling mormolika off to the table, casting a suspicious glance at me on the way. I sensed a certain degree of annoyance in it. This noble-born, cultured lover of art didn't like having his thoughts read. Especially by me.

The Faryartos had every right to feel offended because Felicia had brought a telepath. My presence could be interpreted as a clear challenge to the assembled company and a sign of disrespect for the Regenant.

But that didn't concern me.

Suddenly, I felt someone *touching* me persistently with his mind. I looked to the right and shuddered. There was one of the Nachterret, leaning against a wall hung with burgundy fabric in the darkest part of the hall. Johan, the right hand of the head of the House. Massively tall, with great broad shoulders. In his human life he had been a mercenary, a soldier of fortune. His dark, deep-set eyes were half-concealed by thick, bushy eyebrows. His pitch black beard contrasted garishly with his completely bald head. As always, he was wearing a black leather cloak and muddy boots.

The longer I looked at him, the more clearly I saw the true appearance concealed behind that perfectly normal face: it was monstrously ugly, predatory. Repulsively predatory, like an ancient reptile prepared to devour everything in its way.

Acting very cautiously, out of a strangely morbid curiosity, I *touched* him and recoiled in revulsion. It felt as if I'd stepped into thick, filthy, greasy slurry with something wallowing lazily under the surface. I imagined having to immerse myself completely in that stinking murk during the evening in order to catch at least one coherent thought, and I felt sick.

The Nachterret sensed my revulsion. He laughed insolently straight into my face, displaying his magnificently sharpened fangs, and said:

"Greetings, brother."

His voice was hoarse: the intonation was human, but the note of derision was not.

I didn't answer and tried to move away as quickly as possible.

We wouldn't be able to reach any agreement with them. They wouldn't agree to anything. They didn't care whom they ate—us, humans, or one another. The only reason the Nachterret hadn't emerged from their lairs yet was that hunting on the streets of a city was dangerous.

Ah, there were the representatives of the Vricolakos family. I was hoping they wouldn't come. Reading illogical thoughts, clutching at unstable emotions, and experiencing everything in terms of animal instinct for a whole evening was no more attractive than immersing myself in the noxious emanations of the Nachterret.

The werewolves' long cloaks were lined with gray fur, a reference to the name of their house, Vricolakos, meaning "wearers of the wolf's skin." They preferred living far away from cities, at one with nature. This oneness was not just an empty word, either. The Vricolakos really did love the forest; they could *feel* it, and they could stay in it for years, unlike the urban blood brothers, who were accustomed to living only in large metropolises.

As the Vricolakos elder, Ivan Svetlov, walked past me, the edge of his cloak brushed my arm. Suddenly, I was engulfed in a green gloom . . . soft wet pine needles under my feet . . . rustling, whispering, and murmuring, the high-pitched whine of mosquitoes, the smell of wet fur and moldy leaves. . . . The werewolf ran his yellow eyes over me, sensed that I was scanning him, and laughed.

He didn't respect me. Almost despised me, in fact. Because I lived in the city, and when I attacked humans I tried to be careful. Didn't allow the hunting instinct to cloud my reason. Because I served and obeyed women. That was what he thought, served and obeyed.

I knew how incredibly strong and nimble on his feet he was. A large, mature wolf with a thick mane of coarse fur tinged with gray. A stern, cold, somber face with a hint of gray in the beard and mustache, too. Sparks of wild humor glinted in Ivan's yellow eyes. The family's clothing was traditional—suede boots, a linen shirt, trousers of soft leather, and a wide belt with a broad-bladed knife in a scabbard.

The Upieschi had also turned up early. The merchants, businessmen, and deal makers of our world. Three of them. The head of the corporation, Patron Upieschi, Ramon de Cobrero, was dressed in a magnificent Armani suit. Outwardly, the Spaniard didn't seem to have any feelings at all, apart from arrogance, which was written all over his pampered, swarthy face and expressed in his every movement. Ramon nodded in greeting to everyone, waited for one of his men to move out a chair for him, and sat down. He had learned long ago to restrain his southern temperament, and he rarely lost control.

Intelligent, stern, dogmatic, determined. His House was the only one that didn't have any special abilities, so instead of devoting his time to training his pupils in magic, he taught them to play the stock market. But I could *feel* a charge of energy in Ramon that I didn't understand, a vague blur with a sharp, fresh scent of ozone. His companions looked like copies of their leader, and on the inside they were like empty safes, all locked with the same key.

I had heard that once, in ancient times, this family used to be very powerful. But even now, although they had no magic powers, no one quarreled with the stock market brothers. If only because most of the blood brothers' money was deposited in their banks. The well-being of the other blood brothers depended to a large degree on the prosperity of the Upieschi.

That was everyone. There wouldn't be any Cadavercitan. They had stopped coming to the general assemblies a long time ago.

The side door swung open, and the Regenant appeared. A tall man about thirty-nine years old. More than anything else, he looked like a successful businessman—a superbly tailored dark gray suit, the gold cap of a fountain pen peeping out of his breast pocket, an expensive watch under the snow-white cuff of his shirt. A businessman or a politician, or maybe both. He held an important position in a ministry and turned over big deals on the stock exchange. He owned several factories, two shipyards, lived in a magnificent mansion in the best part of the city, and had a wife and two children.

He wasn't human, but he wasn't a vampire, either. It was an ancient curse on the royal line of Cornelis that every second child in the family would be born as a Regenant—a non–human being with the powers of a vampire.

The House of the Regenants possessed a strange kind of power, effective with both humans and all the blood brothers. But Regenants died like ordinary mortals, and not even they could say if that was a blessing or a curse.

A long, long time ago, during the Dark Ages, the blood brother families grew tired of constant internecine warfare and appointed the Regenants from the Cornelis family as their supreme judges. The ones they could turn to for a decision in cases of dispute. Judges whose decision was final and not subject to discussion.

I sat beside Felicia, facing the gloomy Vricolakos.

I prepared myself.

"Greetings, ladies and gentlemen," said our judge, Belov, in a tone of voice better suited to a cabinet meeting than a council of vampires. "I am glad to see you all in good health."

I picked up a half-formulated thought from Amir in response to this greeting: "good health" was the very last thing he would like to wish most of those who were present. To his mind, a long, painful death had a sweeter sound to it. And that applied in particular to me, the Dahanavar whelp. I was used to it. The high-blooded brothers and sisters were always annoyed by the presence of a telepath, and they showered me with enough ill will to almost make me physically sick.

"I don't see the honorable Miklosh Nachterret," said the Regenant, looking around the assembled company. His eyes met mine, and for an instant I felt his calm composure, self-assurance, and gravitas. Also the sense of duty, lying like a heavy stone in his soul. The Regenants were born with that. It determined all their actions.

Johan shifted lazily on his chair. "Nachttoter Miklosh has other plans for this evening. He sends his regrets that he is not able to be present at this honorable gathering."

But I caught a black thought, a greasy glimmer that had sharp barbs: *He's got better things to do than waste his time with these dumb blautsaugers, who aren't even worthy to step in the dust of his footsteps.* The Nachterret made no secret of how he felt about all of us, and he didn't even try to suppress his emotions. *Blautsauger.* The German word for "bloodsucker" and a pejorative term for a vampire. Johan couldn't give a damn.

"Come on, let's get down to business," Amir said irritably. "No one cares why the honorable Miklosh Balza has not graced our modest meeting with his presence." And he thought rather loudly: *That lousy idiot.*

The Regenant sat down in his armchair. He looked at Felicia.

"Would anyone care to make a statement?"

Our First Lady inclined her head imperiously and started speaking.

"The Dahanavar family wishes to charge the House of Asiman with unjustifiable aggression against the human section of the population."

The Vricolakos snorted loudly. Alexander frowned, correctly assuming that now he would have to wade into yet another quarrel between relatives and take one side or the other. Johan Nachterret amused himself by mentally undressing Constance in a perverted and bloody fashion. Ramon was in principle indifferent to humans, but he had no objection to the Asiman getting their tails twisted.

"What exactly do you mean, dear Lady?" Amir inquired cautiously, protecting himself against the persistent probing of my sensors with a heavy-duty *shield*. But I could still sense his irritation and anger.

"What I mean, dear Magister, is the increasing frequency of attacks on humans. With a fatal outcome."

"I beg your pardon," Amir hissed through his teeth, his nostrils flaring in outrage, and he shook a menacing finger at everyone there. "This is unproven. What makes you think this is our doing? But even if it were, we have not signed your convention on the humane treatment of mortals."

"You live on our land," said the leader of the Upieschi, looking down at the polished surface of the table, and his black Spanish eyebrows knitted together above his nose. *Kill as many mortals as you like, but why leave the corpses lying around?* I heard the thought clearly.

"The eighteenth century," Felicia continued, staring intently at her furious opponent. "As you recall, that was the time of the First Vampire Epidemic. The period between 1725 and 1732 is the most famous epidemic and the one most thoroughly studied by the scholarly circles of the time. That was what the humans called it. It resulted in the mass extermination of blood brothers. Do you remember the 'vampire hunt' that the mortals organized? And all because the honorable Nachterret"—a glance filled with contempt in the direction of Miklosh's deputy—"felt it was beneath their dignity to clear away the dead bodies."

Amir narrowed his eyes in response, and a clear picture came floating across to me. A small street in an old town. Houses with roofs that almost touch one another. Filthy mud, a fetid odor in which the aromas of rotting garbage and the rank stench of decomposing flesh mingle, and human bodies with necks torn open and limbs twisted out of their sockets, piled in a heap beside the wall.

That's the Nachterret idea of heaven: one part of humanity lying dead in the streets, the remainder held in reserve.

I had a sudden feeling of grateful respect for Felicia, for holding this insanity in check. At present, only the Dahanavar family was capable of preventing our degenerate brothers from holding another bloody massacre.

"That Vampire Epidemic didn't lead to anything. The attempt to hunt down the blood brothers was a total fiasco." Amir looked around for support for his statement.

All the leaders who were present remembered those times. Ramon Upieschi gave a slight nod, and I read his thought: *But how much money and effort it cost to appease the mortals.*

Alexander was gazing fixedly at Felicia, and in his mind I read half-formed thoughts about how the human population had started to realize there were dangerous alien beings living beside them, beings who killed in the night. In the popular imagination, the dead had risen from their graves to drink their blood. Legends thousands of years old had come to life. Vampire myths were deeply ingrained in human culture, and the humans panicked.

"We do not wish this 'fiasco' to be repeated," Felicia declared. "We are opposed to mortals discovering who controls them. If they do, they will start to question and rebel. They obey authority more calmly when they themselves have chosen it than when it is imposed on them. Especially by beings whom they fear and hate. That is an essential part of human nature."

"We understand the word 'control' in different ways, Lady." Amir clasped his fingers together and cracked the joints.

"Yes, we know that your position on this matter is close to that advocated by the House of Nachterret."

"We have no desire to control humans," Johan interjected, leering smugly. "We eat them."

"Ladies and gentlemen," intervened the Regenant, who had been calmly following the conversation so far, "please speak to the subject of today's meeting."

Felicia inclined her head in agreement and looked at her companion. Constance shook her red mane of hair and took several sheets of paper out of a file.

"Allow me to read several extracts from the press for the last month. They all have a direct bearing on the subject of today's meeting. This is yesterday's *Capital Gazette*: 'A vicious killing took place in the Seven Parrots late on Thursday night. A girl was found in the toilet of the club with her throat ripped open.'" Constance cast an expressive glance at Amir and continued. "'The *Criminal Gazette* wishes to warn its readers that today the body of the tenth murder victim with stab wounds in the region of the neck was taken to the city morgue. The same maniac is apparently responsible for all of these cases.' And then this is absolutely intolerable—I request the honorable assembly to pay particular attention: 'The *Oracle* is alarmed! The bodies of three men have been found in the central graveyard. They were completely drained of blood. Could this be the aftermath of the supernatural rituals of some devil worship sect? The police are at a loss.'"

Amir smiled condescendingly. "My child, these are nothing but the usual human fairy tales. They used to spread stories of attacks by the blood brothers by word of mouth, and then they would go and tear open the graves of their own deceased relatives to make sure their bodies were decomposing as rapidly as they ought to. Now they write about it in the newspapers. And they make those absolutely idiotic films. That Wallachian prince

Vlad Dracula—the historical one who defended Chris lands against the incursions of the Ottoman Empire—would turn over in his grave if he knew what kind of bogeyman they've turned him into."

"These are no fairy tales!" Constance exclaimed this with a passionate fervor quite impermissible for a high-blood Dahanavar Lady. "You know they are true. Everyone knows it."

Human whore, Amir thought, still smiling. I was glad Constance couldn't hear that. For hundreds of years, the Ladies of my family had successfully influenced human politics. They had manipulated diplomats by becoming their mistresses, beautiful éminences grises. Our red-haired Irishwoman, for instance, lived with the minister of communications.

"If we do not want a repetition of Augustin Calmet[2] and his odious book, we should all exercise caution, ladies and gentlemen," said Alexander.

Ramon permitted himself a wry grin as he recalled the financial outlay he had had to make in order to appease the impressionable mortals on that occasion. The stormy debates about whether the blood brothers really existed had concluded successfully ten years after the publication of Calmet's book. After that, scholars were interested in only one question: What made people believe in unreal beings like vampires? A triumphant conclusion to years of work. Nobody could explain who we were and how we had appeared in the human world. Which was just fine.

"We must not repeat the mistakes of the past," Felicia declared. "We must not give humans even a single chance to discover that we are living among them."

---

2 This is a reference to a book by the eighteenth-century French scholar Dom Augustin Calmet, *Reflections on Appearances of Angels, Demons, Spirits, Regenants and Vampires in Hungary, Bohemia, Moravia and Silesia*, in which he argues that such creatures are real.

"Let me clarify that," Ramon said with a smile. "Honorable Amir, imagine a virgin forest. The wild game is not frightened, and can easily be approached. It doesn't run or shy away from you. But if you start shooting game indiscriminately in this forest, hanging the bodies on the trees and hunting the creatures down with dogs, not a single animal will let you come anywhere near."

He suddenly smashed his fist down on the table, transformed for a moment from a levelheaded, slightly ironic businessman into a bloodthirsty, vengeful blood brother.

"We may not know who leaves the corpses in the city, but I support the Dahanavar family's demand to stop sawing off the very branch on which we sit. Mortals are essential to the Upieschi political agenda. I work with humans. They have to trust me and my brothers."

He said something else as well, but I suddenly *felt* and *heard* and actually *saw* Amir remember. Several dead bodies in a metro station. Bites—"stab wounds"—on their necks. A massive loss of blood. Two survived. They were sent to the intensive care ward of municipal hospital number fifty.

I suppose I must have spoken this out loud, because I realized everyone there was looking at me. Felicia in delight, since I had justified her hopes. Alexander in annoyance. The Vricolakos with vague contempt. Ramon with a smile of encouragement. The Nachterret with intense concentration, as if he were watching a jester.

"There's your proof," said the Upieschi.

"A scanner's ramblings aren't proof," said Amir, scarcely able to restrain his fury.

"You know he doesn't lie!" Constance interrupted vehemently. "When he's working, he can't lie. He only says what he hears and senses. He is completely detached from his own emotions and desires."

Felicia stopped her with a gesture of her hand. "With the consent of all here present, I move to demand a halt to the aggression against the human population by the House of Asiman."

"I support that unreservedly," Ramon declared.

"I agree," Alexander said immediately.

"The decision of the honorable Nachterret?" the judge inquired.

"You know the opinion of Nachttoter Miklosh on this matter," Johan replied, examining his fingernails. "We need humans as food. And we treat them as food. We eat what is fresh and discard what is rancid. We're not concerned with the problems of the slops, and we don't negotiate with fodder."

"Ivan Vricolakos, your opinion?"

The werewolf's eyes glinted with yellow fire, and he grinned as he said, "I don't agree."

"With whom?" the Regenant asked patiently.

"With the position of the Dahanavar family."

"But in the past you have supported it . . . ," Felicia began, unable to conceal her surprise.

The Vricolakos smirked. "I don't like that redhead girl."

Constance blinked in astonishment and spilled the papers out of her file.

"I'm sorry, I don't quite understand . . . ," the Regenant began, his imperturbability slightly dented. "How is that connected with the question that we are deciding?"

"Directly. I don't like her. And I disagree."

Ramon slammed his palm down on the table. "Stop playing the fool, Svetlov. It makes no difference to you what the girl looks like."

"I don't like redheads."

"Mr. Svetlov," said Felicia, closing her eyes for a moment to recover her inner composure, "the question we are deciding today is putting a stop to the Asiman family's killings of mortals, which jeopardize the secrecy of our existence among them. And I fail to understand what my assistant has to do with that."

Of course she didn't understand. Our First Lady was too consistently logical. She could never appreciate the Vricolakos leader's feral sense of humor. All he had wanted was to make a joke. Have a bit of fun. Anyway, he really didn't like redheads. Unlike the others, the Regenant either understood or sensed this just as I did. After all, he was human to a certain extent, and I already knew that humans, at least some of them, could be amazingly sensitive.

"Amir Asiman, I support the Dahanavar family in its demand that you cease and desist from your acts of aggression against the human population. We cannot force you to abide by our agreement, but we require you to keep in mind the law on the maintenance of neutrality."

This meant: You can kill humans as before, but don't leave the bodies lying about. And if you fail to comply, severe measures will be taken. The Dahanavar, Upieschi, Vricolakos, and Faryartos families will find a way to restrain anyone who goes too far in killing humans.

"Allow me to make a point," said Ramon, taking out his Parker pen and mechanically unscrewing and screwing back the top. "What are we to do with those two in the hospital? It would be a good thing if the Asiman finished what they started. We don't need any unnecessary witnesses."

Amir didn't say anything, but he was thinking loudly. Mostly in obscenities, addressed to me and Felicia. And for some reason, he recalled Flora. My dead mother. It was only a thought in passing, her face flashing through his memory, but this recollection grated painfully on me.

The Regenant rose to his feet, which indicated that the council meeting was over.

3

A DIFFERENT STAGE

The world is a stage, but the play is badly cast.

—Oscar Wilde, "Lord Arthur Savile's Crime"

September 15
Darel Dahanavar

"That miserable gold digger!" said Vance, and his low, vibrant voice broke into a hoarse croak. "The rotten bitch!"

I frowned in automatic response, moved the phone to my other ear, and rubbed my aching temple with my free hand. As always after serious psychic exertion, I had a raging headache. All I wanted was to stay in bed for a couple of days. And not feel any emotions.

Unfortunately, I'd forgotten to switch off the phone.

I could even feel it at a distance—Hemran was trembling in fury, despair, and, strangely enough, love. I glimpsed the image of a woman moving in and out of his thoughts. Vance simply couldn't concentrate on anything else. He was in a wretched state, really upset, and he was looking for help from me, but I didn't know what kind.

"It's all coming back," he said indistinctly, then cleared his throat, and his voice became strong and vibrant again. "I can feel the old insanity coming back, but there's nothing I can do about it. She's found me again. I thought it was all over, dead and buried a long time ago. But now I find it's still there. It's impossible to forget her." Then he added without a break: "Sorry, I don't know why I'm telling you all this."

Of course he didn't know. Humans never understood why they started feeling fond of me and trusting me. Wanting to bare their soul. And why they felt so much at ease in my company.

"Darel, I'm going to a rehearsal today . . . in a so-called theater. Maybe we could meet up afterwards and have a proper talk?"

I thought about Loraine. This would be an excuse to see her again.

"Why don't we meet right there at the theater? You don't mind if I bring Loraine, do you? It would be interesting for her to watch."

"The fan from yesterday? Bring her along. But I can't promise the show will be very exciting. The theater's nothing great. Strictly amateur."

"That's okay. Where and when?"

He dictated the address, and I hung up. Then I looked at the alarm clock—I could sleep for another hour and a half.

The telephone conversation with Vance had helped take my mind off my involvement in the machination of the Houses, and I was glad to forget about the blood brothers' intrigues. Trying to solve Hemran's human problems was far more fun than listening in on Amir's murky thoughts.

Apart from that, I really wanted to talk to Loraine. Take a look at the world through her eyes.

I dragged myself out of bed and wandered into the kitchen so I could make up for my lack of sleep with some food. I opened the refrigerator, studied its contents for a while, and decided that a cocktail of first- and second-group blood would be just the thing.

The telephone summoned me just at the moment when the drink was heated to the right temperature and poured into a glass. As I picked up the handset, I already knew who it was; there was gentle autumn sunshine at the other end of the line.

"Hello."

"It's Loraine. I phoned you yesterday, after the theater, but there was no answer."

The young voice broke into the darkness of my bedroom from a different world, carefree and sunny.

"I was out."

"I wanted to thank you for a wonderful evening and . . ." She hesitated, trying to think of what to say next. She had phoned now because I had *called* her. Of course, she didn't know that. She'd been hoping she could think of something to talk about on the spur of the moment, but inspiration failed her.

"Loraine, would you like to go to a rehearsal with Vance this evening? He just called me and invited both of us."

Her awkwardness was forgotten in her delight.

"Of course! With pleasure! Only . . ." She hesitated again and then asked quickly, afraid that I would say no straightaway: "Can I bring a friend with me?"

Ah. So she has a boyfriend, I thought, but decided not to jump to any hasty conclusions.

"No problem. I'll come by at half past eight."

She told me where to pick her up, and I put down the phone to wait.

The blood in the glass was cold, but I downed it and went to get dressed.

THEY came out of the doorway at precisely half past eight. Saw me standing by the car and hurried over. They were both wearing warm sweaters, jeans, and thick-soled shoes. But Loraine somehow managed to look elegant even in that outfit.

They were both radiating excited impatience, but Loraine's friend also had an aura of curiosity and vague unease.

Loraine smiled at me happily. Her friend shook my hand firmly and looked me up and down, taking my measure.

"Hi," said Loraine, "this is Max. We're at college together. He's a fan of Hemran's, too. And this is Darel, he knows Hemran."

It seemed that knowing Hemran was the greatest achievement of my entire life.

It took me only a couple of seconds to realize that Max had been hopelessly in love with Loraine for ages. But she treated him like a brother. A younger brother, which he found particularly depressing.

I opened the car door. The girl got in and sat beside me. Max climbed into the backseat. I read in his thoughts Loraine's recent instruction to be nice. Clearly trying to do as she had asked, he struck up a conversation.

"Is this a Pontiac?" He looked at the leather upholstery with the air of someone who knows what he's talking about.

"Yes." I adjusted the rearview mirror and turned the key in the ignition.

"What year is it?"

"Last year."

"Cool. It's a great car. My father's got a Merc, but it's ten years old. It keeps breaking down. We're going to get a new one."

Loraine watched how I reacted, anxious I would get bored with Max's babbling. But she needn't have worried. Humans never stressed me out.

It was funny, they were the same age—only eighteen—but they seemed completely different. Loraine radiated a warm, even glow. There was no chaos in her soul. Max flared up joyfully— *I'm going to see Hemran Vance, I'll talk to him and get his autograph*—and then his delight was enveloped in a black cloud: *Lo seems to like this guy with the Pontiac. . . .* Then there was another bright spot: *At least it's good that we're friends. . . .* And then again that black mourning band encircling his feelings: *But why don't I ever meet people who hang out with celebrities? I can't introduce her to anyone.*

Loraine spread her aura of joy and clear autumn light all around her. It didn't mean that she wasn't feeling anything. She was excited and happy and embarrassed, just like a human being. But it felt *calm* just being beside her. I started settling down after the nervous stress of wallowing in my brothers' emotions the night before.

Max fidgeted in the backseat, looking out into the darkness illuminated by the streetlamps.

"Where are we going?"

I glimpsed his thought: *Now he'll drag us off into the boondocks.*

"It's not far from the riverboat station."

He perked up at that.

"I know it. My brother's always going there for training." He started explaining to Loraine, "It's quite a long way from here. And the main avenue's always jammed with traffic."

"We'll go round the ring road," I replied, taking a turn at high speed.

Max opened his mouth to object, but I turned up the radio and ignored him. Even I had my limits. I pressed the accelerator down smoothly, as far as it would go. My passengers were thrown back against their seats. Inwardly, both of them trembled in delight. Young humans like driving fast with loud music playing.

ON both sides of the road there was dark forest—monolithic walls with jagged upper edges. Lines of streetlamps cast blurred patches of light along the verges. Every now and then, we overtook heavily loaded trucks dragging along clouds of water droplets that settled on the Pontiac's windows. They sounded their horns raucously when my car cut in right under their noses.

"Great," Loraine whispered.

"Can you go any faster?" asked Max.

Sometimes teenagers lose touch with their instinct of self-preservation.

We overtook another heavy tractor-truck, and suddenly a shiny Lamborghini Diablo came darting out of a dark road on the right like some black monster. It raced along beside us for a while and then started trying to force me over onto the hard shoulder.

"What's he doing, the idiot?" Max's voice suddenly sounded shrill. "Is he completely insane?"

"Careful, Darel!" Loraine exclaimed. Neither of them spoke after that; they were petrified. I cast a light stupor over them without even turning around. None of my human acquaintances should ever see whom you can run into on a dark ring road.

I stopped the Pontiac and got out. The Lamborghini pulled up beside me. The door rose up to reveal the spacious leather-upholstered interior, and out climbed Ivan Svetlov, head of the House of Vricolakos.

"Damn automobiles," he muttered. "Coffins on wheels. Greetings, Darel."

"Good night," I said, biting my lip to stop myself laughing. The forest-dweller looked so funny—a big, powerful, gray-haired werewolf dressed in tanned leather, standing beside a magnificent modern motor vehicle.

"Sorry to interrupt your supper," he said with a glance at Loraine and Max, who were sprawling in their seats. "Fine young cubs."

I nodded, accepting the apology and the compliment.

"I have a proposal for you," he went on, peering at me sullenly from under his thick eyebrows. He paused and adjusted his leather scabbard holding his knife.

I didn't try to hurry him, knowing that the Vricolakos needed time to formulate his unexpected request clearly in words.

"Since I'm stuck in this lousy city of yours, I'm getting a bit of business done. I need an interpreter. For one evening."

"An interpreter?"

"I want you to sniff something out a bit." The werewolf breathed in loudly through his nose and moved closer. He had an aura of animal strength—untamable, dangerous, fierce. "I've got a meeting with him today. I want to know what's on his mind. But he jiggles about like an adder on a hot skillet. Can't understand a thing."

A truck went hurtling past. Its slipstream ruffled the fur on Ivan's cloak and flung a handful of raindrops into my face.

"You want me to act as a scanner for the Vricolakos family in negotiations with the Upieschi?" I asked, instantly *catching* his thought.

"Exactly." He stroked his beard and smiled contentedly.

My jaw didn't drop, I didn't gape at him wide-eyed or express my amazement in any other way. But I must still have looked bewildered. Ivan grinned.

"Well?"

"I don't usually act on behalf of other Houses."

"You wouldn't be working for nothing."

He pulled a small bag out from behind his belt, untied the string, and tipped the contents out onto his broad palm. Uncut diamonds.

"This is half. Do the job and you'll get the same again."

"I have to consult with the head of the family."

"Go ahead, consult." The Vricolakos started stuffing the stones back into the bag, muttering in his mind: *Consult, consult. We know how you all chase after her skirt like blind little kittens!*

The right door of the Lamborghini rose into the air, and one of the young guys who had been at the council with the elder got out. His yellow eyes glinted as he glanced at me. I half-expected him to growl and bare his teeth.

"Father, how long are you going to stand in the middle of the road with this—"

"Disappear!" Ivan barked at him. "Sit and wait."

The young guy climbed back in the car with his tail between his legs.

"That's Slaven," the elder explained good-naturedly. "A keen nose, but he's still young."

I nodded automatically and didn't ask any questions. I concentrated and *called*.

Felicia responded immediately.

A picture appeared in front of my eyes. The mormolika sitting in front of a mirror, arranging her hair in a complicated style. Constance sitting in a chair beside her, concentrating on her laptop.

"I'm listening, Darel," said our First Lady.

I briefly described Ivan's proposal. The comb froze for a moment in her hands, then slipped through the bright ash gray hair.

"You must agree. We'll help the Vricolakos, and they won't forget that we did them a service. And in addition, it will be useful to know what links they have with the Upieschi."

I had to make an effort to restrain my sudden feeling of annoyance.

"My Lady, Ivan is not likely to be very pleased if I try to creep into his mind while he's paying me to scan Ramon. I'll have to be very careful reading the Vricolakos. It will be a very demanding job, and I still haven't recovered completely after yesterday's council."

"Darel." There were steely notes in Felicia's melodious voice. "This is a personal request from me."

"All right! Okay! I'll be at the meeting today. But I can't answer for the consequences."

I broke contact without saying good-bye. Ivan had been watching me tensely, trying to *hear* what we were talking about, but he hadn't managed to catch a single word.

"When's the meeting?"

The werewolf grinned in response to my gruff tone of voice, weighed the bag of diamonds in his hand, and put it on the hood of the Pontiac.

"At twelve."

"I'll arrive half an hour early. I need to prepare myself. Make sure no one smokes in the meeting room. And that there are no humans hanging about anywhere nearby."

He listened carefully, nodding at the end of every phrase.

"We'll do everything right."

He wrapped his cloak around himself, looked over my head at the line of the forest, and walked toward his car. Lowered himself heavily onto the seat and closed the door. The Lamborghini roared and hurtled off into the darkness with its red taillights glowing.

I picked up the little bag with my advance fee, put it in my pocket, and got back in behind the wheel of the Pontiac.

When my passengers woke up a couple of minutes later, they didn't remember a thing.

"So why did you buy this car?" asked Max, continuing our conversation as if nothing had happened.

"I like the name. It's almost Pontianak—the name for a vampire on the island of Java," I joked.

They laughed at that, remembering the Goth from the day before—Loraine had already told Max about Vance's interesting friends.

I had to try to detach myself from everything, to relax. Get my bruised and battered feelings back into shape. I would have liked just to be with Loraine, but if that was impossible right now, I hoped that talking to Hemran and the other mortals would inspire me, so I wouldn't have any trouble breaking through my blood relatives' mental shields.

THE building was beside a green square, a small island of forest in the middle of the city. The leaves were rustling, but the gentle sounds were inaudible above the car horns, human voices, and whistling of cables in the wind.

The theater itself was in a semibasement. You had to go down a narrow stone stairway covered with a carpet that was a solid mass of dirt.

Loraine and her friend followed me down. I could feel their impatience, mingled with a gentle excitement and a perfectly reasonable fear of stumbling on the steep stairs. Max took out a digital camera and enthusiastically recorded this sacred spot— a stairway that Vance Hemran himself had walked down only a couple of hours earlier.

At the bottom, we found ourselves in a dark hallway with several rooms opening off it. Two actors—young guys wearing panty hose, satin shirts, and shoes with buckles—were sitting on the windowsill of a false window cut into the wall. As we walked by, they followed us with glazed eyes, no doubt owing to their intense preoccupation with artistic matters.

Another three votaries of the Muse Melpomene, no older than my companions, walked by, talking in loud voices. Their smooth, youthful faces bore the traces of clumsy attempts to portray in makeup the tragic experiences of old age. . . .

The rehearsal hall was tiny. A small stage on which they had somehow managed to install a couple of flimsy cardboard trees, a crooked little gray house representing a temple, and a prompter's box. Hanging above the stage set was a threadbare blue "sky" with silver stars.

And in the middle of all this, a long-legged girl in a short skirt, high boots, and a blouse embroidered with beads was portraying the tragic Greek heroine with frenetic fury. It didn't take a specialist to see that she was good-looking, full of joie de vivre, and delighted to be onstage, but completely devoid of talent.

A young guy was hovering beside an ancient cardboard oak

tree, feverishly leafing through an exercise book that obviously contained his lines.

Sitting in the back row of the hall was a group of performers who weren't involved in this scene. They were chattering and laughing. Laid-back, comfortable, and relaxed.

The general atmosphere was one of mutual satisfaction. People enjoying being each other. As well as a chance to play at being someone else, not the person they were in ordinary life. But in the second row, there was an epicenter of bright negative emotions that were almost out of control. That was where Vance Hemran was sitting.

Max spotted the Brit, pointed him out to Loraine, and started taking photographs again, afraid of missing even a single gesture by this legendary celebrity.

Vance was dressed in the clothes he always wore for informal outings. A pair of worn Voyage jeans and a blue shirt of the same material. Anyone else dressed like that would have looked stylish, but on Vance the fashionable denim reverted to its original function as laborer's work clothes. A light-colored raincoat with a check lining from John Galliano went some way toward correcting this impression. The singer's long, frizzy hair was drawn back into a ponytail. The expression on his unshaven face was bleak.

Sitting beside him was a dark-haired woman of indeterminate age, wrapped in a black poncho. The director of the play. She was overflowing with energy, jumping up and down in her chair.

"Hi, Darel," said Hemran Vance, getting up when he saw me. He glanced at my companions. Recognized Loraine and gave her a brief smile. "Wait. They're taking a break in five minutes."

He nodded toward the stage, where the girl in thigh boots and the guy with the exercise book were locked in passionate dialogue.

The director gave Vance a sideways look; she was annoyed, but she didn't say anything.

This artistic lady had a small, thin face with a pointed nose and an excessive amount of makeup. The lobes of her ears were weighed down by massive silver earrings. The string of beads around her neck looked like good-sized medieval cobblestones, and they were complemented by a varied assortment of chains, amulets, and strings. Her hands and wrists were covered in rings and bracelets, and there was a cupronickel chain with mysterious symbols glinting in her black hair. All this junk jewelry clattered, clanked, and jangled at the slightest movement.

The director herself was ablaze with the fire of creative ecstasy. If she could have jumped up on the stage and played all the parts herself, she would have been up there doing it.

I looked at her for only a moment and then switched my attention to Vance. Everything irritated him. The chattering of the actors in the back row, punctuated by the popping of beer cans being opened. The young actress's manner of raising her head and tossing the hair back off her face at moments of intense feeling. She thought the gesture gave her lines tragic resonance, but in fact it just looked mannered and forced. The girl's voice or, rather, lack of it grated on Hemran's nerves. It wasn't too bad while she was speaking, but as soon as she started singing, the Brit started howling inside. Meanwhile, the director smiled radiantly and looked proudly at her guest to see if he fully appreciated the value of her new artistic discovery.

Vance did. *Unprofessional,* he thought to himself. It was the worst accusation he could ever level at anyone. *Amateur drama circle.*

He glanced fiercely around the hall, thinking about how everyone there was just killing time. None of them would ever get out of this basement.

I used to slave for eighteen hours a day. I was delirious with music, I lived music. . . . Those filthy stinking little bars I had to sing in. Nobody believed I could ever rise above that level. The

miserable pay I had to save up to buy myself a decent instrument . . .
Nobody believed in me. . . .

Nobody believed in him.

Apart from me.

We were sitting in one of those "stinking bars," where he was performing popular hits to earn a bit of money. Vance was drinking beer and looking at me with the angry, hungry eyes of a man prevented from doing the work he loves. He had no money, the group he was working with was falling apart, the girl he loved—the only person who had ever given him any support—had left him. She was tired and disillusioned, and she got a better offer.

"You ought to record an album," I said, pretending to drink my whiskey. He kept his eyes fixed on the foamy head of his beer.

"It's the money. For the studio, for the professional production, the cover design . . ."

"I'll give you the money."

He pulled a sour face, as if he'd bitten into a lemon. "No!"

"I'll give you the money. And I'll take twenty percent of the profits."

Even the Upieschi would have envied my business acumen. Vance looked at me, and his swamp green eyes expressed the turmoil inside. My tactical move had worked. I wasn't giving him a handout. I was lending him money against a percentage of earnings. That meant I believed in him. And what Vance needed most of all was support from someone who believed in him.

He agreed. And I don't think he ever regretted it.

And now Hemran was sitting in a rehearsal hall freaking out because no one there understood what art was all about. It seemed barbaric to him to spend a couple of hours skipping about onstage and then blithely go off home, or to the office, and forget all about your role. He didn't understand that for the young guys and girls in this hall, the theater was no more than a chance to spend a little time being someone else. To be Caesar instead of a bank clerk. A goddess instead of a waitress. Vance lived his music all the time; for him, it was hard work, rigorous effort that brought true satisfaction. But for the others, it was just a chance to relax and have some fun.

Loraine was sitting beside me. She touched my arm gently, rousing me from my reverie, and I glanced at her.

"Is everything all right?" she asked in a whisper.

The girl could sense my tension, but she didn't know the reason for it.

"Everything's fine." I smiled encouragingly and received a warm wave of tranquillity in reply as she relaxed again. Loraine leaned back in her chair and watched the performance curiously. Unlike Vance, she found it interesting. Max was ecstatically offering to photograph everyone. It looked as if he might make a pretty good press photographer.

Hemran looked at his watch. He thought angrily about the friend who had persuaded him to take a look at a promising young actress and then not shown up, although he had sworn he would be there before ten. He finally gave up on the rehearsal and turned to me.

"Listen, Dar, are you free for the whole night?"

He knew about the special conditions of my "job," which meant I was always likely to get up in the middle of a friendly conversation to deal with urgent business.

"Until eleven thirty."

"Then it's time to put an end to this nonsense."

Raising his voice, Vance addressed the entire hall in a commanding voice:

"That's enough! Thank you, everyone."

The actress's jaw dropped in astonishment, and her beautifully made-up face froze. The director was so surprised, she bounced in her seat.

"But won't you just watch . . . one more dialogue . . . ," she said, trying to revive the rock star's interest by making hopeful gestures in the direction of the stage. Vance stubbornly stuck out his lower jaw and took a grip on the armrests of his chair.

"No. That's enough. She doesn't cut it for me. No voice, no ear."

He got up and nodded to Loraine and Max. "Hi. How're you doing?"

For the next twenty minutes, Hemran signed autographs and answered questions from his fans—there turned out to be quite a lot of them in the hall. And he studiously ignored the unfortunate young actress, who hovered around him suggestively.

Once he was free of the fans, he came across and sat beside me. Loraine and Max stayed with the actors, glancing at their idol from a distance, deciding not to interrupt his conversation. Cameras flashed every few seconds, but the Brit took no notice. He was used to it.

"So what other problems have you got, apart from the sudden reappearance of your former sweetheart?"

Hemran gave a grim laugh to show that he appreciated my optimism but wasn't able to reply in kind.

"Not long ago, about three months, I started sensing this strange kind of interest focused on me from all sides. People I didn't know hanging about, offering me contracts. Lucrative contracts, but . . . I got the feeling that there was some kind of trick involved. I can't figure out what it is. It's like they're trying to push me towards some long-term goal of their own. It goes something like this: 'Hey, buddy, you could really have it made. Everything you want. Money. *Real* money. Not the kind you get from the contract with your recording company. Social standing. Not the kind you get from teenagers and young guys and dolls. In *real* society. You can have all this. But not right now. You're not ready yet. Not quite ready.' Strange hints, strange glances, like they're trying to lure me into a Masonic lodge."

Although he usually looked down at the floor during his own monologues, this time he was looking straight at me. With a demanding air, as if he were certain that I knew the answers to his questions.

"And do you actually want real money, real society, real fame?"

Vance smiled. "They haven't mentioned fame yet. But I can always do with money."

"So what were they talking about?"

"I don't know. I just don't know. . . ." He lowered his head and looked at his hands. When he raised it again, a girl was walking toward us along the narrow corridor.

Paula.

A Faryartos.

A light, springy, smooth, rapid stride, flowing from one graceful movement into the next.

A head poised proudly on a beautiful neck. A voluptuous hairstyle. A slim, strong body. A light-colored trouser suit that was a perfect fit for an ideal figure. High-heeled shoes. A brooch on the lapel of the jacket—a silver sunflower.

Overwhelmingly desirable. Magnificent. Magical . . .

Not just beautiful, not just lovely—the fary women are above those simple human words. Divine. She seemed to be poised right on the very borderline between subtle good taste and vulgar extravagance. Her lips were just a little too full for the narrow face that tapered toward the chin, just a little too bright. Her cheekbones were just a little too prominent. Her nose could have been just a little bit narrower and her décolleté a little less deep. But taken together, these details created such a seductive image that I felt all the men in the hall catch their breath and then sigh at the same moment.

A stunning appearance is one of the weapons that make the House of Faryartos so powerful.

Vance's face turned to stone. He swallowed with difficulty,

stuck his hand into the pocket of his raincoat, and hunched over, then immediately straightened his shoulders again.

It was her. The "lost love" I had been speaking about ironically only a minute earlier. The one he had talked about to me on the phone. Paula, who had abandoned Hemran at the start of his career in order to become a fary.

She walked up, casually swinging her little purse on a long strap. Smiled. And spoke in a magnificently modulated voice—sonorous, melodious, intoxicating.

"Hi, Vance."

She looked at me with an impeccable air of polite interest.

"Won't you introduce me to your friend?"

"This is Darel," Hemran muttered, looking down at the floor. "Darel, Paula."

She held out an elegant hand with a thin twisted bracelet around the wrist. I squeezed the slim fingers rather harder than necessary.

"Very pleased to meet you."

"Likewise."

The girl worked the enchanting dimples in her cheeks without showing any annoyance at the deliberate roughness of my handshake. "What brings you here, Darel?"

"The same as yourself, Paula."

—What are you doing here, Dahanavar? What interest could you have in the theater?

—That's none of your business.

While we wrangled in our minds, we smiled politely and pretended that this was the first time we'd ever seen each other.

—So you've come for him now! Do you want to turn Vance?

—That's none of your business!

—Yes, it is. You'll destroy a fine singer. Let him have his life. He wants to live as a human.

—He wants money and adoration. And he wants to be with me.

Yes, Vance had always wanted to be with Paula. He loved her. One reason he had dreamed of making it big was so she would realize how wrong she had been about him—and come back. And now she had come back. Only not as the girl he used to sing with ten years earlier, but as elegant, magnificent bait from her House of artistic bohemians.

She was a highly capable student, taught by the maestro himself, Alexander Faryartos. When she marked anyone down for turning, he never got away. She could enchant, persuade, or buy a man. Act through his wife, mistress, friend, or business partner. This was a family that consumed attractive, talented people. Its aim was to preserve beauty and genius through the centuries. For all eternity. To bottle the spark of magic that flares up in the soul of an artist, to preserve in wax the pain that is born in the heart of an actor, to dry and store the subtle, shifting images that hover above the head of a writer.

Madness. They didn't realize it was impossible. As the years pass by, feelings and emotions are blunted. And thousands of years of life kill all feelings. The soul becomes cold. It can't burn anymore. The farys took away from humans the one thing that I sought and valued in them most of all—their bright, vital feelings.

After a century or two, Vance wouldn't want to sing anymore. His vocal cords would easily strike any note he liked, but the pain and passion would have gone out of his voice. He himself wouldn't even notice how he'd changed. He'd forget what he used to be like before. . . .

The silence dragged on. My eyes drilled into Paula with a gaze full of hate. She pouted her plump lips contemptuously. Vance kept looking from her to me and back again. He could tell there was something going on between us, but he couldn't understand what it was.

"Paula, did you want to talk to me?" he asked eventually, deciding to risk a direct question.

"I did. But unfortunately I see it won't be possible today. You're busy."

Hemran was about to object that he was never too busy for her, but he didn't say it. He didn't want to admit the power she had over him. A few hours earlier on the phone with me, Vance had called this girl a bitch. Now he was ready to do anything she asked. The charm of a fary never fails. It would have been impossible for any man to resist it.

But then, not quite impossible.

Not with the mental support of a Dahanavar.

Paula frowned when she felt me *clearing* her victim's mind. *She abandoned you when you needed her most. Left you for a safe life with a rich idler. And now you're famous, she's turned up again. The rotten, lousy, calculating bitch!* Vance heard these words in his head, in his own voice. Indistinguishable from his own thoughts. Painful and sobering.

Dahanavar, what are you doing? Why are you setting him against me? How dare you interfere? the fary exclaimed.

Oh, I dare! Leave him alone! Go mess with somebody else's mind.

Paula's face suddenly seemed to glow with a magical, glimmering light, like a pearl just taken out of the shell. She became unbelievably lovely. It was impossible to stand beside her and not want her.

This was her response to my crude interference in her victim's mind. Vance groaned inside. The power of the fary's attraction was absolutely unbearable, he was on the point of abandoning his pride, but I *held* him. For his own sake.

She betrayed you once. And she'll do the same again. And you've never forgiven anyone for betraying you.

Paula smiled and looked at him. Tenderly, alluringly.

I don't know how the duel would eventually have ended. But the first to capitulate was the human being—the battlefield for the Dahanavar and the fary. He couldn't stand the struggle between pride and love.

"Paula, let's get together tomorrow. Darel, I'll give you a call. I can't do it today."

He looked as exhausted as if he had just played a big concert. Totally drained. The incandescent heat of the feelings had left behind nothing but apathy in his soul. Vance left without saying a proper good-bye, walking with an impossibly heavy burden on his shoulders. Without looking back.

Paula and I looked at each other. The spite suddenly glimmered brightly in her eyes, as if two black windows had opened in the green scum covering a swamp. Her face was still as beautiful as ever, but there were ripples of hate running under the smooth skin. And I probably didn't look any better myself.

"Don't interfere with my work," the fary hissed, flaring her nostrils furiously.

"Work?"

"He'll have money, freedom, fame, immortal life. Everything that a man could dream of."

"I don't understand what you want Vance for. He doesn't match the Faryartos aesthetic ideal."

"He's incredibly talented and hardworking. That compensates for the shortcomings of his appearance. And our blood will make him more attractive."

"It seems to me it's not just a matter of the interests of the House. You want him personally. Am I right?"

Paula raised her eyebrows haughtily. "I can have personal attachments, too."

"You want to take revenge?"

She was surprised. But she didn't show it. Farys are taught self-control just as strictly as Dahanavar Ladies.

"What do you mean?"

"He has a magnificent voice. Incredible success. Perhaps not everlasting world fame, but quite enough for a live human being. Money. Not billions. But enough. Freedom. Slightly limited, but real nonetheless. He achieved all this himself. With his own human efforts. But you turned coward. You were frightened by a life of hunger and relentless, exhausting work. You went running to a rich benefactor. Sold your mortal essence for a lapdog's warm rug and full bowl. And now you run around carrying out your master's instructions. Taking away other people's human happiness. Seducing them with an easy life. Which is really incredible hard . . . abominably hard and meaningless. But you had talent yourself once. How many years is it since the last time you sang?"

Paula's lips trembled. She pressed them firmly together, but tears gleamed in her eyes. She clenched her fists, struggling to hold back and not slap me across the cheek. She barely managed it. I could have gloated. But what I felt was a wave of such scorching mental anguish that for a second I found it hard to breathe.

I had told the truth. What she had tried not to think about, hiding behind thoughts of the grandeur of her House, her own immortality, beauty, and uniqueness. But now, instead of an alluring, self-confident woman, there in front of me was a young girl with wet eyelashes who had lost herself. Her real self. Out of stupidity, recklessness, or avarice—what difference did that make? What had been lost could not be brought back.

"Bastard!" she hissed, twisting her beautiful lips. "Damn telepath!"

She swung around and walked away from me quickly, almost running. I hadn't scanned her. All I'd done was say out loud what I thought about her. And I'd hit her sorest spot. . . .

"Loraine, Max, let's go. I'll give you a lift home."

They were quiet and thoughtful in the car, sensing my nervous agitation, which blunted their joy at having met Vance. But they attributed their slight feeling of apathy to being tired.

I took Max home first. Then Loraine. As she got out of the Pontiac, she was about to say something, but after a glance at my sullen, gloomy face, all she said was:

"Thanks. See you later."

Once again I felt that surprising breath of warm summer wind, and a ray of sunlight blotted out the vision of those two black windows in a green scummy bog, windows filled with human tears. I looked at Loraine, and suddenly I wanted to see the sun glistening in her wheat-colored hair, caressing her graceful figure, and dancing in her translucent eyes. Just for a second. And I surprised myself by answering:

"Thank you."

"What for?" she asked, also surprised.

Her smiling face seemed to reflect a distant white flame. All the light of a warm August was concentrated in her slender, youthful body.

I got out of the car, walked up to her, leaned down, and took that lovely face in my hands. I looked deep, deep into those eyes, feeling her tremble and sing like a taut string under my gaze.

"What?" her lips whispered soundlessly, looking into my eyes, which were shadowed by her bright glow, unable to read anything in them. But I could see all the shadows cast by the wave of sunlight in the depths of her gaze.

She didn't even try to break away; she was entranced. The magic was too sweet, the feeling too powerful, to be rejected. Loraine's lips trembled when I suddenly released her.

"Thank you for you."

I slammed the car door, leaving her standing on the wet sidewalk in the cold drizzle. Perplexed but happy.

THE address for the meeting between Ivan and Ramon was transmitted to me mentally by Slaven.

I recognized the Vricolakos leader's assistant from his aggressive aura and contemptuous attitude to the "city telepath." The young werewolf casually "tossed across" the information and then cut the contact, managing to squeeze as much disdain as possible into this simple act.

He really was a talented sensor. His technique was only basic, but his abilities were amplified by animal instinct. That was bad. He might sense me trying to reach into his mentor's thoughts.

Before going up into the office for the negotiations, I sat in my car for a few minutes, trying to relax and switch off from everything else. Feel empty on the inside. Ready to pump in other people's emotions, to untangle associations and secret plans. I almost had to tear Loraine's radiant image out of my soul by force.

I got out of the car and faced the modern high-rise building that looked like a pyramid of glass cubes. Among the other automobiles in the parking lot, the black Lamborghini was like a wolf crouching low to the ground, ready to pounce.

I walked into the brightly lit entrance hall, which looked from the outside like the window of some expensive shop. The security guard at reception gave me an inquiring glance. He looked rather dazed, but that could have been because he'd had a hard day, not because there were blood brothers in the building. When he heard my name and what I was there for, he nodded and pointed to the elevator.

The huge window in the corridor on the thirty-fifth floor had a view of the entire city. Streaks of light running along the streets, brightly lit buildings. The slim twin-headed forms of streetlamps, burning with a yellow light, sprang out of the ground in regular rows. Advertisement headings glowed with blinding neon. And far away in the west, a pale, almost invisible haze, melting into the night sky—a constant reminder of the sun that was fatal to me.

I forced myself to stop contemplating that and went to the

office where I was expected. It had a ceiling-to-floor window, too, but it was covered with dark blinds. Standing in the center of the room was an oval table, with four chairs set around it. Ashtrays, glasses, bottles of mineral water. A projector and screen. A whiteboard for writing on.

Ivan was sitting in one of the chairs, and the legs of the modern furniture seemed to be buckling under his weight. Slaven was standing by the window, nervous, angry, and hungry. The Vricolakos thought the sensor would work better on an empty stomach. It would sharpen the edge of his sensitivity.

But then maybe that's the way it worked for them.

The young werewolf's mental shield looked strange—it was woven out of steel barbed wire. The older werewolf was surrounded by the usual monolithic *wall*.

"Sit down," said Ivan, pointing to the chair beside him. "Tell me if you need anything."

I walked over to my place, taking no notice of Slaven's angry glances. I sat down. Took a leather case about the size of an ordinary wallet out of my inside pocket. Opened it as the senior Vricolakos watched curiously. Inside were capsules of thin glass lying in narrow slots. I took one out, broke it open, and poured the contents onto a handkerchief. A fresh, astringent aroma drifted through the room, killing the standard office smell.

The Vricolakos sniffed curiously, drawing in the air noisily.

"Levzeia kubeba." I pressed the handkerchief against my face and took several deep breaths. "It clears the mind and sharpens the thinking process."

"I know what levzeia is for," Ivan murmured, studying me with greater interest. He hadn't expected me to know anything about aromatherapy. Over by the window, Slaven snorted contemptuously.

I didn't normally make use of any additional stimulation, but I was expecting a hard night ahead.

Ramon showed up at precisely twelve. He was followed by two assistants. The Upieschi boss narrowed his eyes at the sight of me, sat down facing us, clicked open the locks of his briefcase, took out a folder of documents, and set it down in front of him.

"Honorable Ivan," he began without any greeting, and not actually looking at anyone, "I don't recall you warning me there would be a telepath at the meeting."

The Vricolakos stroked his beard smugly. "I warned you."

"You were talking about him," said Ramon, pointing at Slaven, who was scowling at everybody there in turn. "But nothing was said about Darel Dahanavar."

I sensed that the financier was angry.

"All right. Let's get started." Overcoming his irritation, he opened the folder and pushed some documents across to his opposite number. "You need to sign these. Three copies of each."

The long, tedious negotiations began. The Upieschi wanted to rent a plot of land that belonged to the Vricolakos family. And each side was trying to get the most advantageous deal possible.

My awareness divided. With one part of it, I studied Ramon. The other part felt out Ivan, while screening itself from the elder and his assistant at the same time. Slaven tried to reach into my mind, but he received a sharp riposte, like a painful electric shock. His fur bristled up in fury. I could hear him snarling loudly all the time, but he could no longer distract me from the most important part of my job.

The Upieschi's head was full of numbers. Long strings of calculations, virtual images of real profits. The thick line of an imaginary graph crept along in his mind, moving up or down depending on the result of each calculation. It was actually quite interesting. He was calculating the outcome of his actions ten moves ahead. Irreproachable logic.

Realizing that I wouldn't be able to remember the increase in percentage returns from the use of the Vricolakos land over a seven-year period, I reached out, took a sheet of paper off the table in front of me, and, without looking at it, started writing down the columns of figures that appeared in front of my eyes.

Ramon squinted at my crooked notes and grinned patronizingly. He had nothing to hide in this department.

Ivan looked through the documents, knitting his brows in concentration. I could tell he found it hard to understand the subtleties of legal language.

"Another copy," I said, holding out my hand toward the Upieschi's folder, and he handed me a copy of the agreement with a condescending smile.

"Clause one. Obligations of the parties . . ."

Then began the difficult work of translating the dry terminology into images that the Vricolakos could understand.

Ramon gradually started to get irritated. Time was passing, and we had got only halfway through the agreement.

"Gentlemen, perhaps you should take the documents and study them in detail? We can meet tomorrow. Or are you prepared to accuse me of devious practice on some specific points?"

"The price of this land is too high," I said, interrupting the Upieschi. I didn't know why I'd said it. What business of mine was the value of the land that was being leased? The district was a poor investment proposition. The infrastructure could be developed in ten years. But it would only start producing a return in fifteen or twenty years.

"I'm aware of that." Ramon gestured, dismissing my statement as inconsequential. The platinum watch on his wrist flashed.

"There are no roads. A high-voltage power line—"

"I know! Dear Darel, you were invited as an emotional monitor for these negotiations. The two parties can draw their own conclusions."

Slaven smirked, sending me a repulsive, spiteful thought about my professionalism. I ignored him. Ivan muttered something vaguely reassuring and approving to me and reached for the pen.

"I'll sign. It suits me. I knew you wouldn't cheat me, Ramon, but I still had to check."

I lifted the handkerchief soaked in levzei to my nose again, my mind beginning to skew from the incompatible feelings of the two family leaders, and suddenly I *saw*. Before I reimmersed myself in the other men's emotions, I had a moment of faintness and dizziness, with a ringing sound in my ears. The vision came from Ramon.

The figure of a man on the ground. The body arched, the eyes rolled up and back, the mouth open in a scream . . . Bared fangs—so it was one of the blood brothers. His hands were tearing the clothes off his chest, the nails of the hooked fingers scratching the skin. And standing opposite him, another figure in an immaculate business suit. Observing.

The picture blurred and was replaced by Ramon's furious impatience. He leaned forward, as though he wanted to grab me by the lapel of my jacket.

"What did you see?"

"Nothing," I muttered, crumpling the damp handkerchief in my hand. "Nothing to do with the business. It was personal."

The Upieschi wasn't satisfied with my answer. But before he could demand any further explanation, Slaven's furious cry echoed around the room.

"Father! Father, he—"

I didn't let him finish. My patience was exhausted. After the events of the last two days, the insolent cub's attempt to reach into my mind was enough to throw me into a fury.

I *struck out*. Hard, abruptly, taking pleasure in it. Without any warning. Slaven howled, grabbed his head in both hands, and collapsed to his knees. He started whining like a beaten dog. But I kept turning up the pressure of the Neuron Attack. It must have been painful. I've been told it feels as if your brains are starting to boil.

"Darel. Let him go. Stop! That's enough!"

Ramon's shout drowned out the young pup's howls in my mind, but in addition to the desire to halt the punishment and part in peace, the Upieschi was feeling a keen curiosity as he observed the aggressive display of Dahanavar power. Ivan was holding me by the shoulder, and there was a wave of gentle warmth flowing from his fingers. He was trying to calm me down. Strange, he ought to have attacked.

"Let him go. . . . Let him go."

Slaven was sobbing, trembling on the brink of blankness, but he couldn't collapse into unconsciousness. They say that animals can't faint.

"Stop!"

I released him. Not because I was sorry for him. But it was sickening. I was disgusted with myself. The young Vricolakos doubled up on the floor, his head against his knees. Ramon leaned back in his chair.

"That was what I meant when I said I didn't want a Dahanavar scanner involved in the negotiations."

Ivan lowered himself heavily into his seat. He signed all three copies of the agreement with a flourish. Took out a little bag from behind his belt and tossed it across the table to me.

I took the diamonds and walked out of the office without saying a word. I was staggering.

Almost Immortality

> The world is simply divided into two classes—those who believe the incredible, like the public. And those who do the improbable.
>
> —Oscar Wilde, *A Woman of No Importance*

September 15
Darel Dahanavar

I tried not to think.

As I watched the wet road come flying in under the wheels of the car, I tried to distract myself by thinking about other things. About Paula and Vance. Even about the bank where I would deposit the money from the diamonds I had been paid and what the interest rate would be. But the cursed thoughts kept crowding into my head. I was bogged down in them like quicksand.

Why had the Vricolakos invited me to the negotiations? What had he really wanted? If Ivan didn't understand civil law, he could have called in a solicitor to explain all the subtle points in the documents.

Why pay a huge amount of money for a worthless piece of land?

And what did my vision mean?

No, our First Lady could think about that. My job was the telepathy. The emotional monitoring of the negotiations, as Ramon had put it. I didn't want to know any more than that.

The road, with the streetlamps and the headlights of the other cars, suddenly swam in front of my eyes. I had to make a serious effort to refocus. I was tired. Sick and fed up with all my relatives and their business. I didn't want to think about them.

It was funny. In two days I'd managed to earn three enemies: Amir, Paula, and Slaven. And maybe Ivan, too.

Felicia called unexpectedly. And loudly. As if she were right there beside me on the next seat. A young, resonant voice, vibrating with inner strength. She had had a good rest and eaten well, and she was feeling wonderful. I was annoyed and surprised to find that I disliked the sound of her voice.

"Darel."

"The negotiations are over." Of course, that short phrase wouldn't be enough to get rid of her. The Lady wanted a full, detailed report.

"I'm expecting you."

"No. I haven't got enough time. Or strength."

She paused, wondering whether to take any notice of my impudence. Thought of the importance of what I could tell her. Remembered that insolence was not a regular fault of mine.

"All right, let's talk now. What did you learn?"

"Maybe tomorrow? I'm tired."

The attempt to get time for a little rest was futile.

"I need this information today." She wasn't ordering me. She was insisting gently. But I knew that, if necessary, Felicia would turn me inside out to discover the facts that interested her.

A BMW with dark-tinted windows sounded its horn in annoyance as it overtook my Pontiac. The note was low, almost verging on infrasound. I was driving too slowly, and I'd occupied the middle lane. I had to move over to the far right.

I didn't have much mental strength left, but with a vindictive, despairing determination, I set up a blind tunnel between us, a defense against anyone else listening in. Although she could have done that herself.

Overcoming my sense of revulsion, I gave her a brief account of the meeting.

"I don't understand why the Vricolakos needed me. He could have managed without me."

I pulled up at a traffic light and waited for the arrow for my turn to light up. "And what was that farce about leasing the land all about? The Upieschi have thrown away a heap of money on that."

I wasn't expecting any response to these questions, but Felicia unexpectedly condescended to give me an answer.

"They didn't throw it away. Ramon paid Ivan for services rendered. The leasing was a pretense."

"Even so, he could have handed over the money without getting an outsider involved in the elders' business."

"He needed you. . . . What's that sound?"

"Brakes. I'm in the car. I was driving, but now I've stopped. It's hard for me to watch the road and talk with you at the same time. So why did Ivan want me to be there? I could have seen something that compromised them both. And I did see something."

"Ivan's not as wild as he seems. I believe that vision wasn't meant for you. The Vricolakos knew you would report every word of his conversation with Ramon. And all the images you saw."

"I don't understand."

Felicia paused, as if she were wondering whether she ought to fill me in on the fine details. I lowered a window slightly, and cool air with the sharp smell of the city flowed in through the narrow crack. The occasional cars driving past lit up the interior of the Pontiac with their headlights.

"The Upieschi have no magic. You know that."

Not a question, but a statement. Only I wasn't quite so certain about it. The financier-vampires couldn't hurl fire or create zombies, but how could I explain to Felicia that feeling of prickling, sparkling electricity inside Ramon? He had power, I just couldn't define its essential nature.

"They tried to acquire some magical potential from the Vricolakos. As you saw, it didn't work. The vampire in the experiment was killed."

I gazed obtusely at the instrument panel. I needed to go and get some gas. I was almost on empty.

"Are you telling me that the Upieschi are holding experiments to combine the powers of the two families? But that's insane!"

"Who knows," the Lady replied evasively. "The negotiants don't think so. Ramon doesn't want to advertise his secret business, and so even the simple payment of money was disguised as a leasing agreement."

She stopped speaking, distracted by something happening in the room. I didn't want to *look* at what it was. My blind irritation grew stronger. I was being used. As a live video camera. Recording the required information and conveying it to my master.

"You worked well today," said Felicia, coming back to me and radiating satisfaction. "I'm pleased. Thank you."

I could take that as permission to go home.

I went back to my dark, empty apartment, walked into the parlor, and sat down in an armchair without even taking off my jacket.

My head was buzzing with white noise—an excess of information. Rustling, ringing, squeaking, meaningless echoes of other people's emotions. Around my eyes the skin felt inflamed, across my cheekbones it was stretched so tight that it hurt, and it was gathered in deep folds from my nose to my lips.

Fatigue had exceeded its usual limits. Instead of dull apathy, there was a nervous inner trembling. I needed to get some sleep. Switch off from my thoughts and memories.

I wondered whether, if Ramon offered Felicia really big money to open up my head and see how I read other people's thoughts, she would agree. No, hardly. It would be stupid to sacrifice a first-rate scanner for vulgar material gain. But I wondered if she would sacrifice me if the interests of the House were involved. And justify the sacrifice in the name of vital necessity.

How sick I was of them. Greedy, farsighted, wise, despicable, empty. Dried-out, desiccated, frozen entities inside young, attractive bodies. Weighed down by the memories of centuries gone by. With no genuine, vivid feelings left. Old.

Outside, on the other side of the wall, the day was beginning.

Day. A blazing disk in the hot haze of the bright autumn sky. Dense shadows with sharp edges lying on the concrete. Buildings flooded with light. Every pane of glass reflecting a small, blinding sun. In this light, human faces look pale. Pale.

I went into the bedroom and got undressed, dropping my clothes on the spot. I climbed into bed, laid my cheek on the cool pillow, and closed my eyes tight. Hot red spots floated behind my eyelids.

I couldn't fall asleep. I skipped from the edge of one dream to another, but I couldn't get a grip on any of them. I was choking and drowning in gray sludge. I tossed and turned in the bed, trying to find a comfortable position in which my tired body would relax, but I couldn't.

They say the Ligamentia can control the space lying between reality and the world of dreams and that they draw power and knowledge from it. There's a huge amount of information dissolved in that thin layer between the states of being fully asleep and fully awake; the passage of time keeps shifting every moment, and it's easy to get lost there. That's why Ligamentia children can foretell the future and see the past. That's why they're so strange.

The phone shrilled piercingly. Deafeningly. I was shaken and tossed up out of the deep darkness I had sunk into what seemed like only a minute ago. The anger and weariness that were only just beginning to dissolve into a dream came back again.

"Hello, Darel?"

I stifled a yawn with an effort. "Hello."

"It's Loraine. What are you doing?"

"Sleeping."

"Sleeping?"

She laughed, and I thought a stream of blinding light came flooding out of the phone straight into my face. I had to close my eyes.

"Sleeping? At four in the afternoon?"

"God, is it that early!"

She laughed again, thinking I was joking. "Wake up. The weather outside is wonderful."

"Is it? What's it like?"

"Warm. Calm. A clear blue sky, sunshine . . ."

"How horrible," I muttered, and was rewarded with another burst of miraculous laughter.

I opened my eyes, and there in the darkness of the room I *saw* her—a slim, delightful young woman. She was calling from a pay phone on a corner in the park; that was why there was a feeling of immense open space filled with light and the rustle of falling leaves.

"I love the fall," Loraine said, and then added quietly, amazed at her own boldness, "Let's meet right now."

I realized I was smiling, even though my irritation wasn't easing off yet.

"If you're in a bad mood, I'll try to cheer you up. We can go into the park. It's really beautiful in there." She paused and then added in a voice that was trembling slightly: "I'm so happy today. I'll wait for you on the bridge where you came up to me."

Loraine paused again, and for a few long seconds I heard nothing but resounding silence. And then a timid question:

"Will you come?"

"Yes, at nine in the evening."

And before she had time to object, I hung up and then pulled the adapter plug out of the socket.

There were five hours left, enough time to catch up on my sleep. If only I could sleep.

I feel better when I talk to her, don't I? The sheer joy that the girl radiates washes away my poisonous bitterness, and now my head's not buzzing so badly. . . . But she probably won't come now. No girl would forgive that kind of insult. She invited me into her world of trees turned gold by autumn, clear skies, and ripe rowanberries, and I hung up.

I lit candles. All the candles I had. Lots and lots and lots of candles. The golden glow rose out of the white wax and floated around the room, rising higher and higher. It bathed my sore eyes, my dry lips, my entire face.

I sank into a chair and allowed the golden light to play with my imagination. The trembling spots fused together, and in them I saw a beautiful, luminous face.

Why am I drawn to you, tiny spark of light on the bridge? You give no warmth or light. I can extinguish you with a single movement of my hand. Why would I want you? Why does my heart, which has been still for so very long, suddenly recall that soaring thrill, that sweet anxiety of anticipation? How good it was to be human, how good . . . not to be alone. . . .

Raving nonsense.

I swept the candles off the table with an abrupt movement of my hand. The candlestick from the bedside table followed them to the floor. I kicked over the candle ends on the floor.

If only I could have trampled out the sparks of light in my soul as well, I would have done it long ago.

* * *

SHE came.

I was standing on the bridge. The dark water was swaying and heaving far below. A cold wind was throwing the first sparse drops of approaching rain into my face, and the white light of distant, icy Vega was shining through a gap in the clouds. I looked at it and remembered a futile conversation with well-intentioned Chris:

"Darel, can you answer one simple question—why do you have this constant urge to associate with mortals? What for?"

I could have answered honestly that I didn't know, if only he hadn't been acting like that.

"You treat me like you're my guardian, Chris. I'm sick of it."

"I am your guardian. Ever since Flora was killed, I'm responsible for you."

"Well, look at that, he replies."

"No irony, please. You still have a lot to learn before you can impress me with your sarcasm. Leave that girl alone. Stop messing with her head."

"Chris, leave me alone! And stop following me, will you? Don't you have anything better to do?"

"One day I'll shorten that insolent Dahanavar tongue of yours."

"Just you be careful no one shortens yours first, Cadavercitan."

I grinned as I recalled how the exchange of pleasantries had developed into an undignified tussle both guardian and pupil had enjoyed hugely. We had exchanged a couple of harmless spells, which left me with green circles floating in front of my eyes and Chris frowning and smiling as he massaged his temples.

I heard a quiet breath beside me, and when I turned around I saw the subject of our argument standing there. Twin reflections of cold Vega sprang up in her eyes.

"I don't understand why you had to hang up. We didn't have to meet today," she said, pronouncing every word slowly and precisely in a hurt, trembling voice.

I looked at her closely. Resentment, surprise, bewilderment, anticipation, that quiet trembling. And what else is there? What else is it that flickers through your feelings so quickly that cheeks don't even have time to flush in embarrassment?

"I'm sorry, Loraine. I've got serious problems at work."

Her annoyance with my loutish behavior dissolved into sympathy and concern.

She remembered that my job was connected with my empathic abilities. She started feeling worried. Her overdeveloped imagination created pictures of what could have happened, and for some reason most of her visions featured tough young guys with shaved heads, fierce faces, and pistols under their leather jackets. Guys annoyed with me because I'd forecast the foreign currency exchange rates wrong. And she had wanted to go for a walk in the park.

"Very serious?"

"Tolerable."

"Please, don't be upset," said Loraine. And suddenly she moved close and hugged me tight.

I felt as if I could hardly breathe. I felt as if I were suffocating in the circle of those slim, supple arms, because in a single second my game had stopped being a game. What had I done? I'd tried everything to make this young, impressionable girl fall in love with me. I was only playing at romantic meetings in the night. But I'd played so convincingly that she had believed me. And believed *in* me—the mysterious, attractive stranger who could guess her desires. Her shoulders suddenly trembled.

"Are you cold?"

"A bit," she said with a nod. "It's the wind."

"Let's go somewhere warm."

"Do you want to see where I live?"

I suddenly felt uneasy. I remembered the ancient superstition. Until you invite a vampire into your home, he can't enter. He can't do you any harm. It was an unpleasant feeling. I felt like one of those greedy, farsighted, wise, despicable old creatures.

Loraine looked at me in calm anticipation, not knowing what was going on in my soul. And I answered:

"Yes."

SHE lived in Botanical Lane, in a new sixteen-story building. On the tenth floor.

"Please, come in. Take your coat off. This is the sitting room."

I walked past her and drew the curtains. Cozy and warm. Comfortable, beautiful furniture. Shelves with elegant ornaments, books, photographs.

I examined the smiling, carefree faces of people I didn't know. This delightful woman in a light cotton dress, under a striped umbrella, she must be her mother. Loraine had her eyes and hair. And this man with the dog was her father. And there she was—a girl with a tan, wearing a short white skirt, holding a tennis racket, and laughing, the eyes in her dusky face looking as transparent as water.

Loraine had disappeared into the depths of the apartment, but I could hear her in the kitchen, clattering dishes, and in the next room, where drawers scraped as they were pulled open. Then she appeared again and explained, touching my shoulder with her light hand.

"That's us at the seaside last year. And this is me with a friend from my class at school. That dog was given to me for my tenth birthday."

"Can I have this photograph?"

I was holding a photograph in a simple wooden frame. The sunlight had settled on her hair like matte gilt, and the strings of the white tennis racket cast narrow diamonds of shadow.

"That's me at the school tennis tournament. Third place. Take it, if you want. So, you like it?"

"Very much."

Loraine was slightly embarrassed. She disappeared into the kitchen again, but a minute later she looked out and asked:

"Darel, do you drink coffee?"

I liked the smell of coffee, and the blood of people who drank it acquired a very pleasant, heady taste.

"I won't have any today."

I put the photo on the shelf and looked around. There had been a few changes in the room. There was a bottle of white wine, two glasses, and a bowl of fruit standing on the coffee table between the two armchairs.

I opened the bottle, we sat down, and I asked Loraine to tell me about her life. She talked and I listened, with an avid craving that surprised me. In sixth grade, she had been sick: "Nothing serious, but I missed a lot, and I studied at home." In seventh grade, she fell in love for the first time: "But he liked talking about football, and I liked studying history and playing tennis.

"You know," she said out of the blue, "I don't know anything at all about you."

"Does that bother you?"

"It's just strange spending time with someone when all you know about him is that he's an empath and he knows a famous rock singer. Well, and his name, too."

She looked at me demandingly—she had decided it was finally time for me to lay my cards on the table.

"Darel, sometimes I have a very strange feeling when I'm with you. As if you can tell what's going on inside my head. Is that possible?"

"Yes."

Loraine thought about that. "Is it hard, always feeling other people?"

"Yes."

"Today, when you were standing on the bridge and looking at

the stars, I suddenly felt as if you had nothing to do with me or absolutely anybody at all on earth. And I felt frightened. Really frightened, in case it was true."

"It isn't."

This girl had a rare gift. I could sense her sincere interest in people, the desire to share their problems. That was what I used to be like, in my human life.

"And can you tell what I'm thinking about now?"

Of course, Loraine couldn't resist asking that question. She was trying to think about something else in an attempt to test whether I really could read her thoughts. But I wasn't going to do that.

I took hold of the girl's shoulders, pulled her toward me, and kissed her, very gently, on her warm, slightly parted lips. So that all she could feel was the softness of my own.

Loraine clung to me, sending a wave of rapture, happiness, excitement, bewilderment, and tenderness flooding over me. I was about to make another big mistake. It wasn't just because she'd already planned the way this night was supposed to continue. Apparently I wanted it to continue like that, too.

I was woken by a sharp, stabbing pain in my shoulder.

Sunlight.

A ray as thin as a knitting needle was shining in onto my shoulder through a gap in the curtains. I thought it must have burned all the way through. Daylight—the light of the sun!

"Damn! Damn!" I tumbled off the divan bed and into the safety of the shade, waking Loraine with my howl of terror.

"Darel, what is it? What's happened?" she murmured, batting her eyelashes sleepily. "What's wrong with you?"

"Pull down the blinds! That light could kill me!"

Loraine gazed in horror at my face contorted in pain, at the long smoking scar on my shoulder, and finally she saw my pale face by daylight—my glittering eyes, my fangs. She jumped up, dashed to the window, and slammed down the blinds.

Shadow—soft, gentle shadow—caressed my scorched skin and blinded eyes. I felt a bit better. I could still feel my breath trembling as I heaved a deep sigh. I relaxed and looked up.

The girl was standing there, pressing her hand to her throat, looking at me with huge eyes full of fear.

"Darel, you . . . No. It's not possible!"

She sank gently onto the bed and put her hands over her face. In her place, I would have opened the window as wide as possible and waited for the sun to reduce me to ashes.

"Listen . . ."

She shook her head desperately and threw up her hands to stop me trying to come any closer.

"Don't. Don't say anything, please."

Loraine was trying to calm herself down, but the scar on my shoulder from the sun defied all logical explanations. Her normal human world had collapsed with the appearance of a monster straight out of horror films and ancient legends. The kind you had to drive away with holy water or kill by sticking a stake through his heart.

"But, Darel, you know vampires don't exist! You laughed at that Goth. You made him look like a total idiot."

"Loraine . . ."

"No. It can't happen. It's simply impossible!"

"Loraine!"

"Why? Why should it happen to me? Why should the only boy that I liked so much, that it felt so good to be with, be a . . . Darel, tell me it isn't true. It's a joke, isn't it? You were just fooling with me?"

"Yes, it's a joke, a stupid joke. Does that make you feel better?"

She shook her head, and her hair fell across her face. I heard a sound from behind the soft curtain. Was she crying? Or laughing?

In her place, I would have laughed. There were plenty of attractive young men in the city, and she'd fallen in love with a vampire.

So now where was my overhyped supersensitivity?

I *reached out* to her gently, very carefully, trying to make my touch warm, trying to *feel*. There was pain, stupefaction, fear, resentment, and something else. That something else was what I had to cling to.

"Loraine, I know I have to go. But I can't go right now. I'll have to wait for night, otherwise . . ."

I looked at the wound that was still aching, and she raised her head.

"Does it hurt? There's a bandage in the bathroom, and iodine . . . No, I'll go. It's light in there."

She brought a first-aid kit, put it on the floor beside me, and sat back down on the bed. After her initial fear, she wasn't afraid of me the way she ought to have been. There was no disgust or revulsion or horror in her feelings, no desire to just turn and run.

"This is why you didn't come yesterday afternoon?"

"Yes."

"And if I hadn't gone out so late that time, we would never have met?"

"No."

She touched her neck, as if she were trying to find scars that didn't exist.

"Why didn't you tell me anything? Did you think I wouldn't believe you? Or did you not want to scare me?"

I pressed the back of my head against the cold wall and closed my eyes. "You are scared."

"I could have imagined anything at all, but this. Darel, tell me it isn't true."

"Check. All you have to do is open the blinds."

Loraine lowered her head so far that her face was completely covered by her wavy hair.

We sat there, Loraine on the divan with her knees pulled up to her chest and me on the floor in the darkest corner of the room. Which was exactly where I belonged. It was good that everything had turned out this way. There'd be no more daytime phone calls, no hurt feelings and implausible explanations. There wouldn't be anything.

I opened the first-aid kit and ripped open the bandage with a crack. I tore off a piece of cotton wool, took a bottle of antiseptic, pressed the moist swab to the wound, bore the stinging pain, and bandaged my shoulder tightly. It probably wouldn't help, but there was still something human left in me. Even if it was only a body that could hurt in such a very human way.

Loraine was watching me. I could feel her sad, uneasy gaze.

"Are we still friends?" she asked quietly.

"Yes," I said, smiling my usual smile. I didn't have to hide it any longer.

Loraine sighed, and in that sigh there was relief, a little bit of the old fear, and a tiny bit of a new one. It was the new fear that made her ask:

"And you . . . you won't . . . you won't do anything bad to me?"

I looked at her seriously. "Don't be afraid. I'll never hurt you."

"Darel, tell me, why . . . why me?"

"Perhaps because you're like a clear sunny day. There's so much light in you, but you don't burn. Perhaps because I'm tired of being alone, and when you were standing on the bridge, you looked so lonely yourself."

Loraine walked over, sat on the floor beside me, and pressed her warm side against me. I felt myself slowly beginning to sink into sleep. I knew it would be a deep sleep; there had been too much of everything all at once—fatigue, fear, pain, sunlight . . . love. Loraine whispered something, but I couldn't hear her any longer.

Brief fragments of some vivid dream floated up out of the darkness, together with the scent of her hair. My cheek was pressed against it, and through the tangle of images I felt the touch of gentle fingers on my face and warm rays of sunshine that didn't burn me.

I woke up at the very moment the sun sank below the horizon. As if an alarm clock had gone off.

And I realized I'd had a wonderful sleep.

The room was lit up by the matte glow of a laptop screen. Loraine was sitting in front of the computer, biting her lower lip in concentration as she clicked through pages on the Internet. She was looking for information on vampires. Naturally, there was a huge amount of it.

For a while I just watched her hands, her slim fingers moving over the keyboard, her hair, which was almost dark in the semidarkness, and the black shadow of the bookshelf falling across her exposed neck.

Loraine looked around when she felt me watching her, saw that I wasn't asleep, and smiled.

"Hi. You slept all day long, like a log. You didn't even move about in your sleep. It's eight o'clock already."

Something in my face must have changed, because she asked in alarm:

"Darel, is there something wrong?"

"I'm hungry."

Yes, that was what I had been dreaming about—hunger, pain, and sunshine. Warm, gentle sunshine that I didn't have to hide from.

Loraine sat on the divan and watched as I got dressed.

"Are you going right now?"

"Yes."

"But I . . . is there nothing I can do for you?"

I grinned and touched her feverish cheek. "No." I cast another quick glance at that dusky neck and hastily looked away. "No."

"I'll go with you."

The idea had obviously only just occurred to her, and she found it tremendously attractive.

"No, you won't."

"Darel, please."

First she had stopped being afraid of me. Now she would cajole one small concession out of me, then another; after that she would ask to be introduced to my friends. Then I would realize I couldn't refuse anything she asked.

"Listen, girl, don't make me angry. You're not going anywhere."

Then something incredible happened. The docile girl who only a few hours ago had been frightened out of her wits threw back her golden hair and declared:

"Yes, I am going. And don't shout. You have no right to stop me."

WE walked out together. Loraine breathed in the cold night air through her nose with an anxious air and looked around as if she were in a forest full of dangerous predators and expected to be attacked at any second. Beyond my annoyance with her stubbornness, I felt sorry for her.

"Do you remember the bar we went to the first time?"

Loraine nodded and squeezed my hand tight.

"Go there and wait for me. I won't be long."

"No, I'm coming with you."

When I heard her tone of voice, I took her by the shoulders and turned her toward the light of a streetlamp.

"You're afraid, I think?"

She was frightened by the cold gleam in my eyes, but even more by the emptiness of the streets, which didn't seem mysterious and attractive any longer. Now it concealed shapeless shadows that followed her movements with cold, glittering eyes from behind every corner. Almost like me.

"All right, let's go. We'll walk to that corner."

I set off quickly along the dark street, without looking around or stopping or thinking about where I was going. Loraine could hardly keep up with me. It was the first time she had seen me hunting. And she still didn't know if my cold concentration frightened or fascinated her.

There it was, creeping up on me—the calm indifference, dissolving my memory of the girl and my feelings for her, of the Vega in her eyes, of autumn and the sunshine. In the darkness, the world was shrinking to a narrow strip that I had to walk along quietly without being noticed. Then I would be able to hear snatches of thoughts and feelings; I would be invisible and almost all-powerful. At moments like that, I am no longer subject to the mortal desires that are still strong in me and become genuinely free.

"Darel! Darel, can I wait for you here, on the bench?"

I turned to look at her, and when Loraine met my gaze, she shrank away. A confused, helpless smile sprang to her lips and immediately disappeared. It seemed to me that she wanted to run away, shout for help, or do something else stupid. But the girl simply touched my hand timidly and asked again in a quiet voice:

"Can I?"

I came back an hour later.

Loraine was sitting there like a sparrow with its feathers fluffed up against the gusts of icy wind that were sweeping over her from head to toe, tousling her golden hair and forcing their way up into the sleeves of her jacket. Every now and then, she lifted her head and looked into the darkness of the side street out of which she imagined I ought to appear. And her expression was so agitated, tense, and despairing that I felt the stab of an old, long-forgotten pain in my heart.

She saw me. Lifted her head abruptly and jumped to her feet.

"You were gone so long . . . is everything all right?"

"Yes. You're frozen. Let's go."

"No, wait."

She was tired, chilled through. What she wanted most of all was to press herself against me and not think about anything. But for some reason, she had to know the truth. The whole truth.

"You want to know if I killed anyone? If I kill every night?"

Loraine nodded, looking at me eagerly.

"No. No, I didn't kill anyone. Now let's go. I'll tell you about it."

WE were sitting in that same bar, the first one. I'd chosen it a long time ago as the final halt on my nocturnal wanderings around the city. It was very like another bar in another city. The one where long, long ago Chris had split an oak table with a single blow of his hand for a bet, where the enchanting Lidia—a young maid-in-waiting to the empress—used to arrange assignations with her lovers, where one day Ferenz had played the piano that stood in the far corner. The one where, almost a century later, Samuel had taught me to smoke marijuana.

That was where Flora had taken me. Confused, tormented by doubt, hungry . . . that was when I first learned what genuine *hunger* was like. And she sat me down at a table and smiled affectionately and told me I was no longer human.

We were sitting at the table farthest from the door, by the wall, under a copper lamp that looked like a withered flower. Loraine was holding a big cup of hot chocolate in both hands, looking at me with eyes full of concern, and listening carefully to what I said.

Flora had sat in that same place many years ago, and I had twirled the cigarette lighter in my fingers in the same desultory manner, trying not to meet her eyes or see that expression of tender care for her foolish child. Trying not to notice that she could read me like a book. The small flame flared up above my fingers and was reflected as a bright patch on the table. I still loved her then.

My second mother. I was twenty-five when Flora took me into

her family. I was young, arrogant, and searching recklessly for new experiences and sensations. And that's just the beginning.

Loraine reached out to me; I felt the hot touch of her hand on my wrist but kept looking at the tiny flame in my hand.

"I am Darel, a telepath from the Dahanavar vampire family. I am one hundred and twenty-nine years old, and I am the dream come true of teenagers and young people today, a veritable treasure trove of superhuman superpowers. In the same category as the X-Men or Spider-Man."

The slim fingers were still burning my wrist, but Loraine didn't take her hand away, and for a moment it seemed . . . yes, she probably felt sorry for me. For me, who was almost immortal and almost all-powerful.

SOMETHING had changed. I ought to have realized that everything would change after she learned the truth. Loraine looked at me with wide-open eyes full of amazement, curiosity, and a new kind of tenderness. I had expected her to be more afraid of me or at least be a bit apprehensive or respect me for my boundless abilities; but she felt sorry for me.

"Darel, you haven't seen the sun for a hundred and four years. That's awful!"

I shrugged indifferently, watching as she entered columns of figures in her iPhone and marked in bold the most amazing details of my life story. There were already more than a dozen phrases like "hasn't seen," "hasn't tried," "hasn't wanted."

"You see the world in black and white. The dark, shapeless blotch beside a river is trees, the brighter patch is houses. A black sky, a gray river."

I grinned. An astonishing knowledge of her subject. So she had read up on it on the Internet. But I looked at her golden hair, her smoky blue eyes, and still couldn't admit to myself that the world became brighter when she smiled at me.

She wanted to know as much as possible, and I told her the truth as far as I knew it myself. Dark legends thousands of years old. Rumors and traditions about families of vampires fighting an endless bloody war. About the inhuman appearance of the Nosoforos, the intelligence and diplomatic skill of the Dahanavar Ladies, about my Cadavercitan friends and the cruelty of the Nachterret. I told her about our sanctuaries—catacombs and labyrinths deep below the streets of the city that had collapsed during the last century. About the treasures collected by the Asiman and hidden somewhere in the East; about the mysteries of the Ligamentia, none of whom I had ever met, although I had heard many strange stories; about the Vricolakos, who could turn into wolves. About the long winter nights with a short period of daylight, when I slept for only a few hours.

Loraine listened with bated breath as I told her about the time when mortals worshipped us as gods, about the families that had died out and the beautiful ruined cities, and the wonder in her eyes was mingled with sadness.

She was incredibly quick to step across the borderline beyond which fantasy and reality became one. And she accepted the existence of this fantastic reality.

Humans so often imagine my brothers and sisters as completely different from the way they really are. What they're afraid of is not at all what they ought to be afraid of. And they try to use our help to realize the wrong values, not the ones that are worth living for.

I must have thought this too loudly. Loraine seemed to have heard me, because she answered my thought:

"Darel, I wouldn't like to live in your world."

I know you wouldn't.

That's strange. Or, at least, unusual for a human—but you really don't need the strength and power that being nonhuman brings. For you the sunlight is more important.

CAVALIER OF THE NIGHT

What is a cynic?
A man who knows the price of everything and the
value of nothing.

—Oscar Wilde, *Lady Windermere's Fan*

September 18

Miklosh Balza was fond of comfort. So for his rare trips around the city, he always chose a limousine. Despite his abhorrence of everything new and progressive, this kind of automobile met his aesthetic requirements perfectly. In a limousine, the Nachttoter,[3] as the members of the House of Nachterret respectfully referred to their leader, did not feel like a rat in a cage, as happened when he had to abandon his own preferences and switch to a less comfortable and less prestigious automobile.

This evening, Mr. Balza instructed Roman, his personal servant, to select the black Rolls-Royce from the range of cars standing in the garage. Over the last hundred years or so, the Nachttoter had developed a stubborn aversion to cities, but driving into the capital from his residence in this miracle of engineering was actually quite enjoyable.

In his opinion, during those hundred years the human anthills had become vastly overcrowded. The stench of human bodies in them sometimes gave Miklosh a headache. Of course, he

---

3 Nachttoter, "he who kills by night" (German): the official title of the head of the House of Nachterret. From *nacht* ("night") and *töten* ("to kill").

had come to terms with this annoying fact—"you can't slaughter all the sheep (at least, not all at once)"—but he had cut down the number of his outings on the streets of the megalopolis to a fifth, or even a seventh, of what they used to be.

It was all so much simpler before, Miklosh thought irritably as he sat on the soft, comfortable chair in the luxurious automobile. Before anyone had even heard of cities with populations of millions. Life might have been dirtier, but it was far freer and unhampered. The Nachterret were kings of the night then. But now they were more like ghosts who came creeping out of their hiding places. The civilization of the sheep was destroying the wolves. Transforming the blood brothers into toothless calves. Look at what the Cadavercitan had turned into, for instance. And that was the awesome House of Death that had the citizens of Prague running for home as soon as night started to fall.

Miklosh looked out the window and watched as he drove past a huge monument on the far side of the river. He almost swore out loud. What point was there in putting up something like that in the capital? To Mr. Balza's eyes, the bronze giant in the three-cornered hat, mounted on the empty shell of a sailing ship, looked like some huge, ugly monster. And what was the creature on the lookout for in Miklosh Nachterret's city? he would like to know. The Nachttoter wasn't concerned about the artistic side of the matter, he just thought to himself: If I ever meet the sculptor, we'll discuss it seriously.

But then, Miklosh didn't like the historical center that the limousine was driving through now, either. Piles of red brick and flat surfaces. Colors that were far too cheerful. For him personally, the only architectural style worth anything at all was somber Gothic, or at least pseudo-Gothic. The Nachttoter's beloved Prague was far better from that point of view. But unfortunately, Prague had been inaccessible for several centuries now. And it would stay that way.

"Those damn Cadavercitan," he muttered, grinding his teeth.

The next curse was addressed to the Dahanavar family, who roused the Nachttoter to a fury by daring to defend the sheep.

Miklosh chuckled contentedly. He had done right to send Johan to the council instead of going himself. He could do without the dubious pleasure of listening to Felicia's hysterical whining. Mr. Balza preferred to spare his nerves and his ears. He despised the female First Elder of the Dahanavar family with a vicious hatred, and sometimes after he was obliged to meet her, it was two weeks before he was able to write music again.

The Nachttoter thought the mormolika had too high an opinion of herself altogether. The most disgusting thing of all was the way she tried to make the other families live by her rules. The leader of the Golden Hornets,[4] as Miklosh's pupils referred to him, thought it was absurd that any of the blood brothers should accept Felicia's proposals, let alone put them into practice. The House of Asiman and the House of Nachterret were the only ones who had not yet signed a single agreement on the regulation of hunting.

Mr. Balza was firmly convinced that all humans were legitimate prey for the blood brothers. And he had no intention of bowing and scraping to every sheep before he fastened his fangs in its neck. And he certainly wasn't going to leave them alive.

Miklosh looked out the window again and noticed a girl standing near the entrance to a nightclub. Short, but with an excellent figure and, even more important, an immensely thick braid of straw-colored hair hanging down below her waist. She was dressed with style, but not flashily. Only the basic minimum of makeup and—to judge from the lovely complexion—she didn't smoke. The very thing. This little poppet was very much to his taste.

---

4 The crest of the House of Nachterret is three gold hornets on a black field.

He immediately ordered the limousine to stop. Keeping his eyes on the girl, he reached for his raincoat and told the driver:

"Wait."

"But, Nachttoter," the driver tried to object, "we have a meeting and—"

"I said wait," the head of the House of Nachterret repeated without raising his voice.

The driver shut his mouth and hurried to open the door for Mr. Balza.

The Nachttoter got out of the car. Breathed in the night air, which smelled of a thunderstorm and exhaust fumes from the main highway. Repulsive. And Johan was always tearfully imploring him not to just stay at home, but to take a stroll in the city at least once a week. The Nachttoter wasn't inclined to indulge in the pleasures of strolling. He emerged from his lair only very rarely, and only on business. Even his food was delivered to his mansion.

Thinking about food, Miklosh looked at the girl again. She was standing on the far side of the road, clearly waiting for someone. Well now, the little poppet had no idea who was going to show up tonight. Humming one of his own symphonies to himself, the Nachterret was just about to walk across and get acquainted when his cell phone started pealing loudly.

Mr. Balza raised his eyes imploringly. Everyone seemed to have conspired against him today. They just wouldn't let him relax. All his subordinates must be in on it. He took out his phone and put it to his ear without saying anything.

"It's me, Nachttoter," said Johan's voice.

Speak of the devil. Sometimes Mr. Balza found his number one assistant infuriating. It happened very rarely, but fairly predictably.

"Nachttoter, it's me!" Miklosh replied, trying to suppress his anger.

There was a second of bewildered silence. Then an uncertain question:

"Where are you?"

Instead of answering, Miklosh looked up at the sky. The full moon was apparently still a long way off. But Johan was behaving exactly like some mental retard.

"You know why I hate cell phones?" Balza hissed. "The question I'm always asked on them is where am I. Don't you rather think that's my business, my friend?"

"I'm sorry, Nachttoter. You didn't arrive at the meeting."

"If I didn't arrive at the meeting, it means that more important business came up."

"Svetlov is worried."

Miklosh shrugged. So the lousy blautsauger wasn't pleased. What a disaster.

"My heart melts and I could weep. Well, give him my apologies. And conduct the negotiations yourself. You're a big boy now. I'm busy."

He switched off his cell phone. The business that the Vricolakos wanted to discuss while he was in town wasn't all that important. Balza didn't really want to see Ivan's hairy face and smell that faint doggy aroma given off by his moth-eaten cloak. Svetlov wouldn't be any worse off if he didn't go. Johan was perfectly capable of resolving all the issues on his own.

While the Nachterret was talking on the phone, two other girls came up to the one he was watching, and all three of them went into a six-story red-brick building right there beside the road. It was the well-known B-9 Club. Quite a popular establishment. And certainly not the cheapest.

There were humans jostling in the entrance. Lots of people wanted to get in. The only way to bypass them was with a club member's card. But Miklosh didn't intend to stand in line.

One of the two massive security guards blocked his way.

"Where do you think you're going, son?"

Mr. Balza didn't like it when people stood in front of him. But this time, he decided not to punish the insolent roughneck. A gentle touch applied to the hulk's brain changed the situation fundamentally. Suddenly the security guard wanted to allow this frail young man in. He apologized profusely and stepped aside.

Miklosh walked into the club.

A vestibule with another two security guards. A bit farther on, a huge aquarium covering an entire wall. A corridor with mirrored walls. The first dance hall. Blue green light and the roaring of so-called music.

A cacophonous wall of sound slammed up against the vampire's pitch-perfect hearing, but for the sake of that girl he was willing to tolerate even this assault on his ears. He looked for her among the many faces of the crowd but failed to find her. She wasn't among the dancers or at the bar, among the eager crowd jostling to get a drink. The Nachttoter didn't despair. It was a big club. The blonde would show up sooner or later.

Another corridor with mirrored walls. Another dance hall. Everything here was wreathed in mist, pierced by shafts of violet light. The music sounded different, but it was just as unpleasant to a sensitive ear. Ignoring the entrance of the video game hall—the girl was not likely to go in there—the cavalier of the night walked through into the third dance hall, the biggest one, which occupied two stories.

Another change in the style of the noise—to the roaring of a chain saw. Another change in the design of the hall—to a spaceship. And another failure.

Miklosh walked up the spiral staircase to the second floor, across a balcony, along a corridor with leather armchairs and palm trees, across another balcony, and into the bar and restaurant. He looked around quickly, and his gaze settled on a couple sitting at a table by the wall. To the Nachterret's surprise, one of them was Felicia's telepath. The girl he was with was not a member of any blood brothers family.

A human being.

A rather attractive-looking girl.

Had Darel Dahanavar decided to fatten up his own supper? That wasn't really his style.

Miklosh didn't like telepaths. He felt uncomfortable in their presence. You had to keep up your defenses all the time, so that they wouldn't go rummaging in your thoughts. And that was incredibly tiring.

Right now, Flora's pupil was telling the girl something and she was listening avidly. He was so involved in the conversation that he hadn't noticed Balza, and there were others he apparently hadn't noticed, too. Miklosh recognized the three men ensconced in the farthest corner of the bar counter as Amir's protégés and grinned spitefully.

Why, the B-9 was positively packed with blood brothers today!

The Asimans didn't notice the head of the House of Nachterret, either. Their attention was focused entirely on the telepath. Miklosh wondered what the pyromaniacs wanted with the Dahanavar. They probably weren't planning to invite him over to their table and stand him the first glass of rhesus negative. Johan had described very vividly how furious Amir had been at the latest council.

But then, what happened to Felicia's protégé was none of the Nachttoter's business, and it wouldn't bother him in the least if the Supreme Magister of the Asiman took revenge on the telepath for some real or imaginary insult. Darel Dahanavar didn't like Miklosh, and the feeling was mutual.

Once he was sure the girl wasn't in the restaurant, Mr. Balza went out onto the stairs and walked up another floor. Searching only whetted his appetite. The longer the hunt, the sweeter the prize when you found it. He knew that he wouldn't wander about like this for much longer. The hunger was becoming almost unbearable.

The next hall had spheres covered in mirrors hanging all over its ceiling. There was a 1965 pink Cadillac set into the bar. Miklosh hated human music, but he knew the different styles. Here, instead of the rock 'n' roll that the design demanded, they were playing disco. There were far fewer people than downstairs. This kind of music wasn't as popular nowadays as it used to be.

The Nachttoter spotted the blonde's girlfriends straightaway. They were chattering gaily about something with three young guys. But the girl he was looking for wasn't there. He swore. Then he felt the fear, horror, despair, pain, and, a moment later, the final agony. Almost hissing in disappointment and fury, Balza set off toward the girls' restroom.

He was too late.

The head of the Nachterret was just about to take hold of the handle when the door opened and an Asiman appeared. Obviously from the same group as the three at the bar. He had spotted the cute little thing and decided to take a snack. This young whelp had killed *his* prey!

The blautsauger gaped wide-eyed. He hadn't been expecting to run into such a famous celebrity. Enraged, Balza took advantage of his rival's confusion to push him back inside. He followed him in and closed the door firmly behind him.

The collar of his brilliant white shirt was ruined. But surprisingly, this annoying fact failed to spoil the Nachttoter's good mood. He glanced at himself in the mirror and tossed the hair back off his forehead. Laughed. The fit of uncontrollable fury had evaporated without a trace.

Miklosh had fits like that occasionally. He liked it. You had to relax and let off steam sometimes, or else life simply became too boring. The fact that anyone unfortunate enough to be within reach suffered when he flew off the handle didn't bother him at all.

Now that the fury had gone, he was in a good mood again. The girl and the Asiman were forgotten. Well, almost forgotten.

Mr. Balza glanced sideways at one of the washroom cubicles, where both bodies were lying. The Asiman had deserved to be dispatched into darkness. Perhaps the Nachttoter had been just a bit hasty, but he didn't regret it. Yes, of course there would be an outcry from Amir, but Miklosh had acted within his rights. Someone had taken his prey, and he had punished the smart-ass as he thought fit. Unlike the other families, the Nachterret never bothered observing the stupid diplomatic niceties.

The door of the restroom opened. The girl who came in saw a young man standing by the washbasin, squealed in fright, and disappeared again. A pity. They could have found something to talk about. His hunger hadn't gone away, it had only been blunted.

After skeptically studying the blood on his collar, Miklosh opened the cold-water faucet wider, tore off a paper towel, and tried to wash off at least some of the stain. While he was busy doing this, the next visitor arrived.

This time, the Nachttoter didn't turn around. He just glanced quickly into the mirror and immediately set up a heavy-duty mental shield. Then he chuckled and added some broken glass to that shield—to teach certain people not to go reaching into other people's thoughts.

"This is an amazing night, Dahanavar," said Mr. Balza, still working on his collar. "All the blood brothers seem to have conspired to visit the girls' restroom. You're the third."

"Miklosh?" The telepath was tense, and he didn't pick up on the jocular tone.

"I can see a question in your eyes. What am I doing here? Isn't that it?"

"What are you doing here?"

"Trying to clean my shirt," the Nachttoter replied imperturbably. "Do you happen to know how to wash out blood? And by the way, asking me what I'm doing here is impolite, to say the least. I was here before you. You wouldn't argue with that, would you? I'm the one who should be feeling curious. So what brings you to such an unusual place, Dahanavar?"

Narrowing his eyes, Darel surveyed the room. Miklosh really disliked him. Who did they tell me he was? A Scandinavian? thought Balza. I don't believe that. In the modern world, the blood of my ancient ancestors has been defiled with such a huge number of vulgar impurities, maybe even dissolved away completely. He's not a Viking just because he has blue gray eyes and light brown hair.

The sensor eventually completed his study of the tiled walls and floor.

"One of the brothers has just died here."

"There are times when I don't envy you. Being a telepath must be such a headache," Balza said, chuckling. "None of us is without sin. Yes, your instinct is correct. Felicia's quite right when she says you're the best. He's in there. In the cubicle. You can take a look if you like."

Miklosh gestured invitingly. Darel hesitated but accepted the invitation.

The Nachterret watched him carefully in the mirror. There—he had opened the door. The bodies had fallen out at his feet. The dead girl in the embrace of the dead Asiman. Hunter and hunted, united by invisible death. Highly symbolic. Edgar Allan Poe, with whom the Nachttoter had chatted informally on occasion, would no doubt have written a magnificent story about it. Full of mysticism and horror. He knew about such things. He had a feeling for the otherworldly. The "invisible," as he called it. But unlike the Cadavercitan necromancers, who worked with dead flesh, the human had been fascinated by the magical moment of transition from living to nonliving, the fading away, the decaying. The helpless fluttering of the soul until the precise moment when the fine thread binding it to the body snaps. That was what interested Miklosh, too. It was a shame that Edgar died after being so frightened by what he had learned. He had been a talented writer. But then, it had to be admitted that his talent developed only under the brilliant influence of the leader of the House of Nachterret, who had revealed to the mortal the enchanting magic of death.

The Dahanavar's voice roused him from his reminiscences.

"This is an Asiman."

"Bull's-eye." Mr. Balza chuckled, and his eyes met the eyes of Flora's pupil. He really enjoyed making this prude angry.

"Why did you kill him?"

"That's my business," said the Nachttoter, closing the faucet. "If Amir al Rahal asks politely, I shall think about my answer."

"You have just violated neutrality."

"I have not concluded any agreements with the Dahanavar!" snapped the head of the Nachterret. "Members of my House can kill blautsaugers if it's in the family's interest. The conversation is over."

He guessed, rather than felt, that the telepath was trying to break into his memories. Chuckling to himself, Miklosh weakened his shield and thought about the girl he had recently seen sitting at the same table as this bothersome fly. He imagined very vividly thrusting his fingers into the mortal's eyes, tearing off her face so that the flesh hung down from the bones, and then sinking his fangs into her trembling neck, tearing it open, and greedily gulping down the blood, trying to cause the dying girl as much pain as possible.

The telepath shuddered at what he had seen and recoiled. Naked hatred blazed in his eyes.

"That's better," the Nachttoter said in a soft voice. "You shouldn't go creeping into other people's heads, or you might come across very specific dreams."

"If anything at all happens to her, you deranged sadist . . ."

"Then what? What will you do to me, Dahanavar? Nothing, without an order from the elders. They keep you on a tight leash. You're a puppet in that kingdom of women. You won't jump until the mormolika tells you to jump. Which makes your threats absurd, at the least. Anyway, I have no interest in your girlfriend. But I advise you to get back to her as quickly as possible. The bodies could be found, and you don't want any problems with the police, do you? Good evening, brother."

He walked over to the dead bodies and held out his hand with the palm facing down.

". . . and Death came to them with a beautiful and youthful face. He led them away into fragrant gardens, and every step removed the shrouds from their bodies . . ."

In the original it said, "removing the shrouds from their souls," but Mr. Balza liked to improvise.

The bodies began to decompose. The skin covering them bubbled up and liquefied, exposing the muscles. In places, bones protruded. A foul-smelling cloud rose into the air.

The Dahanavar backed against the wall. Miklosh enjoyed seeing the grimace of disgust that appeared on his face.

"Your friend the Cadavercitan and I are almost related," said Miklosh, putting more effort into the Wave of Thanatos emanating from his hand. "Except that he controls dead flesh. Transforms the dead into the living. While I effect the opposite transition—from the living to the dead."

Skeletons lay where the bodies had been. And then the bones crumbled into dust under the Nachterret's destructive magic. A minute later, there were only two irregular patches left on the floor.

Miklosh slowly lowered his hand, enjoying the sight of the

telepath's pale green face. His weak annihilation spell had clearly produced a very powerful impression on the fastidious sissy.

"Oh, do the Dahanavar clear away the bodies in some other way? Ah, yes, you don't kill, do you?"

He walked out of the restroom without waiting for an answer, losing all interest in the sensor. The dead girl's friends were already starting to get worried. In a little while, they would come to check on what had happened to her. There was nothing left for them to do in the club. It was time to go home.

Balza forced his way through the heavy wave of music and the crowd of dancing sheep and walked out of the club. Surprisingly enough, this time the air outside in the street didn't seem so foul and suffocating.

The phone in his pocket rang, and the Nachttoter's mood started deteriorating again with catastrophic speed.

"Well, who is it now?"

"Hello, Miklosh? We need to talk," said the head of the Upieschi corporation.

"That's all I've been doing all day, talk. I'm tired of talking. If you want to talk, get yourself a psychoanalyst."

Ramon took no notice of Balza's rudeness. For the negotiants business always came first, and manners were less important. And anyway, the Upieschi had long ago got used to the fact that when Miklosh talked on the phone, he was insulting and excessively sardonic.

"We should meet."

"Not today."

"Tomorrow, then. I'm thinking of offering your family a very profitable contract."

"Good. Johan will be in touch."

The Nachttoter dropped the cell phone into his raincoat pocket in a gesture of annoyance. Crossed the road. The driver was already standing beside the politely opened door.

6

THE METRO

Experience is the name everyone gives to their mistakes.

—Oscar Wilde, *Lady Windermere's Fan*

October 1
Darel Dahanavar

Chris had sacrificed one of his evenings in order to pay me a visit.

We were sitting in my sanctuary. The Cadavercitan was lounging in an armchair, with one elbow propped casually on the armrest, making small talk about nothing very important, while I was thinking how eight hundred years ago, his manners were nowhere near as elegant and he used to spend most of his free time staggering around the taverns with a group of boorish, pushy Burgundians just like himself, swilling cheap wine by the bucketful and wading into every fight that came along.

"Listen, Chris, how many of you wise, noble Cadavercitans are there left? Fifty? Twenty? Even fewer than that? Why don't you want to continue your glorious line? Resurrect your House?"

Chris leaned forward toward me, and a dark, shadowy flame lit up in his eyes.

"Because we are dead, my Dahanavar friend. Dead for centuries already. Our blood is too old, and we are too tired. That is why no one bothers us. Several centuries ago we ceased to be competitors in this interminable struggle for power. We always wanted to be left in peace. The Asiman long to be the most powerful House, do they? By all means, we have no objections. The Vricolakos seek unity with nature? Let them have it. We want peace. We are tired because we have lived too long. All I want to do is sit here in this armchair and calmly watch the candles burn."

"But you're talking nonsense!" I exclaimed the moment he finished talking. "Why, if I had your knowledge, your powers . . ."

The Cadavercitan stared at me with frank curiosity. "Then what would you do?"

"I don't know. But I certainly wouldn't just sit here dreaming about the past."

"Dear Darel, I would be only too glad to hand over all my knowledge to you, if only I could have just a few days of my former life in exchange."

He stopped speaking, and I suddenly saw him as the human being he used to be—a soldier standing on the ruins of ancient empires. Still young and fresh, unburdened by the secret knowledge of the world of night.

"We all yearn for our former life," said Chris, turning back into an elegantly indifferent aristocrat. "And we take our revenge on mortals because they are so blithe and carefree, because their life is so short, because they can see the sun. That is why we transform them into creatures like ourselves—so that they will live forever and suffer just as we do. That is why you are so attracted to that girl."

I looked at him thoughtfully. "I'm not sure you're right. She's not like us. She's not like all the other mortals."

"It's dangerous, Darel. You've become too attached to her," Chris said with a smile, and the smile lightened the tone of his warning. "You spend every night with her, you've given her the key to your sanctuary, revealed so many of our secrets to her . . ."

Sometimes the sorcerer's gentle concern made me furious.

"I am simply trying to warn you that sooner or later one of the elders will object to you running around with this mortal girl. And they won't allow you to make her one of us. You know as well as I do that she has nothing to offer you, the House of Dahanavar. She is too young, too inexperienced, too weak. Edgar was accepted into the House because he knew how to use a sword; in those days you needed skilled warriors. Flora was enchanting and highly intelligent. You possessed rare psychic sensitivity. Ajax is a diplomat from the very highest political circles. But this girl of yours—"

"You know," I interrupted my friend, "she's like me. Like the person I used to be in human life. I can't explain more clearly than that. There's something very familiar."

"Are you trying to say she could be a scanner? A scanner like you?" Chris leaned forward, raising his interlocked fingers to his mouth in an expression of extreme interest.

"I don't know. I don't even want to think about it. Anyway, Chris, that's not important. But could you, you know, if it suddenly became necessary, take her in yourself?"

"But I don't take pupils, Darel," the Cadavercitan said slowly. "I gave up bothering with neophytes several hundred years ago."

"But if I ask you to?"

"Not even if you ask me to."

"Why?"

"Have you never had a pupil of your own? You haven't. You don't know what it's like to transfuse part of yourself into another being and watch every day to make sure that tiny particle grows into something worthy. And if that creature commits some kind of willful abomination, to agonize over whether it does so because your blood corrupts it, or because it was already corrupted by nature. And you can never be certain if, in the end, you will receive genuine gratitude for all your trouble, or a knife in the back."

I suppressed an impolite smile and cautiously suggested: "Perhaps you take this too seriously?"

"Perhaps. But I don't want a House of Cadavercitan that consists of these modern young idiots who choose Pepsi or MTV. You may think me old-fashioned, but I refuse to tolerate an impudent, brainless creature who comes barging into my home, sprawls in my armchair, puts his muddy shoes up on the polished table, calls me 'dude,' and tries to tell me how to live my life. He thinks that just because he was given a few drops of ancient noble blood a month ago, he has the right to consider himself my friend. Why, he shouldn't even dare to speak to me without my permission!"

It sounded as if one of the young brothers must have hurt Chris's feelings. I'd have liked to see that unfortunate individual now.

"And what did you do to him?"

"I gave him a moderate reprimand."

I laughed, imagining this "reprimand." The overbearing pride of a noble knight should have made my friend seize his sword and teach the impudent fellow a good lesson on the spot. His ideas of the complicated system of subordination and authority in the old families were so strict that probably even I had no right to sit in his presence, but the sorcerer apparently made an exception for his friends.

"Do you know what your problem is, Chris?"

"I'd be curious to hear," he replied rather sharply, still fuming at his recent insult.

"You—and not just you, all your people—you're tied too tightly to the past. I realize that the ancient code of honor requires you to fling the unfortunate youth down the stairs immediately, but just think for a moment. He didn't mean anything bad by it. The young clown was simply delighted with his new abilities and new friends, he felt all-powerful. How could he know that the

House of Death still lives according to rules that are a thousand years old? You live in the past, but to survive, you have to adapt to the present."

"Probably." Chris leaned down and adjusted the candle that was about to go out in the candlestick at his feet. "Very probably you are right. But it's not just a matter of my own personal dislike of modern life and the rules of decent behavior. I don't trust the young people nowadays. I can't pass on my knowledge to them, because I don't know what they will use it for."

This was a subject that had always fascinated me—the secret mystical knowledge of the Cadavercitan.

"You don't have to reveal all your secrets to a pupil."

"But what would I want with an empty-headed dummy created in my own image? I need a friend, a helper I can rely on, one who won't start intriguing behind my back so that he can take my place or discover my secrets. No, Darel, I have already been through all that."

"But Loraine isn't like that."

"I don't know. Who can tell what she would be like, once she sensed our power? I have known sweet boys and girls who turned into ravening beasts once they received only a small measure of power."

"She doesn't want power. She doesn't want anything, apart from . . ."

"Apart from what?"

I didn't answer, because I heard the click of the lock opening. Loraine came into the room. Joyful and glowing, carrying a bundle of yellow maple leaves. My mother used to collect them in autumn, I heard her voice say in my memory. She used to iron them, and there was always a big colorful bouquet standing on the table in the sitting room until winter.

"Darel . . ."

When she saw the sorcerer, she stopped talking and halted in the doorway. But he glanced at her with his green eyes glinting, waiting for her to continue.

"Loraine, this is Chris. Chris—Loraine."

The girl nodded and tried to smile. The Master of Death rose from his chair with inimitable feline grace, walked up to her, and took her hand as if he were about to kiss it. Loraine started and several leaves fell on the floor, but the Cadavercitan turned her hand over with the same quiet composure, inspected her perfectly smooth wrist without a single bite mark on it, then turned to look at me, and in his glittering eyes I read: *So, it's like that?* Then he said:

"Very pleased to meet you."

Loraine freed her hand from his grasp and clutched the maple leaf bouquet more tightly. Still looking at me, Chris picked up one of the fallen leaves and smiled ironically.

"All right, Dar, it's time I was going. It's getting late and I'm hungry. Nice to have met you, Loraine."

When the door closed behind him, the girl dropped all the leaves and came dashing across to me, taking no notice of them rustling under her feet. She hugged me hard, pressing her body against me and burying her face in my chest.

"Darel! I'm afraid. Afraid of your friends. And you too, sometimes."

I ran my hand through her hair, which gave off the aroma of maple leaves, and repeated the promise I had made only recently:

"Don't be afraid. I'll never hurt you."

And she believed me again.

"Who is this Chris?" she asked a little later, settling herself more comfortably in the armchair. "I thought he was rather . . . strange."

"He's a Cadavercitan, and they're all rather strange."

Loraine raised her head, and a thick strand of hair fell across her face, covering one of her curious eyes.

"Why?"

I reached out and tried to tuck the strand away, but the girl shook her head and the rebellious hair tumbled back down again.

"Today we'll go to visit him and you'll understand why."

"The Cadavercitan are strange," she said slowly. "The Asiman can fly. The Nosoforos make themselves invisible. And you. What can you do?"

I sat up, examining her serious face.

"I can love you."

WE were walking through the center of town. It was late, but the area was crowded. The air seemed unusually warm and fresh. And the people of the city were enjoying the last fine autumn evenings.

The light that evening was amazing. An intense orange light surrounded the streetlamps in broad, glowing halos, trembled around the buildings, and rose upward in columns of pale, misty radiance. The sky was flooded with purple and lilac. In this radiance, the blazing colors of the ad billboards looked pale. The cars racing along the highway reflected back this unreal light from their polished sides.

Loraine kept looking at me with avid curiosity. Very carefully, as if she thought that I might turn into a bat or disappear into thin air at any moment. She was becoming more and more aware that the person beside her was a supernatural being. She wanted to know what was going on inside my head. She was trying to understand what I felt, what I thought about. How I differed from an ordinary human being.

I was keeping my promise. I was taking her to visit Chris.

"Let's go on the metro."

She looked at me in surprise, although I didn't think there was anything unusual about my suggestion.

"But where's your car?"

"Being repaired."

Another glance of suspicious amazement. The girl genuinely believed that vampires repaired their vehicles exclusively by magical means. Or they abandoned a broken-down automobile in the middle of the street and bought a new limousine half an hour later. Just like in the gangster movies.

Well, naturally, there were some who did that kind of thing. But I wasn't in the habit of throwing money away.

"All right, let's go on the metro." Her voice still sounded suspicious.

We walked down the steps into the underground passage. We got into a train that pulled up.

The car was full. All the seats were taken. People were standing, holding on to the handrails, and there was an atmosphere of evening tiredness and vague irritation. Someone was reading—I *heard* voices muttering indistinctly, and blurred images that had nothing to do with reality flickered in front of my eyes. Several people were dozing, swaying in time to the movement of the train, enveloped in the vague, shapeless clouds of half-formed dreams. If I were a Ligamentia, I'd work in the metro, I thought. The people's dreams looked very accessible at that moment. It would probably be easy to get inside them.

The couple standing at the far end of the car radiated a bright, scorching desire to get home and into bed as quickly as possible. The group of young people who had tumbled in through the door a few seconds after us were sparkling with high spirits and a desire for music and good times.

Loraine occupied a spot that was free beside the door opposite the entrance, leaned back against the rail, and took her cell phone out of her pocket.

"Look, Darel. A commercial message. 'Send a text to your favorite musician and get a free cell phone! Every week the writers of the two most original messages win a free phone.' Do you think it's true? Would Vance really read texts from hundreds of his fans?"

"I'm quite sure they'll never even reach him," I said with a smile.

Then suddenly, from somewhere—from out of the first car, I was struck by a sensation of acute pain. Before I even had any idea of what it meant, I grabbed the girl, pushed her to the floor in the corner by the door, and followed her down. There was less than a split second, a period of time that only blood brothers could feel. The silver cell phone went flying out of her hand and seemed to hang in the air. At that instant, the train braked hard. Rasping and screeching, a heavy blow, the sound of metal tearing, glass shattering, people howling as they were thrown to the floor, falling on one another. The lights went out. Pain, terror, a rising wave of hysteria, minds flickering on the border of consciousness. I forced myself to shut down and not hear the human emotions; I *cut them off*.

"Darel . . . Darel, what is it?" Loraine exclaimed. "What happened?"

"Take it easy," I said in a quiet voice, "it's an accident. Accidents often happen on this line. The cars come off the rails, or the ground slips. It's close to the river."

"But how are we going to get out? How will we get out of here?" She tried to jump up and go dashing away, although she had no idea where to go, but I held her back.

"Don't be afraid, we'll get out."

"I can't see anything!"

"I can see."

The people lying on the floor started stirring feebly, feeling around themselves with their hands as if they were blind. I heard groans and weak voices. Someone hesitantly tried to persuade the people near him not to panic; several women started sobbing. A hysterical voice from the far end of the car said the person next to him was dead; another particularly hysterical individual started wheezing, imagining there was no air and he couldn't breathe. Loraine pressed herself tight against me, and I could feel her shuddering. She was very close to panic.

"We're only a few dozen meters from the station," I said, and a wave of calm reassurance flowed out to the people with my voice. "It's on the surface. They'll get us out in half an hour. At the most."

The people quieted down, mesmerized by my magic.

"Has anyone got a flashlight? Or switch on your cell phones— at least there'll be some light."

Timid patches of light started appearing at various spots around the car. Orange, blue, yellow. The passengers tried to look around, searching for their things.

"My cell phone's broken," Loraine whispered.

"I'll buy you another one."

But then I was jolted by another wave of panic and pain even more powerful than the first.

And this time, the danger was far more real.

"Loraine, we have to get out of here now."

"What? Why? You said the station isn't far away, the rescuers will be here to get us in half an hour."

"It won't be rescuers, and they'll get here much sooner than that."

"What are you doing?"

"Opening this door."

"Darel!"

"I sense Asiman."

She stopped talking, but I was lashed by a horror so strong that I had to turn back to her and put my hand on her forehead to calm her down. To block the fear that was hindering me.

The fit of panic started to fade.

"I'm afraid."

"We'll get out of here in a moment. Stay beside me."

She took a tight grip on my jacket. I stuck my fingers between the rubber flanges of the doors and started pulling them open. Very slowly—the locking mechanism was probably jammed. Meanwhile, the Asiman were getting closer. Six walking through the cars, the others in the tunnel. Four of them were high-level magicians.

"What are you doing?" asked a woman with curly hair, moving right up against me. She grabbed hold of my sleeve, radiating fear and anger. "What are you doing that for?"

"I want a breath of fresh air," I muttered, bracing my foot against the side of the door that was slightly open and heaving hard. The locking mechanism gave way with a plaintive squeal, and the way out was open.

Then suddenly the car was filled with the acrid, choking smell of burning plastic, and some idiot howled: "Fire!" A panic began. People started trying to escape, floundering about in the darkness, maiming and crushing one another. Someone gave a quavering, high-pitched scream of pain, there was a crunch of breaking glass, and the separate cries fused together into a single howl of panic. And through this insanity I could sense the calm composure of the Asiman at work. They were selecting human material for their experiments.

A lamp lit up at the end of the car. Probably it was a short circuit in the wiring, or the emergency lighting had come on. The weak light made the door that I had opened visible. All the passengers turned their contorted faces toward us. As if someone had put blinkers on all of them at the same moment, and there was only one thought left in their clouded minds, a single, clearly defined goal—the open door at the center of the car. And they flung themselves at it, blind to everything else.

Loraine gave a faint cry. Holding one half of the door open

with one hand, I grabbed her around the stomach with the other arm and *struck out* at the berserk crowd. The woman who was closest to us screeched. A red weal appeared on her narrow forehead under the black curls. A trickle of blood ran down her face and started dripping off her chin. She screeched again, stepped back, and slumped to the floor. The physical effect of my magic shattered the glasses of a young man at the front. Lots of other passengers started bleeding from the nose. But the most important thing was that all of them froze for a second, staring into space with blank indifference.

"Loraine, climb down, quickly."

But the girl suddenly started struggling in my grip.

"Darel! What about the others? They'll kill them."

"Yes, probably."

"But we can't let them! We can't! Do you hear?"

I stood her on her feet and slapped her lightly on the cheek, while still holding the door open. I needed to save my mental strength. The girl's head jerked and she gasped in surprise, but the revolt was crushed.

"There are ten Asiman. Four of them are top-level magicians. I'm not going to fight them. The important thing is to save you. I don't care about the others. Now move it, jump down!"

Loraine got out without another word. I followed her. The door closed. Now we were in the space between the train and the wall of the tunnel. I grabbed the girl's hand and pulled her after me toward the front of the train.

But before we had gone even a few steps, a magician from the House of Asiman jumped out of one of the niches in the wall. He was young, about twenty years old, with a pretty kind of face. Wearing a flashy suede jacket with lots of shiny studs all over it. He raised his hand, and his open palm started glowing red.

An instant before I *struck*, the vampire's eyes opened wide in astonishment. And then they went blank. Blood poured out of his nose, mouth, and ears straight onto that expensive jacket. He staggered back and sank gently onto the rails. My narrow-focus psychic ray had torn his mind apart, demolishing his brain.

Loraine's hand gripped my hand in her icy palm as tightly as she could. "Did you . . . did you kill him?"

The car we had just escaped from started swaying on its suspension. The bright fire of Asiman magic lit it up from the inside. Howls of pain and horror lashed at my nerves. A human body was flung against the window, and it slid slowly down the glass, leaving bloody streaks from its hands and face. The Asiman vivisectors moved on unhurriedly, continuing with their work.

I grabbed hold of Loraine's hands, concealed us behind a thick *curtain,* and ran. The girl held on tight, panting for breath. Her head was spinning, and there was a ringing in her ears. It's not easy for the human body to keep up with the speed vampires move at. And we really had to run fast.

The tunnel widened out, and side branches appeared. I turned into the first one. There were bundles of thick cables running along the walls. Puddles of water lying on the stone floor between the rails. Several times, rats squealed as they ran out from under our feet. I heard the rumble of a train in the distance. It looked as if this were an offshoot from the main line and trains didn't run here very often.

We weren't being followed. They were too busy, or they hadn't found their brother's body yet. The flashes of human pain faded away and disappeared; I could barely sense the Asiman anymore. It took real distance to blank out a source of powerful emotions, so for the time being we had nothing to fear. I stopped and listened again. Yes, everything was quiet. We'd managed to get far enough away. We could make our way out of the metro now, but Loraine started sobbing and struggling. I had to set her on her feet. She sat on the ground and huddled into a ball with her forehead pressed against her knees. Her shoulders started shaking.

"They'll kill . . . they've killed . . . all of them," I could just hear her say through her sobs. "The brutes . . . the sadists . . ."

I squatted beside her and reached out, but she shook my reassuring hand off her head.

"Don't touch me! Get away from me! You're just the same! You left them all!"

She started shuddering and sobbing in silence again. Shock. It would soon pass. A few minutes later, Loraine wiped her cheeks with her hands, and then, without looking at me, she asked in a voice that was faint and indistinct after all her tears:

"Why do they do that?"

"They need material for experiments. They carry out experiments on living matter."

"What kind of experiments?" Loraine asked, looking at me. The tears had lightened the color of her eyes and stuck her eyelashes together.

"I don't know. I haven't been invited into their laboratories."

"But when the rescuers get here . . ."

"They'll find a wrecked train and heaps of burned bodies. Nobody will realize that they have some parts missing. The Asiman don't leave any clues behind. Usually, at least."

Loraine squeezed her eyes shut and put her hand over her mouth. She was feeling sick. She was in pain. The fairy tale about the mysterious life of the blood brothers that I had told her had nothing to do with this hideous reality.

"You think of us as cattle, don't you," she whispered with a feeling that was almost hate.

"I don't."

"That's a lie!" The girl didn't know what to think. "That's a lie! All of you . . ."

She said something else, but I wasn't listening any longer. I heard a vaguely familiar voice ranting inside my head: *Darel! You scum! I know you can hear me. You killed my pupil. I'll roast your brains, you louse.*

"What's happened?" Loraine asked in a trembling voice.

"We're leaving. Right away."

"Have they found us?"

"No. Not yet."

Ernesto. That was the one who had sent me the message. A powerful and very dangerous magician. One of Amir's deputies. And I'd just happened to run into his pupil. But how did he know it was me? Had the pupil been in constant contact with his teacher?

He couldn't find us. Not unless he sent his men out to comb the entire neighborhood. Or ran across us by chance.

"Darel!"

"Let's go."

I pulled her to her feet and led her after me. I wasn't frightened by the Asiman's threat. But there was an unpleasant prickly sensation in the region of my solar plexus. Amir, Paula, Slaven, Ernesto . . . It seemed I had a real talent for making enemies.

A light flared up at the end of the tunnel, and the rails started trembling. Loraine screeched. I grabbed her, threw her across my shoulder, and set off again at a run, looking for a niche or a passage in the wall where we could hide while the train that was chasing us hurtled past. It would be just too stupid to escape from the Asiman and then get run over by a train. A narrow corridor appeared on the left.

I turned sharply and crashed at full speed into a protective spell stretching across the narrow tunnel. A split second before contact, I sensed something was wrong and pushed Loraine aside, but I couldn't stop myself in time.

The pain was agonizing.

I was pierced through by sharp shafts of ice, paralyzed,

twisted into a knot, and flung to the ground, trembling and soaked in sweat.

"Darel!"

"Don't come close . . . don't touch . . ." I seemed to hear my own voice through a wall of cotton wool. The train rumbled past behind me, searing me with a blast of hot air.

It was an old spell, and its magical power had weakened considerably over time. I wondered who had put it there. Clearly not the Asiman. If the fire magicians had created it, I would have been roasted. But this . . . no, I couldn't classify it. I'd have to ask Chris.

I got slowly to my hands and knees and shook my head. Loraine was standing an arm's length away, looking frightened.

"What's wrong with you?"

"Nothing, now."

I stood up cautiously, holding on to the wall, and rubbed my neck. The girl tried to support me.

"What was it?"

"An old spell. Very old."

My head was still buzzing and my knees felt weak, but I started off confidently, tuning in to the wavelength of human feelings as I went. Loraine walked beside me, glancing at me in concern.

About twenty minutes later, we came out at a station, and I was astonished when I saw which one it was. The underground passages had led us to a completely different line from the one on which we had started our journey.

"I've had enough of the metro," I declared, looking at Loraine's pale, grimy face. "Let's take a taxi."

She didn't object.

7

MASTER OF DEATH

It is personalities, not principles, that move the age.
—Oscar Wilde, *The Picture of Dorian Gray*

October 2
Darel Dahanavar

For the last thirty years, Chris had lived in a luxurious mansion on the embankment, in which his apartment occupied all three floors—second, first, and basement. The layout of the rooms was so strange that I still hadn't managed to figure out how many of them there were. And apart from them, every couple of years the Cadavercitan moved the furniture around "from the drawing room to the bedroom and vice versa."

I had been on the first floor quite often and visited the second floor occasionally, but he had never let me into the basement. I wasn't all that keen on getting in there anyway. That part of the house contained the laboratory where the necromancer conducted experiments that I couldn't even understand.

Chris opened the door himself and stared at me without saying a word. He actually stared. He had a way of looking at you with a somber, grave expression that made you feel very uncomfortable.

We had arrived at a bad time. The Cadavercitan was dressed in perfectly modern white overalls, there were suspicious reddish brown spots on the thin surgical gloves that he casually shoved into his pocket, and there was a sweetish, unpleasant, and very familiar odor coming from somewhere inside the house.

"Hi, Chris. Should we go away?"

He transferred his gaze from my exhausted, dirty face and torn jacket to Loraine's equally grubby and weary features. Then he raised one black eyebrow.

"All right. Come in."

We went in. Chris waved an arm in the direction of one of his many sitting rooms and went out through the door that led to the basement, almost running. Loraine gave me a curious look.

"Was he angry?"

"No, more likely surprised."

I pointed to a black leather armchair and went into the kitchen. As well as the refrigerator with his supply of blood, Chris had a few cupboards containing human food—a bottle of good whiskey and one of slightly less good wine, packets of spices, a box of almond cookies. I wondered what the Cadavercitan needed these stores for. Whom was he entertaining?

I opened a bottle, poured the wine into a pan, put it on the stove, brought it to a boil, and added some spices. Judging from the smell, it turned out quite good. I poured it into a mug and took it to Loraine.

As she drank the hot mulled wine, she gradually calmed down. Young girls' minds may be vulnerable, but they are also very re-silient. Some inconsequential trifle can leave a scar that never heals, but serious events can be forgotten very quickly when they are displaced by more vivid impressions.

Loraine finished her wine and started looking around curi-ously. I couldn't understand what there was to look at. The mag-nificent, windowless room seemed rather gloomy—black wood and greenish bronze—and then, against this dark background, a sudden bright spot, a huge bouquet of yellow tulips in a round black vase.

I raised my eyes higher. On the wall there was a picture in a massive wide frame with a matte glint of gold—a knight with a scarlet cloak thrown carelessly over his burnished steel armor. The hand in the heavy metal-scale glove seemed to be resting right on the massive frame, and the edge of the cloak had been thrown back by a light gust of wind. The other hand was resting on the handle of a huge battle-ax. My eyes met that cold, intent gaze, and then I looked back at Loraine. She glanced around and saw the portrait. Her blue eyes opened wide.

"He looks like Chris."

"It is Chris, in his young days."

The portrait was smiling faintly into empty space.

Once there used to be a picture hanging on the opposite wall, a portrait of a delightful young lady in a low-cut green dress, holding a crimson rose in her hands. She looked at the knight through the narrow slits of a half-mask, and her eyes shone. Flora in the time of Louis XIV and young Chris in his dress armor. Then the portrait of the dark-haired beauty had disappeared.

I didn't know, I wasn't supposed to know, how things had been between them. But I remembered very well. When he heard that Flora had been killed, the imperturbable, elegant Chris seemed to lose his mind. He started smashing up his magnificent mansion in a wild fury, sparing nothing, not even his unique collection of Etruscan vases. Then he shut himself in the basement for months and refused to answer a knock at the door or a mental summons. No one knew what he was doing in there. Was he trying to get drunk, had he turned to strange magic, or was he contemplating vengeance? Nobody knew, not even me, although I had always thought that Chris trusted me more than anybody else.

When the Cadavercitan finally rejoined us, he was almost his old self: calm, levelheaded, cool, only with an even fiercer hatred of the Asiman clan, even more resolutely bitter. He kept nothing that could have reminded him of her. He made himself forget, or perhaps he really did forget.

"Darel."

I started at the sound of the quiet voice that called me back to the present. Loraine had got out of her chair and come closer, alarmed by my long silence and blank gaze.

"It's so strange in here, so dark. In that corner there's an Egyptian statue, and in that one there's a sarcophagus. The tapestries on the walls are dark and gloomy, and you don't say anything, as if you were sleeping with your eyes open."

"There's nothing to be afraid of here." I moved up to let her sit beside me and put my arm around her.

She calmed down immediately and asked the question that had been bothering her all this time.

"What kind of spell was that? Back in the metro?"

"What spell?" asked Chris, adjusting his cuffs as he walked rapidly into the room.

He had changed, replaced his coveralls with his usual clothes, styled to look medieval. A shirt with broad cuffs, breeches, soft leather boots. My friend sat down in a chair and crossed his legs. In the dark sitting room, his eyes glowed an intense emerald green. The statuette of an Egyptian cat standing on the shelf above his head had exactly the same gaze: wise, calm, piercing.

Loraine forgot about the mulled wine and the frightening interior and gazed at the sorcerer.

All the Cadavercitan were distinguished by a certain inexpressible air of elegance, refinement, and mystery. The allure of death. A stupid phrase, but I had never been able to think of a better definition. They were shrouded in a mystical, magnetic haze that attracted others to them. I saw the way women looked at Chris whenever he socialized. It didn't matter whether it was with humans or vampires. My Loraine was no exception.

"Well?" the sorcerer asked pointedly.

"We were in the metro," the girl said, blushing at her own audacity.

Chris raised his eyes slightly and looked at her. A faint shadow of surprise flitted across the necromancer's face, almost as if some inanimate object had spoken in his presence. But the sorcerer immediately controlled his response, making the mental effort to upgrade the status of his visitor from a creature of low intellectual capacity to an individual capable of conversing with him.

"And what happened in the metro?"

"The Asiman attacked the train," I said, taking the empty mug out of Loraine's hands. I put it on the table beside the bouquet of tulips. "I expect we'll read all about it in tomorrow's newspapers. The train came off the rails. Damaged electric cables set three cars on fire. The number of people killed is not yet known. The catastrophe was caused by metal fatigue, failure to observe standard operating procedures, subsoil erosion, subsidence, and so forth."

"They killed everyone," the girl said morosely, looking at her scratched hands. "Darel said they need people for their experiments. What kind of experiments are they?"

The Cadavercitan gave a deep sigh and took a tight grip on the armrests of his chair. "I believe they are trying to synthesize from human flesh a substance capable of protecting them from the sun."

"But is that possible?" Loraine exclaimed.

Chris grinned good-naturedly, leaned forward, and scrutinized his female visitor, who was embarrassed by his gaze.

"Why does that surprise you? Your skin is stimulated by ultraviolet light to produce melanin. If it became possible to synthesize a chemical substance that could endow the skin of the blood brothers with the properties possessed by human skin, that would give them very great power indeed."

"I understand . . . it might be possible," Loraine said cautiously. "But in practice . . . surely it would take them a very long time to do it?"

"They have an unlimited amount of time. Darel, you have a suspiciously thoughtful look about you. Are you imagining what a successful outcome of the experiment would mean to you?"

"It would be rather good," I said, not quite sure what to make of the Asiman's grandiose plans. I didn't really believe that they would succeed, but . . . "I think it would be easier to experiment on Regenants, not humans. They have immunity to the sun, too."

I thought Chris would appreciate my sense of humor. But he carried on looking at me seriously, tapping his fingers on the armrest of his chair.

"Darel, do you know why the Obaifo family died out?"

"Did they think they'd developed a defense against the sun and all go outside during the day?"

The sorcerer shook his head with an expression of complete surrender in the face of my frivolity. "They decided to become all-powerful, almost exactly like the Asiman now. And they carried their experiments too far. Every family dreams of increasing its potential. The ideal thing would be to combine the powers of several different masters. For instance, the mental power of the Dahanavar, the fire magic of the Asiman, and the hardiness of the Regenants."

"Wait! Do you mean to say that the Obaifo actually worked on Regenants?"

Pleased with the impression that he had produced, Chris leaned back in his chair and examined his fine lace cuffs. "Yes, but that was a long time ago."

I could tell Loraine was desperate to know who Regenants were, but she kept quiet in order not to interrupt the conversation.

"They died as a result of their experiments?"

"No, they were exterminated. The other families united and . . ." He clenched his fist, then opened it again and blew imaginary dust off it. "It is the only occasion in history when all of us acted in unison."

"Had they really achieved something significant?"

"I was not present at the experiments, but I don't think the elders would have panicked for no reason. Can you imagine what could be created by combining the power of several Houses and adding the distinctive features of the Regenants? By collecting together every conceivable kind of power? The Obaifo would have become invincible."

I had a flashback of my recent vision. Ivan and Ramon standing over a dying blood brother. I recalled Felicia's words: "The Upieschi have no magic . . . they tried to acquire some magical potential from the Vricolakos."

"Were the results of the Obaifo experiments destroyed? Completely? Or was there something left?"

Chris waved his arm in the gesture of a tragedian concluding his final monologue. "Who knows."

"So it seems the interest in combining various powers has been revived recently."

"Perhaps."

He didn't want to talk about it anymore. He had unpleasant memories of his own. Personal memories. Which I had never attempted to probe. I tried never to scan Chris in general. Probably I respected him too much. I didn't want to tear away his veil of Cadavercitan mystique. And I was quite certain that he was honest. He was probably the only person I always trusted completely, with no reservations.

The sorcerer caught my eye and nodded at Loraine with a smile. The girl had fallen asleep, with the side of her head resting against the back of the divan. That was why she had been so quiet for the last few minutes. I hadn't noticed because I was absorbed in the conversation.

"You had a hard day today."

"Yes."

I told him about our adventures, complete with dramatic descriptions of the Asiman slaughter and our flight through the tunnels.

"By the way, Chris, what was this?" At the second attempt, I managed to convey the full impact of running into the spell.

The Cadavercitan winced at the harsh naturalism of the sensations, thought for a moment, and stated confidently:

"Nosoforos. It's their style. If you'd run into that trap three hundred years ago, it would have reduced you to dust."

"There wasn't any metro three hundred years ago."

"But there were tunnels under the city. The metro took over and reconstructed some of them."

"But what about the humans?"

"The trap is only designed for blood brothers."

Chris never used the word "vampire." He considered it degrading.

"Take the girl home. It's getting late. And find some time to eat. You look like a ghost. And another thing—be careful. Try not to let any Asiman catch sight of you. Just to be on the safe side."

"Yes, sir, Mr. Teacher. Definitely."

THE ASIMAN

Those who see any difference between soul and body have neither.

—Oscar Wilde, "Phrases and Philosophies
for the Use of the Young"

October 17

Loraine had never experienced so much in a single evening before. Her walks had never been like this; she had never imagined the night could be so beautiful—it didn't seem dull and black, the way it used to be, anymore. The nights that Darel revealed to her were pale green and dark blue, purple and orange, the color of fallen leaves. They were as deep as wells. Or else completely flat, like a drawing on a saucer, so that it seemed as if she could reach out her hand and touch the most distant tree on the riverbank.

Every day became the anticipation of a new night, and every one of them was different. Beautiful, amazing, magical. And every time, the girl's guide to the period of darkness disappeared for an hour or two. He went away, and when he came back that hungry glow in his eyes was gone.

The dangerously reserved Darel knew dozens of nightclubs, small restaurants, and cafés. He would suddenly stop on some completely dark, desolate street, look around, and say:

"There's a great bar somewhere round here. They used to serve really good hot chocolate. Let's go in, you're frozen."

And it was only after he said it that Loraine realized she really was chilled right through and just longing for some hot chocolate.

Sometimes they came across others like Darel, and they smiled at each other or walked on by, turning their eyes away indifferently.

She ought to be afraid of her strange friend. Anyone else in her place would soon have stopped meeting him. Max, for instance. If anyone had even hinted to him who this young guy she was seeing really was, he would have done absolutely anything to put an end to the acquaintance.

But Loraine couldn't follow the dictates of common sense. She just couldn't give Darel up. Perhaps because, deep in her soul, she craved adventure. Or perhaps because she was simply afraid of going back to the boring, empty bustle of everyday life.

How could she study, read, and discuss everyday details with her friends when this incredible, unreal, fantastic life was going on right beside her? It had always been there, for hundreds and thousands of years, but people had never even suspected.

And now only the chosen few knew about it.

Every now and then, of course, Loraine felt scared. She felt as if she were glancing into a bottomless well in an archaeological museum. A round hole, its walls covered with mosaics showing ancient people, mammoths, fossilized mollusks, with mirrors at the bottom and the top. Look down and you see layer upon layer of colors receding into infinity, and somewhere in among them you can see your own tiny face. Merely the effect of a double reflection, but still breathtaking.

Sometimes Loraine was overwhelmed by fear and dread. She remembered the wide, staring eyes of the vampire Darel had killed. The way they had bulged out of their sockets, like boiled eggs, and then the blood had started pouring out. From his nose, his ears, his mouth. Several times at night she dreamed about that bloody face, and the screams, and the network of tunnels they had run through. After nightmares like that, she didn't want to go outside at all. No matter if it was day or night. She saw monsters with bared fangs in every dark corner.

When she told Darel about this, he looked at her intently and put his warm, dry palm on her forehead. And something inside her head clicked. A switch tripped. What had happened in the train became a distant, blurred memory, and the sense of constant danger disappeared. It was possible to live normally again. Almost normally. Especially when he was with her.

Loraine realized that she was asking her supernatural friend lots of stupid questions. But she couldn't stop herself. For example, when she was eating ice cream in a café, it was impossible not to ask:

"Tell me, how do you relate to human food?"

Darel had looked at the slowly melting vanilla ice cream with chocolate crumbs in her sundae glass and shrugged. "I don't relate to it at all."

"But if you ate something, what would happen to you?"

Darel grinned and gave a very amusing impression of dying from strangulation.

"No, really, what would happen?"

"Well, what would happen to you if you ate a handful of soil?"

"I don't know, I've never tried it. Have you?"

Darel laughed.

His fangs were really quite conspicuous. The genuine article. But he knew how to smile so that no one noticed them.

And it was always interesting being with him.

"Confess, why do I always feel so calm and secure with you? Do you do it on purpose?"

He looked up for a moment from the new cell phone that he had bought Loraine an hour earlier, then stuck his nose back in the menu.

"No, that's just the way I am."

"And does everyone feel it the same way I do?"

"Yes."

"Wait, that's wrong. Press here, then here. Haven't you ever had a cell phone?"

"What for?" He selected the wrong option again, and the cell phone started beeping indignantly.

"It's the twenty-first century, you know. People talk to each other."

"With my specialty I can communicate without a phone."

Loraine nodded understandingly and narrowed her eyes mockingly.

"And being a telepath's so very convenient."

LORAINE's human life had suddenly been divided into two halves.

Her unexpected encounter with a supernatural being was rapidly changing her view of the world. She tried to live during the day, to study and see her friends and put up with the complaints from her parents, whom she had started to see very rarely—they could see that something strange was happening to their daughter, but they couldn't understand what it was. And she waited for the sun to sink out of sight behind the horizon.

Darel never even hinted that he would like to control her daytime life. It was as if it didn't exist for him. As if real life began only after sunset. Sometimes the girl wondered if she ought to withdraw into the world of shadows, darkness, and multicolored nights forever. To feel the power that Darel spoke about, to free herself from human doubts and fears, to become quite different.

But the vampire never actually suggested this.

"Giving up human life is too painful," he said once. And he didn't even notice how very hopeless that sounded.

THE Dahanavar's home was in one of the oldest districts of the city. People with any sense tried not to wander in there after eleven o'clock at night. Only every second streetlamp worked, and the narrow alleyways and dead ends were just made for ambushing people out walking late. Once it had been a lively locality, but the bright life of the capital had gradually crept farther and farther away, moving into new districts beyond the river, abandoning the old houses and fences, the crooked little streets, the battered and broken roads.

Loraine often wondered why Darel wasn't afraid to live here. Apart from the real live thieves and murderers, the dark alleys seemed to be inhabited by the ghosts of past centuries with swords or axes in their hands.

But the telepath didn't seem to be afraid of anything. When she cautiously asked if anyone had ever tried to attack him, he replied indifferently:

"Yes, last week, I think. It was very helpful, actually. I was feeling really hungry."

She didn't feel like asking any more after that.

The Dahanavar lived on the first floor of an old stone building, in a very spacious three-room apartment that was highly unusual. Not only because there were absolutely no windows: instead of the usual wallpaper, the walls were simply covered in white plaster, and in places the brickwork had been exposed.

The huge sitting room contained a very modern leather sofa, several armchairs, and a beautiful carved mahogany table. And candlesticks. Lots of candlesticks. All different kinds. Simple metal cups on slim legs, complicated glass structures that looked like frozen flowers, with slim candles growing out of their petals, ceramic candleholders that looked like Etruscan vases. Candleholders made of bronze or carved out of chunks of semiprecious stone.

These were not simply trinkets that Darel had laid out all over the apartment to impress visitors with his originality. They all contained candles that were partly melted away or burned right down, and there were frozen rivulets of wax on the supports.

* * *

To Loraine's surprise, Darel's home did not contain any huge collection of ancient artifacts accumulated in the course of his long life: the interior was simple and empty. Apparently, Darel had never collected old pictures or furniture or anything that would now have been considered valuable antiques. Only candlesticks.

And the girl had always imagined that a vampire's bedroom should be dark and gloomy, built of stone so that it resembled a vault. Like in the horror movies, with the compulsory coffin for resting during the day and all the other attributes of the non-human life. But once again, she was wrong.

The bedroom was very light. The same white plaster walls. A wide bed of light-colored wood. A cordless phone the color of baked milk standing on a little low table. And bright spots that seemed almost out of place against this blank background, like several books in blue bindings, lying in a neat pile. And a black leather jacket tossed casually onto the creamy white bedspread.

For some reason, this jacket shocked the girl most of all. She suddenly pictured Darel as a perfectly normal, ordinary young man who slept in an ordinary bed, who could toss his clothes onto the floor with casual indifference or not put a book away after he'd read it, just like Max, just like her. Yet even with all these perfectly human characteristics, he still wasn't a human being.

Completely confused, the girl turned around to look away from the bed and saw a huge picture covering the entire wall, painted straight onto the plaster—beautiful girls in long Greek tunics, slender graceful columns, blindingly white marble steps, clouds, a clear sky . . .

"Do you like it?" Darel asked, suddenly there beside her.

"Yes, I really do. It's an incredible fresco. Who painted it?"

"A friend of mine. Monet."

The girls seemed to be floating over the smooth marble surface, holding flowers and green laurel branches in their arms.

"Incredible. Monet . . . you knew Monet?"

"Yes."

"Amazing."

He had known a lot of famous people. In the past and in the present, too. Take Vance, for instance.

Strangely enough, just recently Loraine's interest in the British star had faded a bit. The rock singer's rating in the charts of the most popular individuals in her life had dropped from number one forever to a modest third. First place belonged to Darel now. After their visit to the Cadavercitan, he shared it with Chris, but he was still slightly ahead.

Loraine had to admit that she felt a bit shy in the Cadavercitan's presence. The necromancer looked at her as if she were an empty-headed little girl, and Loraine suspected that his opinion was unlikely to change anytime during the next fifty years. But that didn't bother her; after all, she had Darel beside her.

"Let's go for a walk, shall we?" the Dahanavar suggested. And, of course, the girl agreed.

THEY were walking through a park.

The leafy crowns of the trees were already noticeably thinner. The yellow maple leaves fell slowly, gliding on the wind and then settling on the cold ground, covering their withered brothers and sisters with their thin, fresh forms.

The sky was clear. The round yellow moon was shining brightly. Sometimes it was covered by a faint haze, and then it seemed as if gentle ripples were running across the surface of the glowing disk.

Her breath didn't leave little clouds of steam in the air yet. But the air felt cool already. The girl pulled her hood up over her head, and the sounds she heard became slightly muffled. The wind was a regular, monotonous drone. Every now and then, cars drove along the nearby street.

They made small talk about nothing in particular. The conversation had just turned to werewolves when Darel suddenly stopped walking. Loraine looked around and saw several figures standing around a bench. They were looking in the opposite direction, but for some reason her vampire companion was suddenly alert and uneasy. His face turned to stone, the way it had that time in the metro train.

"Loraine, you get out of here now."

Her heart started pounding rapidly and then skipped several beats. "What's happened? Who are they?"

"Nothing's happened. They're old acquaintances of mine. But I don't want you to meet them. Be a good girl now, don't let me down. Go home."

His voice was very soft, very calm, but his eyes . . .

"Go."

"Darel—"

"No. I'll call you. Later."

The group started moving toward them slowly, and it became clear that they weren't humans.

"Go. Go on now!" Darel pushed the girl in the direction of a dark side alley. And she *heard* his thought that she was his weakness, that the telepath couldn't protect her. And he didn't want any help. All he wanted was to know that she was safe and as far away from here as possible.

The Dahanavar suddenly pushed Loraine, so hard that she almost fell, and shouted: "Do as I tell you! Run, get out of here!"

And the girl ran, jolted into action by that crude shout. She dashed away as fast as she could, without looking back.

CHRIS lived in the center, on the embankment, not far from the art gallery.

Loraine's heart was in her mouth as she flew up onto the porch and pressed the smooth round button of the doorbell. He has to be home at this time. It's almost dawn. My God, dawn! Not much time left! She rang the bell again, then again and again . . . and then the door swung open.

At first Loraine thought that Chris was wearing fancy dress—a white silk shirt with lace cuffs and silver embroidery, black trousers, also embroidered in silver, and high boots. Then she remembered that it wasn't a masquerade costume. The Cadavercitan had been wearing clothes like this for a hundred, two hundred, three hundred years.

"What a surprise. To what do I owe the pleasure?"

The green eyes glittered. The smile on the lips was supremely sardonic. But Loraine forced herself to remember that he was Darel's friend, and she shouldn't be afraid of him.

"Chris, Darel's in trouble!"

"What kind of 'trouble'?"

"We were in the park and we met some blood brothers. I think he knew them. He told me to go, but he stayed there."

The sorcerer suddenly turned serious. He grabbed his visitor firmly by the shoulder and dragged her inside.

"Come with me, girl. Tell me everything clearly and simply."

There was a huge, dark, empty room ahead of them, but before Loraine could get a good look at it, the Cadavercitan suddenly turned to the left into a low stone corridor. It led into a large room with an arched ceiling, dimly lit by candles that looked like torches.

In the yellowish light, Loraine could make out tapestries on the walls, long benches, and tall black vases on the floor. There was an old cupboard, too, covered all over with intricate carving, a hexagonal table in the center of the room, and a strange elongated object covered with a burgundy-colored cloth in the far corner.

And then her eyes fell on Chris's guests. There were two young men and two young women in the room. One of the men was lying on that strange long object, and the other was stretched out full length on a bench. The young women were sitting on the floor. They were having a cheerful discussion about something. The sudden appearance of a human broke off the group's merry laughter and they all froze in astonishment.

"Chris, what's this, dessert?" asked a girl with a magnificent head of blond hair.

Chris shook his head. "No, Dona. This is a friend of Darel's. And she has bad news. Our brother has encountered Asiman."

Loraine didn't know why Chris was certain they were Asiman, but she didn't argue.

The young man on the bench whistled expressively, and the girls exchanged glances. Chris casually pushed his new visitor toward a bench. "Sit down." He hurried over to a cupboard and started studying its contents, giving instructions at the same time.

"Samuel and Viv, come with me. There's not much time left until dawn. Are you armed?"

One of them turned back the flap of his jacket to reveal a holster. "Of course. Always."

The other nodded without speaking. Chris turned around.

"Loraine, will you show us the place where you left Darel?"

"Yes. Of course."

"Then this might be useful."

In an instant, the Cadavercitan was behind her back, and before she could even feel surprised, he had fastened a broad collar, made of something like metal fish scales, around her neck. The thin steel plates lay tightly against one another, protecting her throat securely. The astonished girl touched the cold scales. Chris chuckled darkly in response to her inquiring glance.

"I hope someone breaks his teeth against that. Girls, you tidy up everything here."

"Be careful," the blonde said to no one in particular, and when Loraine looked at her, she smiled back.

* * *

OUTSIDE, the predawn air was cold, the stars were absolutely white and so bright that not even the streetlamps could outshine them.

A black BMW with dark-tinted windows glided smoothly up to the porch. Vivian, the taciturn, light-haired young man, was driving. Sam, dark-haired with dark eyes and slightly irregular features, was sitting beside him.

It took them about ten minutes to reach the park.

"Stay here," Chris told Loraine.

"No! I'm going with you!" she declared firmly, clambering out of the car.

The necromancer smiled ironically, but he didn't argue with her.

The Cadavercitan left their car at the entrance to the park. And they didn't even bother to lock it, thought Loraine. But then, it probably has a special spell on it to stop anybody stealing it.

Chris set off quickly, looking perfectly calm, as if he were out for a brief bedtime stroll. Viv and Samuel hung back a little bit. Hearing their light, stealthy footsteps behind her, the girl suddenly realized that something terrible had happened to Darel.

Her head suddenly felt dry and hot, but her palms were moist. Loraine started trembling, and she couldn't control it.

"Stop that," Chris said without looking at her.

To the girl's amazement, his words had an instant effect.

"We need to hurry," the Cadavercitan declared in a calm voice.

"What will they do to him?"

"I don't know."

He said that in an indifferent voice, too. Almost indifferent. Looking around as he spoke.

Loraine glanced around at their companions and only then realized that one of them had disappeared somewhere. But that didn't seem to bother the others at all.

Vivian appeared as unexpectedly as he had disappeared, emerging from behind some trees. He walked up to Chris and whispered something quickly. Chris's face darkened and he uttered a short, resounding phrase. It wasn't hard to guess that it was some kind of oath. In French. Incorrect French. Loraine didn't ask them exactly what it meant; the expressions on their faces didn't need any translation.

"I hate the Asiman," Chris hissed through his clenched teeth, and Loraine saw his fangs for the first time.

"Why?" she asked, struggling to control her nervous trembling again.

"They're treacherous, cunning brutes. You already know that their favorite pastime is experimenting on humans. But a while ago they started hunting blood brothers, too."

"Why would they do that?" the girl asked, shuddering inside.

Chris shrugged. "Every family manages its gift in its own way, and seeks its own way to perfection. We don't interfere in each other's business until our neighbors become a real threat."

Loraine remembered what Darel had told her and asked: "Is it true that the Asiman can fly?"

"Yes."

The Cadavercitan grinned and gave her a strange kind of look, and she realized he was answering her questions only because he wanted to distract her from her disturbing thoughts. Which was exactly what she needed.

"Why do you call each other blood brothers?"

"Some of us don't like the word 'vampire,' it doesn't sound very nice. When we receive the dark gift with the blood of our teacher, we leave the world of mortals behind forever. And join a new family."

"That's terrible!"

Chris laughed. "I see you're not attracted by strength, power, and eternal youth, then?"

Loraine shook her head. "I didn't even believe you existed until I met Darel. Even now I don't entirely believe it."

"A good tactic," the sorcerer commented casually, as if he had lost interest in the conversation. "Vivian, check, they should be going towards the tunnel."

Viv nodded without speaking. And Sam made sure his pistol came out of its holster easily.

The group turned another corner, leaving the narrow alley behind. They walked through a low arch and found themselves in the darkest and most remote part of the park.

Loraine thought they must be somewhere close to the piece of wasteland that ran along the brick wall of the old cemetery. When she was little, she and her friends had once climbed in there to look at the grave of a wizard who was buried under a fir tree hundreds of years old. All the kids in their yard used to tell one another scary stories about that place. They never found the fir tree or the grave, because they ran off, frightened by the gloomy silence of the ancient graveyard and the bloodthirsty expression on the face of a stone gargoyle sitting on one of the gravestones.

The memory of her childhood experiences sent shivers down her back, and she really didn't feel like going through them again. But now they were walking straight toward that waste ground. And now the girl wouldn't have been surprised to learn that some kind of vampires lived there, too.

Chris suddenly stopped and looked around slowly. As if he were sniffing at the cold morning air. There was a gentle clicking behind him as pistols were cocked. The blood brothers seemed to have sensed something or someone. They prepared.

The girl listened closely to the darkness, but she couldn't hear anything. A strong hand grasped her shoulder and pulled her back.

"Just make sure you don't get under our feet," Vivian whispered.

Loraine immediately felt grateful for this advice, because she had finally noticed the figures that the Cadavercitan had already sensed. This was all a lot more frightening than anything she could have imagined.

They didn't look unusual—just figures. But Loraine felt she wanted to scream and run away. And she simply couldn't move. She was hardly even breathing, hypnotized by the gaze of those strange beings standing at the other side of the patch of wasteland, and she began to regret that she hadn't stayed in the car.

There were five vampires. They looked like ordinary people, one in a black bush jacket, three in leather jackets, one in a raincoat. Darel's body was lying beside the nearest Asiman.

"Don't look into their eyes," Vivian whispered, rescuing her again. "Especially that one, in black."

They're all in black, the girl thought in a panic, and as if he could read her mind, the young necromancer squeezed her shoulder and pointed out the vampire standing slightly in front of the others, in line with Chris.

"That's Jacob, a very powerful magician."

"And Chris?" Loraine whispered with an effort. "Is he a powerful magician, too?"

Vivian snorted very quietly but didn't say anything, because Chris had started walking forward at a leisurely stroll.

Loraine saw one of the Asiman slowly take a knife out from behind his belt and raise his hand equally slowly to throw it, aiming at the necromancer. The Master of Death walked as if he hadn't noticed anything.

The girl wanted to shout out and warn him, but before she could, the sharp blade whistled past just a few centimeters away from Chris's head. It made no impression at all on him: it didn't halt his steady stride or even make him duck.

There was the sound of a shot. The Asiman who had thrown the knife clutched at his shoulder, then immediately straightened up, regenerating instantaneously.

That was the signal to begin. Sam fired a few more shots. Vivian took out his sword. Chris stopped walking.

And Loraine saw the most incredible fight of her life.

There were moments when she thought she was watching a movie with fantastic special effects. Because all this couldn't really happen.

It couldn't.

But it did.

The waste lot was lit up by flashes of vampire magic. The blood brothers moved so fast that the human eye couldn't keep up with them, and sometimes the girl thought she saw the same person in several different places at once. They appeared and disappeared right in front of her eyes, just like trick shots in a movie: Sam, blazing away with his pistol; Vivian with the blade of his sword glowing green; Chris . . .

Chris was facing Jacob. His face was pale with effort, and there was a poisonous green fire blazing in his outstretched hands. Drops of this liquid fire were streaming from the necromancer's fingers and landing on his enemy, searing him with their green splashes. The Asiman's clothes and hair were smoking, but he didn't seem to notice, and he was responding with flashes of scarlet light that lashed Chris like blows from a whip.

No one took any notice of the girl, and her stupor began to pass. As if her heart had suddenly started beating faster. And she remembered.

"Darel!"

Ignoring everything around her, she dashed across the waste lot to the wall of the cemetery.

"Darel! Wake up!"

The Dahanavar's face was pale, and his body was too heavy to lift.

"Darel! We have to get out of here!" Loraine grabbed the collar of his jacket and shook him with all her might. "Wake up!"

She smacked him on the cheek in despair. Then again. And again.

And then suddenly someone grabbed her from behind, squeezing her so tight that she couldn't breathe, and lifted her off the ground. Her jacket was ripped off her shoulder. And it was only then that the girl realized what they could do to her. She screamed in horror and anticipation of pain.

"No! No-o-o!"

Sharp fangs scraped on the metal plates protecting her neck, and she heard a brief curse.

"Chris! Chris! Help!"

A splash of green flame came hurtling out of the ball of fire enveloping the two battling sorcerers. Loraine heard a loud howl. Her panic and terror dissolved in the realization that these horrific beings could also feel pain. She twisted free of the Asiman's weakened grip and fell, and then, still stunned after her fall, she saw Vivian appear in front of her. The sword scattered green sparks as it whistled through the air, and she squeezed her eyes tight shut in order not to see the headless body sinking slowly to the ground.

"You make good bait," she heard a laughing voice say. "Now I know why Chris brought you with him."

She wasn't offended, because he was right.

"What about Darel? He's unconscious! We have to help him!"

"Not right now!"

Vivian picked up the girl as if she were as light as a kitten and tossed her onto a pile of dry leaves, then raised his blade just in time to block the sword of an Asiman who had sprung up out of nowhere. He missed the second blow, and the Asiman's sword sliced open his chest. Viv fell, but he must have managed to call for help, because Chris threw another ball of lightning. But this time the Asiman ducked, and it demolished one of the gravestones, lighting up the wasteland with a green glow.

The triumphant enemy raised his sword, taking good aim before he split Vivian's head open.

Barely even aware of what she was doing, Loraine picked up a thick stick that looked like a broken fence pole. From behind the Asiman vampire, she smashed it against his waist with all her strength. The vampire started in surprise and turned around. The girl's knees buckled under his fierce gaze, and the useless weapon fell out of her hands. Instantly hypnotized, she stared into that predatory face, and then suddenly an expression of astonishment appeared in the Asiman's eyes. He swayed. Tried to turn around. And collapsed on the ground.

When Loraine dared to lift up her head, Vivian was standing there with his jacket ripped across his chest. He winked at her.

"Well, now we're quits."

Before she could answer, he suddenly jumped forward, grabbed her by the scruff of the neck, put his hand over her mouth, and pressed her down against the ground so that she couldn't breathe. Startled and frightened, she tried to break free, but the cunning Cadavercitan didn't even seem to notice. And Loraine froze anyway when she heard the low howling in the distance.

It got louder and louder, until it became a deafening screech. Some *thing* that was barely even physical hurtled low across the open space and turned in a circle, and then she heard human screams through that eerie screeching, screams full of appalling agony. And Vivian's hand trembled ever so slightly.

Is he really afraid, too? Loraine thought in surprise. The leaves beside her rustled as someone else dropped to the ground, and she heard Chris's second pupil say:

"He summoned the Dark Hunter. I barely managed to get out of the way."

Viv shushed his blood brother, and he stopped talking. Then suddenly it went quiet. So quiet that Loraine's ears started ringing.

Vivian's grip eased. He helped Loraine to her feet.

"It's over. Now it's definitely over."

Sam got up after them, still excited.

"It's the first time I've seen him do it. Imagine, he just raised his hand and then, straight out of the void . . . that creature . . ."

Vivian apparently didn't share his enthusiasm. He winked swiftly at Loraine, then suddenly swung around and slapped his friend across the face. Any ordinary man's jaw would have been broken by a blow like that, but Sam just took a step back, completely stupefied.

"Viv, what was that for?"

Viv, who had so far been calm and smiling, jumped at him, grabbed hold of his collar, and almost growled in his fury:

"It was because of you that he summoned that vile brute. We were almost eaten alive, you cretin! I saw the way he was constantly covering you. Why the hell did you have to go playing at soldiers again? Jacob almost roasted him."

Bristling with resentment, the young Cadavercitan threw off his blood brother's hand.

"And why the hell did he bring that girl here? You were the one acting as her personal nanny."

"That doesn't concern you."

"Vivian! That's enough."

The sound of the sorcerer's voice came at exactly the right moment. A little later, and Loraine's new acquaintances would have been locked in a mighty tussle.

The Master of Death looked very tired. His snow-white shirt was torn and spattered with blood, the fire seemed to have gone out of his eyes, and his face was paler than usual. When they saw him, Sam and Viv lowered their heads like naughty little boys.

"Chris, how are you?" Vivian asked cautiously.

"He hurt me."

"I'm sorry," said Sam, hanging his head even lower. "It was my fault. Is there anything I can do?"

The sorcerer didn't answer, because he had spotted the anxious question in Loraine's eyes. He walked up and put his hand on her cheek, and the girl trembled involuntarily at this touch.

"They got away from us. Jacob managed to grab Darel and take him."

"What's going to happen?"

The Cadavercitan looked at her without speaking for a few moments, as if absorbed in thoughts of his own, then he turned abruptly toward his friends.

"I need blood."

Viv and Sam started, and both of them made a movement that was almost unconscious, reaching toward their left wrists in order to unbutton their cuffs.

Chris nodded to Vivian, who held out his hand to him, and then Loraine saw how it really happened. Viv winced slightly as the sharp fangs pierced his wrist, and then an expression of grateful rapture appeared on his face. Probably in the Cadavercitan family it's regarded as an honor to give your blood to an elder brother.

Samuel confirmed her guess by biting his lower lip in disappointment. The girl still didn't understand what he'd done wrong, but she realized that Chris had punished him quite severely by preferring Vivian's blood.

The sorcerer released his pupil's wrist with a deep sigh, and sparks seemed to run across his body. Then he stretched and became the old, imperturbable Chris once again. He turned around, wiping his lips on his cuff, and said:

"Let's go. We don't have much time."

No one asked where they had to go to. They all obeyed without a word. Loraine looked back. There was no trace left of the fearsome supernatural beast. The Asiman had disappeared. There weren't even any dead bodies.

The girl was tormented by a hundred questions, but she waited until they had left the park before falling in beside Vivian, who was clearly feeling pleased, and asking quietly:

"And who is the Dark Hunter?"

"A creature from the World Beyond," Vivian answered in an equally quiet voice. "A very dangerous brute. It devours everything living in its way and obeys only its master."

That means the vampires who didn't get away were eaten by the beast, Loraine thought with a shudder.

"And who is its master?"

Vivian cast a silent glance at his teacher. And the girl felt herself beginning to feel seriously afraid of Darel's mysterious friend.

"Why didn't the Hunter eat him?"

"Because Chris has paid it with his own blood."

"Can you summon it?"

"No. And if I could, I wouldn't. It's too dangerous."

"And Sam?"

Vivian laughed, looking at his gloomy friend, and shook his head.

"Are you Chris's pupils?"

"Let's just say that we're relatives," Viv answered with a smile.

The girl stopped talking, but she thought about all the strange things that had happened. They got back into the car and then wove their way through the dark back streets. Then they stopped in front of a gray five-story building where some of the windows were lit up. Some people were already awake and getting ready for work.

Chris strode into the entrance and set off confidently down the stairs that led to the basement, toward a pair of tall metal doors. It reeked of old rubbish and cigarette smoke.

"Get ready," said the sorcerer, and kicked out the heavy door with a single blow of his foot.

Someone yelped in fear in the dark corridor behind it, and a vague shadow went dashing away. The Master of Death dashed after it, and a few moments later they all heard his abrupt, imperious voice and a faltering, frightened voice answering indistinctly.

The girl looked inquiringly at Vivian. He shook his head, which clearly meant: *Keep quiet and wait.*

She didn't have to wait long. Chris appeared in the doorway, holding a very young vampire tightly by the neck. Loraine had never seen such perfect features and such a frightened expression before. She even felt sorry for him.

But the Cadavercitan kept squeezing the thin neck in his leather-gloved hand and asking questions in some incomprehensible language. The boy answered them quickly, and the expression on his face suggested that he was willing to confess to absolutely anything. But the Master of Death didn't like his answers.

The girl turned away in order not to see the young vampire choking without even trying to defend himself. The boy shouted something in a desperate voice. The sorcerer laughed out loud.

"Let's go," said Chris. "We're all ready."

He kept a tight grip on his prisoner's collar, but judging from the boy's miserable, bewildered face, he wasn't even thinking of trying to escape.

The corridor was very narrow, with stone walls and a vaulted ceiling. It led smoothly downward under the ground and was lit by widely spaced lamps, like kerosene lamps, that gave a bright light.

Loraine had passed beyond the bounds of fear a long time ago, and now she merely felt empty. Chris strode on as confidently as if he were at home, keeping a tight grip on his hostage, who was stumbling at every step and gazing around wildly. The sorcerer's metal-shod boots clattered defiantly on the stone floor. And Loraine could have sworn that the Cadavercitan was doing it on purpose—only a short while ago, he had been moving without making a sound.

Squinting sideways at his confident movements, Loraine

couldn't help taking heart. Behind her, Sam and Vivian walked along as quietly as before, without speaking, and the girl got the idea that now they were something like the sorcerer's bodyguards. Or, rather, escort of honor. Because there was no doubt that the necromancer could take care of himself.

The corridor gradually grew wider. Cracks appeared in the stonework of the walls, and tree roots that had forced apart the stone slabs of the ceiling hung down into the tunnel. There was the gurgling sound of water and a cool breath of wind with a smell of dampness, rotting wood, and, for some reason, vanilla. The lamps were replaced by round globes that glowed with a diffuse, milky light. The floor under their feet became softer, and the girl realized they were now walking on earth. Chris frowned. He took out a snow-white handkerchief and brushed off a long thread of spider's web that was hanging on the sleeve of his jacket. Loraine was elated to realize that he wasn't afraid at all, he wasn't even concerned, and perhaps it wasn't the first time he had made this journey through the gloomy underground passage.

The long tunnel began branching. They came across side passages, narrow or broad or looking like dark burrows. The necromancer stopped at one of these for a moment, looked back, and pointed confidently: That way. The companions turned into a murky, musty corridor with green mold on the walls.

"It's quite clean here now. Not long ago there were bodies and all sorts of things all over the place," said Chris. Seeing Loraine's expression, he laughed.

"Are these Nosoforos tunnels?" she gasped in amazement and curiosity.

"No," the Cadavercitan said with a smile. "There's no point in hoping you'll ever see one of them. They all departed. A long time ago. All sorts of rabble hang around in here. . . . Stop."

He halted by the wall and started examining the stonework. He was obviously very interested in something, because he left his prisoner in the care of his pupils and started clearing away the mold and moss without worrying about spoiling his cuffs. Then he took a step back, surveyed the surface he had cleaned, and pressed on a slightly protruding piece of stone with both hands.

The wall under his hands trembled and swayed and smoothly moved aside. The girl gasped in astonishment when she saw the space that was revealed.

The companions walked across seven meters of red carpet and found themselves in a spacious hall. It was well lit, the walls were covered with plastic panels, and there were brand-new air-conditioner grilles in the ceiling. "They've certainly made themselves comfortable," Chris murmured as he looked around, and he took a firm grip on his hostage's neck again.

The girl shuddered and only just stopped herself from grabbing hold of the sorcerer's hand when she saw the person walking toward them from the far side of the hall. There was nothing unhuman about him—a perfectly normal big-city entrepreneur. Severe dark suit, short haircut. But Loraine felt tremors of chilly fear running down her back.

To look at, the man was forty at the most, but she sensed he was very old. Perhaps one of the oldest beings on the earth. And he had been alive for so long that he had lost absolutely all human qualities, even those that were left in the blood brothers after they were turned. And Loraine's nervous trembling was caused not by fear, but by the impossibility of being in the same place at the same time with this creature.

When he saw the man, the captive vampire shuddered and started jabbering rapidly in a language that the girl didn't know, with a lot of guttural sounds, but the sorcerer gave him a slight shake. The master of the secret hideaway made a reassuring gesture to him and then looked balefully at the Cadavercitan.

"I know you," the man said to Chris.

"We have met."

"England," said the vampire.

"Ireland," Chris corrected him.

They smiled coldly at each other and started talking in that strange guttural language. Loraine looked around helplessly at Vivian and Sam, who were still standing a little behind her. Realizing what the problem was, Viv leaned over and started translating the conversation in a whisper.

"Let my pupil go. You have already used him to get here."

"I only want one thing," the Cadavercitan replied politely. "Give back my friend. Your brothers took him tonight. He was incautious enough to cross their path."

"Last time the noble Master of Death appealed on behalf of one of his friends, too. I don't recall what became of him."

"That time I arrived too late," the sorcerer said in a cold, almost indifferent voice. "Give back my friend, and we will leave your home."

"What makes you think that he is here?"

"A few days ago, Darel happened to be in a place where the Asiman were carrying out an operation to gather human material. He was a little careless, and I have the impression that some of your brothers felt insulted and decided to take revenge on him for interfering in your family's affairs."

"He was a little careless!" The vampire's social gloss completely deserted him. He bared his teeth and roared, "He killed my best pupil. Incinerated his brain!"

"Amusing." Chris looked at the palm of his hand, which was beginning to glow with a green light. "I didn't know he could do that. Burn out brains. I can't guarantee to repeat his feat, but I can spoil this handsome little fellow's face. Unless I am mistaken, Ernesto, he is the last pupil that you have?"

The prisoner howled, staring at the magical fire in the Cadavercitan's hand with his violet eyes wide in terror.

"Teacher! No! Please!"

"Let him go," the Asiman said in a dull voice. "And you can collect your little friend."

Chris hesitated for a moment, then pushed his hostage away. The young vampire almost flew across the few meters to his teacher and fell at his feet. The teacher helped him up and looked derisively at the sorcerer.

"If you wish to take the Dahanavar out of here, go and collect him." Ernesto nodded toward a passage that had opened up in the wall. His voice was filled with gloating hatred.

The narrow corridor looked very much like a burrow; even Loraine would have had to bend over to walk down it. The Cadavercitan took a step toward the tunnel and immediately recoiled with an expression of revulsion on his face.

"What is this, a stupid joke?"

"I'm very sorry, my dear Chris," said the Asiman, putting one arm around his pupil's shoulders. "But there is no other way to the Repository."

Chris swore briefly and turned to his companions. His gaze came to rest on the girl. A vague doubt seemed to flicker through his eyes and then disappear. He walked up to her quickly.

"Loraine, you'll have to go on your own. We can't get past the trap."

The Cadavercitan took a coin out of his pocket and threw it onto the floor of the corridor. Immediately there was a bright flash of light from the ceiling.

"Daylight lamps, amplified by ancient Asiman magic. They would burn our eyes out."

"All right." It cost the girl an effort to agree, but there was no way back now.

"Don't be afraid, you won't get lost," said Chris, interpreting her nervousness in his own way. "Just keep going straight on all the time. It's a long tunnel. You'll see a lot of strange things, but don't pay too much attention to them. And hurry, it will be dawn soon." The sorcerer closed his eyes, as if he were trying to remember something. "When you reach the end, you'll find a round chamber. Look at the walls. There should be something like a switch. A lever. Or a block of stone protruding from the surface of the wall. Press it, and the lamps will go out."

Loraine nodded and stepped into the corridor, and for some reason she picked up the coin that was glittering in the strip of light. Noticing in passing that it was a gold piece from the last century, she clutched it tight in her hand and walked on.

For a while, nothing about the tunnel changed. It looked modern, with light at regular intervals. There was nothing to be afraid of here.

The plastic covering on the floor and the walls suddenly came to an end, and once again there was earth. Puddles. Roots. A low ceiling. Suddenly a draft of dry air with a subtle, spicy aroma blew into her face. Stone slabs, covered with a fine sprinkling of sand, appeared under her feet. It was quiet, but somewhere in the distance she could just hear a wind droning.

Dark niches from floor to ceiling. Loraine looked closely. There was something lying in them—desiccated, shrunken bodies. They looked like dried-up insects. Skin stretched over bones. Arms like thin branches, folded across chests, heads with the remnants of hair, ribs like spider's legs. Humans? Vampires?

She felt afraid. Her turtleneck sweater stuck to her wet back, and the air started scratching and scraping her throat. Only the thought that Darel might be somewhere among these mummies kept her moving forward. He's here because of me. If he hadn't killed that Asiman to save me, he wouldn't have ended up in here.

It was easier to keep walking if she didn't look around. The important thing was not to let her imagination run riot. Who knew what might be lying there, in these boxes, dried and cracked by time?

The girl cried out when something large and dark, with

wriggling legs, fell onto her shoulder from the ceiling. She brushed it off onto the floor and then looked to see what had attacked her. It was a gigantic black cockroach. Shuddering with revulsion, Loraine rushed on, taking no more notice of the motionless corpses.

The corridor ended suddenly. At the center of the round room's dome-shaped ceiling, there was a hole through which she could see the sky.

Darel was lying directly under it, in a stone sarcophagus. His face looked like wax, his arms were folded on his chest, and his neck was terrible to look at. It had been lacerated. But there was no blood oozing out of the gashes, as if there were absolutely none left.

"Darel, I'll get you out of here. Hang on."

The walls of the chamber were built of irregular blocks of stone. One block did protrude noticeably, but it took a while to find it. She had to walk around the chamber several times before she spotted it. It grated repulsively under her hands as it slid back into the wall, centimeter by centimeter. Then it clicked and locked in place. She could only hope that it really did turn off the lamps.

Heaving a deep sigh, Loraine tried to pull the vampire out of the coffin and suddenly realized in horror that she couldn't do it. He was too heavy.

"It's all right. I can do it."

There was a pale star shining above her head. When the sun rose, its rays would fall straight onto his face. Panic lent her strength. If she took a good grip on his cold, limp hand and pulled . . . No, he wasn't dead, simply in a coma. When they lost a lot of blood or suffered severe pain, the blood brothers went to sleep. That was what all the books about vampires said, and it was in all the movies.

Loraine heaved Darel toward her with all her might. The heavy body tumbled over the edge of the sarcophagus and fell softly on the floor. Excellent. After that it was easier. And there wasn't far to go. First through the corridor with the mummies, then through the tunnel with the magic lamps. She just hoped her strength would hold out.

Trying to breathe deeply and maintain a regular rhythm, the girl dragged the unconscious Dahanavar along the ground. She stopped thinking about the dangers and wasn't afraid of anything anymore. The only thing she felt was the way her heart started beating furiously when she thought about the approaching dawn, and every now and then she brushed away the hair that had stuck to her sweaty face with her shoulder.

About halfway through the corridor with the dried corpses, she had to stop for a rest. Her back was aching. There were colored circles in front of her eyes. It would be dawn soon. She had to hurry. What will happen if I don't make it in time? Darel's arm suddenly moved, and an icy hand grabbed Loraine's wrist. She almost screamed in horror and shock, then told herself not to be stupid. Of course! He's not dead.

"I'll get you out. Don't be afraid. I'll manage it."

The cold fingers clutched her wrist even more tightly, as if they wanted to crush the bones.

"Darel! Don't!"

She couldn't pull herself free. The pain started making her feel dizzy and sick. The Dahanavar began pulling her slowly toward him, and Loraine suddenly realized what he wanted to do. He can sense me. For him I'm just a source of blood. It's a reflex. He doesn't understand what he's doing. In a normal state he would never hurt me, but now . . .

"Don't, I'm trying to help you!"

Tears of resentment and humiliation scorched her eyes. She was not just food.

"I don't want to! No! Don't you dare!"

Loraine jerked again and squeezed her eyes shut, expecting

more pain, but it didn't come. Darel's fangs scraped on the fish-scale collar, making a repulsive sound. How farsighted Chris was. The vampire immediately released his intended victim and relapsed into his stupor.

The girl sobbed loudly, wiped away her tears, and pushed the vampire's limp arm away.

She didn't remember the rest of the journey very well.

In the corridor with the daylight lamps, Loraine realized that she couldn't move another step. But strong arms set her on her feet and took hold of the unconscious body. Chris was standing beside her. Strong, imperturbable, calm. She immediately felt better at the sight of him.

"Quickly, brave Loraine."

The Cadavercitan flung Darel's body across his shoulder with incredible ease and walked toward the way out. The others hurried after him.

THE silhouettes of the trees and houses were clear and sharp in the gray predawn twilight.

Vivian dashed to the car, opened the door for Chris, and helped him put Darel on the seat, then ran around the BMW and got in behind the wheel. Sam got in beside him.

"We don't have time to get to his place or mine. That's the other side of the city. We'll have to stop somewhere else," the Cadavercitan told Loraine.

The car hurtled along the boulevard, ignoring the red spots of the traffic lights. Once a police car started chasing them, but it soon turned off into a side street, "forgetting" about the speeding vehicle. Sam gently tapped his fist on the door handle. He was nervous. Afraid they wouldn't make it before sunrise. Darel was lifeless. His head was lolling against the back of the seat, and the wounds on his white neck were bright red. Chris was absolutely calm.

"Well?" he asked, realizing that Loraine was dying to ask a question.

The girl felt her cheeks growing hot. "Nothing. It doesn't matter."

"Ask."

"Where did Vivian put his sword after the fight in the park?" It could hardly have sounded more stupid, but she had to finish. "It's not on his belt, I can't see it under his jacket. . . ."

Chris laughed. In the rearview mirror, Vivian's serious eyes narrowed in amusement.

"I'll tell you later," he promised, and swung the wheel sharply. The car drove into a courtyard.

Chris got out, put Darel over his shoulder again, and ran into the shelter of the entrance. The others hurried after him. They walked up to the fourth floor without waiting for the elevator. The sorcerer opened a metal door, let everyone in, and turned the key in the lock.

It was a large, half-empty two-room apartment. Which had just been expensively renovated. It still smelled of new carpet and damp wallpaper. Suspended ceilings, magnificent oak shelves, and bright walls that looked like silk in the light of the lamps. There were no windows at all, or they had been brilliantly camouflaged.

Vivian and Sam stayed in the sitting room. Chris put the Dahanavar down on a broad divan in the next room. He rolled up his shirtsleeve with a habitual gesture.

"Hold his head," the Cadavercitan ordered, and bit his own wrist. Blood spurted out onto the white cuff.

"But can he drink your blood? You're from different Houses!" Loraine asked in a quiet voice as she carefully supported the back of Darel's heavy head.

"Yes," the sorcerer replied tersely, and it wasn't clear whether he was feeling irritated by the girl's inappropriate curiosity or uneasy about her excessive thirst for knowledge.

The bleeding wrist was pressed against Darel's mouth, and he fastened on it eagerly. Grabbing Chris's forearm, he drank greedily and hastily for a long time.

The sorcerer looked closely at Loraine. "Not a very pretty sight?"

"No. Not very."

"This is what it really looks like. But when they bite into the carotid artery"—he ran his free hand across his neck—"it's even more disgusting."

"Probably."

The Cadavercitan grimaced in pain, unclasped Darel's fingers, and took hold of his own wrist, stopping the blood.

"He'll come round now."

The Dahanavar started to move. His face had lost that corpse-like look. He sighed deeply several times and opened his eyes. Looked at Chris, then shifted his gaze to Loraine's dirty, disheveled face and her metal collar. He sat up abruptly on the divan and hastily wiped the blood off his lips with his hand. He realized immediately what had happened.

"Loraine, I . . . tried . . ."

"You tried," said Chris, buttoning his cuff. "And you weren't the only one."

Darel gave him a fierce look but made no comment.

"Loraine, I'm sorry, I—"

"I know. You didn't mean to. It's just that—"

"It's just that I'm a vampire. And it's deadly dangerous for you, being around me."

THE ART OF THE FARIES

It is the spectator, and not life, that art really mirrors.

—Oscar Wilde, *The Picture of Dorian Gray*

October 28

The picture was superb.

The column leaning out of the semidarkness seemed suspended above the viewer's head, set to collapse at any moment, crushing the shoots of ivy sprouting at its foot and burying the girl who had halted on the steps of the temple. She seemed about to fall, breaking out a section of the frame, ripping the canvas apart, sending chips of stone spraying up from the marble floor.

Paula looked away to get rid of the feeling of danger radiating from the canvas. Alexander was standing at the far end of the room, beside the false window. The scene beyond the thin Venetian glass was a hot Spanish noon. Dusty crowns of trees seen through a shimmering haze, ocher-colored hills and clouds seething up into colossal heaps in the blinding sunlight.

Against the background of the southern landscape the maestro looked unreal, as if he had been cut out of a sheet of paper and laid on top of the colored picture. Like in the shadow theater. That piazza in Verona. The small pavilion. Entrance fee ten lire. Dark forms moving behind a tightly stretched white curtain. The memory was so vivid that for a moment Paula could smell the resin from the fresh boards of the stage and feel the taste of licorice candy in her mouth. With an effort of will, she drove out the vision of the past.

She looked back at the column about to tear through the canvas, the frail girl who didn't realize that in a second her body would be crushed by the massive monolith.

"A magnificent painting. Perfection," Paula said in a quiet voice, almost a whisper, speaking to herself. But the maestro heard. He turned around, looked past his pupil, and raised one eyebrow ironically.

"They say the tragedy of the artist is that he can never achieve his ideal. But actually, when the ideal is achieved, and completely achieved, that is when even greater frustration sets in. The magical power and mystery of the perfect creation are lost. The work that has been created becomes no more than the starting point for the creation of some other ideal, different from the former."

Paula smiled. She often used to try to understand Alexander's paradoxical musings, but now she just relished them. Accepting every utterance as axiomatic.

"And who does this abandoned ideal belong to?"

"You don't know him. No one knows him yet."

"Are these symbols? The ivy, the Ionic column, the half-ruined stairway in the background . . . Are they painted with deliberate intent, or simply—"

"I don't think he could say for certain himself. An artist's only goal is to record his own experience. But once a work is finished, it lives a life of its own and expresses something quite different from what was put into it."

Alexander walked closer and stood behind Paula. She kept looking at the picture and saw that the colors on the canvas had started to change. Dense cinnabar bled through white, until the light-colored tunic of the girl beside the column was girdled by a scarlet belt.

A tremor of delight ran down her back, as it always did when she saw the maestro work his magic.

"That's better," he declared, and Paula trembled again, this time at the sound of his voice, full of deep, resonant notes. Banal desires, impermissible during a session of high magic, clouded her mind. Her clarity of perception evaporated. There was no longer any meaning in his words, only a sequence of notes in a minor key, like the song of a cello.

"Like life, nature merely copies art. By interacting with a work of art, I change reality."

She tried to concentrate but managed only to hear the beating of her own heart. Regular and slightly slow, echoing through her body.

"Paula, take a look at yourself."

When Alexander pronounced her name, a slight accent appeared in his voice. It came out as "Paola." The young Faryartos looked at her white blouse. A red strip had appeared on the fine fabric of her sleeve, running from the shoulder to the cuff. The same color as on the painting. There it was—the influence of art on reality. Probably, if the maestro had wanted, the column would really have fallen onto the girl in the foreground, and Paula would have collapsed to the floor with her head crushed.

The pupil glanced at her sleeve again. Red was completely out of place in her outfit, and Alexander knew it perfectly well. The joke was in his style. The day before, he had quoted Baudelaire as he knotted his necktie in front of the mirror: "It is irrational to reduce dandyism to an exaggerated partiality for fine clothes and an elegant appearance. For the true dandy, all material attributes are merely symbols of the aristocratic superiority of his soul."

Influencing reality through art . . . sometimes it was impossible to tell if he was being serious or playing a virtuoso game with his paradoxes, teasing his naïve pupil.

She was his favorite pupil. Supposedly the most capable. She could enchant, dazzle, seduce. But she did not have his magical power over the world. Alexander was so intelligent that there was no shame in being stupid in his company. An unscalable peak. If wisdom came with age, then Paula could not even imagine how many centuries you had to live to get close to it.

He said that nature and life were only a reflection of art. She could understand that with her mind. Untangle the complicated reasoning and make it more or less acceptable to her logic. But she couldn't feel it. That was why she had no power in Faryartos magic: she couldn't use imaginary images to influence reality.

Life imitates art far more than art imitates life. . . . That was how it had always been. A great artist created a type, and life tried to copy it. To reproduce it in a popular form. How many young men had killed themselves because that was what Werther had done in Goethe's book? And how many beautiful children had been born in Hellas because their mothers had looked at those magnificent, perfect statues? Even mist had not existed in people's perception until art depicted it.

These were not the maestro's words. But by repeating what the great English writer and dramatist had said, Alexander achieved what was beyond the reach of a human being. He filled a magnificent theory with magic. He found the perfect magical key to an imperfect reality. It was a pity that Oscar himself had refused to accept immortality and could not savor the real fruits of his ideas.

Paula knew that someday she would understand, would feel—and be able to create her own reality. In the meantime, she found beautiful, intelligent, talented chosen members for the elite. Individuals who would have less and less contact with life as time went by, because life was imperfect and cruel and the price that had to be paid for her gifts was exorbitant; in life, disaster struck the wrong people at the wrong time, and it was too short, or excessively long.

Art never caused pain. The world that it created evoked suffering without genuine physical torment, sadness without tragedy, grief without bitterness. It was perfect. Those who created this world had to be like it.

Paula didn't feel perfect. She hadn't created anything. All she did, as Darel Dahanavar had said, was run around carrying out her master's orders. But the telepath didn't know the maestro's theory. All he did was steal other people's thoughts and use them to revitalize his own soul.

As for Hemran . . . She wanted Hemran. She wanted him, and that was all. And she wasn't going to let what anybody else thought stop her.

"Alexander, I'd like to have a word about Vance."

The maestro moved away from the picture, sat down in a low armchair, and crossed his legs. "What would you like to say to me about Vance?"

"I think he could become one of us."

Alexander took a sunflower out of the vase and spun it absentmindedly in his hands. "He could. But he won't. At least, not now."

Paula cast a despairing glance around the room. Everything here was magnificent. Absolute harmony of color and line. It was so comfortable to sit on this divan, with her legs pulled up onto its springy cushions; this lamp gave the most delightful golden light; the carpet was caressing and springy under her feet; the round mirror on the wall was made of polished silver; and the person reflected in it seemed to be surrounded by a heavenly radiance. And that hot Spanish noon painted behind the false window—it seemed as if the rays of sunlight were shining into the room and lighting up every corner. This sensation was produced by the precise selection of colors. Lemon yellow curtains, a cream carpet, light-colored tapestries. The picture was the only dark patch on the wall.

"But why? Why are you against it? He's very talented, and so popular with the public."

"Yes." Alexander casually set the flower back in the vase. "The public always feels quite wonderful face-to-face with mediocrity."

"Vance is not mediocre."

The maestro's only reply was a suggestive smile, expressing his doubts concerning his pupil's objectivity, mistrust of Hemran's success, and weariness from watching the constant parade of various kinds of artists flitting past in front of his eyes every day. There were so few genuine talents to be found among them.

She wanted Vance. Alexander was beyond her comprehension. His intelligence, magnetism, and magical power were sometimes too much for her to bear. She wanted to divert to herself at least part of the admiration that he received, and that way Hemran had looked at her: with love, adoration, longing.

Paula walked up to the chair that the maestro was sitting in and knelt on the floor, not worrying about whether she might crease her fine English suit. The soft nap of the carpet yielded gently under her knees. Alexander took hold of her chin, forcing her to raise her head and look him in the eye.

"Thinking is the most harmful pastime in the world. People die from it, just as they do from other illnesses."

She smiled in reply. She didn't want to, but her lips obediently stretched out into a smile.

"Do you want me to think less?"

"I want you to feel more."

He ran his thumb across her forehead. She wanted to close her eyes, press her cheek against his knee, and try to get all these thoughts out of her head. Every last one. But she couldn't.

The phone rang. Alexander leaned across the armrest and picked up the receiver with one hand, holding on to his pupil with the other. She had half-risen, about to go out in order not to interfere with his conversation. But now she stayed, frozen in an unsteady position on one knee in front of the maestro. His eyes were at the level of the low neckline of her blouse, but the Fary-artos remained disinterested, intent, undistracted.

"Hello," he said in a changed voice, dry and unpleasant. "Yes . . . yes. I remember."

Paula couldn't hear whom he was talking to, but she imagined it was someone confident and powerful. Alexander's frown grew deeper and deeper; he gazed gloomily at the picture, and it suddenly started to change. As if the canvas had been generously splashed with solvent. The colors ran, transforming the composition into a messy daub.

The young fary cautiously laid her hand on her teacher's wrist, sensed his tension, and tried to calm him mentally. Looking at her in response to this timid expression of affection, he saw the anxiety in her eyes and gave a slight nod: a moment later, the picture had resumed its normal appearance.

"Yes. I understand."

The other party ended the conversation. Alexander hung up the phone. Rose to his feet rapidly and went over to the false window.

"Who was it?" Paula asked, turning in his direction. Thinking that she was like a sunflower, following the movement of the sun across the sky.

"The Upieschi."

She didn't need to ask who exactly. It was clear anyway. Ramon de Cobrero.

"What does he want?"

"Get changed," the maestro replied abruptly. "You've got forty minutes left."

SHE got up without a word and went to get dressed. The presentation of an exhibition of work by a promising young photographer was due to start in two hours. The photographer was still human. So far.

The event had been organized under the patronage of the House of Faryartos. Inspired by Alexander and managed by Paula.

She arrived an hour early. Checked once more that the tables were laid for the buffet meal and the price lists were ready for the press. Showed the TV men the best spots for their cameras.

Everything was perfect. Several halls of the art gallery were brightly lit. The huge ceiling-to-floor windows caught glimmers of light from the nighttime street. From outside, it looked as if the people inside were slowly floating past without touching the floor, surrounded by halos of light. Their voices were inaudible through the thick bulletproof glass, but every change in an expression, every wrinkle, smile, or grimace of dissatisfaction, was visible. A theater of mime.

The walls were hung with photographs in 90-by-120-centimeter format. Social scenes, lyrical compositions, ironic comments. One of them was her portrait. Paula standing right on the edge of the sidewalk. The cars rushing past are broad smears of bright color, quivering bursts of light; the whole world seems to be blurred. She is the only real thing in it, a sharply defined image, standing there motionless in a long black coat. Her pale face is glowing like a pearl, her eyes reflect the glitter of the shop windows.

The photographer was already there. He had arrived in a great hurry, three hours early. And the first thing he had done was start rehanging the photos, because he thought the overall composition had been disrupted. Paula had already been informed about his excessive diligence. He still hadn't realized that there were staff members ready and waiting to carry out his every demand. He was used to doing everything himself. But he'd get over that. In time.

Vladar was standing in the manager's office, running an electric razor over his hollow cheeks and talking to someone on the phone at the same time. When he saw her, he beamed and immediately cut the conversation short.

"Paula, glad to see you! Sorry, I'll just . . . this . . ."

"It's okay," she said with a smile, and pressed her lips lingeringly against his freshly shaved cheek. "The TV's already here."

Since their last meeting, which had been the week before, the photographer had gotten even thinner. It was amazing how he managed it. His face seemed drawn and his nose looked sharp. But the bright green eyes still glittered with their eternal optimism, and the vibrant human energy was literally gushing out of him. He was excited and happy. And so he should be, with an exhibition in the most important gallery in the city. A rare stroke of luck. His work had been noticed by the well-known philanthropist Alexander Danville Milo himself. The same man who had lifted the popular artist Ilya Kmar out of obscurity, out of near poverty, in fact. There was no doubt that after this exhibition Vladar's name would be known even outside artistic circles, and another couple of exhibitions would make him famous.

Paula liked him. But then, so did everyone. His friends, the models he worked with, his colleagues. Even people who hated to be photographed admitted that he knew what he was doing. His energy was infectious, inspiring, convincing. Magnificent qualities for a future Faryartos. Amplified by the magic of art, they would become a weapon of great power.

Vladar was crazy about photography; he seemed to see the world through a camera sight all the time. This was one person who would definitely master the ability to influence reality through art very quickly.

Charming, kind, considerate. Very talented. A real find for the House of Faryartos. In a few more years, when he had acquired more experience and fine-honed his skills, he would be ready to join the family. Then Paula would come to him and make the magnificent, generous proposal that was hard, almost impossible, for any intelligent man to refuse.

Every mortal had his weak spot. A secret desire. Money, celebrity, world fame . . . Vladar wanted to live for a long time. To a hundred and twenty, as he admitted with a smile. He wanted to see if the art of photography would change during the next century. He dreamed of following the changes and finding out what the modern digital camera would become in fifty years' time.

A human weakness that could easily be taken advantage of. Instead of a pitiful sixty or seventy years of life, he would receive immortality and eternal youth. It was quite unbearable to refuse an offer like that. And what would he lose in this world? Only the ability to take shots by daylight.

She spoke to Vladar for a few minutes. He liked everything. The lighting, the spacious halls, the dishes for the buffet, the guest list, and Paula herself. But then, he always felt a genuine interest and liking for everyone he talked to.

Paula straightened Vladar's necktie, smiled, and set off into the hall.

The guests were gradually arriving. As usual, the TV men had all come in a group. They said hello to two journalists. Both of them were human, and both were fated to stay that way. The Faryartos family had no interest in them. One was supposedly famous, and the other tried very hard to act as if he were.

Paula glanced past them and noticed Elvis. A handsome man, she had to admit, but not to her taste. It was annoying, really. There was the idol of millions standing right beside her, and she had the feelings of a sister for him. All the girls still went crazy over him, even now. His fans didn't believe that he was dead. They invented absurd legends about him being kidnapped by aliens. That swarthy face, the dark, wide-set eyes and broad bridge of the nose, that black wavy hair generously anointed with gel. A formal suit that was a striking contrast with his former white, red, and silver jackets and shirts with rolled-up sleeves. The inimitable charm and sexuality that the king of rock 'n' roll used to wind up his fans. Every now and then, Paula felt she would like to know how a star from the fifties felt in the modern world. But she thought it was tactless to ask.

The singer gave her a brief wink and turned back to the photograph that he was studying thoughtfully. And he doesn't sing anymore, either, she suddenly thought. Just like me. . . . That damn Dahanavar! As if Darel were the one who wouldn't let her sing. She forced herself not to think about it and went over to the other guests.

Freddy Farah gallantly kissed her hand and whispered a sweet obscenity in her ear. Paula laughed and looked her blood brother up and down, pretending to be taking his measure. It seemed unlikely that he was capable of what he had suggested.

He had never been short of fans, either, and especially male ones. The Faryartos had saved him from an incurable disease, the plague of the twentieth century, and now he was enjoying his new afterlife, as he called it. He never mentioned the name he had used as a star and had gone back to his modest family name.

A popular author was standing against the opposite wall, surrounded by female journalists. One of the people they were intending to turn in the near future. Unfortunately, or perhaps fortunately, he wasn't aware of that. Unlike most of the other men there, who were dressed in formal suits, the writer was wearing black jeans and a gray T-shirt with the inscription "Death to vampires!" He was obviously still under the impression of his own latest book. She remembered that after Alexander read it, he had paused and then commented: "In art . . . such a viewpoint on the question of the blood brothers can also be meaningful."

The TV people loved the writer. Now he was waving his hands around casually as he expounded his views on modern literature and its undeniable links with the moods of society. From there, any intelligent person could go on to draw the conclusion that photography also reflected the life and problems of society. The female journalists nervously clicked the buttons of their Dictaphones and hung on every word.

The well-known poetess Olga Artemeva appeared, surrounded by her admirers, then a pair of young TV presenters in extravagant outfits, a fashionable artist with a retinue of followers, a movie director . . .

Paula played the customary role of hostess, moving from one guest to another, smiling, accepting compliments and kisses. She introduced Vladar to useful people. Including vampires, naturally. Radiating his unfailing charm, the photographer immediately found the right words for everyone and seemed to make the required impression.

At precisely ten o'clock, the fary took the microphone and walked out into the center of the hall. The guests broke off their chatter. Looking at their politely interested faces, she announced that the exhibition of work by the young and talented photographer Vladar Bondar was open. The bright spotlight set colored lights dancing in the diamonds on her hands and chest, and the silvery stripe in her dress glowed with a radiant sheen.

Then Vladar said a few words. And fifteen minutes later, the official ceremony was over. The cameraman wandered off to mingle with the celebrities, and Paula went back to work. Talking to the guests, listening to what they thought of the photographs. Making sure that empty dishes on the buffet tables were refilled promptly. Cultural events usually gave the humans among the guests an incredible appetite. The others would satisfy their hunger later.

So far, everything was going splendidly. Alexander would be

pleased. And she could take pride in her organizational abilities. As always.

Vance appeared at ten forty-five. The relaxed TV men suddenly came to life again and made a dash for the rock star, finishing off their sandwiches on the way. Hemran was gloomy and dressed casually—jeans, a T-shirt with a picture of a grinning wolf's head, a leather jacket. He blew off the journalists in that ironically cynical manner of his, then stopped and looked around the hall. When he saw her, his sullen face lit up.

She didn't have to be a telepath to sense the painful breakdown he was going through. He looked just about ready to fall apart, start playing in low dives, drinking hard, and taking heroin. And Paula knew who was to blame. She was.

The singer walked over to her.

"You're looking great." Hemran stared at her with an avid yearning. Examined her carefully, gazing at her naked arms, the low neckline of her dress, her lips. She didn't need to use any magic to enchant him. It was enough just to move one step closer, so that he could smell her perfume, and smile or put her hand on his arm.

"Can we talk?" Vance's voice sounded dull. Under the three-day growth of beard, his cheeks looked very hollow.

Paula was going to talk to him straightaway, but a low murmuring started up behind her. She sensed the tension with her back and turned around. A short, frail-looking young man of about twenty was standing in the center of the hall. He had light blond hair, blue eyes, and an indescribable expression of mingled arrogance, disdain, scorn, and conceit on his thin face. All the blood brothers at the exhibition were looking at him nervously. The human half of the guests didn't know the young man, so they gave him only a quick glance and went back to talking or eating.

The fary gripped the stem of her glass convulsively. She looked icy cool, but there were sharp little needles pricking at the inside of her temples.

Miklosh Balza. The head of the House of Nachterret.

She was scared.

But she would rather have died than show it.

Hovering beside the young man was a massive hulk with a huge black beard, an unpleasant smirk on his face, and a bald head that gleamed brightly in the light of the lamps. He was wearing a black leather cloak and boots that left muddy tracks on the marble floor. Paula thought she felt the glass crunch in her tightly clenched fingers.

She hadn't been expecting this guest. She could never even have imagined that he would turn up.

"So, can we talk?" Vance repeated, unable to understand why she had suddenly tensed up, stopped dead, and turned away from him.

"Not right now."

"When?"

"Tomorrow. I'll call you."

"What time?"

"Eight. In the evening. And now, please—"

"I get it. I picked the wrong moment, as usual."

Vance swung around abruptly and headed for the exit, angry and offended, but she had already forgotten about him.

The fary walked forward in welcome, radiating charm and sexuality from the top of her head to the tips of her toes. Smiling.

"Nachttoter Miklosh." Despite the treacherous tremor in her throat, her voice sounded just as it should—deep, resonant, entrancing. "What a pleasure to see you here."

The Nachterret laughed, appreciating the frank flattery. He appraised her body, tightly encased in the silk evening gown, looking her over from head to toe.

"Would you like to take a look at the exhibition? I can show you some works that might interest you."

He narrowed his pale eyes.

"And do you know what might interest me?" He had a strange voice. Young and clear, but with occasional hoarse, low notes.

Two-faced. Deceitful. Dangerous. But, like everyone else, responsive to her allure.

"I can guess." Paula smiled, and she took the Nachttoter by the arm with a spontaneous, natural movement and gently led him in the required direction.

He grinned crookedly again but allowed himself to be led. Miklosh was apparently in a good mood today. Johan wandered after them, sniffing loudly to express his contempt for everyone there.

Vladar also noticed the new visitor, looked at him in interest, and was about to come over. Paula shook her head, only slightly, but clearly saying no. He understood and stayed where he was, watching her go with a surprised expression. It would have been difficult to explain to him just how contemptuously Mr. Balza regarded mortals.

Walking beside Miklosh, sensing his touch and his desires, was disgusting. Black, stagnant water with broken glass on the bottom. And she walked across it, smiling, smoothly swaying her hips, and remaining calm.

Paula knew that the Nachterret preferred blue-eyed blondes, and she was a brunette, with dark, almost black eyes. Italian in her old life. But every now and then, his interested glance touched her. If you like one thing, it doesn't mean the time will never come when you fancy trying another.

"After you," she said, gesturing into the hall containing works devoted to war and other social disasters.

The photos were black and white, making them all the more expressive. Dead, empty houses with broken windows, heaps of broken stone, tracks left by tanks. Men in dusty camouflage uniforms, with indifferent expressions on faces and beards growing right up to their eyes. Automatic weapons in their lowered hands. Against the background of a white Oriental palace, a young soldier, pressing a heavy sniper's rifle against himself with one hand and holding a mug of hot water in the other. Broken children's toys trampled into the mud. A table in a room with one wall destroyed and bullet marks on the ceiling. In close-up—the face of a dead man with shell cases scattered all around it. Small black dots—combat helicopters moving into the attack over a village. Armored personnel carriers flying past at high speed with assault troops clinging all over them. Refugees carrying their remaining belongings on a cart. An old woman crying. A factory burning. A shattered tank with its turret torn off and the charred bodies of its crew. A man wearing a turban squatting in the ruins of a building with a grenade launcher.

Paula took her hand off the curve of Miklosh's arm and moved aside, so as not to irritate him with her presence and to avoid seeing the bloody details in the photos. Johan stood at the far side of the hall, leaning back against the wall. He wasn't interested in the exhibition. He was keeping a keen eye on his lord and master. As if he expected somebody to try to do him harm.

The Nachttoter moved from one photograph to the next, examining them with evident enjoyment and lingering in front of the ones that he particularly liked. To an outsider he looked like a refined, likable young man who was interested in modern art and never missed a single new event in the cultural life of the city. But the initial impression evaporated with the first glance into his eyes. A murderer and sadist, a cruel degenerate. Paula smiled calmly and good-naturedly when he glanced at her. And obeyed when he jerked his head abruptly for her to go over.

"Not bad," Miklosh concluded. "This one."

A dirty, disheveled little girl in a ragged dress sitting beside some ruins, holding an equally dirty doll and gazing into the camera lens with sad, wise eyes. People rushing about all around her, rescuers carrying a wounded man out of the rubble, relatives weeping, curious onlookers whispering in a tight little group. But the child looks out at the world with an adult's expression of calm resignation, clutching the rubber doll against her chest.

"That reminds me . . . ," said the Nachterret, turning to Paula, his vacant gaze seeming to look straight through her. "Do you remember the materials from the Nuremberg trials? The photograph of a girl from a concentration camp. She's waiting to go to the gas chamber with the other prisoners. They're all undressed, and she's sitting in the foreground, naked, covering her breasts with her arm. She has such sad, resigned eyes. A twentieth-century Madonna. And this"—he nodded at the photo—"is a twenty-first-century Madonna."

Paula felt a catch in her throat. She hadn't expected a reaction like this from Miklosh Nachterret.

"The photographer would be flattered to hear what you say. That is high praise."

"No. The photographer only took what he saw. He wasn't the director of the play, he didn't put the pain in the child's eyes. He is not the creator of the catastrophe."

Now Balza was looking straight at her, attentively, not as if she were some toy that it would be enjoyable to play with for a while. He wanted to talk, to share his impressions.

"But he did *see*, Nachttoter. Not many are capable of seeing those moments that become the portraits of an age. Like Leonardo's *Mona Lisa*. On the canvas there is just a woman. But in her eyes there is the reflection of the age. Slow and unhurried."

He laughed. "Who else should one talk to about art, if not a fary! The sixteenth century was just as bloody and cruel as any other. It was a time of wars. Italy was transformed into the field of an endless battle, in Spir there was one rebellion after another, the Algerian corsairs terrorized the Spanish and the entire Mediterranean. Europe was one big bonfire. The conquistadors baptized the Incas with fire and the sword, there were bloody battles over the New World, and religious wars brought France to its knees."

"Who else should one talk to about war, if not a Nachterret!" Paula said with a smile, returning the compliment, if that was what it was. "I have read about the events of that time, but in the eyes of the *Mona Lisa* there is peace and calm. A concentrated expression of the tranquillity that people have always sought . . ."

The cell phone in Miklosh's pocket rang. The Nachttoter's face contorted in furious annoyance, and he took out the phone and flung it into a rubbish bin. It jangled pitifully as it struck the bottom and fell silent. Johan, still keeping his eyes on his master, walked over imperturbably to the bin, put his hand in, and fumbled around, snorting in concentration, and fished out the cell phone.

". . . the state that embodies the supreme value for them," said Paula, concluding her thought and pretending that she hadn't noticed Balza's outburst.

"Peace does not embody any values," he growled discontentedly. "Peace is repose—that is, the absence of movement and development. Catastrophes are the impulse that arouses the creative energy in humans, that shakes them up and makes them see something new. Not sloppy landscapes and still lifes, but this."

The Nachterret gestured around the photograph exhibit with his open hand.

"It is what quickens their very soul. But a still life can only induce nausea or indigestion. What?" he exclaimed, abruptly interrupting himself. "What is it?"

Paula hastily fluttered her eyelashes, trying to recover from her amazement and even a certain degree of admiration.

"It's a pity the television crew's already gone. It would be interesting to repeat what you said for the camera."

If he was flattered, he didn't betray any pleasure at the compliment.

"War has its own aesthetic. It is beyond the comprehension of farys, yes, and everybody else as well. I would like to meet the photographer."

Paula hesitated for only an instant. "But, Mr. Balza, he is human."

"I know. Where did he see all this? Where did he take the pictures?"

"The Middle East, the Balkans. He worked as a news photographer for several months."

"Excellent. Call him." And he turned back to the photographs.

Paula walked out into the central hall, where the guests were crowding along the wall with the society photos. Vladar was standing in the middle of them, talking animatedly about something. She moved closer, caught his eye, and beckoned to him discreetly. The photographer nodded, and a few seconds later he was there beside her. He was absolutely happy.

"Paula, everything's magnificent!"

He hugged her and put his forehead against hers, unable to express his delight in any other way.

"It looks like a success." She laughed and hugged him back, but the tension left by her conversation with the Nachttoter only increased.

"Then let's go and have a drink to our success."

"Wait. I want to introduce you to a certain . . . person." She delicately removed Vladar's arm from her shoulder and straightened his necktie, gently hinting at the importance of the meeting. "And please, be as polite as possible, but not to excess. Be attentive, but without being sycophantic; don't try to get too familiar once you feel that he's bored with the conversation—just say good-bye and go. And if he's a bit gruff, or even rude, don't take any notice. That's just his manner."

"I understand. Don't worry. But who is he?"

"That's hard to explain in a moment. Come on, let's go. He doesn't like to wait."

When they walked into the hall with the war photographs, the Nachttoter was talking to Johan in a low voice. His first deputy was hunched over with a frown on his face and his hands stuck in his pockets, hanging his head as he listened to his lord's complaints. Then he turned and walked back to his former position—to observe and protect. It was funny, there was nobody else there apart from them, as if the humans could sense the danger emanating from these two. Of course, the blood brothers knew.

Paula waited until he noticed them.

"Mr. Balza, allow me to introduce Vladar Bondar, the photographer. Vladar—Mr. Miklosh Balza."

The Nachterret examined the human for a few seconds and was about to say something, but the photographer beat him to it with his usual directness.

"Balza? Are you Serbian or Croatian?"

All of Paula's warnings had been forgotten. She froze, expecting an outburst of fury, or at least irritation with the curious mortal, but the Nachttoter reacted incredibly calmly.

"My ancestors were Marcomanni, an ancient tribe that lived where Bavaria is today from the fifth century. And before that they fought rather well against the Romans, who remembered the Marcomannic Wars for a long time. So I'm neither a Croat nor a Serb."

"That's very impressive. Not many people know their ancestors that far back."

"I like your works," said Miklosh, nodding at the photographs.

"Thank you," Vladar responded happily, as if he couldn't sense Paula's anxiety and the other man's oppressive aura. "I'm glad to hear that. But you have only looked at the war photographs. The society photos are in the next hall. I think they're just as good."

"This was quite enough for me to form an opinion. Do you sell your works?"

"Usually only in book form."

"I would like to buy a couple of photographs. For myself. This one, this one, and that one there."

Vladar looked at Paula, and she nodded quickly in reply.

"All right."

"By the way, if you run out of subjects to report on, get in touch. I can always find something that you could add to your collection." To Paula's great surprise, Miklosh reached out and shook hands with the photographer.

"All the best. Very pleased to have met you. And about the photos . . ." Vladar took a business card out of his pocket and handed it to the Nachttoter. "Give me a call. They can be collected once the exhibition is over."

Miklosh took the card, thought for a second, and put it in his pocket.

"Keep in touch with me through Paula. She can pass on your information."

The fary didn't think that the Nachttoter remembered her name. That was something of a discovery.

When the human had left, Johan stirred impatiently over by the wall, evidently wishing to indicate that enough time had been wasted on visiting the exhibition. But his lord ignored his hint.

"When are you planning to turn him?" Miklosh asked casually, as if in passing. "I'd hurry up if I were you, or I'll beat you to it. I could do with a personal photographer like that."

"Are you joking?"

A satisfied smile appeared on his pale face, and his light eyes sparkled at the agitation in her voice. "No, I'm serious."

"But he's not your type!" Paula blurted out in annoyance, surprising even herself with her loss of self-control.

"Not *my* type?" the Nachttoter asked acidly.

"I mean, he won't make a proper Nachterret. He doesn't have the temperament for it, the right attitude to life and humans. He's a good guy."

"So you think we only take in bad guys?" He was clearly amused by this conversation, and even more by her embarrassment.

"But, Nachttoter! You can't make porcelain out of red clay. The material will be spoiled, and the item produced will be useless."

Miklosh laughed, seemingly enjoying both the simile and her indignation.

"Perhaps I should hire you as a consultant on the selection of candidates to join my House?"

Paula felt her cheeks heating again. She realized that she had gone too far.

"I beg your pardon. I was considering the question of turning from the point of view of the House of Faryartos, but that has nothing in common with the views of the Nachterret."

"Speak more clearly—are you apologizing for poking your nose into somebody else's business?" He narrowed his eyes contentedly and looked at Johan. His deputy had a very menacing air indeed. No doubt he felt Paula was being incredibly impudent by talking to the Nachttoter so audaciously.

"Yes. I am poking my nose into somebody else's business. But I still think that Vladar has no value for the House of Nachterret. Under our influence he would attain the level of a master, but with you he will only be a soldier."

"And the porcelain will be spoiled?" Miklosh's nostrils

trembled. Apparently, she really had managed to make him angry. She could sense Johan approaching her back. But she couldn't retreat now. The professional interests of the House were more important than her personal safety.

"Yes. The porcelain will be spoiled."

The Nachttoter studied her in silence for a few minutes, as if he were trying to decide what the fary deserved—painful punishment or instant death for disrespect. She felt him rummaging crudely through her thoughts, and in her despair she threw all her strength into creating a mental shield, trying to close herself off.

Running into this puny defense, he simply swept it aside. Paula felt a sharp pain in her head, and suddenly a look of boundless surprise appeared on Miklosh's face. His light eyebrows shot up and his jaw dropped, but he immediately controlled himself and shook his head, as if he were trying to get rid of some annoying sound.

"What's this?" he asked irritably.

"Nachttoter, what's happened?" Johan asked anxiously, observing his lord's strange behavior with concern.

"Quiet!" Miklosh roared. He reached out and touched Paula's forehead with his finger. Before she had time to move back, he thrust his fingers into her hair, ruining the style. He pulled her toward him, listening intently. Almost pressed her forehead against his own, like Vladar half an hour earlier. "What is this, damn it?"

Probably in her former, human life, the fary would have blushed. To the roots of her hair, to her shoulder blades.

"Nachttoter Miklosh," she muttered, trying not to look into his eyes, which were only a few centimeters away from her own, "you are sensing my mental shield. It's a side effect. Like the green glow that accompanies the magic of the Cadavercitan. And the smell of decomposition that goes with some of your spells."

"A side effect? I hear a symphony that I composed, inside your head!" He squeezed the back of Paula's neck, and she shrieked in pain.

"I'm sorry! It's not my fault! You enter my mind . . . force your way through the defensive barrier, and superimpose your own thought energy on it. Now it's playing a symphony in C minor. . . . Miklosh, that hurts!"

He laughed uncertainly and let her go. Paula recoiled, almost bumped into Johan, who was standing behind her, and found herself back in Balza's arms. This time he simply held her, with his arms around her waist. But although his touch was cautious, the Nachterret's voice sounded angry.

"Now tell me more about this mental energy."

"My magic is passive. I can't throw you out of my mind, I can't put up a monolithic block, you're more powerful, you'll just break me. So all I do is reflect you back to yourself. You ran into your own music and backed away. I don't know why it was playing in your subconscious. Why it wasn't a burst of machine-gun fire, the screams of the dying, or bombs exploding."

Balza slowly removed his hands from her body, as if he were reluctant to do it. His blue eyes became suspiciously thoughtful.

"Because I always hear music."

Paula gave an intense sigh and pressed the palms of her hands to her cheeks.

"Strange, nothing like this has ever happened to me with one of the farys before," he said in a low voice.

"I'm sorry, Nachttoter. I'm poking my nose into someone else's business again."

He smiled crookedly and ran one hand over his light hair, brushing it back off his forehead.

"Miklosh. You can call me just Miklosh."

10

Good Evening, Nachttoter!

I dislike modern memoirs. They are generally written by people who have either entirely lost their memories, or have never done anything worth remembering.

—Oscar Wilde, "The Critic as Artist"

October 31

Miklosh was rereading *The History of the Blood Brothers,* written by a member of the Dahanavar family who, in his opinion, was not very bright. But then, what could you expect from a lousy blautsauger? Especially one who was under a mormolika's thumb.

Four hundred years earlier, the gloriously delightful Felicia had got the idea of creating a brief outline of the history of the vampire families since their foundation. At first Balza had been amused—it was a case of a fly trying to swallow an elephant. But then he had stopped laughing. She had swallowed it, may the sun burn out her cursed eyes!

Now the *History,* published in modern book format, was on the compulsory reading list for four of the Houses and recommended reading for all the others.

Miklosh had to admit that there was a grain or two of truth in the trashy book. But this truth was swamped by a concoction of innuendo and lies. Felicia had the audacity to create a book that only had anything good to say about her own family.

The pure, snow-white Dahanavar. The lie made the Nachttoter feel sick. Reading it gave the impression that all the members of that House would soon sprout wings.

The author described in tedious detail how, almost since the moment the world was created, the righteous blautsaugers, led by their "far-seeing" elders, had controlled humans "wisely and worthily" in the desire to lead them to universal well-being and prosperity. And also how benign and noble the Dahanavar were. How they were peaceful and wished to be friends with all the blood brothers. But the fact that this friendship was entirely one-sided, and catered only to the interests of the peacemakers themselves, was omitted.

Naturally, this despicable tome paid much less attention to the other families. In addition, it was absolutely riddled with crude errors and distortions of facts that supported the policies of the House of Ladies.

That was Miklosh's opinion.

Some families came in for harsher criticism than others. In Balza's opinion the Nachterret, for instance, were trampled underfoot. It infuriated him that the great family of the Golden Hornets had been transformed into raving psychos who craved nothing but blood and lived only through the sufferings of others. Felicia appeared not to have the slightest idea about the House's profound philosophy, which no rational thinker would ever have tried to dispute. But she did know about it. She understood the logic. She had never been able to refute it. Even so, the thousand-year history of the Nachterret family had simply been thrown out like garbage. Mocked and ridiculed! It was grotesque!

The first time he had opened the book (the seventeenth century was just beginning at the time), Balza had almost gone berserk in his fury. It had cost him a serious effort to suppress the desire to go to the First Elder of the House of Dahanavar and crush her skull with his own hands.

But the Nachttoter's reason had not been disturbed badly enough to confront the cold bitch openly. Say what you like, but she was his equal in strength, perhaps even stronger in some ways. There was no way of knowing how a duel like that would end. Miklosh didn't want to take any risks over some stupid nonsense that had been set down on paper. But he didn't intend to swallow the insult, either.

It was the author who had paid the price for his scribblings. That hideously mawkish, sweet youth had spent a long period as the Nachttoter's personal guest. And Balza had tried as hard as he knew how to explain to the writer that creating books designed to flatter someone by concealing the truth was wrong. It was not art, it was not even honest craft work, it was a crime. The leader of the Nachterret was satisfied only when the Dahanavar finally met his end, shrieking in pain from the rays of the sun. Naturally, everything was arranged so that the Golden Hornets had no connection with the killing.

Felicia, however, had not let the sudden demise of her favorite go as easily as that. She had roused all her minions and turned the whole city upside down. Even called an extraordinary session of the council. But she hadn't managed to hang the crime on anyone, although she had guessed who had done the good deed.

Sometime later, about a hundred and fifty years after these events, Miklosh had come across the book in his mansion, abandoned in a dark corner. He wondered how it could possibly have survived. He had meant to burn it. So he'd finally condescended to reread the masterpiece.

Surprisingly enough, at a second reading he had found quite a lot of interesting things in it. In fact, the Nachttoter had dubbed the volume the most entertaining read of the century. He wondered how the mormolika would have responded to that opinion. But then, Balza was firmly convinced that Felicia had no more sense of humor than her beloved ancient statues. She wouldn't have understood.

"Nachttoter," said Johan, distracting him from his reading, "the car's waiting."

"Take an umbrella. It might be raining." Miklosh regretfully put down the book and thought that he had probably been too hasty in killing that pen-pushing blautsauger. He might have written more masterpieces. Then, when Miklosh was bored, he could have read them. But geniuses were never recognized until after they were dead. And that, too, was in perfect accord with the philosophy of the Nachterret.

Miklosh grinned cynically and glanced sideways at Johan. He had been acquainted with this individual, who had formerly been known as Black Death, for more than five hundred years. Johan had served him faithfully for all that time. Him and the House. Number two in the hierarchy, he was as devoted as a dog, and he carried out the most complicated and delicate assignments, leading the family onward and upward into glory.

Balza had first met Johan the Black Death in the winter of the year 1421, near Kutna Hora. In search of glory and wealth, the cruel German landsknecht, a true professional, had rushed headlong into the Hussite Wars and promptly run into trouble. If not for Miklosh, who had given way to the whim of the moment and turned the mercenary as he lay dying on the snow, no one would ever have heard of Johan the Black Death again. Now the Nachttoter thought it was providence that had made him leave the silver mines that night and led him to the mercenary who had been struck in the chest by a battle flail. The House had benefited greatly from taking in someone like Johan. Cunning, cruel, dangerous. But at the same time, devoted and efficient.

Whenever Miklosh Balza went to an important meeting, his pupil was always at his right shoulder. They made a picturesque duo. The huge, hulking mercenary with his massive black beard appeared to be forty, and the short, light-boned, blue-eyed, blond-haired leader looked twenty years old at the very most. But in fact, the head of the House of Nachterret was one of the three oldest blood brothers alive on earth. Following immediately after Felicia and Ramon.

Miklosh was never irritated by the fact that he was only third. The Nachttoter took an optimistic view of the situation, believing that sooner or later he would overtake the Lady Dahanavar and the Upieschi. He had plenty of staying power. He was happy to wait a bit longer. The multilevel plan had been worked out a long time ago, and the gearwheels of the mechanism were turning smoothly. There was no point in hurrying, when all he had to do was wait for the other players to make their moves and then skim off the cream.

"You've trailed mud on my carpet again," Balza complained.

"Forgive me, Nachttoter, it won't happen again."

Miklosh waved his hand despairingly—it would be easier to teach one of the Dahanavar elders to dance the polka than make his deputy wash his boots before entering the study.

Balza walked out of the room, along the long gallery to the stairs, and down to the first floor, with the sound of intensive sniffing following him all the way—his deputy stuck to him like a shadow.

"How much longer until the start of the operation?"

"An hour. Everything's ready. The soldiers are all in place. And the humans, too."

"Have you checked?"

"And double-checked."

"Well done."

They came out onto the porch. The weather wasn't so good. This year, the second half of October had turned out very cold. There was a bitter wind. And they didn't know what to expect, rain or snow. Mr. Balza congratulated himself on his foresight—the warm duck's-down quilted jacket with a hood and the wool scarf were just what he needed. He couldn't stand the cold. And he felt sorry for the landsknecht, who always went about in his open leather cloak. The huge mercenary apparently had no idea that such things as scarves, hats, and gloves even existed.

"But we do have a little problem."

"You know how I hate problems," Balza replied without turning around.

Tonight he had decided to do without his limousine. This trip required secrecy, and that meant a simple, inconspicuous automobile. The Nachttoter strode swiftly across to the black Mercedes. The driver was already standing beside it, holding the door open.

"What difficulties are you talking about?" the head of the House asked irritably when the car moved off and two jeeps lined up in convoy behind it.

"The money still hasn't been transferred."

For a few seconds Miklosh looked out the window, struggling to suppress his rage. Then, without speaking, he held out his hand and Johan put the cell phone into it, with the number already entered.

Nobody answered for a long time, and Mr. Balza started coming to a boil again. Johan could see this perfectly well from his white eyes and slightly raised upper lip. He did not envy Amir.

"Hello," a disinterested voice said eventually.

"Please call Mr. al Rahal to the phone," Miklosh said, laying special emphasis on the first two words.

"He's busy" was the impolite reply.

"Listen, you creep, call that damn blautsauger, or I'll come round there and rip your heart out!" Balza barked so loudly that the driver flinched in the front seat.

Ten seconds later, he was talking to the head of the House of Asiman.

"What's the problem, Miklosh? I really am busy."

"I'll only distract you for a moment, quite literally," the Nachttoter said acidly. "I believe you commissioned my House to do a little job."

"Yes. And I'm expecting it to be done today."

"Amir," said Miklosh, still trying to be polite, "I respect you, of course, but I won't lift a finger until I get what you promised. Why isn't the money in our account yet?"

"I decided to pay after you deliver the goods to me."

"You won't get the goods until you pay. I don't work on credit. We agreed, and you are the one in breach of the agreement. I haven't trained my men and planned the whole operation just to do it all for nothing! You have"—Miklosh glanced briefly at the watch that Johan efficiently showed him—"fifteen minutes to transfer the money. Unless I receive confirmation, the Golden Hornets are calling off the operation!"

"Wait!" Amir said anxiously. "You can't!"

"I can't?" the Nachttoter snorted. "And just who decides exactly what I can and can't do?"

"But it will take longer than that to transfer the money. It's one o'clock in the morning. What bank will handle a sum like that at this hour? There's nothing I can do until the morning."

"Who are you trying to fool? The Upieschi banks work round the clock."

"Do you know what rate they charge for a cash transfer?"

"That's not my problem. You backed yourself into this corner. You've got thirteen minutes left."

Balza cut the connection and irritably tossed the phone to Johan, who caught it deftly and put it in his breast pocket.

"Do you think he'll pay?"

Miklosh looked at his deputy as if he were insane. "Of course. I haven't got the slightest doubt about it."

He turned back to the window. The back streets and dark yards of the city went flashing by, and then the industrial zone began. Then the car crossed the ring road, leaving the capital and hurtling north along the highway. The highway was empty.

The first fine drops of rain appeared on the windshield. The road surface turned wet. If there was frost early in the morning, it would be a skating rink, but that moment was still a long way off, and the Nachttoter's personal chauffeur didn't even think about slowing down. On the contrary, he speeded up. He knew he was behind schedule.

Johan squirmed anxiously and kept glancing at his watch. He didn't believe that the proud Amir would call back. Miklosh watched the streetlamps standing along the roadside go flashing past. Mr. Balza liked to observe surrounding reality and the way it changed from century to century and age to age. He had an inquiring mind. And unlike many of the blood brothers, he wasn't bored with living. The head of the House of Nachterret derived great pleasure from his life, even though he did believe that the best place for most blautsaugers was a place in the sun.

Right now, for instance, he would happily have arranged a little sunbathing for Amir. That damn bloodsucker had been planning to cheat him. *Him!* He couldn't let him get away with that kind of insolence. The next time the Asiman wanted to employ the services of the Golden Hornets, it would cost them an extra twenty percent. And just let them try to object.

The cell phone jangled repulsively. Johan answered. Listened. Switched off.

"The money has been transferred."

The ghost of a smile appeared on Mr. Balza's thin lips. "Check, and change the ring tone. That tune gives me a headache."

Johan grunted compliantly and started running his thick fingers over the phone's small buttons with their bluish light. Then he called someone's number, waited for confirmation of the transfer, and nodded to let the Nachttoter know that everything was in order.

"The Asiman are proud. How did you know that Amir would back down?"

"I teach you and teach you, but it's just a waste of time," Miklosh said instead of explaining.

The car turned off the highway at a crossroads where there was a traffic police post. After that, the road ran through a forest.

"What about them?"

"Don't worry. They won't see or hear a thing," said Johan, realizing that Miklosh was asking him about the police. "We've paid them."

"That's good. But get rid of them anyway."

They didn't need any witnesses, and money didn't keep mouths shut. That was the prerogative of bullets. Only dead men could stay quiet. Provided, of course, that there weren't any sorcerers from the House of Death around.

THE forest ended as suddenly as it had begun. Miklosh was not interested in the town they drove into. There were plenty like it dotted around the capital. All standard, almost carbon copies, the same houses and roads in need of repair. The industrial zones.

They arrived five minutes ahead of time. The Mercedes stopped in the semidarkness under some poplars that had shed their leaves. The driver turned off the headlights. Soldiers piled out of the accompanying jeeps. Dressed completely in black. Armed. And wearing masks.

"Let's go, Nachttoter." Johan got out, walked around the car, obligingly opened the door, and put up the umbrella.

Miklosh got out into the damp, chilly air with a sour expression on his face. The mud immediately clung to his shoes.

"Where to?"

"The control car."

It was standing nearby. An old Ford van. Balza climbed inside and looked around indifferently at the surveillance monitors suspended from the ceiling, the computer, and the radio transmitter.

"This is the operational control center," Johan explained.

The Nachttoter listened with a bored expression, pointedly ignoring the human mercenaries who had been trained in the ranks of the House as professional cannon fodder.

"Here, put this on, Nachttoter," said one of the controllers, handing him an earpiece.

Mr. Balza took the small item and wiped it down with a handkerchief before putting it in his ear.

"Everything's ready, we can start."

"Get to work!" Johan ordered.

Sitting in a chair, Miklosh started watching one of the monitors. About three hundred meters ahead of their position were the gates. A red-and-white boom. The security guards' glass booth, with video cameras. A tall fence topped with barbed wire. Beyond that, he could see a complex of white buildings. The laboratory and production plant of a human corporation. Animal feed, food additives, and other rubbish not worthy of the Asiman's attention. But they *were* extremely interested in secret biochemical development work taking place in special closed premises. Work of a highly specific nature.

Miklosh watched as a car approached the barrier. A woman got out of it. A human. One of those that the Nachterret had drilled. Much as the Golden Hornets despised humans, some of the sheep were still fit for performing various kinds of duties. Especially during the day, when the brothers couldn't go outside.

A man came out of the security booth to meet the woman. He asked her something. Without replying, she snatched out a pistol with a silencer. Two explosive bullets hit the security guard in the chest. She was forbidden to shoot through the glass, but before the partner in the booth could recover from his astonishment and get his pistol out of its holster, the assassin walked in through the door and cold-bloodedly shot him dead. Then she got back into her car and drove it to one side, clearing the way through. As if on command, a van and two SUVs came tearing around the corner at full speed. They braked to a halt. Four men ran out of the leading vehicle. Miklosh noticed that two of them were dressed in the same uniforms as the dead security guards. The dead men were flung into the van. The false security men took their places in the glass booth.

Balza noted with satisfaction that his people were professionals. In ninety-nine percent of cases, they carried out their work with absolute precision and improvised brilliantly. And it didn't matter who they were, blood brothers or mercenaries who served the House faithfully. That was why the Asiman always hired them.

The pyromaniacs were no mommy's boys, either, of course, but they acted with unnecessary drama and visual effects. It was in their blood. Miklosh thought they worked like refugees from some cheap action movie. In this case, the security guards had been dealt with by a slim girl with a pistol, but the Asiman blautsaugers would have driven a tank up at full speed, demolished the boom and the booth, fired a couple of rounds to frighten everybody, and smashed up a few hectares of forest on every side. They might also have brought along automatic rifles and called in a helicopter. And arranged the kind of massacre that would be heard by the angels up in heaven, let alone the police.

But apart from that, the factory was on Vricolakos territory. It wasn't very likely that the Asiman had asked the werewolves' permission for their incursion. There would be problems if the Vricolakos could prove who had done the job. And why would Amir want any problems? It was much simpler to pay well for the services of the House of Nachterret, which could work without making any noise or leaving any clues.

The boom was raised and the gates were opened. The vehicles drove into the factory grounds.

"Forward," Johan said quietly, and the driver of the Ford started the engine.

The jeeps with the soldiers followed the van. Images transmitted from mini video cameras mounted in the mercenaries' walkie-talkies appeared on the monitors.

"Four in the vestibule on the first floor, one in the toilet. Two on the second floor beside the elevator. They all have automatic weapons. One on the third floor. Working in the office," the co-ordinator said quickly. "Group A, you take them. Group B, advance along corridor 2-13 in the direction of the laboratory."

"Group A—message received."

"Group B—understood."

Miklos watched the movie unfold as the raiders broke into the vestibule and shot the security men with automatic rifles with silencers. The victims didn't even have time to raise the alarm.

"Group A. The man on the second floor has got into the elevator. He is coming towards you."

"Message received."

When the elevator doors opened, the group leader's automatic rifle spat a brief burst of lead. Mr. Balza licked his lips nervously. These killings were getting him excited. After watching sights like this, he always had a ferocious appetite.

"Group B. What is your progress?"

"We are advancing."

"One man. Straight along the corridor."

"Understood."

There was a quiet crackle of shots, followed by screams of horror and pain.

"Group B. What's happening there? Report!"

"There's some kind of beast here! A beast! It's torn two men to pieces! The bullets don't touch it!"

"A-a-a-a-a-a-a-agh!"

"There it is! There it is!"

"Fire! Fire, damn it!"

"Group B. Withdraw immediately! Do you hear? This is an order! Withdraw!"

Flickering images on the screen. Mr. Balza glimpsed the body of one of the soldiers, torn in half, a contorted face, a wall, a ceiling, a wall again, a dark blob that instantly shifted to the right.

The situation was out of control. He needed to take it in hand himself.

"Quickly! Follow me!" The Nachttoter was out of his seat in a flash.

Johan barely managed to open the door in time for him. Taking no notice of the heavy rain and not bothering to wait for the umbrella to be unfurled, Miklosh raced into the building. In his earphones, he heard the panic-stricken howls of the survivors from Group B. But not for long.

"Order Group A to stay where it is," he told Johan without turning around.

He couldn't imagine a worse situation. This was trouble. Big trouble.

The personal bodyguards of the head of the House dashed after him. Johan stepped over a dead body in the vestibule and moved on. Now as he walked he was simultaneously showing the way and covering the Nachttoter against potential dangers. From under his cloak he took out a broad double-edged sword. Although it was not very long, in the huge hands of the former landsknecht it looked like a serious weapon. Like his lord, he had caught a glimpse of what Group B had run into, so he was prepared in advance for a warm welcome.

As they approached the scene of the battle, Miklosh's nostrils started trembling. He could smell fresh blood. The corridor looked like a slaughterhouse. Fragments of bodies and blood, blood, blood everywhere. That was all that was left of the humans. In the middle of it all, the beast was standing on its massive paws. A wolf the size of a large bull calf.

Black, with its face and fangs covered in blood, its mane standing up on end, and furiously blazing amber yellow eyes. One of the Vricolakos.

Miklosh wasn't too concerned about what the werewolf was doing there. It looked as if the blautsaugers of this variety were a lot more sensitive about their territory than had been expected. Could Ivan really have sent one of his pupils to protect the complex?

The wolf might have thought he could deal with any uninvited guests, but the arrival of the Nachterret took him by surprise. He recognized Miklosh and bared his teeth, growling threateningly.

The Nachttoter realized he wasn't facing any young cub here. This was a midranker. Experienced enough to hold his own with many of the blood brothers. But not with the head of the House of Nachterret. In addition to the bestial fury, Mr. Balza could see understanding and fear in those yellow eyes. The Vricolakos knew that Miklosh was not in the foolish habit of leaving witnesses alive.

As if he had read the werewolf's thoughts, the Nachttoter said in a tone of mock sympathy:

"If you think I'm going to let you go, hound-dog, then you are seriously mistaken. I don't want Svetlov's flea-bitten pack on my heels."

The wolf had no choice. He decided to break out or sell his life dearly. But he wasn't allowed to do either. When he leapt, Balza threw up his left hand. A spell that corroded eyeballs hit the black face full on. Nothing more was needed.

Disoriented, the Vricolakos slumped heavily to the floor, almost crushing Johan, who jumped aside just in time. Clattering its fearsome jaws beside Miklosh's feet, the wounded beast howled and thrashed about convulsively. Miklosh kept cool and didn't even step aside. His deputy raised his sword. He severed the wolf's head with three mighty blows.

"You," said Balza, turning to the human mercenaries. "Into the laboratory, quickly. Finish the job."

"What was a Vricolakos doing here?" asked Johan. "I wasn't expecting to see one of their family."

"Neither was I," said Miklosh, looking at the body thoughtfully.

In fact, it was all the same to him what had made Svetlov send one of his brothers to the complex. He was much more concerned about the goods and the delay to the operation. The whole plan had almost been wrecked. Now they had to hurry to make up for lost time.

"Tell them to send someone to the security room before we leave. We have to get rid of the recordings from the cameras."

While Black Plague was giving the order, Miklosh tidied up the corridor. The decay spell would solve their problems quickly. And make sure the police wouldn't be asking questions. No dead bodies from Group B, no giant wolves. No evidence. In the morning, they would find only the dead security guards.

"Nachttoter, can I take the wolf?"

"What do you want it for?"

"I'll make a winter cloak out of the fur."

"It's full of fleas and all sorts of other contagious filth. Highly unsanitary. And anyway, the Vricolakos will not be very pleased if you start wearing the skin of one of their brothers on your shoulders. I appreciate your sense of humor, of course, but it's not very prudent."

"Then I'll take the head. I'll hang it up in my room. I don't have a werewolf's head in my collection yet."

Miklosh shrugged indifferently.

"Thank you, Nachttoter."

"But don't you dare bring that carrion into my car," Mr. Balza warned him, just to be on the safe side.

The smell of decomposition became unbearable, but a minute later, there was nothing left on the floor except dark patches. The decay spell had spared only the wolf's head. Excellent. Johan could carry that himself, if he wanted it so badly.

"Nachttoter," said one of the mercenaries who had come back, "there are men in there. Two of them. At first they returned fire. We wounded one and they retreated into the laboratory. And barricaded the door. We can't get in without dynamiting it."

"Idiots! You can't be trusted to do anything. Have they raised the alarm?"

"No, we cut the cable immediately and turned on the jamming devices. They have no phones, or alarm signals or satellite communications."

"Take me there."

The door of the laboratory upset Miklosh terribly. A good door. Strong. It would take a good drill to get through it. And it would take an hour or an hour and a half.

"What do you think?" the Nachttoter asked his deputy in a quiet voice.

"If they put that there, there must be something to hide. The dynamite's in the cars. But it will be very noisy."

"Out of the question."

Mr. Balza approached the door. Pressed the intercom button.

"Open up. I'm asking you nicely."

The House of Nachterret found the decay spell very useful. Strong steel was no better than living flesh. It was subject to decay and disintegration, too. You simply had to be able to improvise and possess the necessary power.

Spots of rust appeared all over the metal of the door frame. They spread, turning into patches that kept expanding. After a few seconds, the entire surface was covered with a thick layer of rust. Three seconds later, Johan reduced the obstacle to a heap of rusty dust with a single kick.

The mercenaries who burst in encountered fire. But they quickly killed the men in hiding.

Black Plague went in and came back a couple of minutes later with a metal case in his left hand.

"Is that it?" Mr. Balza asked curiously.

"Yes, Nachttoter. It was lying where they said it would be."

"Then let's leave. There's nothing more to do here."

11

PLAYING WITH FIRE

The one advantage of playing with fire ... is that one never gets even singed. It is the people who don't know how to play with it who get burned up.

—Oscar Wilde, *A Woman of No Importance*

November 1

Miklosh was resting. He didn't have anything particularly important to do. Johan was messing about with his Vricolakos wolf head, and the Nachttoter had left him in peace.

He regarded the landsknecht's hobby as a foolish game, an absurd amusement, and refused to understand it in principle. What sort of stupidity was it to collect the heads of his enemies? Who could tell what kind of pestilent contagion might develop in them? But then, as long as it keeps him amused, Balza thought, let him have his fun.

The head of the House of Nachterret decided to switch on the television, purely out of idle curiosity—he didn't watch it very often, since he didn't believe there could be anything interesting to watch. There was only one television set in the entire mansion, and Miklos walked around the rooms for a long time, trying to remember which of them it was in.

All the local news channels were discussing the audacious raid on a production plant belonging to one of the country's largest corporations and the cruel murder of the security guards and policemen at a traffic control post. The cameramen lingered on the bodies of the security guards, the blood, and all the other sights that the average viewer loves to see.

The morose head of the capital's Department of Internal Affairs swore that he would punish the killers of his colleagues. "We already have some leads," he said, "thanks to the security video cameras. But we can't tell you anything about them yet, in order to avoid compromising the investigation."

Miklosh chortled. Not a single video recording had survived. The policeman was lying through his teeth.

The news correspondents were baffled as to why the bandits had chosen to attack a factory producing animal feed instead of a bank. The corporation's representatives raised their honest eyes to heaven and shrugged.

Liars. Liars, every single one of them.

The Nachterret switched off the television in annoyance and tossed the remote control onto the wide bed.

He couldn't think of anything to do. Go into town and have a bit of fun? He didn't feel like it. And anyway, he wasn't hungry.

As he walked out of the room, he saw Raylen. The girl was standing with her elbows propped on the balustrade, looking down at the first-floor hallway with a bored expression. She was rather short, noticeably shorter than the Nachttoter. Her short-cropped hair, the color of molten copper, stuck out in all directions in artistic disarray. Raylen could be proud of it, as she could of her plump lips in their dark maroon lipstick and her large gray eyes. But her eyes and lips were the only really beautiful features of her face. The cheekbones were too broad, the eyebrows were too thick, the chin was too heavy, and the nose lacked character. And her figure was too athletic. She was not Miklosh's type. He preferred tall natural blondes. And anyway, this little poppet was Johan's pupil. And his passion. The landsknecht liked small women.

On several occasions, when Johan was away coordinating the House's coercive operations, Raylen had acted as Balza's personal bodyguard. Her teacher had drilled her well, and the fastidious Miklos had absolutely no complaints about her. She performed her duties competently and unobtrusively, without irritating him. And not to irritate the capricious Nachttoter was a great achievement. There weren't many people who could spend more than an hour in the company of the head of the House without provoking his dissatisfaction. Not even Johan could manage it. But Raylen always did.

In all the time that his deputy's pupil had spent with him, Miklosh had hardly even spoken to her. No more than a few brief, insignificant phrases. He felt no particular hankering to socialize. Yes, she was efficient. Yes, she didn't bother him. But common interests, something they could talk about? Ridiculous. What was there to talk about with a common girl from the slums of Whitechapel?

Raylen finally noticed Miklosh and straightened up.

"Good evening, Nachttoter."

Balza looked her up and down with morose curiosity.

"Can you play chess?" he asked.

"Yes." It was clear that Raylen was a little confused by such a strange question, but she answered without any hesitation.

DURING the next hour, Miklosh fundamentally revised his opinion about Johan's pupil. She proved to be nobody's fool, ironically and emphatically obsequious. During the game, she easily maintained a conversation on practically any subject. She played quite decently, even well, although she lost very quickly after allowing herself to be tricked on the sixth move, and then on the thirteenth in the second game. But with a great effort, she just managed to hold the third game to a draw. Johan really had educated her well. It had taken him a long time to reach this level. It was a hundred and fifty years after the mercenary first saw a chessboard before he was able to give a good account of himself in the game of sages.

The fourth game also looked as if it were going to end in a draw. Raylen opposed Miklosh's cunning with a competent, finely balanced defense and rapid counterattack against the Nachttoter's exposed left flank.

Mr. Balza was enjoying the game tremendously. In fact, he was so absorbed that his somber mood actually started to lift. The girl had genuinely surprised him.

Just as the head of the House had got completely carried away, Roman walked into the study.

"I'm busy!" Miklosh barked without looking at him. "Get out."

Roman loitered uncertainly on the spot and cast a persecuted glance at the imperturbable Raylen. But then he decided to speak after all:

"Nachttoter, you're wanted on the phone. Amir. He says it's very urgent."

Balza ground his teeth and moved his rook. "Sometimes I almost believe that the humans' devil actually exists," he muttered angrily. "Only he could have invented the telephone."

Miklosh abandoned his game to answer the phone. "What's the problem, Amir?"

"Now you're the one who's not fulfilling his obligations. When will I receive my goods?"

"I have fulfilled my obligations," Miklosh objected. "As I think you are very well aware. Come and collect them."

"That's not the way businessmen do things, my friend."

"I'm not a man." Miklosh laughed, and his fangs glinted. "And as yet I'm not your friend, either. I'm busy today."

"I don't believe it's in your interests to damage the reputation of the Golden Hornets, is it? There might suddenly be no more commissions."

"Don't make me laugh," the Nachttoter snorted.

"Balza, I am well aware," Amir said patiently, "that neither you nor your House is in need of money. Operations like this one are merely an amusement to you. But I need the goods today. We agreed that your brothers would deliver it immediately."

Miklosh laughed. "Very well. As a personal favor to you, I'll bring it myself."

"Today?"

"Possibly."

Mr. Balza put down the phone before Amir could turn indignant again. And he cursed.

"That impatient bloodsucker! He could easily come here, but oh, no. He's not leaving his warm nest and going out in the cold," he muttered, not without a certain satisfaction at having found something to keep himself busy.

"Roman! Have a car at the door in ten minutes. Get a move on."

Balza went back to his place. And studied the chessboard. During his negotiations, Raylen had made a move. A decisive one.

"Checkmate, Nachttoter."

Miklosh narrowed his eyes. And chuckled again. He was beaten. Johan's pupil had managed to exploit her opponent's mistakes to her own advantage. Well now. One more thing to add to the list of her merits.

"Do you think you're very smart?"

"Oh really, Nachttoter. How could I possibly?"

Her face remained absolutely serious, but there were imps of mischief dancing in her eyes. He snorted ironically in reply. Got abruptly to his feet. Stretched.

"We'll continue later. Find your teacher. Tell him to stop messing about with that lump of carrion. I need him. You might come in handy, too. So get ready. And quickly. I don't like to wait."

RAYLEN was back in the Nachttoter's study in less than three minutes. He cast a quick glance in the mirror without looking around. The girl had already changed into her standard outfit for going visiting.

Nothing but black leather. A rather revealing corset, a skirt reaching to midthigh made of broad horizontal strips, lace-up knee boots, fingerless gloves.

A leather coat, hanging open down to her heels, of course. That was in direct imitation of her teacher. A collar with metal studs and round metal earrings of black onyx. Her high heels made her significantly taller.

To Miklosh's old-fashioned taste, this kind of getup was very far from aesthetic perfection, but he had to admit that it had its own style, even if it was one that he didn't really understand.

"All you need to complete the image is dark glasses," he said with gentle mockery.

Raylen took him absolutely seriously. She put her left hand into the pocket of her coat, took out a pair of glasses, and perched them on her nose. Meeting Mr. Balza's eyes, she said something incomprehensible:

"*The Matrix Reloaded.*"

"What do you mean?" he asked, puzzled.

"I'm sorry, Nachttoter," she said, embarrassed. "It's an obscure joke. The name of a movie."

Miklosh immediately lost interest in the conversation. He didn't like the cinema. But he had ordered one of the rooms in his mansion to be made into a movie theater. The soldiers liked movies, especially the new recruits.

The interests of the younger generation left the head of the

House of Nachterret bemused. But he tried to cater to their enthusiasms, believing that small indulgences would not do any harm to the cause of the Golden Hornets. Quite the reverse, in fact.

Unlike Johan, Raylen did not carry a sword, preferring magical weapons to real ones. But, of course, she did have a heavy-caliber pistol—that was why the right pocket of her leather coat was bulging.

"Where's Johan?"

"He's waiting for you downstairs."

"Do you know how to knot a necktie?"

He didn't like this procedure and performed it only when none of his assistants were there to do it.

Again she answered without faltering. "Yes. What kind of knot would you like? Large or small?"

"The right kind."

He followed her movements. Rapid. Confident. Precise. He had never seen anyone tie knots like that before. He assessed the result with a critical glance and praised it grudgingly.

"Not bad."

"I am glad to have pleased the Nachttoter."

"How little it takes to make some people happy. You know an awful lot for a girl from the slums. Chess, neckties . . ."

"I had a good teacher."

"I don't doubt it." He put on his warm coat. "But Johan was never any good with neckties."

She hesitated and her face darkened. But under the searching glance of the head of the House, she replied:

"I sometimes used to tie them for my father. He had a job. For a while. Then we were thrown out on the street."

"A difficult childhood." There was not a trace of sympathy in his voice. "I don't think you have anything to complain about.

The street usually kills or teaches. How old were you when you met Johan?"

"Eighteen."

"Well. We can indulge our reminiscences later." He adjusted the ring of the head of the House of Nachterret on his index finger. "Let's get going."

Johan was waiting for them at the door with the Asiman's goods. Miklosh hadn't looked to see what was in the case. Not that he didn't feel curious. Of course he did. It would be useful to find out what was in there, if only to know exactly why Amir was interested. But he had been warned more than once that the goods could easily be damaged. Perhaps it was a lie, but the Nachttoter had no intention of checking. He had no idea what kind of rotten muck might be inside the case. The Asiman used every possible technique you could imagine in their experiments on humans. Mr. Balza did not wish the contents of the case to be let loose while he was anywhere nearby. Caution was the best approach in dealing with all matters of high science.

"I kept it in the refrigerator. Just like they told us to," Johan rumbled as he picked up the case.

"Don't shake it. I hope it wasn't in the same place as that trophy of yours?"

"Of course not."

They walked outside, and Miklosh turned up the collar of his coat. He shuddered in the cold and looked around resentfully.

"Damn snow. Already lying on the porch. Why doesn't somebody clear it away? If you don't chase them all the time, they never do a stroke of work.

"Roman, do you really want to go wading through snowdrifts? Make sure that's cleaned away."

"No, Nachttoter. Yes, Nachttoter. I'll make sure of it, Nachttoter," jabbered the servant who happened to have caught Miklosh's eye.

He clearly could not understand how a light sprinkling of snow could prevent Balza from walking across the porch.

The Nachttoter walked over to the limousine with a disgruntled expression on his face. He looked inside.

"Come here," he called to the driver.

The young Nachterret sensed trouble and his face fell, but he did as he was told.

"I won't go anywhere in this car. Look how dirty it is. Have you been transporting pigs in it?"

"No, Nachttoter."

"No pigs? Then why is it such a pigsty?"

"Some soldiers went into town. To get some girls for your supper. On your orders."

"I didn't order you to make the car filthy!" Miklosh was beginning to get angry. "If you bring me a limousine in this condition again, I'll make you pay with your tongue, and then I'll throw you out on your ear. The nerve! You'll end up covered in filth soon, like the Vricolakos."

The unfortunate driver who had borne the brunt of the Nachttoter's bad mood tried to avoid his eyes.

"Bring another car!"

"After yesterday's operation you ordered us to get rid of the Mercedes. We haven't bought a new one yet."

Miklosh raised his eyes imploringly to the heavens. "Of course you haven't bought one. You won't lift a finger until I check up on you. Do we only have two cars in the garage now?"

"No, Nachttoter, there's the other Mercedes, the Lincoln, the second Rolls-Royce, the Jaguar—"

"I don't care how many of them there are. Just bring me a clean one. Quickly!"

While the driver was hastily replacing the car, Balza stood there freezing in the cold, which did nothing to improve his mood. He strode backward and forward and looked irritably at his bodyguards dressed all in black, but it didn't alarm them at all. They had got used to his fits of bad temper a long time ago. Raylen was leaning back against one of the columns of the porch, chewing on a toothpick with a bored air. Johan was talking on the cell phone, coordinating the latest arrangements for a big job in South America.

Snowflakes the size of grains of sugar swirled in the gusts of wind. Repulsive. Winter had come too early this year. It wasn't even halfway through November yet, and just look at the weather! How many of these disgusting cold seasons had there been in his life? He'd lost count a long, long time ago.

Balza walked over to the soldiers standing beside the two escort jeeps. Their first reaction was to tense up, expecting to be served another helping of his discontent, but Miklosh made an exception for them. He was circumspect and polite. He asked how things were going and whether any of them needed any help. The Nachttoter believed that it was good to be chummy with your junior subordinates occasionally. Loyalty should be supported. And encouraged.

Eventually, the Rolls-Royce was brought. The driver jumped out and opened the door. Miklosh took the opportunity to inform him that he was chilled to the bone and very displeased. He got into the back. Johan was already sitting there. Raylen got in beside the driver.

"How can I lead the House to greatness when I am surrounded by such irresponsibility?" Mr. Balza complained to no one in particular.

He didn't get an answer.

THE residence of the House of Asiman was located in the very center of the capital.

When Miklosh first learned the location of the fire worshippers' central lair, he couldn't understand why Amir had chosen this area. It was too busy. Of course, there was food in abundance, but as for living in such a lively district of the anthill, no, thank you. Living with the constant stench of humans—that would have been too masochistic altogether for Mr. Balza.

But it all made sense once he made a thorough study of the area. The Asiman mansion—a three-story building from the early years of the century before last—could be reached only by walking through an archway that led from the main street through a building into courtyards and alleyways. It was set in a small green square, surrounded by cast-iron railings. A pair of large gates. A small gate. The first floor of the pyromaniacs' building was occupied by the office of a company that the blautsaugers used as a front.

But the ground emanated a power that took Miklosh's breath away. This spot was as potent as Vishegrad in Prague. Probably in times gone by, some very bloody and very violent massacre had taken place here. The blood-soaked earth had been transformed into an accumulator that now released its accumulated energy to anyone who could make use of it. Good for Amir. He had chosen the right place to settle when the families moved to the capital after they were forced to leave Prague. The main part of his residence was located underground, on the remains of the Old City and the catacombs.

Mr. Balza generally regarded it as beneath him to deliver goods to various kinds of lowlife. But today was a special case. First, he was feeling bored, and a short outing, even in such repulsive weather, would do him good. Second, it was a chance to visit the Asiman nest, which very few people were ever allowed into.

The car stopped. Raylen, still with the toothpick in her mouth, jumped out and opened the door. The Nachttoter got out, and he and his companions walked into the dark passage, which had a damp smell, tainted with urine. Miklosh grimaced fastidiously. There was the whole of human civilization for you. A bright neon advertisement on the front, but dig a little deeper and there was nothing but excrement. These brutes were so filthy that they defecated beside the places where they lived. Only animals could live like that without being sickened by it.

Johan pressed the bell beside the wicket gate.

"Yes?" the intercom asked.

"Nachttoter Balza. On a formal visit," the landsknecht rumbled.

There was hesitation at the other end of the intercom. Then the lock clicked. They walked along a path, past faded flower beds, until they reached the building, where a young Asiman was waiting for them. Miklosh had a good memory for faces, and he remembered where he had seen him before. In the nightclub. He had been keeping an eye on Darel Dahanavar, while his friend had sucked the blond girl dry.

The blautsauger was clearly nervous and tried not to look at the head of the House of Nachterret.

"The Magister is expecting you. Follow me."

He hurriedly led them through into the elevator, put a key in a lock, turned it, pressed a button, and the cabin dropped downward. But the fall lasted no longer than two seconds. A bell jingled and the doors opened. Raylen followed their guard out. She looked around and nodded to indicate that there were no surprises. Johan stepped aside to let Miklosh out.

The pyromaniacs had done a good job of turning the damp, moss-infested catacombs into a comfortable residence. It must have taken a lot of work. It felt as though they were in the vestibule of some large exhibition center, not under the ground. The floor was paved with gray marble, polished to mirror brightness, the walls were smoothly plastered, there were suspended ceilings covered with small lamps, and there was a huge aquarium with live fish against one of the walls. The desk for a secretary or security guard was unmanned. In the left corner, the green eye of a video camera was blinking. Two rows of columns ran along the sides of the hall.

They walked through a door on the left, then turned to the right and passed the ends of several large corridors, meeting about a dozen blautsaugers on the way. Mikosh thought that if not for the fact that these brothers were required for his plan and they didn't support the Golden Hornets' policy on humans, this little nest could be wiped out. At the cost of blood, of course, but if Mr. Balza started a war, even the large numbers of Asiman and their much-vaunted fire magic wouldn't be enough to save this family from defeat.

Dreams. Dreams. It would be a long time before they could come true. But patience and more patience was the name of the game. Sooner or later, the House of Nachterret would win the position it had deserved from the very beginning. The first task was to exterminate the Dahanavar—the bone that was stuck in his throat. The others could wait.

Amir al Rahal greeted his guests in his personal quarters. A huge plasma TV set was working with the sound turned off, showing the report that Miklosh had already seen, about the attack on the corporation's production plant.

The lamps on the walls reminded Balza of streetlamps in Paris. There were bright flames flickering in the fireplace. In addition to Amir, wrapped in the scarlet mantle of the Supreme Magister, two of his pupils were in the room. By no means the least important magicians in the family hierarchy. Or the weakest, either. Ernesto and Jacob.

Mr. Balza knew both of them.

He had clashed with Ernesto once over territorial interests. On that night, Miklosh had been seriously angry. Ernesto had always been inclined to act on the spur of the moment, and his brigade had started hunting around Vishegrad—the residence of the House of Nachterret in Prague—without asking permission.

Such offhanded insolence had deserved immediate death, and only Amir's personal intervention had saved the audacious young Asiman from his fate. On this occasion, Ernesto was leafing through some documents and making notes in the margins with a thick felt-tip pen, and he didn't even glance up at the visitors as they walked in.

The Nachttoter had never had any direct dealings with Jacob, who never did anything without orders from Amir. The blautsauger was certainly looking terrible today. His black hair was limp and tattered, his skin was deadly pale, with an unhealthy sheen, his eyes were red, his lips were cracked and bleeding, and his cheeks were hollow.

Miklosh frowned. Was he sick? Infectious? He had never heard of any illnesses among the brothers before. But there was a first time for everything. Especially with the Asiman.

The idiots. Messing around like that with human materials. What if they caught something? It wouldn't be hard; humans were well-known carriers of infection. And such a huge number of experiments was bound to turn out badly. Constantly using all those new drugs, chemicals, and other dangerous garbage. Who could tell what effect it would all have on the physiology of the blood brothers? Jacob could easily have spilled some kind of filth on himself. Perhaps something like what Johan had in the case.

They ran riot all over the city with their experiments, stuffing themselves and the humans full of their rotten scientific brews, trying to get closer to the ideal. Miklosh despised the blautsaugers' attempts to become better than everyone else. You couldn't change what was foreordained. The dreams of being able to tolerate sunlight were nonsense. Raving nonsense. It was not the body, but the spirit that needed to be improved. They had to become tougher, more cunning, and more dangerous. That was where the guarantee of victory lay. Not in a test tube filled with a mess of chemicals. On the other hand, if the idiots wanted to amuse themselves with science, let them. Maybe they would all drop dead. Just as long as they didn't take the Nachterret with them. And if they did get a result, that wouldn't be a bad thing, either. The Golden Hornets would always find a way to steal the new knowledge and use it to their own advantage.

"Miklosh," said Amir, getting up out of his chair, "I am surprised that you have come yourself."

"I like surprising people," said the Nachttoter, throwing off his coat, which Raylen caught deftly, and sitting down without waiting to be asked. "I didn't want any misunderstanding to arise between us. Johan?"

His deputy set the case on the table.

"Magnificent," said Amir, making no effort to conceal his delight. "This is exactly what we needed."

"I'm sure it is. You always need something. I hope this whole disgusting business will get you what you want."

"What do you mean?"

"Amir, if you believe that no one in the city knows what you do with humans in your torture chambers, then you are profoundly mistaken. You work too sloppily. Sooner or later the Dahanavar will take you by the throat."

"Just let them try."

"They will, don't you worry. As if you didn't know Felicia. She's worse than a flea—once she takes a grip, there's no way to shake her off."

"That is a private matter for my family. If Felicia starts trying to play the great defender of human rights, I shall know what to say to her."

"Whatever you say. You are our allies. I was only trying to warn you. As a friend."

"I see you have a new bodyguard with you. I haven't seen her before," said Amir, changing the subject.

Ernesto looked at Raylen, then put down his papers, picked

up the case, and walked out of the study. Jacob glanced sideways at Amir for permission to leave, then rose to his feet with an effort and also left.

"He's not looking well," said Miklosh, not seeing any need to introduce Raylen. "Aren't you feeding him properly?"

Amir's face darkened. "The magic of the House of Death has never been good for anyone's health. Jacob has been given a thorough battering. And apart from that, he was almost eaten by the Dark Hunter."

Johan was unable to refrain from a quiet whistle of surprise.

"Hmmm," the Nachttoter mused. "Your pupil decided to take on the sorcerers? Rather impetuous, if you ask me. The Dark Hunter . . . Chris, I presume? What were they arguing about? A couple of corpses from the morgue?"

"Felicia's telepath."

"Darel? How did that happen?"

"The sorcerer is a friend of his."

"I still don't see the connection. What did Jacob want with the Dahanavar?"

"He killed one of Ernesto's pupils."

Miklosh could barely control his irritation. He couldn't understand what Jacob had to do with it, if the motive for personal revenge belonged to someone else. Amir failed to notice his visitor's somber expression and went on.

"He has become quite unbearable just recently. And he has got under our feet more than once."

"Then get rid of him if he's bothering you," Miklosh advised Amir with emphatic indifference.

If the Asiman could actually do it, Miklosh would be only too delighted. Felicia with her telepath and Felicia without her telepath were two completely different propositions. Her family would be weaker without the scanner.

"He's hard to catch and keep. We almost had him in our

hands. Jacob's lads caught him all right, but then Chris and his pupils turned up. And I lost some good warriors."

"Yes, Chris's not one for making polite conversation," Mr. Balza said with an affected smile.

He didn't envy Jacob. To be caught in the viselike grip of the House of Death was not a pleasant experience.

"But there's nothing to stop you trying again."

"There is just one little obstacle," the Magister replied dourly. "The telepath is under the sorcerer's protection. And there's Felicia, too. The Dahanavar's hard to reach now. Ernesto is ranting and raving. His pupil was killed for nothing."

"I didn't think the pampered telepath was capable of killing brothers."

"Nobody thought so. If not for that damn human girl, we would have rid the city of that scum a long time ago."

"You're rambling. We were talking about Chris, and now it's some girl."

"First Chris got in Jacob's way, and then he turned up at Ernesto's lair to collect his friend. Everything had already been prepared. None of the brothers could have reached the Dahanavar, not even the elders. But we hadn't prepared any defenses against a human. That girl, the sensor's friend, dragged him out all on her own."

NOTHING had changed outside while Miklosh was in the Asiman residence. Except that the snow had started falling more heavily. The wet snowflakes glittered in the light of the streetlamps and settled silently on his collar and cap. At least the wind had died down.

Mr. Balza put on his gloves. "Johan, go to the car. Tell the driver to wait for me on the next street. In front of the theater. Go with him. I'll take a walk through the back alleys. I need to think a bit."

"Nachttoter, you might need us."

"I don't think I'll be in any danger, I can manage to walk three blocks on my own. Call the Upieschi about that job. Find out if everything's ready."

"At least take Raylen."

"All right," the Nachttoter agreed after thinking for a moment.

Johan disappeared into the darkness, and Miklosh and his escort set off along an alley.

The head of the Nachterret was thinking furiously. Fate seemed to have just done him a great big favor. The Asiman had a serious grudge against the telepath, and that was good. Now he wouldn't have to rack his brains about how to neutralize Felicia's trump card. The pyromaniacs would do it for him. All he had to do was channel their ebullient energy in the right direction.

So now where did that leave him? There was a new player in this unexpected game. A human. A girl who was not afraid to come to Ernesto's lair with a Master of Death and drag the Dahanavar out of a fatal trap. How very audacious young maidens had become these days.

But wait.

He had already seen Darel and this girl together. In that night-club where the appetizing young blonde had become someone else's supper. The telepath had been having a friendly chat with her, and Miklosh had thought the little poppet was dessert for Flora's pupil. But now he saw he had been mistaken. It was something more than just feeding that bound the Dahanavar and the girl together. But what was it? What could bind a blood brother and a human together? What?

Mr. Balza didn't understand. He could only try to guess. The girl saved a bloodsucker's life. She obviously knew who they were, and she wasn't afraid. Also, she was with him all the time. Darel treated her as an equal. Amir said the two of them had been together for a month already. Miklosh recalled something of the kind. Telepaths were sentimental and could easily become attached to any low creature. Even one as repulsive as a human. Now what could he do with this?

He could turn it to his own advantage.

The mormolika's minion might be under her protection, but the girl was not. Just how important was she to the Dahanavar? What would he be willing to do to keep the girl alive and well? What risks would he take? Would he do something as stupid as what Miklosh had in mind?

Questions. Nothing but questions. And not a single answer.

This girl seemed to be the lock on the door that led to the great victory. The important thing now was to find the right key. But it was already clear that he had to act through her. To strike at the telepath where he would not be expecting it. He had to do it. He had to act.

Of course, not with his own hands. No need for that. There were more than enough willing volunteers. The entire pyromaniac community was at his disposal. He ought to phone Amir and give him the idea. But not too bluntly. With appropriate caution. Under no circumstances must the girl be killed. That was too simple, too crude. It had to be done more elegantly than that. To back the Dahanavar right into a corner. So that he would do something stupid. What if it really could work?

Miklosh thought he knew what he needed to know to have an extraordinary council meeting convened. Provided, of course, that all his assumptions were correct, and as far as he could tell, they were. Although there could just be some mistake. In any case, tomorrow Amir would hear his ideas on this subject.

Suddenly Raylen was right there in front of him, almost under his feet. Mr. Balza was about to abuse her for distracting him from his important thoughts when he noticed the reason the girl had acted so presumptuously.

Two figures were walking slowly toward them.

Miklosh was surprised to recognize Chris Cadavercitan and one of his young pupils.

They spotted the Nachttoter and slowed down. They had obviously not been expecting to see Mr. Balza here. He wondered what the sorcerer was doing in this part of town. And so close to Asiman territory.

To judge from the expressions on their faces, the Master of Death clearly thought they had been followed and that Raylen was about to leap into the attack.

"Good evening, sorcerer."

"What are you doing here?" asked the necromancer, looking Miklosh up and down.

"Taking a stroll. It's fine weather for a stroll today."

Chris glanced at his pupil to tell him to stay back and walked closer. Raylen jerked up her hands, and suddenly she was holding the short handle of a gray, semitransparent battle-ax. Mr. Balza noticed that she had used the decomposition spell and woven it together with the Structure of Disintegration or the Spiral of the Metal Phantom. Apparently her own invention. The girl really did have natural talent. Johan had done all that he could, but now it was time for Miklosh to give her some attention. Serious attention. She would go a long way and bring great benefit to the House. If she survived this encounter, of course.

Chris didn't react to the appearance of the weapon. He kept his eyes on Miklosh.

"Take your rat out of my way."

Miklosh smiled politely and shrugged disarmingly, as if to say, *It's nothing to do with me. This is your business, sort it out between you. I'm not going to lift a finger.*

Mr. Balza felt curious. Had his deputy managed to instill hatred of the Master of Death in his pupil? If he had, this could be interesting. And amusing.

Chris frowned as if all his teeth had suddenly started aching.

He walked up to the female bodyguard, stopped just one step away, and looked down at her. He deliberately paid no attention to the dangerous spell in her hands, as if it didn't even exist. She had to raise her head in order to see his eyes.

Miklosh could read her thoughts. Chris is standing almost right against me. From the right. One blow. If it succeeds, there is no way to survive the spell.

"Get out of my way, girl," the sorcerer said at last.

Mr. Balza decided to hurry events along.

"Attack," he said.

Raylen immediately threw her body to the right and lashed out with her magical battle-ax. A rapid gray blur. An excellent attacking move. Magnificent. Most opponents would have been killed on the spot. But not Chris. The sorcerer who had spent his entire human life in battle avoided the danger simply by stepping aside.

Before Raylen could raise her weapon for a second blow, the sorcerer attacked. He didn't feel the need to generate any kind of weapon. A poisonous green flame sprang to life on his open palm and he struck the girl in the chest.

Miklosh saw that the Cadavercitan stopped his hand at the last moment, transforming Death into Pain. Raylen shrieked and collapsed on the ground. Convulsions ran up and down her body. Foam bubbled up through her plump lips. Then she went limp, but she didn't lose consciousness.

Chris prodded the battle-ax away from her with the pointed toe of his boot and turned the furious gaze of his green eyes on Miklosh.

"Why did you do that?"

"I was curious to see what she can do," the Nachttoter replied calmly.

"If she gets in my way again, I'll kill her," the sorcerer promised.

"As you wish," the leader of the Golden Hornets said with an indifferent shrug.

He waited for Chris and his pupil to walk past and disappear into the maze of alleyways before going over to Raylen. She had managed to get to her feet and was spitting blood.

"Get up," he said without even looking at her. "Have you learned the lesson of this encounter?"

"Yes, Nachttoter," she wheezed.

"I'd be interested to hear what you've learned."

"I was too clumsy."

"Rubbish!" he snorted. "That's not the important point. Remember. You should never pick a fight with a Cadavercitan unless you have a clear advantage, preferably at least three to one. That's the first thing. The second is that going up against the Master of Death himself is absolute madness and the quickest way of committing suicide. Only idiots try that. Compared with him, you're like a louse facing an elephant. He'll crush you without even noticing. Perhaps in about seven hundred years you might have just the ghost of a chance of attracting his attention, but not before then. And not in a duel of magic. He usually kills insolent fools like you."

"Then how did you know that he wouldn't kill me when you ordered me to attack?" she asked, now completely in control of her body again. She was quite steady on her feet, although she still looked terribly pale.

"I didn't know," Miklosh answered calmly. "There was a very good chance that you wouldn't survive. But since you did, we must assume that Chris is in a good mood today." He giggled. "That's very instructive. At least now I know how far you are prepared to go."

"With all due respect, Nachttoter, now I know how far you can go," she said dryly.

"Believe me, my little chick. You have no idea just how far."

12

GREENHALL

Art is the only serious thing in the world.
And the artist is the only person who is never serious.

—Oscar Wilde, "A Few Maxims for the
Instruction of the Over-Educated"

November 2
Darel Dahanavar

I was sitting in an armchair in Chris's magnificently somber drawing room, with my feet up on the low table. The sorcerer couldn't bear to see his furniture treated in such a vulgar fashion. But he didn't make any comment. Just once, as he was walking past, he gave me a kick to make me assume a more acceptable position. I was idly leafing through the magazine *Around the World* and listening as Viv and Loraine talked.

I found the spectacle amusing. The young Cadavercitan was demonstrating his weapon to her.

The pupil of the Master of Death got up from his chair, reached out his hand, and muttered something that I could hardly hear. A small green, glowing sphere appeared on his open palm. After a moment, it stretched out into a long, glowing ellipse, and then it changed into a sword with a beautifully curved hilt. And only the green sparks running along the blade betrayed the Cadavercitan's magic.

Loraine sighed in delight.

"How do you do that?" she asked, reaching out for the weapon, but then she pulled her hand back. "Can I have a look?"

Vivian held out the sword to her handle first.

"It's heavy. When I was little I used to dream about fencing. But then I got addicted to tennis."

I must say I was surprised to learn that Chris's pupil had already reached the level of such complex combat spells. It didn't seem so very long ago that he was completely defenseless. But then, just how long ago was that? It had to be twenty years.

"You're making good progress," I said, watching the sparks scatter from the blade as Loraine waved the sword around. "Chris can be proud of you."

Vivian smiled. He enjoyed praise.

I always picked up a strange feeling from him. A profound inner dichotomy. As if there were two personalities battling each other inside him. The result was that Viv was constantly dissatisfied with himself, yet at the same time he craved special attention. But on the surface he looked absolutely calm, imperturbable, and coolheaded. And he always behaved with perfect decorum.

He chatted with Loraine, and I started thinking about my recent encounter with the Asiman. A very humiliating memory. I was trying hard to block it, but every now and then Ernesto's grinning face appeared in front of my eyes, mangling everything inside me with the sensation of his triumphant gloating and malicious delight. Now he had that insolent upstart, the Dahanavar telepath, sprawling helpless at his feet.

I couldn't even attempt to resist after he hit me with a spell from the higher Asiman magic. Not fatal, but excruciatingly painful. And while I was lying there doubled up on the floor, feeling my insides being devoured by worms of fire, he drank his fill of my blood. That lousy bastard. That damn blautsauger. Miklosh Nachterret's favorite term of abuse was never more appropriate.

If it hadn't been for Loraine . . .

It was incredible that she hadn't stopped seeing me after all that. She'd dragged me all the way out of that underground chamber, and I had almost killed her. Perhaps Chris was right, and I ought to leave her in peace.

The sorcerer appeared beside me as if in response to my gloomy thoughts.

"Darel, take your feet off the table, will you? Viv, take the sword from Loraine. Loraine—" But before the Cadavercitan could think of something to reproach the girl with, she interrupted:

"Chris, please tell me how you were made into a vampire."

Chris frowned. He didn't like this subject, and he hated being called a vampire. But then he smiled. Apparently, for Loraine's sake, he was willing to recall that old story. He gestured for his curious listeners to sit down. Then he waited for Vivian, who was just as interested as the girl, to put away his sword.

"At that time the House of Death needed skilled warriors. And I used to earn my living as a mercenary. A warrior. And a rather good warrior, too. To be quite frank, fighting was the only thing I knew how to do and enjoyed doing. One day when I was carousing in a tavern, a suspicious-looking individual came up to me and told me in the most disrespectful terms that a certain gentleman had asked him to inform me that in his opinion I was a worthless nonentity and an insult to the aesthetic sensibilities of decent society. As he said it, he pointed to a tall gentleman in a black cloak, who gave me a very bad-humored look. Of course, I picked a fight with him. And, of course, the gentleman gave me a thrashing that I prefer not to remember even to this day. No one had ever humiliated me like that. I had never encountered an opponent who was stronger than me. And I had never felt so angry. The only thing I could think about was revenge."

Loraine smiled understandingly. "And so you challenged him to another duel?"

"Worse than that. I attacked him late at night, when he suspected nothing—or so I thought. The second fight ended even worse for me than the first. And I realized that he had either sold his soul to the devil, or he was the devil himself, because no ordinary man could possibly possess such monstrous strength and agility and fight with such incredible virtuosity."

Chris laughed, remembering himself as an insolent twenty-eight-year-old rogue.

"When my wounds healed, I decided to go and demand that he teach me his skills. And didn't I happen to turn up at his house just when he was in the company of other noble ladies and gentlemen like himself. Blood brothers—as I know now. How they laughed at me! At my manners, and my clothes, and the way I spoke, and most of all at the purpose of my visit. I put up with all of it without saying a word, although I was absolutely furious. Eventually the master of the house, who had been observing me closely, stood up and invited me to his study, where I pressed him once again to train me in the art of combat.

"'People say that I am a warlock,' he said. 'Do you know what that is?'

"Of course, I didn't know a thing. And I didn't want to know anything. The only notable qualities I possessed were bravado, bumptious conceit, and inordinate pride. And so I replied accordingly: 'That doesn't frighten me!'

"'But what about your immortal soul? Your church forbids you to accept advice and help from dark spirits and the devil.'

"I thought about that. But I soon found my answer:

"'I shall save your knowledge for a good cause. For fighting the enemies of humankind.'

"'You mean for fighting me?' he asked with a cunning smile.

"I thought again for a moment and decided to be magnanimous:

"'I won't touch you, unless, of course, you force me to. . . .'

"The gentleman laughed. He laughed heartily for a long time, and when he had calmed down, he looked me over from head to toe and said:

" 'I like you. You're crude and unpolished, but something can be made of you. I have guests today. Come back tomorrow and I'll make you one of my pupils.'

" 'I'll come,' I promised. And so the next day I went."

Loraine and Vivian learned forward eagerly in anticipation of what would come next, but Chris was staring thoughtfully into empty space. Did he regret that he had gone to the head of the House of Cadavercitan with his naïve desire to be taught how to fight better than anyone else, or did he think of that day as one of the most fortunate in his life? I couldn't tell.

Chris got up and took down a crudely carved Cadavercitan cross of painted wood from a shield hanging above the mantelpiece. Over the centuries, the paint on it had faded and the wood had cracked.

"I got what I wanted. Volfger gave me his strength and taught me the simplest spells. At first that was enough for me, but then I wanted more. The brothers and sisters stopped laughing at me. Many of them were already too old, they no longer had the furious joy and vitality that was raging inside me. I realized that being able to fight with a sword was not enough, and I threw myself into learning the higher magic. As time passed, they learned to respect me. Then to fear me. And some regretted that they had ever let me get close to the Mentor."

"Why?" asked Loraine.

"I became the right hand of the head of the House."

"And how did you come to have the Dark Hunter?" Vivian asked in a quiet voice.

"I stole the spell for the Dark Hunter."

"Really?" Loraine asked in amazement.

"Yes, that was how it happened. And when I summoned it the first time, I almost died. I didn't have enough blood to feed it or enough strength to control it. If not for Volfger, the Hunter would have eaten me."

The sorcerer paused, examining the wooden cross.

The head of the necromancers had disappeared about thirty years earlier. And nobody knew where he was. Chris had searched for his teacher but failed to find him. He had even asked me to try to *sense* him. But I hadn't caught even the faintest echo, as if the Mentor had been swallowed up by his own dark sentinel. I hadn't been able to do anything for the Cadavercitan, but while I was working with them, I was surprised to discover that I liked their company. Their thoughts, feelings, and desires were somehow streamlined. Level and calm, a gently quivering backdrop. They were completely cool, benevolent, and self-confident. They smiled, joked, and laughed, but inside they remained cool. Elegant and imperturbable—not indifferent, but somehow abstracted, carrying within them the eternal burden of many centuries of death. They themselves were death.

I used to think about this all the time when I talked to Dona, whom I had met thirty years earlier. Dona arranged the initial meeting through the First Lady of the House of Dahanavar. Felicia asked me to help with the search for Volfger, and I found myself sitting in a bar not far from Chris's house, examining one of the necromancers with almost indecent curiosity. She had come there on his instructions. I thought that her enchanting appearance must be a mask that concealed her true face—the ugly face of death. Eventually, she sensed my unhealthy curiosity.

She stopped talking, straightened her hair, pulled down her sweater, and cast a brief sideways glance at the mirror hanging on the wall. Basically, she behaved exactly like any woman who suspects that she is attracting attention because her clothes, her hair, or her makeup are a mess. Then she frowned.

"Darel, you're looking at me as if you'd seen Anpa."

"Sorry, who?"

She smiled, crossed her legs, and leaned back in her chair.

"In the Middle Ages, that was what they called the phantom

of death who walked around in a shroud, with a hood over his face, carrying a sharp scythe. The same image that they use for death nowadays. But in actual fact, it was only the last person to have died in the year. It was his duty to make sure that all the dead reached their place of rest safely. And after twelve months he handed on his authority to the Anpa who came to take his place. Another dead person."

My jaw dropped in surprise, and I looked at this mysterious young woman, unable to tell if she was joking or being serious. It was strange, but I was having difficulty *sensing* her.

She touched her wavy hair again, adjusted an earring with a large diamond, and said thoughtfully:

"There are many legends like that in Cadavercitan folklore, and even we don't know how much is true and how much is myth."

"Interesting," I said, watching her white hands, studded with diamond rings (there were ten in all, one on each finger and thumb). The slim bands of gold glittered, and the gleam of the stones blinded my eyes.

"Do you think so?" Dona asked coolly. She noticed my curious glance and put her hands under the table. "I think it's all nothing but human make-believe. But we've got off the subject. Chris Frederick Alabert would like to meet you today sometime before twelve. He will tell you what he wants to ask in person, I am only here to settle the amount of the fee."

The young woman had a long chain encrusted with diamond dust around her neck. It shimmered brightly, and there were transparent stones glittering in her hair, too.

"Dona," I said, interrupting her before she could finish, "before we discuss the details of my remuneration, please do me a favor and take off one of your rings."

She opened her cornflower blue eyes wide in surprise for a

moment but immediately put on her imperturbable expression again. She clasped her hands tightly together, as if I were threatening to take away one of her ornaments by force.

"What for?"

"You're hung all over with diamonds. And they have all been cut in a rather unusual way—only the top half is faceted. The lower part, in the setting, has been left untouched. I won't read you a lecture on the magical properties of minerals, but diamonds like that create a solid shield that conceals your feelings. I could break through your defenses, but it would take a little time, and I'm afraid your jewelry might suffer in the process."

She laughed quietly, took the ring off her index finger, and tossed it across to me. The ring skidded across the table, scattering sparks of light, and one of the customers walking by glanced at it covetously. I picked up the gold bauble. Yes indeed, half of the stone was rough and opaque, the other half was magnificently polished. An ideal combination. The uncut stone embodied chaos, and the polished stone embodied harmony and order. The combination of the two provided the wearer with a defense against any intrusion into his mind.

Dona took off the rest of her rings, and her emotions started streaming across to me. She was anxious, concerned, missing her Mentor, afraid that he was already dead, she blamed herself and Chris, and she was hoping, although she knew that hoping was pointless. No, it wasn't likely that she would remember or feel anything useful. But you could never tell.

"An amusing little trinket," I said, placing the ring on my open palm and holding it out to her.

"Upieschi work," said the girl, taking the ring but not putting it on. "The ancient Upieschi. The modern ones have forgotten a great deal of what they used to know. They never had the normal kind of magic, so they used the power of minerals, plants, and animals. But that was before. You'd be surprised, Darel, if you knew how much we have all changed. And how do you come to know about the magic of diamonds?"

"In my line I have to. I try to know about everything that affects my work."

She nodded and closed her fist around one of the rings.

"If Volfger really is dead, then our world will lose another little bit of knowledge, of memory about magic. He taught us what he knew, but it's not possible to transfer every last little drop."

"I'll try to find him, Dona."

"Do. And the House of Cadavercitan will be grateful to you."

The young woman got up abruptly, showering me with her pain and grief, and walked out of the bar. In the doorway, a burly, aggressive young drunk tried to molest her, but she simply shrugged off his hand and gave the poor guy a fit of violent nausea. He turned green and reached for the wall, then doubled over and lost interest in his surroundings for about ten minutes. The Cadavercitan are virtuosos in the art of controlling human physiology.

She actually loved Volfger. Not as a man and a lover, but as a father and a teacher and also, strangely enough, as a part of her past that she found unbearable to lose.

Chris met me in the magnificent hallway of his equally magnificent mansion. He didn't think it necessary to conceal his feelings. The Mentor's best pupil was seething inside. I hadn't the slightest idea that old, wise blood brothers burdened with centuries of life were capable of such powerful, vivid, searing emotions. But then it became clear later that he was an unusual Cadavercitan. He could certainly have used a few rings with half-processed diamonds.

As soon as we had said hello, he started telling me all about his Mentor's disappearance.

"Volfger left home on September twelfth, as soon as it got

dark. He said he had some business that would take about an hour and a half. He said he didn't need anyone to go with him. If only I'd known!"

During the next four weeks, Chris and I combed the entire city. Crowded streets, dark passages, dubious fast-food joints, the slums. But I didn't *feel* a thing. I promised Volfger's pupil that if I ever happened to sense his Mentor, I would let him know. But I still hadn't *felt* a thing yet.

After a month of fruitless searching, however, I realized how interesting I found the Master of Death's company. And he came to appreciate my friendship, too.

I was distracted from my reminiscences by a voice in my head.

Darel!

What a surprise. Paula. I wondered what the fary wanted from me.

I'm listening, I replied mentally, watching Loraine examining the Cadavercitan cross like some holy relic.

You must come! I mean . . . could you please come here straight-away?

This was something new. I was being asked. And in a most ingratiating manner.

To Alexander's place?

No! To mine. Please. It's very important!

I *switched off* and noticed that everybody was watching me, Chris and Vivian with understanding expressions, Loraine in amazement.

"I have to go. Urgent business."

While I drove Loraine home, she was silent and thoughtful all the way, and then at the entrance to her house she said:

"You know what? Get yourself a cell phone. It will be simpler. Press a button and talk. Press a button and switch off. Seeing you engaged in mental conversation is pretty scary."

"Why, what's wrong with me?" I inquired peevishly.

"Next time try looking in the mirror," the girl advised me, then she kissed me on the cheek, got out of the car, and ran home.

Okay, maybe sometime I will take a look.

I swung the Pontiac around and set out for Paula's place. The fary lived at the other side of the city in a pleasant green district. Both sides of the highway were lined with two- or three-story houses with red-tiled roofs and windows with rounded arches. The drive leading to each one of them was covered with gravel. It crunched under the wheels as I carefully drove up to the entrance.

There was an intercom by the door. A few seconds after I rang, the door clicked open. Stepping inside, I found myself in a small hallway. The walls looked as if they were made of crudely dressed stone blocks. I touched them to check, and it was real stone, not cunningly designed wallpaper. The floor was made of long polished oak boards.

The stairway led upward, lit by lamps in the form of dragons. In its paws, every dragon was holding a wire-mesh sphere with a lightbulb burning inside it. It was like the vestibule of some medieval castle. In miniature.

The mistress of the house met me at the top of the stairs. I had to walk up toward her, feeling like the hero of some chivalrous novel arriving for a tryst with a beautiful princess. And I had to admit that Paula did look magnificent. She was wearing a long, body-hugging, very revealing green dress. Her white skin was positively radiant, and the comparison with a pearl came to mind again. The fary was standing with her slim hand resting on the banister, and her elegant figure arched very slightly. The dragons seemed to be staring in delight at the girl with their bulging eyes.

"Hi," she said in a melodious, enchanting voice. "You got here quickly."

"Paula, tell me the truth. Did you call me here to seduce me?"

My words killed all the romance stone dead. The emotional background that I had sensed as a light, pleasant efflorescence around the girl suddenly sprouted prickly thorns—and she instantly lost half of her feminine charm.

"Don't flatter yourself. I hope I never find myself in a situation so sad that I have to resort to anything like that."

Paula turned away and walked rapidly into the house. I followed, realizing that I had offended her again, and the fary had no reason to have any warm feelings for me.

There were several doors leading off the broad corridor on the second floor. Paula opened the first one and let me go in ahead of her.

It was a spacious sitting room decorated in green and brown tones. There was a sofa that looked like a moss-covered boulder. Several armchairs that were smaller boulders. A thick shaggy carpet on the floor. The lamp hanging from the ceiling looked like a carnivorous tropical flower. I felt like keeping as far away as possible. As if any moment now it would suddenly straighten out its stem covered in fine scales and throw itself on its passing prey with a predatory rustle of sepals.

There were green cushions shaped like water lily petals scattered around the floor. The low table was supported on massive, widespread feet that sank deep into the nap of the carpet. Instead of curtains, the false windows were decorated with some kind of shaggy lianas. Or waterweed . . .

I looked around at the wild interior for a few seconds. I would never have agreed to live in a room where I felt my own curtains might attack me at any moment. I wondered which of Paula's internal vices this incredible décor expressed. Latent aggression?

There was someone in the room. I didn't sense him immediately and saw him only after a few seconds. And when I saw who it was, I was flabbergasted yet again. The person who got up to greet me was Vance.

"Hi, Darel," he said with a smile.

His face, his movements, and his glance had all changed.

He had become different. Pale skin. Glowing eyes. He had never moved so smoothly before. Except onstage, when he became someone else. And his inner essence was not the same, either.

I flung myself into a boulder armchair, and it yielded springily under the weight of my body.

"She's turned you. She went ahead and did it anyway."

Still smiling, he said: "Now I'm the same as you."

No, you're not the same, but you don't understand that yet.

"You were my friend."

"Darel, I still am your friend, just like before. I've started to understand you better. I understand your world! Everything's changed! I've started feeling more, this strength inside . . . it's absolutely incredible."

He radiated joy and happiness. He felt all-powerful. It's always like that at first, when the human feelings have not yet been forgotten and the contrast between weak mortal existence and immortal nonhuman existence is felt most strongly.

"She's opened up a whole new world to you, has she?" I asked quietly. Something dark, wild, and vicious was slowly starting to stir inside me. "Given you love and thrown in immortality for good measure?"

Vance looked at me in silence with new eyes, in which the light of human genius had been extinguished.

"But did she tell you what this new life would cost you? How all the joy, the freshness of vision, feeling, and desire, will desert you, at first slowly, then faster and faster. People don't think of us as dead simply because we really are dead. There's no life in us. We're nothing but walking, talking bodies. You used to be a magnificent singer, a great guy, a good friend of mine. Now you're a Faryartos, and I'm a Dahanavar. Different families, different tastes and preferences. I'm sorry, Vance, but I'm not interested in you anymore."

I jumped up, took a step forward, and jostled against Paula.

"Why? Tell me why? You believe art is the most important thing, the most serious thing in the world. The thing that gives life meaning. But you've taken that meaning away from him. And you'll regret it."

I elbowed the girl out of my way and dashed out of the room. Ran down the stairs and out through the door. Got into my car. My anger needed an outlet. Even I didn't understand why I had reacted that way to Vance being turned and was so full of rage.

Had Paula invited me in order to relish her victory? To see how I would react? She was so pleased with herself, smacking her lips like a cat that has just lapped up the forbidden cream. I suddenly wanted to go back and do something that would cause her a lot of pain. But instead of that, I hammered my fist on the steering wheel several times and turned the key in the ignition.

The Pontiac was hurtling down the highway. Cars swerved out of the way and honked at me angrily as I roared past. Had she turned him just to demonstrate her power over him to me? Just because he was my friend? She had wanted him like a new dress or a pair of earrings. She'd just reached out her hand and taken what she wanted. Vance hadn't even put up a fight. Or perhaps he'd wanted it himself, once he found out who his Paula really was? She had seduced him with her beauty and the promise of eternal love, fame, money, and power. How wrong! How insanely wrong! A fine human being and remarkable singer had been turned into an ordinary vampire. I wondered how many years he would hold out. When would he feel the chill in his soul and start to forget his former self? Exactly when would he get *bored*?

The traffic light at the crossroads turned red, but I took no notice and drove straight on. And just at that moment, a large black Jeep came flying out of the other street. I hit the brakes. The Pontiac groaned in protest, then shrieked as its tires scrabbled the slippery tarmac. I was thrown forward into the steering wheel, and the seat belt bit into my chest. But I already knew it was hopeless. The front bumper of the Jeep crunched into the side of my car.

The sound of tearing metal. Broken glass spilling onto the road, like glittering silver blood from a torn artery. A searing wave of human panic.

And silence.

I swore under my breath, borrowing a couple of words from the Nachterret vocabulary. Unfastened my belt, opened the door, and got out. The drivers in the cars going past took no notice of the accident. I had *screened* us from the rest of the human world. The last thing I needed right now was an interview with the police.

There was a dent in the side of the Pontiac, and the windshield was missing.

The powerful Jeep hadn't suffered so badly. A young man was getting out of it with an expression of brutal fury on his face. In the car a dog was whining pitifully, pressing its miserable face against the window. From the folds of black velvety skin and the red eyes, I recognized a Neapolitan mastiff.

The young guy limped across to me.

"Why, you . . . what were you . . . on a red light . . . you motherfucker. You almost killed my mastiff!"

His eyes were white with fury and fear that was only gradually receding. His fists were clenched, his lower jaw was thrust out aggressively, and his short-cropped hair seemed to be standing on end above his sweaty forehead. His leather jacket was wide open.

He smelled of Lacoste, sweat, and adrenaline. The mastiff whimpered in the backseat, smearing its slaver across the window.

"You bastard. I had the car fixed yesterday. I'm going to call my buddies, they'll take care of you!"

At that moment I realized I was going to smear this man, who had got in my way by pure accident, across the surface of the road. Him and his dog. For Vance, for Paula, for Ernesto, Amir, and Slaven, for Loraine, who had dragged me out of the underground vault and I had almost killed her. The young guy suddenly recoiled and started blinking and muttering soothingly:

"Hey, cool it, take it easy. What's wrong with you?"

My black, insane fury had crushed his will, paralyzed it. He was very young, only about twenty. His clear blue eyes looked bewildered.

"Take your dog and clear out. Your Jeep must be working. Go on, get moving!"

"But . . . this . . . ," he said indecisively.

I rummaged through my pockets and found a scrap of paper. I looked closer and saw it was a ticket for Vance's opera. I went back to the car. The door of the glove compartment was jammed, and I got it open at the third attempt. The contents poured out onto the floor—an empty Coke can, sunglasses, an old map of the city, CDs, a pencil. I caught it in midair, scribbled the number of my phone on the ticket, and took the note to the driver of the Jeep, who was still standing in a daze beside his car.

"This is my number. Call me. I'll pay for the repairs."

He nodded, staring blankly at the piece of paper. I turned away, removed the protective *cover* from the Pontiac, and set off along the edge of the highway, walking with my hands stuck deep in my pockets. Leaving the damaged car standing on the side of the road.

A few dozen meters farther on, a Jeep with a bent bumper drew level with me. The front window wound down, and a glum human face appeared in the gap.

"Hey! Where you going?"

I told him the address.

"Get in."

I got in. The interior of the Jeep smelled of polish and conditioners, a pine air freshener, and dogs. The dog on the backseat started fidgeting and growling, then whined and tried to move as far away from me as possible.

"I'm taking him to the emergency vet," driver informed me trustingly. "He ate something he shouldn't have. The rubber rabbit, I reckon. So now he's got a bellyache. Nikita."

The last word was obviously the driver's name and had nothing to do with the state of his dog's health.

"Darel."

Keeping one hand on the wheel, he took a business card out of the breast pocket of his jacket and handed it to me.

"My contact details."

"Breeze Commercial and Industrial Association," I read. "Nikita Ivanov, director. So what do you trade in?"

He laughed contentedly and told me: "What do I trade in? Fresh air!"

I didn't feel like going into the details, but on his own initiative, Nikita started telling me all about his latest deal. To judge from his expensive auto, the trade in fresh air was going pretty well.

What incredible trust humans all felt in me. I'd damaged his car, almost crippled his beloved dog, and here he was talking to me as if I were his best friend. Vance had trusted me, too, and Loraine. What kind of curse was this? I made them like me, and I brought them disaster. They ought to keep as far away from me as possible, but instead they all reached out to me.

"Stop here."

"But you—"

"Stop."

"Okay."

Nikita stopped the car at a bus stop. I got out. A happy dog's face appeared in the rear window. The mastiff was glad to be rid of the dangerous passenger. The Jeep flashed its headlights and went dashing off along the highway.

It had got cold. There were tiny, sharp crystals of ice drifting through the air. I thought I could see their jagged edges glittering in the light of the streetlamps. Huge, heavy piles of cold blue clouds crept sluggishly across the sky. The smiling moon disappeared into them and then surfaced again, beaming brightly.

The people at the bus stop shuddered in the gusts of cold wind and turned up their collars. A group of teenagers with their jackets unbuttoned was standing under the plastic shelter. Pale white faces and thin, naked, defenseless necks. They were chatting happily, as if they didn't feel the cold at all—a peculiarity of adolescents and vampires.

I raised my hand to hail a taxi.

All the way home, the talkative driver fed me a detailed account of the situation in the Middle East and his own ideas about it. It took us about half an hour to reach my house, after plenty of winding through dark, dirty back streets and alleyways. Dead ends, long side streets, old churches, houses due for demolition, a boiler-house plant with a tall chimney that puffed out clouds of steam around the clock. Also—an essential part of the landscape—a vandalized automobile standing on bricks instead of wheels, which had been stolen. Some young guys had taken it for a ride without asking the owner's permission, then dumped it, and the thrifty locals had removed everything that could possibly be sold.

I paid the driver and got out of the taxi. My apartment was in a building on the edge of a small green square. The huge poplar by the entrance seemed like some passing traveler who had halted to think beside the gray stone wall. Its leaves had already fallen, except for the last few way up on the very highest branches, fluttering in the wind like dirty scraps of paper.

The grass of the square was littered with broken glass and empty beer cans. In May, this spot was a riot of blossoming lilac. It scented the air of the entire neighborhood. And the screeching of the female cats was deafening. Crazed by the spring, the slinky, furry creatures scurried about right under people's feet; they weren't afraid even of me. But now everything was cold, empty, dead.

There was a huge puddle extending across the road, its edge frozen in the first fragile covering of ice. It was impossible not to step on it for the pleasure of hearing the thin, glassy crust crunch under my feet. Water spurted up through the crack and rushed toward the sole of my shoe. I stepped back onto the dry surface of the road. Raised my head. The moon emerged from behind another heap of clouds, glowing with a pure, bright light. Its reflection appeared in the puddle.

At that moment, I caught the smell of fresh pine needles and wet fur and heard the low, exultant growl. I barely had time to swing around before a huge, snarling shadow threw itself at me and knocked me to the ground. Its teeth snapped shut just short of my throat. The powerful paws pressed me down against the road. I saw the red tongue and the long fangs in the hot mouth. The eyes glittering like two half-moons. A huge gray wolf.

Squeezing his throat just below the jaws to prevent him from getting a grip on my throat, I *struck*. With an intense, focused beam of power. The beast whined, jumped off me, and started helplessly rubbing at his eyes with his paws. The next *blow* knocked the wolf to the ground. He collapsed beside the puddle, shuddered, and started changing. The transformation was very rapid. In just a few seconds, there was someone standing on his hands and knees in front of me—a vampire. The pose looked very familiar.

"Slaven?"

Ivan Svetlov's assistant certainly knew how to hide. He had

camouflaged himself against the natural background of the square. I had heard the rustling of the leaves and the creaking of the trees and caught the smell of the forest. But I hadn't guessed there was a Vricolakos there. I had let down my guard.

"Come to try your strength? All right. You've persuaded me. I'll show you some real Dahanavar magic."

My anger with Paula was merely a pale shadow of what I felt now. Invisible trembling threads reached out and thrust into the overconfident boy. He cried out in his mind, because he couldn't make any sound out loud. Slaven was no longer in control of his own body. It obeyed only me. Completely, every last nerve. He got to his feet, gazing at me with huge, frightened eyes. A pitiful twisted puppet.

There was a long knife hanging on the Vricolakos's belt. I made him take out his weapon. Slowly, centimeter by centimeter, the glittering blade slid out of its sheath. Slaven's fingers gripped the handle tightly. The young cub watched in panic-stricken terror as his own hand obeyed my will and brought the sharp blade up to his neck. He couldn't stop it moving. Just a little farther and . . .

I didn't feel any anger or sadistic pleasure, only a cold satisfaction that I had finally managed to vent my corrosive fury.

The narrow tip of the blade was already scratching Slaven's throat.

No! No! Don't! I didn't mean it! I was only joking! he cried out in his mind. It wasn't the pain of the knife cutting into his skin that frightened him, it was his own total helplessness.

Now it's my turn to joke. We'll swap jokes, the way good friends do.

The first drops of blood appeared. They ran down the blade, staining its clean metal surface red.

Don't, Darel!

Suddenly there was a new message in Slaven's cries: *Wait! My father asked me to tell you he wants to see you. He invites you to visit Greenhall tonight. I'm supposed to take you there.*

I came to my senses.

What was I doing? What did I want with this foolish, help-less boy? *But he attacked you!* cried the remains of the anger quivering deep inside me. *What could he have done to me?* my common sense replied. *This stupid little cub?* Objectively speaking—nothing. Especially since he was here on Ivan's in-structions.

I broke off the mental connection. Slaven sank to the ground, trembling all over: his legs wouldn't hold him. He threw away his knife. The ritual weapon splashed into the puddle and sank out of sight, but the Vricolakos didn't even notice. He felt his face with both hands, as if he were trying to convince himself that it was still the same.

"A fine guide," I said with loathing. "Try another joke like that, and I'll kill you."

He got to his feet with a great effort, tugged down the suede jacket that was almost the same color as a wolf's fur, dusted off his trousers, and asked, avoiding my eyes:

"Do you accept the invitation? The Vricolakos family guaran-tees your absolute safety."

After the trick Slaven had pulled, words about safety had a hollow ring, to put it mildly.

"All right, let's go. I'd better find out what Ivan wants."

Svetlov's Lamborghini flew along the empty highway. Slaven concentrated on driving the car, and I looked out the window at the trees rushing past. Wondering if I ought to tell Felicia about my unexpected trip.

It wasn't a consultation between the heads of two Houses or an official reception. After thinking for a minute, I decided I didn't need to tell her.

"How did you do that?" Slaven asked unexpectedly, gazing at

the white beams of the headlights running along the road ahead of us.

"What, exactly?"

"It was like you got inside my skin. I could feel your anger, your fury, inside me, in my head. It was like you *were* me. Even my face . . ." He took one hand off the wheel and touched his cheek again.

"Keep your eyes on the road."

"What? Ah, yes. But how did you do that? How did you control my body?"

"Dahanavar magic."

"Really?" There was more doubt in his voice than respect for my sorcery. "Only the Cadavercitan can control bodies."

"Dead bodies."

"All the same," Slaven said, knitting his brows. "It's not natural."

The Vricolakos didn't explain exactly what it was that didn't seem natural to him. Soon after that, the car turned onto a narrow side road leading into the forest. And about fifteen minutes later, we arrived in front of an immensely tall wooden fence made of logs with one end sunk into the ground and the other end sharpened to a point. The fir tree and pine trees ran right up to this stockade, and I could see a roof behind it.

The gates slowly creaked open, and the Lamborghini drove into the yard. Greenhall was an immense wooden palace, with walls built of light-colored logs, a spacious porch, and towers topped by pointed domes. A massive, solidly built, beautiful building.

The yard was completely overgrown with tall dried grass, with just a patch of asphalt for cars. Slaven walked ahead of me along a narrow path through the yellow grass that was wilting in the cold. I followed. The werewolf walked up onto the porch, pulled on the metal ring to open the door, and gestured for me to go in.

It was warm inside, and there was a smell of dried herbs. The walls, floor, and ceiling of the spacious hallway were all made of golden wood. I wanted to go over to the wall and run my hand across the honey-colored planks to feel their smooth coolness.

Slaven walked straight through the hall, opened another door, waited for me to go in, and slipped in after me.

It wasn't large, but it was comfortable. Wood, animal skins, low benches along the walls. On the right was a stove covered with brown tiles. The door of the stove was open, and there was a heap of hot charcoal glowing inside.

Ivan was sitting on a low bench with carved legs. As usual, he was wearing a loose linen shirt and trousers of soft leather. His celebrated cloak was nowhere to be seen. The Vricolakos was staring intently into the stove, breaking up the charcoal with a long poker.

When he saw me, he nodded somberly and glared at Slaven, who seemed to shrink and suddenly become very unsure of himself. As if the only thing he really wanted to do was hide behind me or, even better, just slip away unnoticed.

I heard light footsteps and sensed the approach of another Vricolakos. When the woman came into the room, the sight of her took my breath away. She was savagely beautiful. The features of her face were somehow sharp and smooth at the same time, combining enchanting softness and wild ferocity in the same way as a cat's face. Her movements were rapid, yet graceful and relaxed.

She had green slanting eyes, like a lynx's, thick black eyebrows that shot back toward her temples, and high cheekbones. Proud, stubborn, plump lips and a thick mane of silky ash gray hair. I gasped silently when, just for a moment, I imagined that hair slipping across my skin. She exuded danger. And passion. Every muscle in her magnificent, svelte body rippled under her thin leather dress as she walked. Her long neck was encircled by a string of wooden beads.

As I—a civilized, reticent town-dweller—looked at her, I suddenly felt an echo of my own animal nature quivering in rapturous frenzy within me. Just to look at this amazing woman was a delight, and her inaccessibility roused me to white heat.

Ivan watched me with a smile, stroking his beard. He nodded at the woman and said contentedly:

"My wife."

It didn't surprise me. All the heads of the families had their lovers, concubines, and intimate advisers. But this woman really only could be the wife of the elder of the Vricolakos.

She walked slowly across to us, then suddenly swung around and slapped Slaven across the face. I thought it was for his impudent attack on the Dahanavar guest. But I was wrong.

"You lost your knife," she said in a deep, resonant voice, looking the young cub up and down. If I had seen contempt in the eyes of a woman like that, I would have wanted to hang myself in despair.

But Slaven proved psychologically more resilient than me. He just sniffed and gave her a sideways glance but didn't say anything. There was no point in making any excuses. His knife was lying in the puddle in front of my house.

Ivan waved his hand to tell his pupil to leave. Slaven immediately did as he was told, radiating profound relief. The boy was as much afraid of the mistress of the house as of the master.

The woman studied me with calm interest for a few moments, then turned around and walked into the next room.

"Sit down," said Svetlov, pointing to the bench in front of him. He pushed the door of the stove closed with the toe of his boot and put the poker down on an iron tray in the corner. "Those fireplaces of yours are no good for anything," he said.

"They just make smoke and soot. All the heat flies out the chimney."

I didn't answer. The stove gave off a dry warmth, and the charcoal inside it crumbled with a quiet rustling sound.

"The day before yesterday, one of my men was attacked," he said, gazing at me sullenly from under his shaggy brows. "I think he was killed. He was on guard duty not far away from here. I want to know what miserable dog did it."

"What do you want from me?"

"I need you to sniff things out. At the scene."

He wanted me to find out who had killed his relative. If they had killed him.

"Perhaps he's still alive. There was no body. There was a smell of blood, but he could have just been wounded."

Everything is repeated. It all comes round, as Vance used to say. Now Ivan was looking at me hopefully. As if I could bring his cub back to life again.

"All right. I'll try, but—"

"That's great," he said, slapping his knees and getting up. The wife of the head of the House came back in from the next room. She was carrying a tall clay mug and had a white linen towel across her arm. She came up to me.

"They say it is your custom to eat before work."

The blood was fresh. Not reheated, but freshly extracted from some young, strong, healthy victim. Group one, with an indescribable aroma of grass, berries, and honey. The taste of summer lingered on my tongue for a long time afterward.

"Thank you."

The woman nodded, smiled, and walked out.

"Let's go," said Ivan.

When we were in the car—an ordinary Toyota, driven by Slaven again—I looked at the brown hair on the back of the young werewolf's head and said to his elder:

"I'll do what I can, but I think you ought to ask the Cadavercitan for help. They can sense death more keenly, and if there were other casualties . . ."

Ivan frowned and shook his shaggy head in disgust.

"Rotten grave diggers! They reek of carrion. You're on good terms with them, are you?"

I said nothing. Svetlov didn't like the Masters of Death. In fact, he absolutely detested them. He was suspicious of them, and his animal instincts told him to give the Cadavercitan as wide a berth as possible.

We drove out onto the highway. There had been a frost after the previous day's sleet, and the road was a sheet of ice. The trees along both sides of the road seemed to be standing deathly still. Not just motionless until next spring, but dead. I tried to detach myself from my unpleasant thoughts. For some reason, today most of them seemed to be linked with death.

We drove for more than half an hour, then the car turned off onto a side road. Another five kilometers, and our destination appeared in front of us. A high-security factory of some kind. A concrete wall topped with barbed wire, a boom across the entrance. A security guard in a glass booth.

Slaven stopped the Toyota and got out. Three security men with automatic rifles slung across their chests walked up to him. There were people all around, in the building and in the grounds. Darting here and there, going up and down in the elevators, talking on the phones.

The icy chill of an imminent vision pricked the skin on the back of my neck. Without paying any attention to Ivan, I got out of the car and walked slowly toward the guard post. The world around me started turning gray. I think someone tried to stop me, but Slaven said something to the guards and they left me alone. Bright, slightly blurred pictures flashed in front of my eyes, and other people's feelings exploded in my body.

"Here. Two humans were killed. Men. First one, then the other."

Ivan was walking close behind me. I could hear him breathing heavily through his nose.

"Who killed them? Can you sense it? Who?"

"They were shot with a pistol. In the chest. In the head. A human shot them. A woman."

The gates opened. A four-story concrete building. The doors open wide. Another four deaths in the hallway. I sensed them immediately. All at once. The pain pierced through my body. I clutched at the desk as I waited for another vision.

"Humans. With automatic weapons."

I was scanning too deep. The human pain, fear, and despair were deafening me. Farther along the corridor, another death. And another.

Then suddenly, in one of the vestibules—animal fury and triumph, the wild pleasure of the hunt, the sweet taste of blood.

"He was here. He killed five of them, a sixth one was killed here, three over there. And then . . ."

Surprise, panic, fear. The Vricolakos had wanted to run, but he had attacked his new enemies. He hated them and he feared them. His hatred had proved stronger.

"What?" Ivan asked furiously. "Tell me."

"He's dead. First he was hit with a decomposition spell. Then they broke his neck. They took his head away with them. All the bodies were destroyed."

"Who?"

"Nachterret. Miklosh. Johan."

Ivan started growling, and the low, rumbling sounds in his throat brought me around. The world around me acquired colors, smells, and sound again. The past went away.

"Where was he lying?" Svetlov's voice sounded remarkably calm.

"Here." I pointed to the place on the floor. He walked over and stood in silence for a moment over the nonexistent body. Then, without looking at me, he asked:

"Why did they take the head?"

"As a trophy."

The werewolf slowly turned to look at me. He seemed to be balancing on the very brink of transformation into a wolf. His eyes were glowing bright yellow.

"Will you help me take revenge?"

Don't *even think about it!* Felicia's icy voice echoed piercingly in my poor, long-suffering head. *Don't you dare, do you hear me? Taking revenge on the Nachterret is an internal matter for the Vricolakos family. It has absolutely nothing to do with the House of Dahanavar. And it must stay that way.*

After Slaven drove me home, I had collapsed on the sofa, intending to rest, but I couldn't help myself and I'd told Felicia what had happened. Naturally, she knew about the attack on the laboratory, but the additional details I told her made quite an impression.

Our Lady was riding in an automobile. Or rather, she was being driven in a luxurious, spacious Cadillac. I could hear other voices, music, the sound of traffic. With a bit of effort, I could have found out exactly where she was going, but I couldn't be bothered.

It's excellent that Svetlov trusts us. You. But you must not assist his insane plans for revenge under any circumstances.

I know, but . . .

Darel, we have enough problems. What answer did you give?

I didn't say yes or no. I promised to think about it. I couldn't refuse straightaway. Ivan was too upset.

What stupid sentimentality! None of us like the House of Nachterret, but . . .

I sat down abruptly on the sofa, almost knocking one of the cushions onto a lighted candle in a tall candlestick, but I managed to grab it a couple of centimeters away from the flame.

He doesn't just dislike them, he hates them. There's a difference. They killed one of his family. And Johan cut off the head.

I'm not interested in these details. I've warned you, Darel, don't dare to help Svetlov. Or you'll have my displeasure to deal with.

Wonderful. Magnificent. I cut the link first and flung the cushion I had just rescued against the wall. I hadn't been planning to help Ivan. There was no need for her to take that tone with me.

Svetlov had thought about his revenge all the way back to Greenhall. He was dreaming about taking the high-handed Nachterret down a peg or two and making Miklosh feel the pain that he was suffering. I didn't want to upset him by suggesting that there was nothing in the world capable of making the cavalier of the night feel any kind of suffering.

"If you agree to help me, you can always count on my help. You personally."

What could I say to him?

Miklosh was one of the oldest blood brothers in the world. He possessed formidable power. He was intelligent and cunning and had absolutely no principles. It was insane to act against him openly. There had to be a plan. A very cunning and subtle plan. A perfect plan. The kind of plot that the Dahanavar Ladies wove so skillfully.

I didn't want to meddle in the politics of the Houses. Ivan's feelings were no concern of mine. But isolated details, surmises, and associations started flashing through my mind. Nothing serious. I was only amusing myself, playing an entertaining game of logic, thinking up ways of getting at Miklosh.

13

The Golden Lady

A little sincerity is a dangerous thing, and a great deal
of it is absolutely fatal.

—Oscar Wilde, "The Critic as Artist"

November 10

Felicia was standing at the window, watching the snow that was
slowly covering the city.

Yet another city. How many of them had there been over the
millennia? Prague had been the last one, but it had been destroyed. The living soul had been burned out, leaving nothing
but a dead empty shell. The mormolika accepted part of the blame
for that. She was always coolheaded in assessing her own actions: she honestly admitted her mistakes and acknowledged her
triumphs.

The snow was falling in thick, heavy flakes, covering the roads,
the trees, the buildings. Killing the smells, deadening the sounds,
transforming the world into a silent, cold desert. Intensifying her
sadness.

She had never been able to forget that city. One of the first.
The great and beautiful Mohenjo,[5] standing on the border between two lands.

---

5 Felicia is referring to Mohenjo-daro (meaning "mound of the dead" in the Sindhi
language), a city in the Indus River valley founded in 2600 BC. Excavations revealed to
Europeans the high level of development of ancient Indian culture.

Its towers and canals, sultry nights, and ferocious winds. People with hot blood, dark, blazing eyes, and swarthy skin.

They worshipped her as a goddess.

The jungle had advanced right up to the walls of the city, stubbornly clambering up the stonework and sinking its roots in between the blocks. In the shelter of its semidarkness, wild animals howled; white, waxy flowers exuded heady scents; and rotting leaves covered the ground.

Felicia closed her eyes and saw it.

A night lit up by hundreds and thousands of torches, their light shimmering on the stones of the walls and the roadway, the flanks of the horses, the slim trunks of the palm trees. The air filled with the smell of incense, hot resin, magnolia, and the sultry jungle. Fragrant rose petals falling like rain under the hooves of the four horses pulling the magnificent chariot.

She sat smiling, on a throne, under a fine canopy that fluttered in the wind. That hot wind caressed her skin and jingled the little gold bells in her hair, tossed petals and little star-shaped flowers up onto the dais. The ecstatic crowd saluted her with crazed exuberance. The warriors were scarcely able to hold back the human flood. The humans were ecstatic, reaching out their hands to her, dreaming of touching at least the hem of her dress. They saw their living goddess. Their swarthy bodies gleamed with sweat, their faces glowed with an almost childish happiness. The goddess had descended to them from her palace. Terrible but just. Wise. The one to whom it was an honor to give their blood. The one who could choose the most worthy among them and make them her equals.

Her city. Mohenjo, destroyed in ancient wars. Leaving behind nothing but heaps of stones, articles in historical treatises, and her memories. For millennia she had wandered the earth seeking its equal. But never found it. She never would. Her world had died.

A quiet knock at the door interrupted her reminiscences. Constance peeped into the room. Constance, her last child.

"I'm sorry, my Lady. Am I intruding?"

A fiery child. Curly hair like flames. Young, audacious, strong, naïve, gullible, rapturous.

"Come in, my dear."

She came in. Rapidly, but rather tentatively. Modern girls weren't taught to be feminine and graceful. They had no use for that. Almost like the Spartan women of her own youth. They also thought of themselves as equal to men. Felicia, being an Athenian, had been raised as the future mistress of a large house. A dutiful wife and caring mother.

Flora had been immoderately impulsive, too. And very young. One more child lost. How many had Felicia outlived, and how many more would there be?

"My Lady, I was looking through the documents and I found something."

"What, exactly?"

"It's the long-term program called the Golden Billion."

Felicia sighed, turned away from the window, and looked carefully at her pupil. The girl was agitated, bewildered, and embarrassed.

"Sit down."

Constance sat down, nervously rolling up the sheet of paper into a tube.

"Did you understand the essential nature of this program?"

"Yes. The elimination of the human population," Constance said without looking up at her teacher. As if she were ashamed.

"Not elimination, reduction," the mormolika said in the gentle, patient tone of voice that had long ago become a habit. "The reduction of the number of humans to one billion."

"But, my Lady! The official policy of the House forbids the killing of humans. You taught me—"

"Calm down, my dear."

"I'm sorry." Constance sat down again and smoothed her hair, as if neatness could help her maintain her equilibrium.

"We do not kill humans, and we are not going to kill them. The Dahanavar will not go out in the streets with machine guns to shoot down the human population." Felicia paused, went back to the window, and looked at the cold street, where half an hour earlier she had seen the ghosts of an ancient city strangled by the jungle. "There are too many of them. And they themselves realize that. The population of the earth is growing at a catastrophic rate. Resources of energy and other vital necessities are almost exhausted. All the mortals' wars are society's natural response to a demographic explosion. An unconscious attempt to reduce the numbers of people. The Golden Billion is their program. Drawn up with the assistance of the Dahanavar and approved more than ten years ago. The ballast has to be discarded. And we have tried to suggest how this can be done most effectively."

"I understand," Constance muttered, smoothing out the crumpled sheet of paper on the leather skirt across her knees.

She didn't understand. Once, a long time ago, Felicia had cherished every single human in *her* nation. But the old world had died. And now she had no one left to cherish.

"We have been guiding the humans for many thousands of years. And we have the right to do that. We are older, wiser, stronger, more farsighted. They try to seek harmony, but unfortunately they are not capable of achieving it on their own. Humankind is heading for catastrophe, and our purpose is to avert it. Otherwise we shall perish together with them."

"Yes, I understand," her pupil repeated, but Felicia could see that something was still bothering her. In the mirror, Constance's reflection toyed with a curly lock of hair falling down to her shoulder and looked at the mormolika tensely. "But doesn't that still mean that the family has a dual policy? Everyone thinks that we protect humans, but in actual fact—"

"You reason like Darel."

The young woman abruptly straightened in her chair and shook her ginger mane furiously. Comparison with the telepath always had this effect on her.

"You know that isn't true, my Lady. I'm just trying to get things clear."

She doesn't like the scanner, Felicia thought, not for the first time. She envies him. Thinks I value him more than her. And she thinks she's smarter than him.

"Then think with your reason, not your feelings. If the House of Dahanavar officially announces the Golden Billion program, there will be a horrendous massacre. The Nachterret and the Asiman will turn this world into hell. We wish to reduce the population peacefully, not cause a global bloodbath."

Constance thought, frowning and biting her lower lip. "And what methods would be used for the elimination—I mean, reduction?"

"We do not intend to use any physical methods. We are pursuing a policy of psychological pressure. Disaster movies, books about impending catastrophes, articles, interviews, and studies of the question by well-known and respected members of the human race—constant reminders that the end is nigh. Through the relentless repetition in the mass media and other sources of information accessible to humans, that there are too many people, we are acclimatizing them to the idea that it is time to cut back their own numbers."

Felicia never begrudged the time needed for an explanation, but she was not allowed to finish teaching her pupil this lesson.

There was a polite tap at the door, and in walked Sebastian, the mormolika's personal majordomo. He had no magical capacity, but he was pleasant to look at. A magnificent figure and a beautiful face. A tall, smooth forehead. A straight nose, a rounded chin with a dimple, plump lips. The tight curls of his hair were like fresh shavings of pine wood. His blue eyes were as transparent and pure as a child's. It was clear that behind their transparency there was nothing but open space, with nothing in it for a thought to cling to. But then, Felicia had other companions for intellectual pleasures; Sebastian was strictly a source of aesthetic delight. As strong and handsome as a Cretan bullock, willing in his endearing trust to follow her to the sacrificial altar and the priest's knife. And terrifying when his rage was aroused.

"My Lady," Sebastian said in a deep, resonant baritone, "there is someone to see you. A Nachterret. He said he has brought some very important information."

He seemed to be repeating the visitor's words. Trying to reproduce them as precisely as possible.

"For your family and for you personally. He asked me to give you this letter. He will wait until you have read it."

"Who is he?" Felicia asked, reaching out to take the letter.

"I do not know him."

Sebastian handed her a long black envelope sealed with wax. Constance stood abruptly and walked up to her teacher.

"My Lady, perhaps it would be wiser not—"

"Don't be silly, my dear. The curses of the Nachterret do not work on the Dahanavar. At least, not on me."

After carefully adjusting her tunic, the mormolika sat on the chair at the writing cabinet, opened the lid, and took out a little paper knife. Sebastian brought a table lamp and turned it on, then retreated to the far end of the room.

The envelope was as smooth and cold as a piece of polished stone. The four circles of wax at the edges bore images of hornets: the insects were arched predaciously, ready to thrust their stings into anyone who touched the letter. The image on the fifth circle of wax—at the center—was the face of Medusa, the Gorgon. Not the monster with snakes on her head, but the beautiful girl she was before she desecrated the temple of Athena. The personal seal of Hranya Balza. Miklosh Nachterret's sister.

Felicia slit open the envelope with a swift stroke of the knife. Took out the sheet of fine, silky paper and started reading.

Ten minutes later she got to her feet, still holding the letter in her hand, and gave instructions:

"Sebastian, ask the guest to come up. Constance, I need Darel. Immediately."

The majordomo bowed slightly and set off. Felicia's pupil pursed her lips angrily, which made her face ill-tempered and unattractive, but she didn't dare to disobey.

Hranya's messenger came in and looked around the room, which was decorated in the Hellenic style that Felicia was so fond of. His gaze slid over the elegant Corinthian columns decorating the walls and came to rest on the weaver's loom with an unfinished piece of canvas on it. The visitor's face expressed nothing at all, not even elementary curiosity. He was dressed simply, in a gray suit bought at some ready-to-wear shop. White salty streaks on his black shoes. Nothing remarkable about his appearance. A lowly clerk, one of thousands of similar faceless office workers. But there was fire burning in his black eyes. A powerful magician. Very powerful.

"My Lady Dahanavar," he said, bowing his head respectfully to Felicia. "My Lady . . ." Another half-bow in Constance's direction.

"Please," said the mormolika, indicating a chair. She nodded to Sebastian, who walked out quickly, closing the door firmly behind him. The Nachterret sat down and cast a brief glance at the window. The elder of the House of Dahanavar sat facing him, and her pupil took a seat some distance away.

"Have you read the letter?" the messenger asked abruptly.

"Yes."

"Destroy it."

"Naturally."

"Immediately. In front of me."

Constance shifted uneasily in her chair. She hadn't had time to look at the letter.

"If you insist."

Felicia got up and walked back to the writing cabinet. She lit a candle, showed her visitor the black envelope and the sheet of paper covered with Hranya's fine handwriting. Lit them and dropped the burning paper on a bronze platter. When it had turned to a black lump of ash, she went back to her seat. The Nachterret, who was watching her closely, relaxed, leaned back in his chair, crossed his legs, and lowered his heavy eyelids, hooding the black fire in his eyes.

"My name is Algert. I am Nachttoterein Hranya's personal assistant."

"As far as I am aware," Felicia remarked cautiously, "Madam Balza is not the head of the House and has no right to the title by which you name her."

"A perfectly fair comment," the visitor said with a smile, if his grin could be called that. "But we wish to correct that slight mis-understanding."

He looked around again, as if he were trying to tell how thick the walls were.

"I hope everything that is said here will remain between us. Indeed, within the confines of this room."

"Mr. Algert, you can be absolutely certain of it."

The Nachterret looked at her quizzically for a few moments and then nodded.

"Nachttoterein Hranya assures the Dahanavar family and Lady Felicia personally of her absolute fidelity and requests their help and support," the messenger said in a voice completely without expression. The mormolika had already read this in the letter.

"Exactly what help does the esteemed Madam Balza require?" she asked in an equally indifferent tone.

At this point, Algert's self-possession deserted him. He stood up. Walked around his chair and leaned on its back with his hands, as if it were a lecturer's podium. A purple amethyst glinted on the index finger of his left hand. On his right hand, half the little finger was missing. Strange hands. Knotted and gnarled like roots, but their former elegance was still obvious. They had been beautiful once.

"We wish to eliminate Miklosh. That vile scum! I beg your pardon, my Lady. There are very few of us. The personal friends and soldiers of Madam Hranya. We have no right to leave the area where we live, we cannot turn mortals, we do not dare create human servants. This is humiliating, and it cannot continue indefinitely."

Felicia knew the story of the downfall of the sister of the head of the Golden Hornets. Her magical power was weaker than Miklosh's, and she had been defeated by him in a struggle for dominance. But he had not eliminated her. He had exiled her instead, together with a small number of her supporters. So far, everyone had believed that she was completely under his control.

No one knew why the Nachttoter had not killed Hranya. Perhaps it was because their blood ties were so strong. Or he regarded her as a pitiful nonentity who posed no danger. In any case, Felicia believed that she must not compromise her own interests.

"My esteemed Algert, Miklosh Balza is very powerful. It seems to me that any active opposition to him would be foolhardy, to say the least."

"No, no!" The Nachterret raised both hands as if defending

himself against her audacious suggestion. "On no account. We only require the assistance of your telepath."

The door swung open without any warning, and its handle banged loudly against the wall. Darel strode into the room. His tangled hair, soaked by melting snow, hung down in matted icicles; his jeans were daubed with mud almost up to his knees; his leather jacket was covered in gleaming drops of water. He was breathing loudly, as if he had run all the way from his apartment to Felicia's house.

As he walked in, he slapped the gloves that he was clutching in his fist against his thigh, narrowed his eyes, glanced briefly at Constance, nodded to Felicia, and started staring at the visitor in a challenging manner that was almost insulting.

"Nachterret," Darel announced instead of greeting everyone. "Hranya Balza's senior pupil."

And this was the scanner, assistant to the First Elder, the face of the family. The mormolika sighed hopelessly. Sometimes he behaved impeccably, but sometimes he seemed deliberately to forget the rules of decorum. Was he trying to assert his sense of freedom and independence from the family and from her?

"Mr. Algert, this is Darel Dahanavar. The telepath you were talking about."

The messenger laughed and tightened his grip on the back of the chair.

"I realized."

Sebastian came in without making a sound and delicately took Darel's gloves. Keeping his eyes fixed on the Nachterret, Darel pulled off his jacket and thrust it at the majordomo. He took the nearest chair and dragged it noisily across to where Felicia was sitting. Sat down with his back to Constance, breathed in loudly, and said:

"Close the window. It's stressing Algert out."

The messenger smiled, obviously pleased, and said: "I would be most grateful to you."

Sebastian lowered the heavy protective screen, and the room immediately felt cozier with the sight of that black rectangle with white streaks of flying snow no longer provoking a vague feeling of unease.

"So, this is my scanner," Felicia repeated when the major-domo had closed the door behind him. "How can he be helpful to you in this matter?"

The Nachterret swayed the chair onto its back legs, as if he were testing its balance.

"Miklosh is very powerful. We want to know the limits to his abilities. How far his power exceeds the power of Madam Hranya. If it really does exceed it."

"You want me to scan the Nachttoter in order to assess his mental powers?" Darel's face was stony and his gaze seemed blank; only his lips moved. Slowly, with an effort.

"Yes."

"And if Hranya is more powerful, will you kill him? And if she isn't, will you carry on waiting?"

"Madam works hard every day. Her potential is increasing. But we cannot take any risks. I have to be certain."

The messenger looked at Felicia, who had not said anything.

"Help us, and the House of Nachterret—the new House of Nachterret—will demonstrate its gratitude."

My Lady. Darel's agitated voice broke through the thoughts swarming through Felicia's mind. *I can scan Miklosh. It would be no problem for me.*

Felicia disliked the scanner's unhesitating enthusiasm. He was sitting there, impassive and motionless. But on the inside, he was seething and sparkling with furious energy.

No problem? Are you sure?

He bristled in response to her irony. *Yes. I'm sure.*

Tell me, Darel, would your desire to go rummaging behind Balza's mental shield have anything to do with Svetlov's request to help him take revenge?

Algert was studying his ring with exaggerated concentration. He realized that an internal dialogue was taking place between the First Lady and her follower and waited patiently for the elder's answer. Constance was feeling nervous, clenching and unclenching her fingers. Her hair seemed to blaze more brightly with every minute that passed.

I have no intention of taking revenge on anyone, Darel replied calmly. And it was impossible to check if he was lying or telling the truth.

Felicia considered the proposal. If Hranya managed to destroy Miklosh, the new Nachterret would be in the House of Dahanavar's debt. If Balza killed his sister, the Dahanavar had nothing to lose in any case. Tempting.

"Mr. Algert, you will have our final answer tomorrow. I shall expect you at the same time."

The messenger nodded dourly, walked around the chair, kissed Felicia's hand, bowed to Constance, and looked intently at Darel. The scanner got to his feet and, without emerging from his working trance, said slowly:

"On the right one, a half-moon shape."

"Correct," the Nachterret said with a satisfied nod, and walked out of the room.

Constance jumped to her feet with a flourish of her fiery red curls. "What nonsense was that? What half-moon?"

Darel stretched, yawned, and rubbed the nape of his neck.

"He asked me what was the shape of the birthmark on his mistress's shoulder. He put up a *shield* and tried not to think about it, so that I couldn't read the answer in his mind. He was trying to catch me out."

"How stupid," said Constance. She started striding about the room, the tight leather skirt around her hips creaking.

"Not really." The telepath rested his head on the back of his chair. "Anyone who doesn't know my true abilities should find it quite impressive."

"You imagine that you can scan Miklosh?"

"That's not the main point," said Felicia. She got to her feet, walked across to the writing cabinet, and put out the candle that was still burning. The smell of hot wax immediately drifted around the room. "Will he be able to *evaluate* his power? As yet he has nothing to compare it with."

Darel arranged himself more comfortably in his chair. His face, an amazing combination of sharp-edged Scandinavian features and southern mobility, darkened slightly.

"First I have to spend some time with Hranya. Take her power as the starting point for comparison. Then read Miklosh and go back to his sister."

"Are you sure you can manage it?" asked Constance, sitting opposite the telepath and examining him like some rare curiosity.

"Yes, I'm sure," he declared in his usual categorical manner, then thought for a moment and added: "But I think I should do a bit of training. On someone neutral."

Constance looked inquiringly at the mormolika. "I could call Archie," she said.

The Lady smiled. This was all just a game for the two of them, and they had already started playing, without a thought for the consequences.

"Very well. Call him."

While the children played, she could think.

Constance's pupil arrived a few minutes later. He lived somewhere not far away and always showed up quickly when his teacher called. He was still completely a boy. Skinny, gangling, awkward.

Felicia took a sheet of paper out of the writing cabinet and pretended to be busy with serious work. But in fact she was simply trailing the pen aimlessly across the paper.

Archie squinted at the Lady and relaxed a little when he saw that she was paying no attention to him. They sat him down in the chair where the Nachterret had been sitting and called Sebastian.

While the junior Dahanavars amused themselves by comparing mental powers, the elder pondered the benefits that the House would reap if Hranya seized power. First, the new Nachttoterein would put her own family in order, relish her power, punish those who had helped banish her, build a new residence or refurbish Miklosh's so-called Fortress of the Moon. She would set about educating the newly turned members of the House of Nachterret. During the initial period, the Golden Hornets would be easy to control. Their alliance with the Asiman would be shaken, although Amir would certainly go running to Madam Balza with offers of friendship and collaboration. But that would come later. First of all, Felicia would make Hranya sign an agreement on terms that were highly advantageous to the Dahanavar.

Her musings were interrupted by Constance's ringing laughter. Darel was standing there, shaking his head with a serious and thoughtful expression on his face as he carefully examined the subjects of his experiment.

"This one is weaker magically," he said, pointing to the embarrassed Archie, "but his capacity will increase. But this one"—a nod in the direction of the smiling majordomo—"has already reached his ceiling. And here's the funny thing. It's as if his power has been put on standby. It will obviously erupt when he gets aroused. Sebastian, get angry. Think about something unpleasant. Come on!"

The scanner grabbed a chair and threw it at his imperturbable subject. Sebastian, still smiling, caught it and carefully put it back in its place.

"All right. Leave him alone." Constance laughed. "Now what can you say about me?"

Darel narrowed his eyes, glowered at her, and said in a strange, hollow voice: "You are a deep well. And it will take many thousands of years before it is filled."

The telepath slowly turned his head and seared Felicia with an icy glance that could pierce any defense.

"And you, my Lady, are a bottomless abyss."

The mormolika stood up, slamming down the lid of the writing cabinet, and he immediately lowered his eyes, realizing how tactless his remark had been.

"I beg your pardon. I am willing to scan Miklosh whenever you consider it necessary. Good evening."

He turned and walked out. Constance nodded peremptorily for Archie to follow her and also left the room, realizing that her teacher wished to be left alone. Sebastian switched off the ceiling light, moved Felicia's favorite armchair closer to the low table, put a lamp on it, and left without making a sound.

Once she used to love spending the time before sunrise in semidarkness. She used to love the velvety shadows slipping over the walls and lying across the floor beyond the reach of the round lamp, the rustling of the flames in the fireplace, and the blackness outside the window. But now ghosts had started visiting her in the dead hours before dawn. Reminiscences of dead children and friends. Too many of them had accumulated over the centuries. They all jostled in her memory, trying to break back through into reality.

She could have told Sebastian to leave the ceiling light turned on, but that would have been weakness. And Felicia could not afford to be weak.

The one who came most often was Catherine. A friend, almost a sister, who thought in the same way she did. Her charred black face, arms like gnarled branches, body crumbling to pieces. That was how she had remained in Felicia's memory. Saint Catherine of Alexandria. She had been burned. First they had tried to break her on the wheel, but a miracle had happened: the instrument of torture had broken down. Then they had beheaded her and committed her to the flames.

The fire had scattered sparks through the air and shot red tongues of flame up into the sky. The black smoke had billowed across the ground.

The Dahanavar magic had given her amazing powers of persuasion, and she had tried to convert humans to the Chris commandments, tried to tame the wild herd and give it human laws. They had killed her and then canonized her. And invented a wonderful legend about how Catherine had laid her own head on the executioner's block.

My poor sister. You would oppose me, if you knew what I want to do. The Golden Billion? They cannot be educated and taught; it's only possible to select the best of them and let them live a peaceful, contented life.

Felicia stood up, adjusted the folds of her tunic, and ran her fingers over the combs in her hair—they were all still in place, not one had fallen out. She walked slowly to her bedroom.

"WOLVES SHOULD BE KILLED"

There is no sin except stupidity.

—Oscar Wilde, "The Critic as Artist"

November 14

The crash of breaking china made the brush in Mr. Balza's hand tremble. Struggling to suppress his fury, he turned to the guilty party, Roman.

"Nachttoter," the servant mumbled guiltily, "I was only trying to dust it. As you told me to. But it slipped off and—"

"It would be better if your head had slipped off! That's Chinese porcelain you're smashing, you miserable wretch! What is it I've lost this time?" Miklosh gloomily surveyed the shards on the floor. "I see. Well, as a matter of fact, if it's of any interest to you, your butterfingers have just cost a unique dinner service one of its finest serving dishes. Do you realize what a rare thing that is? It's three times as old as you are! Where am I going to get another one like it? Carve it out of your body? I'd be more than glad to, if I only knew how. The only thing you're good for is killing rats! You haven't got the brains for anything else. . . . Get out of here!"

Roman abandoned his daily cleaning of the study of the head of the House and dashed for the door.

"Stop!" Balza called to him. "Where's Johan?"

"He was going to the gym. Shall I send for him?"

"Get out!"

Bonehead! Idiot! Clumsy oaf!

The desire to paint had completely disappeared. The Nachttoter put down his brush and glanced at the picture in annoyance. A green field, a narrow river, a scarlet sunset in the sky. Standing on the near bank, warriors dressed in red. Helmets with crests, long shields, spears, eagles with outstretched wings—the standards of Roman legions. And across the river, on the sandy beach, drawn up in ragged, irregular lines, the men whom the inhabitants of the Apennine Peninsula habitually referred to as barbarians. Mr. Balza had decided to immortalize one of the battles from the Marcomannic Wars.

He washed his hands thoroughly, noting with annoyance that Roman had left without even thinking about clearing up the broken porcelain. The shards were still lying on the floor. What kind of filthy pigs was he surrounded by?

"Roman!" he called.

There was no answer.

"Roman!" Mr. Balza bellowed deafeningly.

A waste of time.

To avoid the Nachttoter's anger, the wise servant had taken off as fast as he could and gone as far away as possible. Holed up in the most remote wing of the mansion, like a snail in its shell. He wouldn't put in an appearance now until tomorrow night. Miklosh shouldn't have thrown him out so hastily. This was like living in a cowshed!

Annoyed and exasperated, Miklosh walked out of his study, slamming the door behind him. The soldiers who were always in the corridor at this time all seemed to have vanished into thin air. They didn't want trouble any more than Roman did. Mr. Balza growled quietly and looked around for someone to vent his fury on.

Not a soul.

"Slobs!" he shouted, choking on his righteous wrath and borrowing a modern term he had heard Raylen use. He thought it seemed perfectly suited to the present situation. "Johan! . . . Johan, where are you, damn you!" he shouted, blinded by his fury.

Remembering that his deputy wasn't there, he strode resolutely toward the stairs leading to the fourth floor of the huge mansion. Where the gym was.

Roman had not been mistaken. He could at least be grateful for that. The landsknecht was holding his regular training session with Raylen, driving her relentlessly from one corner of the hall to another. The girl's muscular body was glistening with perspiration.

Miklosh cleared his throat with an appreciative sound. Making a blood brother break out in a sweat required a real effort.

This time, instead of her usual black leather outfit, Raylen was wearing a brief top of some thin fabric and equally brief shorts of the same material. Instead of high-heeled boots, she had on a pair of worn sneakers. Her copper-colored hair was hidden under a baseball cap, worn back to front, that bore the inscription "New York forever!" But her hands were in the usual fingerless gloves. She was clutching a shortened version of her magical battle-ax and trying to beat off Johan's powerful attacks with it.

He was wielding a heavy sword. Like the girl's weapon, it had also been created by magic.

Despite his bulky figure, Johan's movements were light and agile. He shifted from stance to stance, constantly changing the level of his assault and never allowing Raylen to switch from defense into attack and take advantage of her more formidable weapon. Miklosh could see clearly that the Black Plague was toying with his pupil, and for all her magnificent physical condition, there was no way she could match the landsknecht.

Mr. Balza curled his lips disdainfully. All this energetic pantomiming depressed him. They were fighting with metal weapons, like the sheep, no matter how magical the metal might be. Never mind Johan—he could never be cured. In his day, you had to know how to handle a sword, and he had brought his pathological love of stabbing and slicing with him down through the centuries. But the girl . . . Of course, like teacher, like pupil. She couldn't change anything. But what point was there in all this flashy display? How old was she now? He thought Johan had introduced Raylen into the family in the early forties of the last century.

He took the decision almost instantaneously. Walked out into the center of the hall and said gruffly:

"Raylen. Try me."

Johan immediately put away his sword. It simply dissolved in midair.

"Nachttoter, perhaps it would be better if—"

"Don't worry. I won't do her any harm. Raylen. Attack me!"

The girl looked at her teacher, appealing to him. Then at Mr. Balza.

"Not long ago, the Nachttoter explained very clearly to me that I should never attack the head of a House," she said cautiously.

"I see you learned that lesson well," Miklosh said approvingly. "But I'm not the Master of Death. And I'm not going to kill you! Well? Come on, then!"

She adjusted her grip on her weapon, gathered herself, and came rushing forward. Mr. Balza dodged the blow at the very last moment and maintained his distance so that the battle-ax wouldn't catch him on its reverse swing.

A fine little chick! She wasn't afraid of hurting him. She hadn't held back with her weapon, she'd struck as hard as she could, trying to hit him. She was playing for real. But Johan was nervous. Just look at him scowl. Afraid for his pupil. He could see that Miklosh wasn't in the best of moods. What an idiot. Miklosh had said he wouldn't hurt her. She was valuable material, even if she was still rough and unpolished. In time, something could be made of the girl. Miklosh was convinced of that now.

Mr. Balza didn't let Johan's pupil attack him a second time. To her absolute amazement, her battle-ax dissolved in a puff of smoke and literally slipped through her fingers. The next moment, some invisible viselike hand squeezed her by the neck and jerked her up to the ceiling. It wasn't painful, but it was annoying. Raylen had no doubt that if the Nachttoter wanted, the spell's incredibly gentle fingers could turn to steel at any moment, crushing the vertebrae in her neck.

Miklosh stood there grinning, with his hands in the pockets of his well-pressed trousers.

"Checkmate," he said in a gloating tone of voice. The head of the House had not forgotten that this copper-haired girl had beaten him at chess. "Another lesson for you. Higher magic, as we can plainly see, is much better than that mediocre rubbish you were just demonstrating to me. Nonsense like battle-axes hidden up your sleeve is all right in its own way, but it's no more than a conjuring trick. It's not for someone who has far greater magic potential than that. Yes, yes, I'm talking about you. You're capable of far more, but you keep on playing the same old trump card. Either you're too lazy and you don't want to improve— and the family doesn't need people like that—or Johan hasn't taken the trouble to teach you anything but the basic course for savages."

"I'm not a savage!" Raylen protested furiously.

The fingers squeezed her neck harder, reminding her not to forget her place.

"Did I ask you for your opinion? In any case, starting tomorrow night I intend to take over your training, since your teacher doesn't have enough time for it. It will be some amusement for me, at least. Remember, my little chick—you can only get away with this mediocre nonsense against someone at the very lowest level. There's a time and a place for everything. A battle-ax is only good against a blautsauger who has just been turned. Any blood brother with even rudimentary skill in magic will have you in the position you've been occupying for the last two minutes in an instant. Do you understand?"

"Yes, Nachttoter."

Deciding that this was quite enough for the first lesson, he let her go. The hand disappeared and the girl found herself falling. She pulled in her arms and legs, turned, and landed nimbly on her feet.

Miklosh walked toward the door, still laughing—he was obviously in a much better mood now—and on the way he reminded Johan:

"In my office. In three minutes. With the report."

WHILE he was waiting for the landsknecht, Miklosh found time to take another look at the painting and add a few strokes of the brush. His deputy came tumbling into the study and switched off his cell phone so it wouldn't annoy the head of the House. After asking permission, he reached into the refrigerator set into the wall to get some blood. Mr. Balza was not very fond of concentrates, but just in case the mansion unexpectedly came under siege by friendly families, it maintained strategic reserves that would have been the envy of any regional blood transfusion center.

"Is everything ready for the Colombian operation?" Miklosh asked, looking out the window.

"Yes. All the instructions have been issued."

"Ramon called twice. He's nervous."

"He'll be singing a different tune soon. He's allocated thirty-five of his humans for the job."

"Only humans?"

"Yes," said Johan, taking a gulp of blood. "I decided to put in forty of our mercenaries from the southwest district branch. And twenty soldiers. The plan is to transport the load during the hours of darkness. The plane at the reserve airfield has been made ready. The buyers have been notified."

"I hope I don't have to remind you that all financial operations have to bypass the Upieschi banks?"

"But of course."

Mr. Balza stopped talking and watched the snowflakes falling from the sky. It looked as if there were going to be plenty of snow this season. Those cursed forecasters kept getting it wrong about a thaw on the way. Where was this damn thaw? There was no point in even hoping it would be possible to leave the house without warm clothes at this time of the year for another two hundred years.

Raylen suddenly came rushing into the study, carrying a machine pistol.

Mr. Balza saw fit to raise one eyebrow in surprise. She had come in without knocking, and carrying a weapon, too. This he didn't understand. She might as well have brought a grenade launcher with her. The education of the younger generation really did leave something to be desired.

"Nachttoter, we have an unexpected situation!"

"You've decided to use my soldiers for target practice? How are you getting on?"

"Outsiders have broken into the grounds," she declared, taking no notice of the elder's sarcasm. "The guards at the gate have been killed."

"And you're interrupting us for a little thing like that?" Balza asked indignantly. "You're a big girl. Take the situation in hand. Capture them alive if you like. Fresh food is always welcome. Off you go."

"Nachttoter, they're not humans. According to the reports, they're wolves."

"Ah, well now, that's more interesting," Mr. Balza murmured. "How many are there?"

"We can only guess. Three have been spotted. They're somewhere in the park now. Near your hothouses. Shall I send out search parties?"

"No. On no account. Recall everyone. The soldiers and the sheep. Humans can't handle Vricolakos. We'd just be giving them a free lunch."

"It's already been done. The humans have left their posts."

"Johan, stop guzzling. Order the approaches to the mansion to be left open and say our guests must not be inconvenienced in any way. I plan to meet them in person."

While his deputies carried out his instructions, Miklosh tried to think what Svetlov's brothers could want on his territory. Breaking into Nachterret headquarters was insane. He might have expected it from Ligamentia, but not from Ivan's cubs. Although who could understand those dumb brutes? Nobody knew what went on in those wolf brains of theirs.

"Are you sure you don't need any backup?" asked Johan, taking the liberty of expressing his concern. "There are three of them, and we don't know their rank. What if they're pack leaders?"

"You've been getting too cautious recently. There are three of us, too."

There was a sudden, deafening jangle of breaking glass.

"Wonderful! Those beasts have started breaking the windows now!" Miklosh exclaimed. "Wolves should all be killed!"

They darted out into the corridor and ran past several large rooms. As they ran along the gallery, Mr. Balza glanced over the balustrade and groaned theatrically. Down the hall on the ground floor, it looked as if there were a massacre in progress or someone had just held a bulldozer race. A total shambles. The dirt was knee-high everywhere. Or at least so it seemed to the Nachttoter.

The three huge wolves caught sight of the blood brothers standing above them and made a dash for the wide stairs leading to the second floor. Trampled by the monsters' paws, the burgundy-colored Persian carpet lying on the steps didn't look so beautiful anymore.

Miklosh's blue eyes blazed in fury, and his subordinates were all the more amazed at his whiplash-taut order:

"Don't kill them!"

The first Vricolakos, running almost two lengths ahead of his comrades, flew out into the final straight. Squatting on one knee, Raylen fired two short, well-aimed bursts from her machine pistol. The bullets ripped open the wolf's face and broke his front legs.

Of course, that didn't kill him, but it stopped him for a few seconds. While the uninvited visitor regenerated, the girl skipped back into the safe space behind Johan, who was remarkably calm, and Miklosh, who was raging at the entire animal world.

The Vricolakos healed almost instantaneously and jumped to his feet, growling, and at that precise moment his companions caught up with him. Struggling to stop himself from reducing this menagerie to a heap of dust and ashes, Mr. Balza threw forward the Web of Oblivion.

The wolves became *entangled* in the spell when it fell on them and started whining in pain. Miklosh watched the disturbers of his peace thrashing about convulsively, bloody foam pouring out of their mouths. He smiled vindictively.

"You have an original approach to fighting canines," Mr. Balza said complacently, turning toward Raylen.

"Thank you, Nachttoter."

"Yes indeed. I have never—please note that I come again back to the same subject—never seen such a primitive method used, even by my own thickheaded soldiers. As if it weren't enough for these gentlemen to defile my hallway with such cynical impudence, you have to litter the place with these shell cases, too. As well as almost deafening me. Next time you decide to entertain me with your skill as a sniper, give me advance warning. I'll bring my earplugs."

Miklosh rebuked Johan's pupil more out of concern for the future than for what she'd done. In actual fact, she had helped him, although she almost certainly didn't realize it. The Web of Oblivion could not tolerate other spells in proximity. It lost strength and began to leak. If Raylen had struck with something more effective than bullets, even from the very lowest category of Nachterret spells, it was questionable if the Nachttoter could have restrained these lunatics so carefully and precisely. Anyone caught in the Web certainly suffered a few painful and unpleasant minutes, but that was all. It didn't kill them, and that was the first priority right now.

Mr. Balza had forced the werewolves out of their wolf shape, tearing the skin from the wolves so that he could see what they looked like. They were standing by the wall, holding their arms straight down by their sides. Miklosh was no Good Samaritan; he had no intention of releasing the three intruders.

He scowled as he studied the faces of his uninvited guests again.

Just as he expected, he had been paid a visit by cubs. The tall young man with broad shoulders, brown hair, and the faint beginnings of a thin beard kept throwing back his head, trying to stop the blood seeping out of his broken nose—Johan's fist was responsible for that: the Black Plague had been infuriated by the stubborn refusal of the Vricolakos to answer the Nachttoter's questions.

The strapping young man appeared rather surprised. He couldn't understand why the blood wouldn't stop and his broken nose wasn't regenerating—Miklosh was responsible for that. He had gleefully tossed this young fool who had dared to break into his home a little surprise: a trifling spell that prevented wounds from healing. Sooner or later, of course, the blood would stop and the nose would resume its original shape, but not straightaway. Let him suffer a bit first, the head of the House of Nachterret thought, chuckling to himself.

The second Vricolakos, a pale, skinny boy, kept screwing up his red eyes and glancing sideways at Raylen's breasts under the thin cloth of her top.

How does Svetlov survive when he's surrounded by pubescent cubs? Balza thought. They're almost impossible to control.

The third Vricolakos was a girl. Her biological age could only have been nineteen or twenty at the most. Her face wore the most furiously defiant expression of all. She was probably in charge. Short and beautiful, with slanting blue eyes and brown hair hanging down to her waist in a braid. Credit where credit was due—Ivan's girls were every bit as fine as Alexander Faryartos's women. For some reason, this female Vricolakos reminded Miklosh of Paula. Her body was equally magnificent. But the face was different, more subtle. Her clothes were simpler, and she smelled of raspberries and pine needles, not expensive perfume.

Mr. Balza caught himself thinking how delightful it would be to amuse himself with this little sweetie. Licking blood off her body would be a real pleasure. And he could . . . He pulled himself up short. No. He couldn't do that. A bit of self-indulgence with a beautiful fary once in a while was all right—Alexander turned a blind eye—but Svetlov was very sensitive about any insult to the women of his family. The Father of the Dogs defended the honor of his daughters as if they were fragile china dolls.

So no amusement. He couldn't even kill these animals; he would have liked to, but he didn't know who knew about the cubs' stupid escapade. If their elders knew where they had gone, and he skinned them alive, then it would be public knowledge. Killing fools was a pleasant occupation, but the House of Nachterret was not ready for war just yet. He would have to let them go, alive. It wasn't the same as killing the Vricolakos in the corporation's building. The Golden Hornets hadn't left any tracks behind them there.

The three werewolves were dressed in linen shorts, trousers, and boots. They had ritual knives hanging on their belts.

"So you still don't want to tell me what brought you to my modest abode?" Mr. Balza asked, speaking only to the girl. Her friends didn't have the brains to understand anything.

She withstood his glance in silence. It was clear that she wasn't going to say a word.

"I see . . ." Miklosh sighed. "Perhaps in your family it's in the order of things to enter someone else's home uninvited and spread filth over all the carpets."

"Nachttoter! Nachttoter!" shouted Roman, running up to Mr. Balza. "They went through the southern section of the grounds, with the English park and your hothouses."

"And?" asked the head of the House, turning cold inside.

"Those flowers from the jungle, I think—"

"The orchids are buggered," Raylen declared.

"What do you find so funny, you idiots?" Miklosh roared like a wounded rhinoceros. "Johan! Give me the phone. Quick!"

The first deputy held out his cell phone.

"Switch it on! And dial Svetlov!"

He saw the girl start, the tall young man stop sniffing, and the sexually obsessed boy turn even paler.

"Hello, Ivan? Guess what I'm doing right now? . . . Oh, but it is your business! I've got an entire zoo on my hands here! . . . Yes. Three of your little cubs decided to frolic on the grounds of my mansion. . . . Yes, yes! You're right. They're yours. . . . Don't treat me like a fool! Do you think I can't tell the Vricolakos from any other family? . . . What did they want? How should I know? They won't talk. Perhaps they're feeble-minded. . . . So you don't know? Just as I suspected. Very well. Let me bring you up-to-date. They made an attempt on my life. . . . Yes, I know that's absurd. But apart from that, they have distracted me from important business and damaged my property! . . . What am I going to do? You tell me. . . . Amicably? You have to be joking. . . . You offer me your personal apologies! What good is that to me? My entire stock of breeding plants has been destroyed! Sixty years of work down the drain! Do you know what it takes to raise a decent orchid in this day and age? . . . Yes . . . Yes . . . No . . . Why should I turn a blind eye to their crime? . . . Yes . . . We can . . . What? All right, agreed. . . . No. You can tell them that yourself!"

Miklosh lifted the phone to the girl's ear with a contemptuous gesture. She almost jumped up in the air when she heard Ivan's furious growling. It was only the spell that stopped her.

"Yes, Father. Sorry. . . . All right. Straightaway. We're sorry, Nachttoter. We offer you our apologies."

"How gallant of you to say that, after you've already ruined the Persian carpet. Hello, Ivan? . . . Yes, she did. . . . All right, I'll let your zoo go. But remember that if they turn up here again, I won't go easy on them next time. I'll kill them, or send them to the slaughterhouse. And one other thing! Do something to protect their sanity. Have them inoculated against rabies!"

He broke off the connection.

"Johan, send the bill to the Vricolakos family tomorrow. Payment for the windows, the carpets, the broken vases, for cleaning up the dirt, the ruined hothouse, and the plants that were destroyed. Don't forget to include moral damages. And put in a point specifying the items we have bought for disinfecting the premises. I can't even imagine what pests and parasites they dragged into my house on their paws. And send a complaint to the Regenant for the next meeting of the council. Urgent. The Nachterret protest against the conduct of the Vricolakos family. Raylen, take these smart kids' knives."

"They're our property!" the husky young man exclaimed indignantly.

"Tell me more!" Miklosh shouted at him. "Haven't you got enough problems already?"

The Vricolakos girl growled quietly at her comrade, and he shut up. Svetlov had obviously been really complimentary to her, and the three were in for a grilling when they got home.

Mr. Balza removed the spell.

"Get out of here. If I see you again, I'll hang your skins by my fireplace. Raylen, see them to the gates."

He watched the miserable werewolves leave. They obviously weren't looking forward to facing Svetlov's clear-eyed gaze. But that Vricolakos girl really was good-looking. It was a pity. A great pity everything had turned out the way it did. But he could still have his bit of fun with someone else.

"Johan," Miklosh asked, "do you remember Paula?"

"The Faryartos?"

"Yes. I'd like to have a talk to her. Only not today. And not here. Arrange it. But only after you have the mansion looking respectable again."

15

THE HEART OF AN ARTIST

An artist's heart is in his head.

—Oscar Wilde, "The Millionaire Model"

An idea that is not dangerous is unworthy of being
called an idea at all.

—Oscar Wilde, "The Critic as Artist"

November 24

Paula was sitting in a small, cozy café. The décor had a maritime
theme. There were fishing nets and little ships hanging on the
ceiling, and dried fish, seaweed, and shells on the walls. And
candles in bottles on the tables. From where she was sitting, she
could see a picture of a pseudo-Venetian landscape, with the in-
evitable gondola gliding across the water.

The fary found it painful to look at, but she kept looking. She
hated Venice. A damp, rotten, filthy city. The tourists were shown
only the glossy side—the façades of the buildings and the statues.

She had seen the real Venice. Canals full of sluggishly heaving
stagnant water with orange peels and beer cans floating in it.
Stone walls overgrown with slimy, reddish brown moss. Buildings filled with the smell of damp plaster that fell off and lay in
lumps on the swollen floors. Buildings the sun almost never shone
into.

Paula kept staring at the picture, and her dislike for her native
city was reinforced by her dislike of her vampire brother. She
hated the sight of Darel almost as much as the sight of Venice.

The Dahanavar's mental call had come today, when she was
getting ready to go to the theater.

I have to see you. Immediately! She could feel his turbulent energy pricking at the inside of her head.

I'm sorry, she replied icily. *I'm busy.*

This is important. Believe me. I have a business proposition for you. A very attractive one.

Apart from telepathy, he obviously possessed the gift of persuasion as well. Paula had no idea why she had agreed. The Dahanavar had named the time and the place, and now here she was sitting in this stupid little café, waiting for him. And already thinking for the third time that if he wasn't there in five minutes, she would leave.

"Hi," the familiar voice said close to her ear. "Sorry, I was delayed. There's traffic in the center."

Darel pulled out a chair with a clatter, sat down facing her, and heaved a loud sigh. He smiled at the waitress who came trotting across to their table and ordered a whiskey. The girl in the neat professional apron over her blue dress beamed, as if he had offered her a part in a movie, and ran off to get his order. The Dahanavar telepath had a remarkable effect on humans. After talking to him for just two minutes, they already adored him. It was absolutely incredible.

Usually, other people's unique abilities filled Paula with admiration, but this time all she felt was irritation.

"If you called to criticize me again for turning Vance, then—"

"No." He set his elbows on the table and leaned closer. His blue gray eyes radiated a magnetic attraction, his Scandinavian features—which, she had to admit, were quite attractive—glowed with passionate inspiration. "Paula, you are a beautiful, intelligent, wonderful woman."

What a fine beginning! Her irritation was overlaid with surprise, suspicion, and a little bit of pleasure. Just a tiny little bit.

"You're a perfect fary." He leaned even closer, and now she

could see the spark of insanity glinting in his eyes. "I need your help."

"Help?"

"I want you to seduce Miklosh Nachterret."

Paula dropped her purse, but in her astonishment she didn't even notice.

"Are you out of your mind? I'm leaving."

The fary tried to get up, but he managed to catch hold of her wrist and hold her in her seat.

"Don't you even want to know what I'm offering for this favor?"

"Favor? You call this a favor?"

The waitress came over to the table with a tray. Paula stopped talking. Darel let go of her hand. The girl put down a glass in front of Darel, flashed a blinding smile at him, and walked away.

"How dare you!"

As if he weren't listening, he leaned down, picked up the purse that was still lying on the floor, and examined it as he said:

"If you can win Miklosh's trust, I'll do you a huge favor."

"Yes? I'm afraid even to guess what it might be."

She grabbed her bead-embroidered purse out of his hands and made another attempt to get up.

"I'll help you master the higher magic of the Faryartos."

Paula froze, feeling the palms of her hands turning cold. "You'll what?"

Darel smiled broadly and gazed into his whiskey glass with exaggerated interest.

"You've been in the House quite a few years already, but you still can't grasp the mystery of art. It's beyond the reach of your mind and your heart. You make a great effort, you try your damnedest to learn the magic, but unfortunately . . . and after all, you hoped that if you learned the Faryartos magic, you could get back your desire to sing—you know, that remarkable feeling you get in your chest that makes your voice really *ring*!"

He grabbed her by the hand again, and his eyes blazed with diabolical fire. Paula shuddered, spellbound, and gazed at the Dahanavar.

"You'll be able to alter reality. Create masterpieces in life, not just on canvas. Rewrite people's lives like the plots of books. Kill with your voice, like the Sirens, arouse love with your singing. You'll be a worthy female companion for the maestro!"

Paula tore her hand out of his hot, dry palms and turned her eyes away with an effort. She ran her tongue over her dry lips. "How can you do it?"

"I'm a scanner. I can read Alexander's emotional state and understand the principles of fary magic. Then pass on to you the feelings and thoughts, the subtlest variations in mental vibrations. *Implant* the knowledge in you."

The girl clicked the catch of her purse open and shut without saying a word. The temptation to accept the Dahanavar's insane proposal was immense. He really did know how to convince and tempt. She was on the very point of agreeing, but she still had doubts.

"I'm afraid of Miklosh. He's a bastard."

"A sadist and a thug." Darel put his hand over her wrist, focusing her attention on him again, and she looked up obediently. "I know. But you have caught his eye. That time at the exhibition. Now he wants to see you again."

"How do you know about the exhibition? And about him?"

"I get a lot of information from talking with people and all the others. There's nothing incredible required. I just want to know his weaknesses, his passions, his attachments. All the particulars. And besides that, by spending time with him, you'll find out lots of useful things for your House. You can win the support of the Nachterret. Alexander would be glad to have such a powerful ally."

She still felt doubtful. Instinctively, as a matter of self-survival. But the decision had almost been taken. Darel could feel it. And he carried on persuading her.

"I don't think he would find me interesting."

"Let me repeat. You are an intelligent, beautiful woman, and you're a fary."

Paula stopped trying to free her hand. Darel's fingers were holding her wrist, and there was an electrifying current flowing through them, warm and pleasant. The Dahanavar's voice was trembling as his emotions overflowed. How simple it was! He was only being sincere. He believed in what he was saying. He was enthralling her, drawing her into the whirling vortex of his feelings.

"There's something about your suggestion I don't like at all."

"I have no right to insist. You don't have to agree. But someday you'll regret it. Sooner or later he'll come for you himself."

"How can you know that?" What infuriated Paula most of all was his cast-iron self-assurance. Darel Dahanavar—the ultimate source of truth.

He smiled. He knew all about her unease and annoyance.

A mirror! He was nothing but a mirror. He reflected what the other person wanted to hear and feel.

"I just know, that's all. You can't possibly imagine how many unspoken thoughts and desires there are just floating around. The simplest word can trigger an entire vortex of associations, emotions, and images from the past. I see them and I remember them."

"That must be hard on you, then." The last thing she wanted was to get into the details of what he felt while he was at work. But just for an instant, she imagined the avalanche of thoughts and feelings that was constantly rushing at him. And a feeling of sympathy for the telepath suddenly broke through her dislike.

He let go of her hand and glanced at the next table, where two men in formal business suits were sitting. He frowned. Looked at Paula again. The translucent springtime ultramarine had faded from his eyes. They were dark gray now.

"Lots of people ask me about that."

Apparently she had asked an improper question. He probably didn't want to talk about the subject. The fary didn't insist on getting an answer. Especially since she was concerned about more serious matters.

"If Miklosh finds out that I'm spying on him . . ."

"He won't. We won't meet, we won't talk. You only need to call me in your mind, and then think about the Nachttoter, remember things. But I'll do the assessment and analysis and draw the conclusions. All very convenient and absolutely safe. By the way, he'll try to exploit you in his own interests, too."

"I know."

Paula shifted her shoulders as if she felt chilly, although she was wearing an angora sweater and it wasn't cold in the room. "But where's the guarantee that after I keep my promise, you won't forget yours?"

Darel was suddenly uncommonly serious. The smile that was constantly straying across his face disappeared.

"I always keep my promises. I give you my word. And apart from that, I'm very curious to take a look deep inside the magic of the Faryartos."

And Paula believed him.

"All right. I promise to think about it."

He took hold of her hand delicately, raised it to his lips, and kissed it. Very gently.

"It's a deal, signorina."

* * *

HE came for her two nights after her meeting with the Dahana-var. That huge bald Johan with the beard, the one she found so disgusting and frightening at the same time.

Paula was getting ready to go to the theater. She was sitting in front of the mirror in her bedroom, carefully putting on her lipstick, when the door swung open and Balza's deputy appeared in the doorway. He looked around the room contemptuously and commanded her:

"Get ready. The Nachttoter wants to see you."

The first thing she felt was surprise. Darel was right! Miklosh was interested in her. The second feeling was indignation. How dare this hoodlum in dirty boots come bursting in brazenly without even bothering to knock? This was her house! And she wasn't the Nachterret's property.

She had not been born when proud, ancient Rome was overrun by the barbarian hordes, who left muddy streaks behind them as they tramped across the white marble in their crude boots. They had just burst in without bothering to ring, too. But the memories of her ancient blood proved stronger than her reason. A red mist of fury appeared in front of her eyes. The fear and weakness dissolved in it.

Paula slowly got to her feet. "Tell Nachttoter Miklosh that if he wants to see me, he can send his invitation in a more civilized fashion."

Johan cursed quietly and spat on the floor in front of his feet, then simply walked up, grabbed hold of her without saying a word, twisted her arm behind her back, and hauled her away.

The fary couldn't possibly have imagined anything more humiliating. She cried out and tried to jerk free and was immediately struck with a mild magical blow. Scarlet circles appeared in front of her eyes, and she gasped for breath.

Her knees buckled. Johan picked her up without the slightest effort, threw her across his shoulder, and carried her downstairs.

The Nachterret's stone-hard shoulder pressed into the girl's stomach, her hair trailed across her face, and the pungent smell of Johan's leather cloak began to make her feel sick.

If I had magic, I could resist! But like this I'm just a puppet! Sweet, pretty Columbina with her beautifully painted porcelain face.

There was a black Mercedes waiting outside the entrance. Johan dumped the fary rather carelessly on the backseat and tossed a fur jacket he had picked up in the hallway onto her knees. He got in beside her and slammed the door. Squeezed her warm, defenseless neck in his cold hand.

"You'll do everything the Nachttoter tells you to do. If he doesn't like it . . ." The fingers pressed down painfully on the carotid artery. "If you get catankerous and start kicking up . . . I'll drain out all your blood and put acid in you instead. Understand?"

Paula closed her eyes.

Alexander! Maestro! Help me! The teacher usually heard his pupil's call immediately. They were tuned to the same wavelength, bound by the kinship of blood.

Paola? Even in mental communication her name had that melodic ring—Paola. *What's wrong?*

Maestro! Johan is taking me to Miklosh. I can't go. I don't want to!

He understood and said nothing for a moment, feeling.

I'm sorry. I can't help you right now.

She hadn't expected any other answer. The magic of the Fary-artos was passive. Alexander would have been helpless in an open duel. He wouldn't put himself at risk even for her. If the maestro was killed, what would happen to the family? Paula understood all this, but her throat tightened in bitter disappointment.

She couldn't feel Alexander's presence anymore. He had gone, no doubt regretting that he couldn't come to his pupil's rescue.

Darel will teach me the higher magic, she thought despairingly, and then no one will dare to humiliate me.

"Understand?" Johan repeated, giving her a gentle shake.

"I understand," the fary said soundlessly, with just her lips.

Paula's neck was released, and the pain and weakness left her body. She threw the fur jacket across her shoulders, shifted along the seat, and turned her face away from the Nachterret. Her eyes suddenly felt hot, and the streets rushing past outside the window began to blur. The girl squeezed her eyes tight shut, took a deep breath, and drove the fury, frustration, and humiliating helplessness as deep inside her as she possibly could. She had to be self-assured, enchanting, and agreeable. Otherwise Mr. Balza would find her company boring.

She was being driven through some dark back alleys. Fine, powdery snow was falling from a gray sky, swirling into little white tornadoes. How early winter was this year!

Paula was not taken to the central residence of the Nachterret. Naturally. Miklosh valued his privacy and safety too much. She may be only a pitiful fary, but who could tell what she might happen to see in the House's holy of holies? Security above all else. Paula's blood was still boiling with hatred: she just couldn't calm down.

They drove along the embankment of the river with its respectable old mansions. She caught a glimpse of the glass cube of the International Trade Center.

The Mercedes halted on a quiet street in front of railings, behind which she could see a two-story building surrounded by old poplar trees. The gates opened slowly, parting with a quiet metallic creak to let the car through. It drove a few meters along a broad drive and stopped in front of the entrance. Johan clambered out first and held the door, waiting for Paula to get out. The icy covering of the tarmac crunched under her shoes. The cold wind scalded her face and tousled her hair.

The silhouettes of the trees cast dark, knobbly shadows of the mansion. As if the frozen phantoms were hugging the gray walls, hoping to warm themselves by drawing at least a little warmth out of the stone. There were stone lions lying on each side of the wide porch. Their good-natured toothless faces smiled, their blind eyes gazed straight ahead. One of them had lost a piece of his playfully curved tail, the other had no ears. Sprawling above the entrance was a mermaid with a broad, flat face and the sumptuous form of a beauty in a canvas by Rubens.

Johan opened the door for Paula, just wide enough for her to squeeze through between him and the doorpost. The Nachterret gave an evil laugh, examining her as if he were thinking what he would do with her if she failed to please his lord.

A spacious empty hall, lit by a crystal chandelier. Ashwood parquet gleaming with polish. An abstract design on the walls. If you looked closely, you could make out the forms of Golden Hornets in the meaningless tangle of lines.

A girl dressed in black leather was sitting on a broad sofa in the hallway. The slits in her skirt revealed the long, muscular legs of a gymnast or swimmer, the corset forced her full breasts up and together, focusing attention on them. A spiked collar. High lace-up boots. A long leather coat. A tangle of short red hair. A coarse-featured face. At any other time, Paula would have acknowledged that the girl was provocatively attractive, but now she just seemed aggressively vulgar.

The female Nachterret cast a contemptuous glance at the visitor, got up slowly, strolled over to her, and looked her up and down.

"The Nachttoter's waiting." She had a slightly gruff voice. Not without a certain sensuality to it. "Upstairs. The second door."

Paula thanked her with a smile, and as she started walking up the steps, she heard the girl sneer derisively behind her: "Filthy whore."

They all think I'm a nobody. Just a little bit better than a human, who's nothing but a dumb animal to them. She suddenly felt passionately grateful to Darel. His proposal gave her at least some hope of winning back her dignity. I have a chance to take my revenge. Remember all the humiliations and pay them back. That's better than swallowing all the insults in silence and playing the part of a seductive Columbina.

Miklosh was waiting in the room, which was lit by the fire in the hearth. On the right, by the wall, there was a huge bed. On the left there was a table: the two goblets standing on it were surrounded by a faint glow. That meant there was blood in them, and the vessels were being kept warm by a special spell.

He was wearing a long maroon dressing gown with a broad belt and, as far as the fary could see, nothing else. A cute, slim adolescent with light blond hair. A smooth, thin face with an exalted expression. But he was actually a malicious, dangerous, vindictive madman. Paula shuddered in loathing at the thought that she would have to sleep with him. But she controlled the expression of her face far too well to show it.

This would have been easier for her earlier, before the conversation with the Dahanavar. She would only have had to play her usual role. Be cautious, smile, grovel to the almighty Nachttoter, guess his desires and his thoughts. That swine Darel had promised her power, and now instead of the old icy calm of "I'm above your contempt," she could feel insane hatred and rebelliousness blazing inside her. I am the same as you. I'm just as good as you! You can't just ignore what I feel. Miklosh, you have to respect me.

"Good evening, Nachttoter."

He examined her greedily, without saying anything. Paula threw off the fur jacket with a shrug of her shoulder. It slid down her body, which was encased in a thin blue evening dress without the slightest hint at any underwear. The fary threw back her head, setting her hair shimmering in a rustling silky wave. It was as soft and dark as the fur lying in a gleaming heap at her feet.

Miklosh came closer, sank his fingers into her hair, pulled her head back with a jerk, and lunged at her neck. His sharp fangs tore through her skin. Paula groaned. It could have been taken for a moan of pleasure, and that was how the Nachterret understood it. His hands ripped the dress apart with a cracking sound. He cast aside the tatters and flung Paula onto the bed. Onto the silk cushions. The girl felt the smoothness of the expensive bedclothes against her naked skin.

The Nachttoter stood over her for a few seconds, and his face slowly contorted into an expression of sadistic pleasure. His pupils distended, turning his eyes black, his nostrils flared, her blood slowly spread across his thin lips. He's going to kill me, Paula thought with calm resignation, and smiled at the Nachterret tenderly and seductively.

Miklosh swung around rapidly, walked over to the table, grabbed a goblet, came back to the bed, and splashed the contents of the goblet onto Paula's body. She shrieked in surprise. The warm blood flowed across her breasts, her stomach, her hips and thighs, soaking into the bedsheets in scarlet patches. Miklosh started growling quietly in excitement and delight. He tore off his gown and fell on her, causing her pain with every movement, touch, and kiss.

The loud scream of despair trembling in her throat could find no way out. She was in a blood-soaked bed with a Nachterret. What humiliation could possibly compare with that? Her welltrained body did everything that was necessary. Arched in passion, thrashed in convulsions of sham pleasure, pressed itself passionately against Miklosh. He greedily licked the blood off her body. And deep in her soul, the girl squirmed in loathing, fear, and hatred.

Then suddenly everything inside her exploded into deafeningly loud music. A cello and a violin. Heartrending, screeching sounds. Miklosh had crushed Paula's shield in order to maximize his pleasure. Curse the sadistic madman! The fary's pain, humiliation, and blood weren't enough for him; he wanted to hear his own music. Immerse himself in it, wallow in it.

Paula didn't know how much time passed before he let her go. He gave a deep sigh of satisfaction and stretched out on the wet, red sheets. Then he yawned, sat up, shook the red droplets off his chest in disgust, got to his feet, and walked into the next room. A few moments later, she heard the loud sound of water from behind the door.

Paula lay on her back, looking at the ceiling. The music stopped playing inside her, leaving nothing but emptiness, weariness, and pitiful crumbs of hate. The blood on her skin was drying. When I have magic, I won't tell anyone about it. I'll lock myself in at home and mix reality with fiction and create a deadly perfect work of art. And the House of Nachterret will have the leading parts in it.

The fary got up. Wiped herself off as well as she could with the sheet. Gathered the tatters of her dress and threw them into the fireplace. The thin material flared up and crumbled instantly into ash.

At home, Paula stood under the jets of hot water for a long time. She tried not to think or feel, just meditate and enjoy the warmth.

Everything around her was made of pink-veined marble. A huge mirror covered one entire wall. There was a shelf stacked with bottles of perfume, aromatic salts, and liquid soap. A pile of fluffy towels. She wondered what Vance would say if he could see her now. If he found out about everything.

She had turned him. Made him her equal. And he was happy. For the time being. Delighted with his new abilities and strength. He had lost his former annoying clumsiness, his human limitations, and the crude simplicity of his facial features. He had become elegant, dashing, attractive.

Paula sank slowly to the bottom of the bath, pulled her knees up to her chest, and curled into a ball. The water beat down on her head and shoulders and ran down her face. She missed Vance. The old, clumsy Vance, madly in love with her, who was like a bear. She missed the human being. She wanted him the way he was. Touching her hand reverently, gazing into her eyes adoringly. Strong, helpless, talented, stubborn, ready to defend her against the whole world, although he knew nothing about that world. But he didn't exist anymore. A new Vance had appeared. Hemran of the House of Faryartos. Her equal. The same as all the others. The old, real Vance was dead. She had killed him. With her own hands.

Paula put her hand over her mouth and burst into sobs.

DAREL'S call caught her by surprise. Through the noise of the water, through her misery and despair, she heard a cheerful, contented-sounding voice.

Paula!

The fary switched off the shower and wiped her wet face with her hands.

Yes.

Has something happened? Of course, as a telepath, he would sense the despondency in her voice.

Happened? She jumped up and tore her dressing gown off the hook on the door, fumbling at the sleeves as she tried to put it on. *You want to know what happened?* She tied her belt tightly. *All right. I'll show you!*

She flung her memories at the Dahanavar. Everything, from the very beginning. From Johan's mocking grin to somebody else's blood flowing slowly across her body. *How about that, telepath? Do you like it? Do you enjoy reading my emotions?*

Darel felt the pain together with her. Paula knew that. And the hideous, repulsive humiliation.

Happy now? Have you found out what you wanted?

I've found out a few things, he said with something of an effort, as if he had been running for a long time and was struggling to get his breath back.

She sat on the edge of the bath. Drops of water fell off her wet hair, tickling her neck.

Now will he leave me in peace?

That's not likely now.

The fary realized she was tired. Living through the memories of her meeting with the head of the Nachterret had been too hard. Her anger and hatred had given way to total apathy.

You need to eat, Paula.

She got up without replying and walked slowly into the bedroom. Lay down on the bed without taking off her dressing gown. *It's not for you to give me advice. You got what you wanted, now get out of my thoughts and my memory.*

Paula fell asleep without even realizing it. Closed her eyes and tumbled down into the darkness. She thought she heard someone call her. It could even have been Alexander, but she didn't have the strength to answer his call.

She slept for the rest of that night and the whole day and woke up the next evening with the kind of intolerable hunger that could turn even an exquisite, enchanting fary into a ravening beast. It had nothing in common with human hunger pains and spasms in the stomach.

She jumped up and dashed for the refrigerator.

Paola, can you hear me?

Alexander. At just the wrong moment. She pictured herself—her hair in a mess, wearing a crumpled gown, pale-faced with dark rings under her eyes, clutching a crudely ripped-open pack of donor's blood, and in an absolutely foul mood.

Maestro! I'm sorry, I can't talk now. I'm very hungry. With your permission, let's talk later. Please!

The minimal proprieties had been observed. Alexander tactfully allowed her time to eat and tidy herself up. He couldn't do anything to help me, Paula thought, still trying to persuade herself, as she squeezed the final drops of blood out of the plastic bag into the glass. He's genuinely concerned about me. But how sick I am of my own weakness! I could almost envy that Nachterret girl in the black leather bodice. She wouldn't have allowed anyone to treat her in such a contemptuous fashion!

Her venomous thoughts were interrupted by a brief ring at the doorbell downstairs.

"Well, now who is it?"

Not Vance. He was supposed to be busy at the theater today. At the evening show. And not Alexander.

The fary walked downstairs, switching on the light as she went. She stumbled over her own shoes lying in the way. One heel was missing. She wondered when she could have broken it. She threw away the shoe angrily. Pressed the button of the intercom and then, out of an innate habit of being courteous no matter what her mood, asked rather politely:

"Who's there?"

"Miklosh," came the absolutely unbelievable reply.

For a moment Paula stood there, staring blankly into space. Then she recovered from her stupor and grasped what was happening. The Nachterret! Here! On the other side of the door! She felt like running away, locking herself into the farthest room, and pretending there was no one in the house. And it was only after this fit of shameful cowardice that she suddenly realized: she looked awful. She wasn't dressed. Her hair was a mess. He had caught her off guard again. But she couldn't possibly put this off.

Paula summoned all the magic she could manage, *splashed* it on herself, unlocked the door, and stepped back. Miklosh came in, followed by a blast of icy air that chilled her bare legs. Through the open door she saw an automobile, a black limousine, parked in front of the house.

Mr. Balza was wearing a long beige coat, casually unbuttoned. And a suit one tone darker. There were snowflakes melting on his shiny brown shoes. He was holding a bunch of orchids wrapped in transparent cellophane. The unexpected guest took a step forward, screwing up his eyes. He couldn't understand why Paula looked slightly blurred, as if she were surrounded by some kind of glowing haze. He could see her general form, but he couldn't make out the details. Her simple magic had helped conceal her disheveled and untidy appearance.

"Nachttoter Miklosh, what a surprise!"

"Are you alone?" he asked, slowly moving forward and continuing to examine her cautiously. The fary retreated slowly in front of him.

"Yes. Go on through. Upstairs, the first room on the right. I'll be there in five minutes. Please forgive me, I wasn't expecting guests."

And she dashed away. It was a rather strange sight as the magically glimmering vision flew up the steps and disappeared into the dark corridor.

If the Nachterret wasn't a complete blockhead, he ought to understand that a girl needed time to tidy herself up. Paula grabbed a red dress and suddenly realized exactly what she had said to Mr. Balza. She had almost repeated what the girl in black leather had told her the night before at the mansion: "Upstairs. The second door . . ." The fary laughed when she realized how absurd the situation was. She had told the head of the most powerful family to wait, and he was willing to do as she said.

I shouldn't be laughing, Paula thought as she pulled on her dress, there's no guarantee that after he's waited a few minutes he won't go berserk and wreck the entire house. Although . . . he didn't break in. He rang the doorbell politely, brought me flowers.

There was no time to make up her face, so she overlaid it with a light cobweb of magical glamour. She combed her hair and went to the sitting room.

Miklosh was sitting in an armchair, examining the toe of his shoe with a bored expression on his face. When she came in, he got slowly to his feet, picked up the bouquet off the floor, and walked across to his hostess, eyeing her with obvious pleasure. He handed her the flowers. The orchids were white, with bloodred centers and strangely curved petals that looked as if they were made of wax. It was hard to call them beautiful.

"Thank you." Paula took the flowers cautiously and looked around for a vase.

"No need to put them in water," the Nachterret said, looking at her neck with a slight smile. "They're already dead."

The fary couldn't tell if he was joking or talking seriously, but she immediately felt like flinging the bouquet away. Naturally, she didn't actually do it. Turning away from Miklosh, she set the pale stalks in the narrow neck of a jug standing on the low table. She straightened up and immediately felt the touch of his cold fingers on her neck. What she really wanted to do was shake his hand off her, but, as always, she restrained herself.

Another light touch. This time on her hair.

"Your perfume is very nice."

"Gucci," she replied, swallowing the bitter lump of revulsion that was stuck in her throat.

"And your blood is sweet."

He swung her around abruptly to face him, and Paula saw his eyes very close. Cold, with that same whitish tinge as the orchids. In her mind she heard the first, timid sounds of violins. Adagio, in D minor.

"Your Alexander phoned me. He tried to defend his beloved

pupil." Miklosh emphasized the word "beloved" with contempt as he continued stroking the hollow on her neck between the collarbones. "Accused me of cruelty. I replied that he created you for pleasure and amusement. Isn't that right? So I used you for exactly what you were intended for. But I think I really was a bit rough. Or do you like to be treated like that?"

The Nachterret squeezed her waist painfully and pulled her against him. He was starting to turn berserk again. The memory of Alexander had infuriated him. So the maestro really was concerned about me? He tried to defend me?

"I don't like the color of your eyes. I can't stand brunettes. I don't like short hair. You're too tall. I despise your House. So then why, *Donnerwetter,* am I so attracted to you? . . . Well? Answer me!"

He flung her away. Paula stumbled over a cushion lying on the floor. Fell into an armchair. Apparently she had managed to drive Balza into a rage after all. The infuriated Nachterret stood over her, looking down. He still didn't understand that it was her charm as a fary that was working on him, but he was already starting to resist.

"The Faryartos are stronger than you think," the girl said in a quiet voice, looking up at him.

Miklosh leaned over her and gripped the armrests of her chair. Paula thought abstractedly that even though he was so slightly built, he could easily throw the chair out the window with her in it.

"You're nobodies. Cowardly, weak, good-for-nothing, miserable wretches. You're nothing! I could strangle any one of you with my bare hands. And he won't even think of defending himself. He'll just whine for mercy."

She looked into his eyes, which were white with fury, and smiled. Realizing that this smile made the Nachterret even more furious.

"But by the way, Nachttoter, you came here with flowers and an apology for being so rough."

The short slap, with almost no swing to it, flung her head against the back of the chair. Her hair swung across her face, and her cheek caught fire.

"I have never had any weaknesses, and I never will," he declared indifferently. Almost indifferently. And walked out of the room.

A minute later, the door downstairs slammed. She heard Balza's angry voice, the slam of a car door, the sound of an engine, and the crunch of ice under wheels.

Paula stood up, straightened her hair, went to the window, pulled back the curtains, raised the steel blinds with an effort, and swung open the heavy shutters. A fresh, frosty wind blew into the room. The fary went back to the table, took the dead orchids out of the jug, and flung them outside into the street. The flowers landed on the snow and merged into its whiteness.

The stream of air went rushing around the sitting room, tangling the curtains, jangling the pendants of the chandelier, ruffling the girl's hair. She stood at the window and looked at the snow clouds drifting slowly toward the city and then cried out loudly in her mind. As loudly as she could.

Darel! . . . Darel!

The reply came instantly. As if he had been waiting for her call.

Yes, Paula?

I need power. Now! Immediately!

The Dahanavar paused for a moment. He was probably trying to make sense of the insane turmoil inside her. And then she suddenly felt a warm touch that wasn't physical. As if a thin stream of heated air had entered the chilled room and slid across the icy hands. Darel was trying to comfort her.

Shall I come over?

No! I don't want you to be seen here. And I don't want any-body's pity! You don't really care what I feel. You're only defending yourself against my pain, because you feel it together with me.

Then let's meet at Alexander's place. His voice sounded less concerned now. *I've got an excellent excuse for going there.*

All right.

See you there, then. And Paula, don't forget to close the window.

She laughed at his concern and slammed down the blinds.

THE taxi arrived in fifteen minutes. In that time, the fary had managed to tidy herself up and calm down a little. Forty minutes later, she was at Alexander's mansion.

He was waiting in the yellow study.

The picture by the unknown talented artist was still hanging on the wall. A girl in a white tunic in front of a marble column about to fall at any second.

Her teacher was not alone. But his guest was already leaving. Paula started when she saw who it was. She hastily stepped aside to let the great master out. As he walked by, he looked right through her with his piercing blue eyes, smiled at something, and quietly closed the door behind himself.

The girl had seen him only twice. She hadn't talked to him. She hadn't dared. She had only looked at him adoringly from a distance, delighted that she could be in the same room as a creative genius. Leonardo lived a very solitary life. He met with almost no one in this world that was alien to him. Alexander said he had retreated into mysticism. Almost created his own reality, where he spent all his time.

When the visitor's steps had died away at the end of the corridor, the fary hurried over to the maestro. And he did the thing that always soothed her. Hugged her and kissed her on the temple. But this time, he pulled her against himself a little more tightly.

Paula pressed her neck against his velvet jacket, breathing in the familiar scent of his perfume, and whispered, without knowing why:

"Aren't you angry anymore?"

He had good reason to be angry. Paula had turned Vance without permission from the head of the House. Even worse than that, against his express instructions. He had rebuked the young fary quite sharply for that offense. And punished her by ignoring her completely. But now he seemed to have forgiven her.

"I'm not angry."

"Just to hear that makes all the torment from the Nachterret bearable."

The fary felt the maestro's hands that were holding her so tenderly suddenly tense, and she added hastily:

"I'm sorry, I understand. You couldn't defend me."

The magic of the Faryartos was passive. A duel between a Nachterret and an Asiman would involve powerful spells, explosive flashes of light and fire, wounds. The weaker one would die. Two blood brothers equal in power would both survive. In a duel like that a fary would certainly be killed. Quite definitely. They had no battle spells capable of decomposing an enemy's flesh or consuming it with fire. Their power was of a different kind.

Paula pressed herself even closer against Alexander, trying not to think any more about Miklosh or Johan. She even tried not to remember about Vance. Why couldn't she be as calm as she used to be? Before that conversation with Darel. What had happened to the iron self-possession that even the mormolikas could have envied?

Alexander stroked her hair affectionately and said quietly, as if he were talking to himself:

"Life is imperfect. Its disasters are always the wrong disasters, that happen to the wrong people. Its comedies are filled with absurd horror, and its tragedies often degenerate into farce. The moment you get close to life, its starts hurting you. Everything in it either lasts too long or is too short."

" 'The Decay of Lying'?" Paula asked, breathing in his subtly expensive scent delightedly.

" 'The Critic as Artist,' " Alexander replied, and kissed her on the temple again. "We had a very interesting talk at that time."

"Why wouldn't Oscar agree to become one of us?"

"He was too world-weary. Disenchanted with life."

Paula looked up. She was always amazed by the casual way in which the maestro spoke about the illustrious and famous people he had known. For her they were characters out of textbooks, but for him they were friends and acquaintances he had talked to and known well.

Alexander smiled and looked at her tenderly. "Feeling better?"

"Yes, I'm better now."

He frowned and pushed his pupil away slightly without letting go of her, as he listened to something that only he could hear.

"It's Darel Dahanavar. He wants to see me."

Paula suddenly felt tense. "Should I go?"

"No, stay. It won't take long. He's brought some documents from Felicia."

"Documents?"

"Yes. I requested a few things from the mormolika's personal library."

Darel showed up a few minutes later. As always, slightly disheveled, surging along on the crest of his own irrepressible seething energy. His jacket was open, his light hair was tangled, and he was breathing like a man who had just run up the stairs. But then, perhaps he had. He gave the impression of having too many things on his plate, as if the First Lady's personal psycho-scanner could barely keep up with his work. But the fary could remember him looking quite different. Extremely focused. Calm. Cold. That was what the Dahanavar was like when he was working.

Paula sat in a chair, pretending to be absorbed in a book, but she didn't read a single line during the conversation. Darel spoke with Alexander, standing beside the picture at the far end of the room. Smiling and looking around with an interested expression. He cast only a brief glance in her direction once.

He certainly didn't give the impression that he was reading the knowledge of higher magic from the mind of the head of the House. At the council meetings, it was all very different. The telepath appeared abstracted and indifferent, and his eyes acquired an intense depth, as if they were piercing right through you. But this time, he had come only to pass on greetings and best wishes.

The fary herself didn't know what she was expecting. She couldn't understand what the Dahanavar ought to be doing. But it certainly wasn't gazing around, shifting from one foot to the other, and waiting for the courtesy call to come to an end.

He had promised to help her.

Paula slammed the book shut and immediately heard a voice inside her head: *When you leave the room, wait for me.* Darel didn't look at her, he just carried on talking to the maestro.

She got up, smiled apologetically at her teacher, and slipped out into the corridor. She walked a few meters, turned off into a small hall, walked up to the table with a vase of roses on it, and started mechanically rearranging the flowers. Her gentle excitement rapidly developed into nervous impatience. After she pricked her finger painfully on a thorn, Paula left the flowers in peace.

When Darel appeared, she was wandering aimlessly from one end of the hallway to the other, constantly stumbling into pouffes and armchairs. When she saw him, she stopped and clasped her hands together. He wasn't walking very fast. But not very slowly, either. He wasn't hurrying, just moving smoothly, not making any abrupt movements. As if he were carrying some heavy but fragile load, something that could smash or spill at any moment and send bright-colored fragments scattering in all directions.

The Dahanavar's face looked stiff, his gaze was blank, turned inward toward the precious thing that he was *holding*.

The telepath walked up, took Paula's hand in a strong, masterful grip, and pulled her after him. He opened the first door he came to and pushed her inside. There was no light in the room, and she didn't get a chance to switch it on.

Darel pushed her back against the wall and took her head in both hands, pressing it firmly against the marble bas-relief. She gasped and clutched at his wrists, trying to break free. But the Dahanavar didn't even notice her feeble fluttering. His pale face was so close that the dark, dilated pupils of the two eyes seemed to merge together, and she gazed, horror-struck, into that dark, deep well. There was a glittering, shimmering, entrancing madness swirling in its depths. Then suddenly a seething torrent came gushing out of those dizzying depths, straight into her mind.

Sounds. Jingling and murmuring, tearing her eardrums apart. Melodic, flowing in a single continuous stream. Colors. The entire palette of hues in blinding gold flashes. Smells. The play of light and shade. The steel structures of logical formulae with visions of unimaginable beauty swirling around them. Shapeless chunks of material light congealing into patterns woven in the air. Pain, happiness, yearning, love, despair. Everything! Everything that could possibly be felt or seen!

Paula felt as if she were choking, burning, and turning into a lump of ice. That she was going to die right there on the spot. That she wouldn't be able to support the weight of this power that the telepath was pouring into her.

Alexander's face. Distant, familiar, mysterious, close, the one and only maestro, the one who knew her through and through. His quiet, trembling whisper: "There is no such thing as reality. . . . There is only you. The world of your soul . . . Your powers are infinite. Do not be afraid. Do what you want. Reality does not exist! It is a coarse, clumsy replica of your desires. Reach out your hand, touch it, and you will see how its forms flow beneath your fingers. . . ."

Sounds. Colors. Smells. A void with a thin white beam darting about in it. Darkness narrowing down to the two black pupils of the Dahanavar's eyes. A bright flash, splitting apart her old superficial rigid limitation, her insensitivity and blindness. She understood, she felt. Immediately. In a single instant.

Darel released her with a hoarse gasp, leaned against the wall on his open hands, lowered his head, and broke off the mental link. But the fary didn't even notice. Slowly, very slowly, she walked over to the statue standing in the center of the room. Raised her hand. Reality does not exist. That monolithic, unchangeable reality that I used to see before.

The marble siren sitting on the tall plinth stirred, turned her indifferent face, fluttered her wings, and froze again. Stone, but not dead. Ready to come to life at any moment.

The fary pressed her hands against her cheeks and laughed. Quietly, almost silently. But in her soul, she was shouting at the top of her voice in ecstasy and delight. Darel leaned back against the wall and looked at her. With an expression of weary satisfaction.

SETTING the long sheet of coarse, rough paper in front of her, Paula picked up a thin stick of charcoal and traced out the first line. She had never taken any great interest in drawing, but that wasn't important. It didn't matter what you drew, what mattered was what you felt while you did it. Precise, black outlines. Brisk strokes. She didn't think about how hard to press or the correct positioning of the shadow. The fary's movements were confident. Her fingers stippled the lines, she erased unsuccessful details with the edge of her hand and drew over them.

There was a frantic joy seething inside her. It didn't matter what you drew, what mattered was what you saw in it.

Miklosh! My powers are not strong enough for you! I'm still too young and inexperienced. Perhaps someday I'll take my revenge on you, too. But in the meantime, your faithful dog and bodyguard will feel the humiliation that you made me suffer. Not this very moment, not today or tomorrow. But I'll tie the lines of your destiny together, Johan, so that you feel the pain just when you're least expecting it.

The magic of the Faryartos was passive. But the extent of their power was beyond the understanding of the other blood brothers.

The charcoal rustled across the paper, leaving black lines and small crumbs behind it. The paper seemed to sing with the power pouring into it from Paula's hands. And somewhere in reality, invisible forces were weaving together above the unsuspecting Nachterret's head.

A warm, strong hand was laid on the fary's shoulder. She swung around sharply. Alexander was standing beside her, looking at her drawing. Paula froze, expecting to be punished for attempting to assassinate a member of a family with a policy of neutrality toward the Faryartos. But her teacher suddenly smiled gently and raised one hand to the sketch. A few ill-shaped strokes turned blacker and fused into a precise, serrated line.

"I think that will be better," the maestro said in a matter-of-fact voice. He took out a handkerchief and wiped the charcoal off his pupil's cheek.

"HERR MANNELIG"

> Whenever people agree with me, I always feel I must be
> wrong.
>
> —Oscar Wilde, *Lady Windermere's Fan*

November 28
Darel Dahanavar

The song "Herr Mannelig," as performed by professional musicians, sounded much better than my rendition. But I was trying really hard, singing at the top of my voice and tapping out the rhythm on the arm of my chair.

> *Bittida en morgon innnan solen upprann,*
> *Innan foglarna började sjunga,*
> *Bergatroliet friade till fager ungersven,*
> *Hon hade en falskeliger tunga . . .*

Loraine had moved a low table up to the sofa and covered it with books on history from my library. She was writing a term essay. Or she had been, until I started practicing my singing skills. But for the last five minutes, she had been staring at me in amazement.

> *"Herr Mannelig, Herr Mannelig, trolofven i mig*
> *För det jag bjuder so gerna*
> *I kunnen väl svara endast ja eller nej*
> *Om i viljen eller ej."*

"What on earth has come over you?" she asked, making no effort to disguise the skepticism in her voice.

"A good mood."

My mood really was excellent. My remarkable—indeed, you might say virtuoso—plan had worked. No Dahanavar Lady could have woven a more subtle intrigue.

"What song is that?"

"An ancient Scandinavian legend."

"Aaaah," Loraine drawled. "And what's it about?"

Early one morning, before sunrise,
Before the first birds began to sing,
A mountain trolless made a proposal to a knight,
Speaking in her forked tongue:

"Herr Mannelig, Herr Mannelig,
Please marry me,
For I can give you anything you want.
Your answer must be yes or no,
Just as you wish.

"I will give you twelve fine steeds,
They have never known a saddle or a bridle.
I will give you twelve mills,
Their millstones glimmer red,
And the millwheels are of silver.
I will give you a sword of gold,
That will strike in battle as you wish,
On the battlefield you will be invincible."

"Gifts like these I would take most gladly,
If you were a Chris woman.

But you are a vicious mountain trolless,
From a line of water trolls and the devil. . . ."

The mountain trolless ran out of her door,
Loudly lamenting and sobbing:
"If I could have this handsome man,
I would be freed of my woes.
Herr Mannelig, Herr Mannelig,
Please marry me,
For I can give you anything you want.

"Your answer must be yes or no,
Just as you wish."

"I see," Loraine declared profoundly, pulling over an encyclopedia. "I thought it was some kind of military march. It's a very martial melody. Are you Scandinavian, then?"

"Two-thirds. My grandfather was a Swede, he married an Englishwoman, and then . . ."

I stopped at that.

The girl squinted sideways at me, then suddenly down at her book. "Is it hard for you to talk about it?"

I wasn't even sure myself what I felt when I remembered my mortal family.

"You know, it's not usual for us to talk about out former lives. It's regarded as vulgar and improper, almost indecent. No one wants to remember that he was once human."

"Is it so very humiliating to be human?" Loraine tossed the pencil she was using to make comments in the book onto the table. And then she declared with surprising anger, "What pigs you all are! You live on us, and you're always calling us humans, mortals, cattle, nobodies."

I could understand her. It's not easy living in a world knowing that it's ruled by soulless, supernatural brutes. It gets a bit scary, and the meaning of everything gets a bit blurred.

"I really like the way you say you!"

"All right, they, you're different, but . . ."

"But what?" I flipped a candlestick out of my way with the toe of my shoe. "Finish what you were saying."

"Oh, it's nothing." She glowered. "It feels disgusting to live when you know that you're controlled by someone else and you're nothing."

"Loraine," I said, sitting beside her on the sofa, "you're not a nonentity. There are very many intelligent, talented, beautiful, strong human beings. Those are the ones they select to keep our numbers up. And no matter what airs my relatives might put on about their blood, and how knowledgeable and wise they are, without you, they are nothing. They'd die of boredom, just hating each other."

The girl listened carefully. She wanted to believe me. And she did.

"I didn't want you to know who I really am. But this way is better. More honest."

"Why do you want to be with me?"

"With you I don't feel lonely."

WHEN I met Flora, I was twenty-five years old, and I was human. I was captivated by the intelligence and beauty of this remarkable and mysterious woman. I didn't notice that I had fallen in love. I always knew perfectly well that she had plenty of admirers, friends, and lovers apart from me. I didn't want to be one of a devoted pack of dogs trailing at her heels, ready to dash to carry out her every wish if she just whistled. But I couldn't help loving her. I never showed my feelings. I remained aloof; I wouldn't allow myself to be tamed and have a collar slipped around my neck. And I thought it was my indifference to her charms that had held Flora's interest. But I was wrong. It was not me she needed, but my abilities.

I was simply being used.

After I was turned, I lost many things, but I also gained a great deal. And the most important thing of all was the chance to live without growing old. Physically or emotionally.

As far as I could understand, Flora had the basic gifts of an empath. Perhaps that was what allowed her to recognize me as a kindred spirit. Her teacher had been killed, Felicia could not take his place, and my "mother" was very lonely. Until she met me.

We exchanged barbed witticisms and argued until we were hoarse. As my teacher, she demanded obedience and submission—and I replied with coarse abuse. Then I would bring her flowers, kiss her hands tenderly, and shower her with compliments, and in the end I was forgiven. I asked her for all the knowledge of the Dahanavar, not just the pitiful fragments that our Lady fed to her pupils. She would get angry and explain that the men of the family were not psychologically flexible enough to master complex spells. Then, little by little, she started slipping me scrolls containing ancient mystical texts from Felicia's personal library.

Instead of amorous human passion for a beautiful woman, I developed a warm, steady, deep feeling of attachment to her. And she felt the same for me. But I could never *sense* her. I could read anybody else, but my own mother remained closed to me. It's a strange peculiarity of all scanners that the teacher and the pupil are blocked off from each other. For the other blood brothers, it's quite the opposite.

If only I'd known what she was planning, I'd have tried to stop her . . . I would have stopped her.

When Flora was killed, I was left alone. The feeling of emptiness and loss simply wouldn't go away. I could feel her inside me every night, every hour, constantly.

Until Loraine turned up.

"Darel. . . . Hey, Darel!" she called, shaking me by the shoulder and snapping her fingers in front of my nose. "Have you turned off again? Have you remembered something?"

"Oh, it's nothing." I smiled, reached out, and ruffled up her hair, then pulled her close to me. Naturally, the response was an annoyed snarl. Loraine couldn't stand to be treated in a casual, patronizing manner.

"Why don't you help me with my essay?" she asked angrily, and pushed the encyclopedia over toward me.

"History?"

"Yes. This is the subject."

"Okay. Write . . . 'The history of world civilization was made by vampires.'"

Naïve Loraine dutifully wrote out the beginning of the sentence and then stumbled over the final word.

"Are you making fun of me?"

I shook my head and tried to control my voice as I said:

"Not at all. Think for yourself. Let's take scientific and technical progress. The telephone was invented so that blood brothers who had no telepathic abilities could talk to each other at night or by day. The cell phone was invented so that busy vampires with no telepathic abilities could talk to each other from anywhere at all. Airplanes are a very rapid means of transport. So it's possible to travel a long way at night. Two hours—and you're in a different city. The computer and the Internet make it possible to gather information without leaving home. Electric light is the artificial extension of the period of daylight for humans. There are always more people on well-lit streets. Shops that stay open at night, casinos, restaurants, and so forth provide a chance to feed calmly without having to wait hours for a victim. . . ."

Loraine listened with bated breath, then suddenly frowned and snorted: "What rubbish! Get away and stop bothering me!"

I laughed and went back to my armchair. I threw my legs across one of the armrests and was just about to launch into the next couplet of "Herr Mannelig" when I heard a *call* inside my head.

Darel? Can you hear me?

Yes.

Loraine, who had already learned to recognize when I start my mental conversations, threw an eraser at me to attract me. She caught my eye and made an inquiring face.

"Vance," I said without any making any sound.

"Who?" she exclaimed, thinking that she must have mis-heard. But I pressed one finger against my lips to ask her to be quiet, and Hemran's fan had no choice but to squirm impa-tiently and chew nervously on the end of her pencil as she waited for the conversation to end.

Darel, I want to talk to you.

Talk. I can hear you perfectly well.

No. In person. Is that possible?

I wasn't planning to go out today.

He didn't say anything to that, but I could feel his sharp dis-appointment. I always used to have time for him when he was human.

Okay. If you want to talk, come to my place.

I dictated my address and *switched off*. Loraine, who had been observing me carefully, immediately came to life.

"That was Vance? But can he talk telepathically?"

"He can now."

"And what did he say?"

"He's going to come here."

"Here? When?"

"I don't know."

"Can I wait for him?"

There was no point in arguing about it, so I just shrugged and she settled herself more comfortably on the sofa with a contented smile.

Vance arrived an hour later. The changes taking place in him were becoming more evident. The coarse, clumsy peasant was turning into an elegant aristocrat. The features of his face seemed to be the same as before, but different. Incredible. I hadn't realized that the effect of the Faryartos blood could be so powerful. The movements, the walk, the angle of the head, the glance.

"What are you looking at?"

He stood in the hallway without taking his hands out of the pockets of his raincoat. Not the old light-colored one with the check lining. This new brown one looked more expensive and more stylish.

"You've changed."

"So have you."

I meant his appearance and inner essence. He was hinting at my sudden vampire indifference.

"Can I go in?"

I moved aside to let him past. Loraine smiled when Vance appeared in the sitting room. But her smile slowly faded away. She looked at me, then turned her eyes back to Vance, then back to me.

"Hemran Faryartos," I said, introducing my visitor. "And this is someone you already know, the same Loraine."

"She's human," said Vance, looking his admirer up and down as she carried on batting her eyelids in confusion.

"Just imagine that. Well, have a seat, blood brother."

Vance didn't understand why I was angry. In fact, my disdainful tone was beginning to needle him.

"Darel, cut it out, will you? It's not my fault I was turned. I didn't want it, and I didn't ask for it!"

"I know."

He was right, it was time to restore a little objectivity.

"Then what's the problem? I'm the same as you are."

"Not quite. And it's not really a matter of different families. I get along just fine with Cadavercitan and Vricolakos, it's just . . ."

I looked at Loraine.

The girl was leaning down over her book, pretending to be busy with her essay, but in fact she was listening avidly. She was dumbfounded by the news that Vance had been turned. And a tornado of the most incredible images was swirling around in her thoughts. I didn't even try to listen to them.

"I suppose Paula laid out all the charms of the new life for you. Immortality, power, beauty, knowledge."

Vance smiled fleetingly, with a flash of his fangs. "Yes. She said something of the sort."

"Then permit me to make a few amendments. I won't bother to mention the internal politics of your family, the passive nature of its magic, and your complete dependence on the Upieschi. As a teacher, Paula is very weak. You will not receive the level of knowledge and power that you want. But that's not the most important thing. As you get older, the human emotions start to fade. At fifty you don't feel as clearly and freshly as you did at fifteen. At eighty, you don't feel things as clearly as you did at thirty. The soul fades. There's nothing new to be surprised at. No urgent desires. Although, of course, there are exceptions. Now imagine that you're a man, and you live for two hundred, three hundred, a thousand years."

Hemran stroked the leather armrests of his chair and asked tensely: "Is that the way you feel, too?"

"I'm a scanner. I'm constantly 'reanimating' my soul through others. My feelings are as strong as they were a hundred years ago. I find it interesting to live, because I'm in contact with them." I pointed at Loraine, who couldn't help squirming under the gaze of two vampires. "You used to be like that. Real. Bright. Alive."

Vance didn't say anything. A black fury was slowly rising up in his soul. Fury with me, with Paula, with all the blood brothers.

"How much time do I have?" he asked abruptly, and added bitterly, "How much time is there left before I start to change?"

"About twenty years."

"Why so little? You said eighty."

"I was talking about humans. You'll change differently. You'll start to find everything human alien, perhaps even disgusting. Your talent comes from that mortal life. I don't know what will happen to it. Have a word with Paula. She'll be able to explain better than me. But perhaps I'm overdramatizing, and you won't suffer too much."

"I'm already suffering."

He got up and walked around the room, with the hem of his raincoat catching on the candlesticks. It was a good thing that the candles in them weren't lit.

"I have to rehearse. Meet people. I can't go outside during the day. The band depends on me. We were supposed to be going on tour. Ten concerts in ten countries. I feel hungry all the time!"

"That's only normal. At the beginning. . . ."

"It's not normal. It's not normal to want to sink your teeth into the neck of your own keyboard player! I can't concentrate. I've got this mess in my head. I need time to understand how to be one of you. To learn to be a vampire! And I don't have that time."

"There are spells that make life easier to bear. . . ."

"I don't know them."

"You have a teacher, ask her."

"But you're my friend."

I jumped up. Grabbed hold of the front of his raincoat.

"Listen! I can't teach you. I don't have the right. Neither Alexander nor Felicia will allow it. You're a Faryartos. I'm a Dahanavar. We have different magic. Different methods of training our pupils. I can't transmit our knowledge to you. Nobody can tell what you'll do with it in two hundred years. Perhaps you'll turn it against me! That's the politics of the families. You don't belong just to yourself anymore. You can't do just anything that comes into your head."

I let go of him and pushed him toward an armchair. Vance sat down and mechanically straightened the scarf that had come out from under his raincoat.

"Right now you're vulnerable. You need to learn to defend yourself. Find the time and ask Paula to teach you. She has to do it."

"She's got some kind of problems," Hemran said in a dull voice.

"That's nothing to do with you. You'll be the one with problems if you don't take some care of yourself."

"Okay. I'll ask her."

He seemed very tired. I could physically sense his apathy and hopelessness.

"Look, Vance. Don't give up. It's hard for everyone at first. If only you knew how I felt when all this descended on me." I circled a hand round my head. "Sounds, voices, other people's emotions, fragments of thoughts. Imagine the pleasure of hearing what people really think about you. But all you have to do is learn to pull the wool over people's eyes. Believe me, the Faryartos are past masters at doing that. After a couple of lessons, no one in your rock band will be surprised that you only arrange rehearsals after sunset."

Hemran's feelings brightened up. His gloomy face took on an attentive, interested expression, and he calmed down. I had calmed him down. With my words and my unobtrusive *influence*.

"You think so?"

"I know so."

"I suppose that's probably what I came to hear. That everything will be all right."

"Have you heard it?"

"I think so." He got up. "So you know all about what's going on, Loraine?"

"Yes," the girl answered seriously, sitting up straight on the divan as if she were about to answer a question in class.

"And you're not afraid?"

"No. With Darel I'm not afraid."

She didn't feel any of the old delight, adoration, and awe as she talked to her idol. This was a new Hemran Vance. A vampire. And Loraine didn't feel any respect for him.

After Hemran left, his fan sat there, gazing forlornly at her book. I walked over and put my arm around her shoulders.

"Why are you suddenly so sad?"

"I don't know. It's all wrong, somehow," she answered with a sigh. "You know, I wouldn't like to be like Vance."

"You wouldn't be like him," I said gloomily. I leaned down over the encyclopedia and looked at the page for a few seconds—it was a picture of a statue. I moved my hand over to it. And concentrated. The knowledge of the Faryartos was still seething inside me. Of course, I couldn't make the picture come alive and move, but a ripple seemed to run across the page. For a moment it acquired depth, then froze again. Loraine gasped when she saw it. She touched the page gingerly.

"How did you do that?"

"I don't understand that myself."

When I was scanning Alexander, I put everything I had into it. It was excruciatingly hard to read the knowledge of the farys from his memory so that he wouldn't suspect anything. And it had been even more difficult to hold on to it. There was one moment when I thought this knowledge that wasn't mine was going to blow my head apart. But I managed it. And I poured the magic of art into Paula.

A magnificent plan. And the execution was perfect.

I felt I had been initiated into the power of my House's elite. A worthy successor to our Lady.

"'*Herr Mannelig, Herr Mannelig, trolofven i mig För det jag bjuder so gerna—*'"

"Darel! You're not letting me concentrate. Can you stop singing for at least half an hour?"

"Okay. I'm sorry."

I went back to my armchair, intending to enjoy doing nothing and contemplate my own magnificence, when I was *called* again.

Can we chat? Ivan's voice said in my head. I caught a sharp tang of wood smoke, wet animal skins, and resin. A picture appeared in front of my eyes—Svetlov sitting in front of the open door of his stove and gazing into the fire.

Yes, we can, I answered. It was strange, but I'd started to like his company. I enjoyed experiencing the unusual sensations of the Vricolakos, immersing myself in his world, so entirely unlike the world of the city.

How much longer? You said the plan was working.

It is working. Wait. We can't hurry it.

I know, I know, he growled with a sigh that sounded like wind inside my head. *But you try explaining that to my boys. Just a couple of weeks ago, three of my brother's cubs broke into Miklosh's place. They wanted to take revenge. He gave them a good battering.*

Did he kill them?

No, he let them go.

That was right; the Nachterret wouldn't openly kill members of other Houses. That was against his rules.

That's right, agreed Svetlov, hearing what I was thinking. *He always does his dirty work on the sly.*

The plan's working, I repeated. *You can't put your family at risk by taking revenge openly.*

I know! Why are you telling me that for the tenth time!

Then be patient. The game has already begun, but Miklosh doesn't suspect a thing. That will only make the blow even more of a surprise when it comes.

I understand. At least give me a hint of what you've done.

I can't. It's a complicated Dahanavar system, a series of moves involving an exchange of pieces. Based on iron logic and virtuoso fantasy.

Every dog barks in his own yard, the Vricolakos mocked good-humoredly, and left.

He trusted me. He was sure I could think of a way to take revenge on the House of Nachterret. And he wasn't wrong.

I didn't know myself why I was doing it. Was it the influence of Flora, my adventuress-mother's mastery in weaving intrigues? Did I want to teach that bastard Miklosh a lesson? Or was it a reaction to Felicia's strict instructions not to interfere in the affairs of the other two Houses? Maybe I'd had enough of being a weak-willed scanner, developed the desire to prove that I was just as clever as our top elite? Or was it my sudden liking for Ivan? Perhaps his pain at the death of his relative had simply been too vivid, too sincere.

And then there was the sudden awareness of satisfaction at manipulating other blood brothers. Including some quite powerful and important individuals. I was a Dahanavar, after all. The urge to rule was in our blood.

I was distracted from my enjoyable self-analysis by the sight of Loraine yawning desperately and trying to settle down to sleep on the sofa.

"Hey, babe. Come on, get up. I'll drive you home."

"But, Darel, I'm not sleepy," she muttered. "I'm an owl anyway. I can stay up all night."

"Come on, come on, get up. And don't forget your notes."

A telephone call prevented any further disciplinary measures against Loraine. I had to release her and go into the bedroom.

I picked up the receiver. "Hello."

"Hi! So how are your wheels doing?"

"Nikita Ivanov, dealer in fresh air," I said out loud. I'd completely forgotten about him.

"The very same," he replied cheerfully.

"How's your dog?"

The young guy at the other end of the line beamed contentedly. The best way to win his trust was to inquire after the health of his dog.

"That mastiff's a wild beast. They wanted to give him an enema in the hospital, and he almost finished off two attendants. Can you believe that? They prescribed some powders. For only ten bucks. Said they were very good. Give them to him twice a day. I told 'em, I said, what do you take me for? Good medicine for only ten bucks? I'll call the guys right now and we'll tear this first-aid post of yours to pieces. . . . Hey, what are you laughing at? I'm serious. I dote on that mastiff of mine! Well then, of course, they prescribed us some decent tablets, for five hundred. And for another three hundred, a special electric blanket. . . . Now look, now look what he's doing. Just look at that! My mother-in-law's turned up. He's already destroyed one of her shoes. Now he's finishing off the other one. Right, what was I ringing about . . . How's your wagon? This friend of mine is selling his. An Alfa Romeo. Do you want it? He'll take five percent off."

"Thank you, Nikita," I said, struggling hard to sound serious. "I've already bought a car."

"A-ah," he drawled in a disappointed voice, but then he bounced back. "Why not buy another one? My father-in-law has two. He goes fishing in one and drives round town in the other."

"Okay, I'll think about it. How much do I owe you for the repairs?"

"Ah, it's nothing. You could spend more in a restaurant."

"Excellent. Then let's go to a restaurant. On me."

He laughed, delighted at how quickly I caught on. "Great. Let's go. I'll give the guys a call. The way it is with our work ... When?"

I looked at my watch. Half past ten. "Let's make it today."

"Okay."

We agreed where to meet and said good-bye, delighted with each other.

"Herr Mannelig, Herr Mannelig, trolofven i mig
För det jag bjuder so gerna
I kunnen väl svara endast ja eller nej
Om i viljen eller ej."

Loraine was asleep. Lying there curled up under the rug with her nose tucked into a cushion. The pages of her unfinished essay were scattered across the table, and there was a half-eaten bar of chocolate lying in the middle of them. I sat beside her.

"Loraine. Wake up."

"No!" she grumbled through her sleep. "I won't go."

All right. Let her sleep. I wasn't going to wake the girl. Her daily routine was already shattered because of me in any case.

I took a clean sheet of paper from a pile and wrote a note, saying that she mustn't open the door for anyone. And if she woke up and wanted to go home, she had to call a taxi. The money was on the table.

The girl wasn't afraid to be alone in my apartment. It was calm and cozy here, not like in Chris's gloomy mansion.

I left the note leaning against a candlestick, kissed Loraine's warm cheek, picked up the car keys and my jacket, and went out.

The snow squeaked under my feet. The frost prickling at my face felt pleasant. Yesterday's snowstorm had left genuine snowdrifts in the courtyard. It had covered the dirty tire tracks, and now the road looked incredibly white.

I leaned down and scooped up a handful of snow. Molded it into a snowball. Squeezed it in my hands so hard that my fingers started to ache.

The stars were shining. Very bright winter stars. Orion was lying flattened across the sky with his arms thrown out wide, and there were three white lights burning on his belt.

The air smelled fresh and clean, like a sheet that had just been laundered.

IT was hard to find a parking space. The lot in front of the restaurant was packed. I literally squeezed the Pontiac in between an Audi and a Honda, almost catching the Honda's mirror. I remembered Loraine, warm and sleepy, and for a moment regretted that I hadn't stayed at home, but a multicolored rainbow of human energy was already calling to me from the open door. I couldn't resist plunging into it.

Nikita Ivanov and two friends were waiting for me at a table on the second floor.

"Kirill." A stocky young guy with deep-set black eyes got up and held out his hand. He seemed to have too many muscles in his face. They bulged on his lower jaw, kept tensing up in his cheeks, and rippled across his forehead, crumpling it into deep folds. His thick neck was squeezed into the tight collar of an expensive shirt. His short, thick fingers were constricted by the narrow bands of a signet ring and a wedding ring.

The main feeling that he radiated was a mixture of aggression and dogged malice.

"Alex," said the second friend. His good-natured face was spoiled by a receding chin and a wide gap between his nose and his upper lip. His thin, light hair was carefully combed backward. He had delicately manicured, slim, nervous hands. He radiated shyness, painstakingly concealed as swagger.

They examined me cautiously for a minute, summing me up,

trying to define my social level. Deciding whether I was worthy to be accepted into their company. But half an hour later, they were already discussing the details of their business and laughing happily at my jokes.

And an hour after that, Nikita was loudly demanding that I come to his dacha near Zelenograd and try his new sauna. Alex was pouring cognac into my glass and trying to croon some song in a low voice. His friends shushed him, jostled his shoulders, and threatened to send him home if he didn't shut up. His hair was a mess, and there were strands of it sticking to his red, sweaty face.

Kirill moved a bit closer and tried to get chummy, putting his arm around my shoulders. He waved the cigarette clutched in his fingers under my nose, blinking at the cigarette smoke as he searched for the words to explain why the four of us ought to stick together. And why only buddies like us could do real business.

I felt good. The human feelings intertwined with my own. I wanted the sauna and the real business, I wanted more cognac, and I definitely wanted to sing. The other customers started giving our group sideways glances. A few particularly cultured people moved farther away.

Alex was jostled again, with cries of "No more of that pop trash." Kirill attempted to launch into something more manly and roguish. But I told them all to shut up and listen to a real song. For the next fifteen minutes, we studied the first couplet of "Herr Mannelig." In Extremo would definitely have choked to death on their envy if they'd heard their hit as performed by three drunk humans and one not entirely sober vampire.

Kirill had a fine, slightly hoarse, baritone voice. Nikita rolled up the menu into a trumpet and blew into it diligently, giving a fine imitation of bagpipes. Alex did a good job of singing the second voice. I tapped out the rhythm on the table with my hand.

After our chorus, a manager came across to our table and suggested in very polite terms that we should go down to the first floor, where there was an excellent karaoke machine.

Kirill felt like taking offense. He started working the muscles on his cheeks, unable to understand how he and his friends prevented people from relaxing in a cultured fashion. But he was swiftly reassured and put back down in his seat, with a glass of cognac in his hand. I promised that we would make less noise.

It felt good. I was happy and free, I felt at peace. I felt like one of them. Human. Having a good time in the company of friends who knew nothing about my wise, powerful relatives. About those who really ruled this world. I almost forgot about my own supernatural nature.

And then Nikita reached for a bottle and I saw the tattoo on his wrist. A precise drawing in fine lines—a hand holding an apothecary's scales. The sign that the Upieschi used to mark their human servants.

The glass in my hand trembled, struck the edge of the plate, and cracked.

They'd never let me forget this.

Nobody would ever let me forget it!

This bright, vital, human world was poisoned, perverted by our power and money. The traces of our influence were everywhere, even on this young guy with the light blond hair.

I leaned across the table, grabbed Nikita by the front of his sweater, and pulled him toward me, overturning the bottles and glasses. I looked into his startled, drink-dazed eyes and hit him in the face with his own wrist that was marked with the tattoo. He had no chance to recoil. The blood poured out of his broken nose. Group two. Rhesus positive.

"Do they pay you well? Your masters? Answer me!"

They tried to calm me down. The sensation of carefree human joy had gone. I felt tired and angry. I pushed away the servant of the Upieschi. Took out my wallet. Put all the money that was in it on the table. Got up and walked out.

Outside, the fresh, icy wind sobered me up a bit. I scraped together a handful of the snow lying on the porch and rubbed my face with it. I took a deep breath and felt the cold air tickle my throat. Walked into the parking lot. And suddenly a deafeningly loud howl of pain and horror exploded inside my head. The car keys fell out of my slack fingers and jangled on the asphalt.

Loraine. She was calling me. Something terrible had happened to her.

17

VITDIKTA

It is the confession, not the priest, that gives us absolution.

—Oscar Wilde, *The Picture of Dorian Gray*

November 29
Darel Dahanavar

The Pontiac flew along the highway, breaking every possible rule of the road. But it still wasn't going fast enough for me. My fear for the girl, my wild guesses at what could have happened to her, my thoughts about whoever had inflicted this pain on her—they were all incinerated by the white heat of my fury.

I walked quickly, then ran, then almost flew.

The door of the apartment was wide open. The result of a hasty retreat or a brazen invitation for me to enter and see the surprise prepared for me—my blood brothers indulging their subtle sense of humor. I walked in, my vision slightly blurred by an elimination spell, ready for immediate use. But there was no one for me to use it on.

Straight along the corridor, past the sitting room, where a swarm of small lights flickered above the candles, past the study. Not stopping until I reached the bedroom.

She was lying there with her arms thrown out wide, her golden hair scattered across the white satin bedspread, and her eyes closed.

My Loraine.

But was she still mine?

A pale face, subtly changed; dry, swollen lips. Two small wounds and a trickle of dried blood at the base of her slim neck.

"Loraine," I whispered in a voice that sounded like a stranger's.

She stirred gently. Her dark red mouth opened slightly, and I saw the long, sharp white fangs.

"Loraine!"

I ran to her, put my arms around her feverish body, held her close to me, and cried out—or perhaps I howled in my pain and helplessness.

What had they done! They had killed her, worse than killed her.

I stroked her hair. She was fragile, like all humans, defenseless. What vile creature had drawn the life out of her, sucked out all her light and joy, and poisoned her with his own corrupt blood? A Nachterret, an Asiman, an Upieschi . . .

I held her in my arms and rocked her gently, gazing into the calm face that had already lost its gentle expression of youth and naïveté.

And then I began recovering from my agonized stupor.

Chris! Chris! My shout sliced through the darkness with a power that set it trembling and pulsing, and it gave back my answer immediately.

I hear you. I'm on my way.

Imperturbable, calm, confident Chris.

He arrived very quickly and strode rapidly into the bedroom, green sparks of Cadavercitan magic darting from his fingers. But that was useless now.

"Who did this? Have you found out?"

I sat on the floor with my head leaning back against the bedpost, looking up at him.

"No. I can't sense anything. Nothing at all."

The sorcerer leaned down over sleeping Loraine, looked into her face, touched her cheek, and straightened up.

"Asiman. Now your little girl is one of them."

"I'll find this bastard, even if it's Amir himself! I'll tear him to pieces! Chris, it would have been better if they'd killed her! It would have been better if they'd killed me! Why do this to her? She's so young and weak. She can't do anything to them! She doesn't know anything! How is she going to live now? She's only eighteen!"

Chris sat in a chair and said nothing as he watched me rushing around the room.

"What am I going to tell her when she wakes up? Sorry, little girl, you can't go home anymore? You don't have any home or family or friends anymore, you can't go to college, and you'll never see the sun again. Never. For the next seventy or eighty years you have to hide yourself away. Crawl into a hole somewhere and wait for everyone who knows you or remembers you to die! And I have to tell her about this savage, insane hunger! Chris, I don't want my Loraine to be a bloodthirsty predator!"

My voice broke off in a screech, but I took a grip on myself. The atmosphere in the bedroom was calm. The gentle illusion that the Cadavercitan had woven for Loraine was working. The girl was sleeping, still unaware of the terrible transformation that had broken her body and her soul. She was lost in a long, sweet dream, a gentle cobweb of deception, with muffled sounds, dear, kind faces, and subtle smells, where happiness jingled like the little golden bell that it was in childhood, when there were no cares in the world. Chris, my friend, how does a Cadavercitan sorcerer like you know what will bring a human being joy? Where do you get these pure images?

"She's an Asiman now." Chris could have kept silent, he needn't have said that, but instead of sweet dreams all he could give me was pain and despair. "In a few generations she could be your enemy."

"I won't let them have her. She belonged to me. From the very beginning."

"She has Asiman blood in her. They won't allow you to keep her with the Dahanavar family. And she won't want to stay."

"She's mine."

"She could have become your pupil, Darel. She could—while she was still human. But the girl Loraine is dead now; her place has been taken by Loraine of the House of Asiman. Let her go, Darel. She has her own life now."

"Chris, sometimes I think I hate you! You know they won't let her live. Because of her friendship with me. They didn't change her like this so that she could be happy in the Asiman family, but to make me settle for this." The Cadavercitan smiled ironically.

"I warned you. I asked you to leave the girl alone. You wouldn't listen. Now it's all over. See how sad love is."

"No, it's not over. I'll go to the Regenant."

Chris leaned back in his chair and narrowed his green cat's eyes, waiting to see what was coming next.

"They turned her into a vampire for revenge. She's very young. She has no special abilities. The House of Asiman doesn't need her. I'll demand Vitdikta."

"What?" the sorcerer exclaimed, amazed, or pretending to be amazed. "You'll demand what?"

"Vitdikta."

"My child," said the Cadavercitan, leaning forward, his eyes suddenly glowing with a dark, murky fire, "are you insane? Do you know what that is?"

"The return of a vampire to human life," I said, confused by that magnetic gaze.

Chris shook his head. "Vitdikta is a curse. It is appalling magic. Darel, you can demand the ritual of Vitdikta, but no one can tell what the result will be. The girl might become human again. Or she might die. The power that you wish to summon obeys no one, it can kill everyone within its reach. It doesn't care who summoned it, it doesn't care who's right, it knows nothing about justice."

"You're not frightening me, Chris."

"You must understand!" he exclaimed in a melancholy voice that was strangely terrifying. "The Dark Hunter is nothing but a harmless scarecrow compared to the Vitdikta. If you're tired of living, then you, Loraine, and your family can find less painful ways of committing suicide."

"What has my family got to do with this?"

"The one who demands the ritual attracts a curse on his entire family. You want to take away from the Darkness a little bit of light that would have given it new strength, and it takes its revenge. That is what the ancients used to say."

"And you believe in that drivel? You—Chris Frederick Alabert, the wisest member of the House of Death?"

"Oh, not the wisest, Darel. Believe me."

"Anyway, I'm going to the Regenant. Right now! To demand that the girl be returned to normal life and the guilty parties punished. I have that right! After all, the Oath is still in force, it hasn't been canceled yet."

Chris looked at me wearily from out of his armchair and raised one hand in a silent gesture of farewell. "Good luck."

"What about you? Aren't you going to come with me?"

"No."

"All right. That's up to you."

I went back into the bedroom, carefully picked up Loraine, still asleep, in my arms, and walked out of the apartment, deliberately not even glancing at the Cadavercitan. I was hoping that he would change his mind and help me persuade the Regenant. Was he a traitor for refusing to help a girl who respected him and thought of him as her friend? I didn't know. I didn't want to know.

THE Regenant was in a meeting. At the human level. The secretary in reception gaped in amazement at my pale face and wild appearance.

"I've come to see Mr. Belov," I told her, making straight for the huge door with the bronze handle.

"You can't go in there! The minister's busy!" She dashed to cut me off, but it was too late. I flung open the door.

Tobacco smoke, expressions of restrained surprise on the pale blobs of faces turned in my direction. I could read them all in a single glance—tired, irritated, and arrogant, with their well-concealed fears. What a pity that you don't have the Dahanavar family's only living sensor in your office, Regenant. So many things I could have told you.

And there he was. Very calm—in fact, rather slow. Not the Regenant; at the moment, he was just a high-ranking human being dealing with other humans.

I stood in the doorway and looked at him. The secretary's frightened face was hovering somewhere behind my back. She began babbling something, then stopped. His eyes gave no sign, and neither did his face, but he understood everything.

"Young man, I think you've had enough time to realize that you have the wrong door," the minister said. *Today at midnight. The northern residence,* the Regenant thought.

"I'm sorry," I said, forcing myself to take a step backward. "I got the wrong door."

The muffled voices started buzzing again in the room. And through the keyhole came a mingled smell of fatigue, chronic fear, and the aromatic smoke of expensive cigars. The secretary hissed at me as if I were a cat:

"Go away! Go away, I told you he was busy."

"Don't worry," I said. "You won't get fired. He likes your neck."

The young woman fluttered her mascara-coated lashes and clutched involuntarily at the pendant dangling on her chest. She must have thought I was mad.

LORAINE was sleeping. I adjusted the cushion under her head, pulled the rug higher, and got into the driver's seat. There was an hour and a half left until midnight.

I drove through the city very slowly and carefully, stopping at every traffic light. I had a girl vampire who still didn't know what had happened to her sleeping on the backseat.

The cars rushed past, and the glow from their headlights drifted over Loraine's head. The neon advertisements painted her face with wild, insane colors, and she dreamed about green grass and bright sunshine.

The northern residence. A huge black castle with pointed towers, surrounded by a fortress wall. Gloomy, empty, dead. Built centuries ago, fifty kilometers outside the capital. Protected by the magic of the blood brothers. I stopped the car in the shade of the tall poplar trees and waited.

The first car was a black Jaguar. It raced up as swift as an arrow, and a moment after it braked to a halt, Felicia was already walking imperturbably up the drive toward the gates. Constance jumped out after her.

The first to arrive.

But of course, the well-being and prestige of the House were under threat.

A few minutes later, the Asiman drove up in two Glentwagens. They seemed a lot less self-assured than usual.

The Upieschi and Faryartos families also arrived.

So all the city families, apart from the Nachterret and the

Cadavercitan, were already here. When the Regenant's limousine pulled up at the wall, it was three minutes to twelve.

At exactly midnight, I took Loraine in my arms and set up along the narrow path.

They were standing in the huge stone hall, where the walls were hung with heraldic flags and ancient weapons. And they were hoping that I would change my mind, that I wouldn't come and wouldn't dare request the terrible ritual.

If I had really known what the Vitdikta was, I probably would have backed down. But I didn't, and when the Regenant pronounced his invariable phrase—"Who demands justice?"—I stepped forward with the half-alive, half-dead girl in my arms, and for the first time in my centuries of life, I said: "I, of the Dahanavar family, demand the ritual of Vitdikta for Loraine, who this night became one of the Asiman."

A nervous tremor ran around the hall. My Dahanavar Ladies froze abstractedly, as if I had suddenly become a stranger to them. Amir bared his teeth and started glowing with a crimson fury. Alexander's handsome face distorted in a grimace of dismay. Ramon remained imperturbable on the outside, but on the inside his strange power grew stronger and thicker. The other Upieschi radiated a desire to run away as fast as possible. Everyone knew what the Vitdikta was. Everyone except me.

The Regenant was calm. The dark eyes in his swarthy face glinted when he looked in my direction. For an instant, I thought I glimpsed confusion in them. But only for an instant.

"Darel Dahanavar, the ritual of Vitdikta has not been performed for several centuries. Are you certain that it is necessary?"

"I am."

"Darel," I heard Felicia's musical voice say, "there's no need to rush this. We can solve your problems without resorting to extreme measures."

The Regenant looked at me inquiringly.

"No."

"Darel . . ." There was a note of impatience and annoyance with her obstinate pupil now. "Darel, you do not understand the nature of the magic to which you wish to appeal. You won't have the strength to survive it—"

"I beg your pardon, my Lady," Amir interrupted. "The young man is still too inexperienced to understand the consequences of the ritual. He is very upset because his friend has been turned too soon. Darel, I understand you very well, I sympathize. I am greatly displeased that one of my brothers has taken this unpardonable liberty. I promise that the culprit will be found and punished severely. We do not accept mortals into our family at such a young age, but for you we will make an exception. The girl shall have a worthy position in the House, she shall have a fine teacher, and perhaps, in the future, she will join the Asiman elite."

That old fox Amir! What magnificent prospects—an ordinary girl, turned by one of the servants, will join the elite and be given access to the higher magic of the Asiman. What a glorious lie.

"Agree, Darel!" Constance shouted. "It's a fine proposal!"

They thought my despair was a mere whim. That my affection was foolishness.

"Stubborn fool," Alexander hissed in fury. "Do you want to kill us all for this silly little girl of yours?"

"Does Mr. Darel Dahanavar believe that our humble family is not sufficiently noble and powerful for this girl? Or does he not believe Amir's promise?"

"Darel, think! The girl is really very lucky. She's being accepted into one of the most powerful families."

They'll all start to hate me in a moment. The Dahanavar because I didn't turn to my relatives for help and brought the matter to a tribunal. The Asiman because I dared not to believe

Amir's barefaced lie, wouldn't humbly swallow the insult and forgive their crime. The Upieschi couldn't bear to be torn away from important business and forced to risk their lives. The Faryartos were quite simply afraid. And none of them could understand what the problem was—they all stopped valuing human life long ago.

"Excuse me, ladies and gentlemen," said Ramon, who had remained silent so far. "I have a question. Your Honor"—he turned to the judge—"who will perform the ritual? As far as I am aware, the honorable Darel Dahanavar does not possess the necessary power."

I felt—in fact, I almost *heard* them all sigh in relief and relax. That was it; the question was decided. The younger brothers didn't count, and that left Felicia, Amir (but he would rather be roasted alive than help me), Alexander, and, perhaps, the leader of the Upieschi. Three . . . no, it was hopeless.

The Regenant also realized this, but he followed the ceremonial procedure through to the end.

"Felicia from the House of Dahanavar, are you prepared to perform the ritual of Vitdikta for Loraine Asiman instead of Darel Dahanavar?"

"No." Spoken firmly and crisply.

She was not going to indulge the whimsies of her younger brother, and what's more, when this stupid farce was all over, she would demand severe punishment for the presumptuous child. For me, that is.

"Amir Asiman?"

"I am very sorry, young man, but I have already offered you too much. Do not ask me to do the impossible."

Blackhearted hypocrite.

"Alexander Faryartos?"

"No." He took pleasure in refusing me. *Everyone should know his own place and what he is worth.*

I hugged the girl closer against my chest, feeling the waves of icy indifference flooding over me from all sides. Curse every last one of them!

"I will perform the ritual of Vitdikta for Loraine of the House of Asiman."

I started and swung around.

He was standing in the doorway. Calm, confident, imperturbable. The sorcerer from the House of Death—my best friend, Chris. Vivian was there with him, holding a black casket in his hands and looking pale-faced and nervous.

The honorable ladies and gentlemen froze in astonishment, then they all started talking at once, pouring out a stream of hatred and fear on us. Chris didn't bat an eyelash, he just gazed at the Regenant with a dour, heavy look in his eyes. The judge paused for a moment and then said in a dull voice:

"I grant permission for the ritual of Vitdikta."

Everybody breathed out and froze again. There was nothing more they could do. From that moment on, the most powerful person in the hall was Chris. Following his curt commands, I laid Loraine on a broad stone slab in the center of the hall and took one step back. Vivian opened the casket and handed his teacher a long stiletto with a black handle. Then he stood facing me. The sorcerer cautiously ran one finger along the slim blade, and in response to his touch it started glowing with green fire.

"He's insane," I heard one of the vampires say in a loud whisper. The final outburst of malice.

Chris walked up to the pale girl lying on the slab of stone and looked at her for a few moments. I didn't know what was going on in my friend's soul just then. I couldn't read anything in the Cadavercitan.

The stiletto in his hand glinted like a faceted emerald, and drops of green fire dripped from it as the sorcerer traced the first line across the floor. He walked around Loraine's body, drawing the symbols of the great Houses. Their glittering images flared up and fused into a circle, with my sleeping Loraine at the center. I recognized the broken arrow of the Dahanavar, the Cadavercitan cross, the crowns and scepter of the Asiman, the three hornets of the Nachterret, the Upieschi hand holding its scales, the sunflower of the Faryartos, the mirror-smooth water surface of the Ligamentia, the wolf's head of the Vricolakos, the shield of the Regenant, the hourglass of the Nosoforos... And then came the ancient symbols of the lost families, whom I had never seen and never would see. The screaming ghost of the Obaifo, the dagger and snake of the Luder, the pyramid of the Lugat, the constellation of Orion for the Leargini.

The bright green glimmering rose off the floor and flooded everything in the hall with its dim light, making us look like a gathering of corpses. The flickering signs began pulsating in sequence, and I heard a voice—slow, sonorous, and spellbinding—and realized it was Chris speaking a language that was already ancient three thousand years ago.

"Chris!" The resounding shout stabbed through the Cadavercitan's monotonous recitation, and I glanced around in amazement. I couldn't believe that it was Felicia—the proud, haughty, staid Felicia—who had cried out.

"Chris, stop!" She hurried toward him but halted at the boundary of the glowing circle. "It's still not too late! This girl isn't worth your life. Stop!"

Chris's voice became louder, and I thought I could hear other entrancing voices answering him.

"You fool. You high-minded fool," our First Lady whispered, and walked away from him.

"This is suicide!" said Alexander, taking a step away from the green light.

"Rest in peace," said Ramon, raising his hand in an indifferent gesture of farewell to the dead.

"Why are they saying these things about you, Chris? What does it mean?"

"It means, my dear Darel, that the noble Cadavercitan is sacrificing himself for your girlfriend. It is possible to tear the inhuman power out of her soul and pour it back into the dark source. Loraine Asiman will die in order to give life to the human Loraine. Chris Cadavercitan will be the channel for her dark soul and will take the full blow of Darkness on himself, together with the fury for the rejected gift. The person who conducts the ritual of Vitdikta dies, crushed by the power that he himself has summoned."

"Chris, is that true?"

"Darel, take your place."

"Chris, don't!"

"Darel . . . everything is just as it should be. Concentrate on your love for this woman and don't interrupt."

". . . Thank you."

He pointed his blade at the center of the circle, and it glittered so brightly that it was almost unbearable to look at. The melodic voices began singing more loudly. As if they were hovering somewhere nearby, circling around above my head, ready to take on the form of flesh at any moment. And a dark shadow, vague and formless, began rising up at the center of the circle of green flame. As it grew, it became stronger and more solid, and a few moments later I could see a furiously swirling vortex hovering above Loraine, covering her almost completely. In the black walls of this whirlwind, I glimpsed flashes of lightning and faces; through its whistling I could hear voices speaking, distant muffled howls, sighs, laughter, and groans. The black, smoky column was pressing up against the ceiling now, and its fearful breath crept slowly around the hall.

I wanted to close my eyes and stop my ears or—better still—turn my back on this dark horror and run as fast as my legs would carry me. But I couldn't move a muscle. I suddenly realized that if I did move, the living tornado would throw itself on me and devour me, draw me into itself, and transform me into one of its disembodied shades. One of those who gave it power and reason. What a good thing that Loraine was still wandering in her dreams, unable to see the black tornado whirling above her.

The symbols of the Houses blazed with a furious green light, holding the Darkness within the circle.

I didn't have to turn around to see my blood brothers and sisters. Pale faces that had suddenly lost all their attractive allure, staring eyes, open mouths revealing fangs . . . the shadows, spellbound by the dance of that immense vortex of death, now clearly visible through their human likenesses. Knowing that any one of them could become a victim, they stood there motionless, scarcely breathing. Only the Cadavercitan—the conductor of this black ballet of death—was invulnerable and all-powerful. For a brief moment this immense power obeyed him, and when that moment was over, it would incinerate him. Chris, forgive me. I didn't know. I didn't think that the magic you possess could destroy you.

The Vitdikta trembled ravenously and turned a crater streaked with lightning flashes toward me. I felt as if I were gazing into the gaping mouth of a gigantic beast, and in another moment it would tear me to pieces. I mustn't move, I mustn't think, I mustn't breathe. A black mist was creeping into my soul, shaking me up, turning me inside out, shuffling me like a deck of cards. The human part of my soul howled in terror, the dark half trembled in an ecstatic desire to merge with this dismal abyss that had given it birth. A few moments longer, and I would have flung myself into that whirlpool. The black jaws closed and the vortex swung around to confront the caster of the spell—Chris.

Could he really be feeling the same things I felt! How could he listen to the siren call of the black abyss for such an eternity and still not respond! Where did he get so much strength?

The vortex was shaken by a powerful vibration, it curved over, and I suddenly heard an inhuman howl of horror, pain, and despair. One of the young Asiman had lost his nerve. He made a dash for it, his eyes glaring with insane fear. The tornado stretched out into a taut whiplash, reached over Chris's head, grabbed the unfortunate vampire, jerked him up to the ceiling, shook him like a limp rag, and swallowed him up. The first victim.

I heard the Cadavercitan's voice again, intoning his ancient spells above the roaring of the Vitdikta. Serpents of fire ran over the walls of the vortex; Chris raised the stiletto and slashed himself across the wrist. The scarlet blood spurted out onto the symbols of the ancient families, and they burst into flame. A wave of prodigious heat scorched my face: my clothes, hair, eyebrows, and eyelashes should have flared up instantly and been reduced to ashes. No, I couldn't bear this. It was far too painful.

Only the shadowy vision of the golden-haired girl sleeping at the center of the tornado made me stay where I was. The raging crater swung around, searching through the hall. In response to that gaze, one of the Upieschi shuddered and swayed. A voracious lash of the whip, and another of our brothers was dispatched forever into the Darkness.

The fire lashed around the hall, transforming us into living torches, making us cry out in pain.

And then it suddenly stopped. The nightmarish heat receded. And I saw Chris again. My friend the Cadavercitan, who had never been more than thirty years old. Cool, mysterious, green-eyed Chris was slowly dying. That accursed Darkness was sucking out his final strength, his life and youth. Only his voice was still the same as ever. His voice, and his eyes.

Darel, everything is as it should be. Don't get in my way. There's not long to go.

The sleeping girl at the center of the magical circle stirred and groaned. Her back arched up sharply, and a dark shadow separated from her body. It flew into the air like a small trembling cloud and merged into the vortex spinning above the tiny human figure.

At that very moment, the sorcerer swayed and started slowly sinking down. The stiletto fell from his fingers and clattered across the floor, cutting through the invisible barrier containing the green flame. The vortex shrieked and exploded. Gouts of Darkness, gray mist, and hissing bolts of lightning filled the hall. I dashed forward, jumped over the line of feebly glowing flame, and covered Loraine with my body.

And then I heard another voice ring out. Vivian's voice. He was standing over his teacher's body, and the green stiletto in his hand was slicing through the Darkness. Swirling eddies of blackness were scattered one after another, and the gray nonlife curling between the columns was reduced to smoke. The Darkness withdrew from Chris, and I saw his burnt, disfigured face, his scorched hair, his slashed wrist still oozing blood. Vivian went down on his knees, and the glowing stiletto in his hand began fading. A final flash of green lightning ran back to the blade, and a cleft opened up in the space of the hall, sucking the remains of the Darkness back into it.

The door opened by the Cadavercitan had slammed shut.

And that was it. Loraine, warm, young, and defenseless, the old Loraine, was sleeping in my arms, and the pale, predatory, hungry shadow had disappeared from her face.

The first to recover his wits was Amir. He rushed past me, hissing a highly tangible curse in my direction. The Dahanavar Ladies raced after him, straightening their clothes and tidying their hair. Felicia stopped beside me. Her face was white with fury and streaked with gray soot, her magnificent peplos was torn, and I could see deep scratches on her arms.

"Tomorrow, eleven o'clock, at a council of the elders." She seemed to have difficulty pronouncing even these few words.

She didn't say what would happen at the council of the Dahanavar elders, and I didn't ask. I couldn't have cared less.

Constance ran past me with her makeup smeared and her eyebrows singed, looking frightened and angry. I was swamped by a smell of scorched hair, expensive French perfume, and the final drops of fear.

Ramon was the only Upieschi left. He left the hall at the same time as Alexander.

The last to leave was the Regenant. I didn't know how he had survived, how his human body had withstood the Vitdikta. He didn't say anything to me, just gave me a long, hard look.

Then I heard muffled laughter, painful coughing, and finally:

"Now, wasn't that fun!"

It was Chris.

The realization jolted me like an electric shock.

"Chris! Are you alive?"

He was alive, but he didn't look it. Vivian was carefully cradling the haggard, emaciated creature that had Chris's voice and green eyes. The withered arms of an old, old man, a body with almost no flesh on it, covered with dirty, tattered rags—it looked as if it would crumble to pieces if you touched it. His dry, cracked skin, scorched by the fire, was cut across by deep wrinkles, and in this terrible face the young eyes were laughing.

"Chris, I . . ."

He smiled. Tried to smile—the misshapen mask twisted into crooked folds, and the green eyes glittered.

"Time for us to go. It will soon be dawn."

CHRIS's car—a long, dark Lincoln with dark-tinted windows—was standing by the side of the road. I got into the back, still holding Loraine. Vivian helped Chris get in and sit beside me.

The Cadavercitan's pupil got into the driver's seat. And it was only then that I found my voice.

"Chris, forgive me."

"For what?" He gestured casually to his face with one hand. "For this? Don't mention it, Darel."

"You could have died. You should have died! Why, Chris?"

"Why did I change my mind and help you? Or why didn't the Vitdikta kill me?"

"Why didn't you tell me what could happen to you, to everyone?"

Chris turned his appalling face toward me and said: "I didn't want you to have to choose."

He was about to say something else, but he stopped, gazing at Vivian. I suddenly realized that we hadn't started moving. Poor Viv couldn't start the car. His hands were shaking so badly that he got the key into the ignition only at the third attempt. Then the motor roared and cut out.

"Vivian," said Chris, "we have to hurry."

The pupil jerked the key again and the car roared, but it didn't move. Then he dropped his arms onto the wheel and lowered his head onto them. The sorcerer sighed, leaned forward, and grasped his pupil firmly by the shoulder.

"Viv, my boy, calm down. Everything's fine. It's all over. Well done. Consider that you've just passed your latest test."

Vivian swung around abruptly. His lips were white, his gray eyes almost transparent. He gazed at Chris for a few seconds, and his eyes were filled with such intense adoration that I instantly pulled in my senses and turned away. I don't know what they talked about, but a few moments later the car started up and set off down the highway, rapidly picking up speed. Chris leaned back in the seat and wearily ran one hand over his face.

"I look terrible, don't I?"

I nodded and asked: "Why did it spare you?"

"Because I knew what the Vitdikta is. Everyone thinks it's a blind, insane force that devours everything it can reach. And that's true, it can be like that. The last time it destroyed all the Leargini elders. The House died out because it couldn't make up the strength and wisdom that had been lost. The Vitdikta is rational enough to read in our souls what we fear, what we are hiding, what we dream of."

"But what kind of creature is it?"

"It isn't a creature," said Chris. He looked at me for a while, trying to decide if I was worthy of the knowledge that he possessed.

AFTERWARD I sat on the edge of the bed, watching Loraine wake up. It was a long, painful struggle. She buried her face in the pillow and tossed about in the bed, muttering something indistinctly in her sleep.

"Darel . . . Darel!"

"I'm here."

"I feel awful, Darel. What's wrong with me?"

"Everything's fine."

"I can't wake up. Wake me up."

I put my arms around her, kissed her closed eyes and hot lips, and thought: What a blessing that you are so young. So weak, helpless, and fragile. The Vitdikta has purged every last drop of the dark power out of your soul; there's nothing left for your memory to latch on to. You'll never know that you almost became my enemy.

THE COMPOSER

For cynicism, sentimentality is just like a day off at the bank.

—Oscar Wilde, *De Profundis*

November 29

Miklosh Balza hated music.

Or rather, he hated human music. In all its manifestations.

It made no difference whether it was a symphony orchestra or a popular rock band—the Nachttoter thought that the sounds made by the musical instruments were appalling. Nothing could satisfy his demanding ear.

But his contempt for human musicians was as nothing compared with his contempt for those whom humans regarded as geniuses. The mere mention of a famous composer was enough to set the Nachterret leader shaking in uncontrollable fury and longing to kill not only the talentless mediocrity who had written such appalling melodies, but also any idiot who attempted to discuss the finest of the arts with the casual air of the connoisseur.

Mr. Balza didn't bother to explain to the sheep where they had gone wrong, he didn't get into arguments, and his retribution was swift. Well, really, how could he possibly try to explain to these idiots that Tchaikovsky had no talent, Chopin composed tedious little tunes, Vivaldi was maudlin, Mozart's symphonies were depressing, and Wagner was too noisy—he wrote operas only to salve his own ego—while Paganini was interested only in fame, and for him music was merely a means to that end.

Miklosh could have extended the list indefinitely. He just couldn't understand how some blood brothers could listen to that for hours, go to ballets and operas, enjoy and even applaud the horrors that some people actually dared to call music.

In fact, of all the immense variety of musical compositions that existed, the Nachttoter liked only those that had been set down on paper by his own hand.

Perhaps to some people this might have seemed like vanity, even gross arrogance, if not for one small thing. Miklosh Balza really was a fine composer. He believed that if he wanted, he could have outstripped the reputations of the acknowledged geniuses of human music, such as Tchaikovsky or that fearsome ghoul Mozart.

But he felt absolutely no urge to do that. It was not the Nachttoter's way to cast his pearls before swine—they would never understand the full depth of the feelings that he poured into his compositions. Fame and recognition among the cattle meant nothing to him. It was empty noise. Miklosh could never imagine himself being so petty and vain, and he made no attempt to take his own creations outside the bounds of his mansion. He played his own works only for himself. And he was perfectly happy with the situation just the way it was.

And right now, Balza was in his study in the Fortress of the Moon, just coming to the end of the cello part in a symphony of his own composition. When the bow had touched the strings for the last time and the melody faded away, the Nachttoter set aside his cello—made by Antonio Stradivari in 1684—and stretched sweetly.

He felt hungry.

The sound of an automobile engine outside the window was like an answer to Miklosh's unspoken prayer. He walked over to the panes of bulletproof glass, moved aside the curtain, and saw a large black Lincoln drive through the English park and come to a smooth halt at the steps leading up into the building. A jolly group got out of the automobile. Three Nachterret soldiers and five human girls.

A champagne cork popped, and the girls all squealed in unison. The soldiers led their guests into the mansion. The human mercenaries guarding the entrance to the Fortress of the Moon made no attempt to halt the unfamiliar women. They had got used to the idea that at night bright-colored moths fluttered inside but never came back out again.

The female visitors to the mansion were young, well-dressed, and attractive. But then, they always were. One more group of seekers of nocturnal amusement and adventures had found both. To their own cost.

Unlike some of the brothers in other Houses, Miklosh Balza had always preferred fresh blood to the packaged kind. Preferably, it should be young. When it came to nourishment, the Nachttoter was just like any other consumer—he liked his products in beautiful packaging. Another preferable (although not compulsory) criterion was that the products should behave quietly and not kick up a fuss while they were being consumed.

Miklosh would have liked to go downstairs to the dining hall, but he was expecting a report any minute, so he had to be patient. Food wasn't the most important thing. He would wait. Business came first.

The head of the House walked across his spacious study and perched on the edge of the desk. One of the soldiers who had brought dinner to the mansion walked in.

"Glory to you, Nachttoter."

"Hello, brother," Miklosh said good-naturedly.

"We've brought the sheep. One of them is a blonde, just as you wanted."

Balza felt hungry again and had to suppress the desire to go downstairs immediately and sink his teeth into the girl's neck.

"Everything in order?" he asked in a calm, steady voice. Without the slightest hint at any kind of hunger.

"Yes," said the soldier, and hastily clarified, "We've checked them."

The head of the Golden Hornets nodded in approval. These idiots had once brought the mayor's daughter into his lair. There had been no end of trouble. The police had turned the entire city upside down, and he had been forced to change the usual way food was delivered to his house. Ever since then, every girl who decided to spend the night at the Fortress of the Moon was carefully checked, to avoid any serious unpleasantness.

"Excellent. You and your brothers have done a good job. Take one for yourselves. No, two."

Miklosh Balza was in an excellent mood today.

"Thank you, Nachttoter!"

Miklosh indicated with a slight gesture of his hand that his subordinate was free to go.

Johan looked into the study.

"Come in. Sit down," Miklosh said briskly, pointing to an armchair with a high back beside his desk. "And take your cloak off."

Without saying a word, the landsknecht took the long leather cloak off his shoulders and hung it over his arm.

"Hang it beside the door. What do you think the hooks are for?" the Nachttoter growled irritably. "And how many times have I asked you to wash your boots before you come in? Who's going to clean the carpet after you?"

Mr. Balza was as precise and uncompromising in matters of hygiene as he was in matters of music. He valued order in all things and found any sloppiness very irritating.

"Sorry, Nachttoter. It won't happen again," the giant replied complaisantly.

That was what he said every time. But he never changed his habits, and he never washed his boots. Either he forgot, or he didn't think it was worth bothering about such trifles. This had been going on for years. Balza glowered in annoyance and rebuked his deputy for being such a swine, but he never resorted to any more serious measures. "Then take your boots off," Miklosh muttered. He walked around the desk and sat in his chair.

While his deputy was removing his footwear, he took a paper knife out of the top drawer of the desk and started twirling it thoughtfully in his fingers.

The armchair creaked pitifully under Johan's weight. The Nachttoter frowned when he saw that his deputy's socks were wet. They had left dirty footprints on the expensive carpet. Miklosh repressed his rising irritation and said nothing, indicating to his deputy that he could begin his report. But then the phone interrupted them.

The Nachterret leader moved only at the eighth ring. He casually reached out and switched on the speaker without picking up the handset. Then he leaned back in his chair, still without saying a word. He didn't like to start a conversation, believing that if someone called him, the caller should make the effort.

The caller at the other end of the line was apparently aware of this habit.

"Good evening, brother."

Miklosh frowned in annoyance, but he replied: "Good evening, Ramon. Glad to hear your voice."

"Don't try to make fun of me. Sometimes I regret that we do any business together."

"Have you got problems?"

The sound of the Upieschi grinding his teeth was audible even through the speaker.

"No. You're the one who's got problems. Big problems in Colombia."

"We're not the ones who trade in that dope the sheep are so fond of," said Mr. Balza, deciding to play the innocent and annoy the other party. It gave him tremendous satisfaction.

"That's not what I'm talking about, as you know perfectly well. Your mercenaries have not met their obligations. And that is costing me money!"

"Gently, Ramon. I might take offense."

"I don't give a damn if you do. You've cost me three hundred million!"

"Don't be so petty." This stupid and pointless conversation was beginning to annoy the Nachttoter. "This lost powder is no reason for us to fall out. Call me back tomorrow. I'll try to sort out this little hitch. If I can't manage it, I'll pay back the money out of my own funds. Good evening."

He switched off the phone without waiting for an answer and then swore.

"Just who does that money-grabbing blautsauger think he is?"

Apart from their legal business, the financier-vampires also had illegal interests, which were the ones that provided the lion's share of their quite fantastic profits. The arms trade, drug dealing, and industrial espionage were the three pillars of Upieschi prosperity. The traders also sometimes employed the services of the House of Nachterret in their dealings. The Nachterret weren't shy of dirty work, and the human mercenaries trained by Golden Hornets could carry out all sorts of assignments. Miklosh sometimes rented out his small army—for instance, to protect goods belonging to the Upieschi. Sometimes the traders also dabbled in politics without the Dahanavar's knowledge. And the amounts of money circulating in politics were absolutely huge; there was no way you could manage without armed security. Two coups in Africa had been carried out by Miklosh's well-trained men. And the Upieschi, if not the Dahanavar, were pleased. The Dahanavar had raised an outcry and called a meeting of the council at the Regenant's residence, but it had all come to nothing. Mr. Balza had just shrugged and said it was nothing to do with him. There was no proof, and the case was dropped.

But this time, the situation was a little more sensitive. The House of Nachterret had misplaced the powder that it was supposed to be guarding. Or, to call a spade a spade, it had simply resold it, after killing the Upieschi's people who were guarding it. Of course, the entire operation had taken place under Johan's control. The dope for sheep had been sold for three hundred and fifty million, not three hundred, as Ramon had wanted to do. The money had already been spread across several different banks, and by tomorrow evening, Miklosh was expecting to transfer the extra fifty million to his personal account and pay the rest back to the financiers. They would grumble a bit when they received the agreed-upon sum, but after a while they would forget all this unpleasantness, while Balza would pocket a large wad of easy money for almost no effort.

"So . . . ," the Nachttoter began eagerly. "Did the council meet?"

He had been deliberately putting off this moment all evening.

"Yes, Nachttoter. Everyone, just as you said."

Miklosh smiled with just the corners of his mouth. Slipping Amir the idea of taking revenge on Darel Dahanavar through the human girl had been a brilliant piece of improvisation. Until the very last moment, he had hardly dared to hope that the Asiman would take the bait. Which made the news that everything had gone as planned and she had been turned all the sweeter when it came. After that, events had played out like a well-written score. The Nachterret had been certain that the telepath was insane enough to demand the ritual.

"And was there a Vitdikta?"

Miklosh hadn't gone to the council meeting precisely because he had been expecting this entirely predictable outcome.

"Yes."

"So, Svetlov couldn't resist after all. He couldn't find any reason to refuse. . . ." The Nachttoter chuckled briefly, feeling delighted that his calculations had proved correct. Now he expected to hear which of his brothers' leaders were missing.

"The Vricolakos didn't come."

Balza's voice was the only thing that betrayed his loss of self-control.

"Then who performed the ritual?"

"The sorcerer."

The head of the House leaned back abruptly in his chair. Outwardly he appeared perfectly calm, but there was a storm raging in his soul.

His plan had gone awry just when he'd least expected it. It had been so right to count on the Vricolakos. Ivan Svetlov was the only one who should have agreed to perform the ritual. The werewolves' animal rules of justice were just too strong.

Miklosh knew that Ivan would not be strong enough, and that was just what he needed. He had been hoping that during the Vitdikta, one of the Houses' heads would be dispatched to the next world. It would have been best if it had been Felicia—the most dangerous of all his enemies. But it would have been pretty good to get rid of Stephanie, the Second Lady Elder. And that young redheaded bitch, Constance—she wouldn't have had a chance of surviving the uncompleted ritual. As for Amir Asiman, Ramon Upieschi, and Alexander Faryartos—the Nachttoter wouldn't have missed any of them too badly, or the Regenant, either. But he hadn't even dared to dream of that kind of success.

But the Vricolakos hadn't even shown up! And that accursed sorcerer had. Miklosh hadn't taken the Cadavercitan into account in his calculations. Chris Frederick Alabert had ignored the council for decades, but now he had suddenly turned up. And performed the Vitdikta, reshuffling all the cards.

"He's dead, I hope?" Miklosh asked in a quiet voice, not really daring to hope too much.

"No, he was mauled, but everyone survived. The Vitdikta gave back what it had taken. The girl's human again."

"Damnation!"

That damn Cadavercitan, of course he would recover from the ritual and carry on being a thorn in Miklosh's side. Curse him three times over.

"What about Felicia?"

"She's very angry. It looks like Darel's in serious trouble."

That was some consolation, at least. One facet of his plan had worked as it was supposed to. That conceited young fool would suffer for putting his family in such an awkward position. The Dahanavar might expel him, and that would be very helpful to the House of Nachterret. To deprive the Lady of the only ideal scanner among the blood brothers was also a victory of sorts.

"Nachttoter . . ." Johan paused, then made up his mind to go on. "Can I talk to the sorcerer now?"

He had been cherishing a dream of getting rid of Chris for a long time. The German landsknecht was just longing to cross swords with the Burgundian knight. Man to man. To see which of them was stronger in the art of wielding cold steel. But Miklosh had forbidden it.

"No," said the Nachttoter after thinking for a moment. "The time hasn't come yet. I have a feeling that sooner or later I shall have to have it out with Chris myself. Off you go."

Trying to conceal his disappointment, Johan bowed and walked out of the study, closing the door firmly behind him. Miklosh watched him go and then started adjusting his plan to meet the drastically changed situation.

He was feeling very hungry.

19

Expulsion

I can't help detesting my relations. I suppose it comes
from the fact that none of us can stand other people
having the same faults as ourselves.

—Oscar Wilde, *The Picture of Dorian Gray*

An idiot in the eyes of God and an idiot in the eyes of
people are not the same thing.

—Oscar Wilde, *De Profundis*

November 30
Darel Dahanavar

At eleven in the evening, I was standing in front of the council of
Dahanavar elders. The large hall was lit by only a few crimson
candles, and in this funereal light, the figures of my judges looked
like dark, faceless phantoms. Immaterial and unfeeling. I looked
over their heads at the huge painting hanging above the fireplace—
white bodies woven together into a strange ghostly dance above a
shadowy abyss.

"Why did you have to do it, Darel?" Felicia asked softly.

I tore my eyes away from the picture and looked at her, trying
to *feel* all of her, all the way through. But there was nothing but
cold. As if I had run into a dark, icy mirror and glimpsed the
distorted reflection of my own gaze.

"Explain what you were trying to achieve!" shouted Constance, annoyed by my silence. Well, well, so young and you already have a vote. I didn't know you'd grown up so fast.

"You wouldn't understand, Constance. None of you would.
It's too long since you were human."

For a few moments, they stared at me. Constance trembling in rage, Felicia abstractedly, Stephanie sadly. She was the first to speak.

"We are not human, Darel. But you are not human, either."

"No," I replied. "Unfortunately."

Constance was about to shout at me and accuse me of trying to condemn the council, but Felicia stopped her with a gesture of her hand.

"I understand, Darel, that your abilities are only possible because of your psychological peculiarities, and I closed my eyes to your unprecedented, insane, unnatural relationship with a human. But what you have done"—for the first time, a hint of some kind of emotion appeared in her voice—"for a human being, a young girl, you put our entire future at risk. Not just my life, but all our lives. We, the House of Dahanavar, are the only force capable of bridling the Asiman and the Nachterret. While we remain powerful, they stay hidden in their burrows. Do you really not understand that their greatest desire is to start a war between the families, so that they can freely kill human beings and our brothers without fear of punishment? The balance is so fragile, and it could all have collapsed simply because a human girl happened to get caught between the two forces, like a grain of sand between two millstones. Nothing would have changed if she had died or become a vampire, the wheels would have kept turning without feeling that tiny grain of sand, our forces would simply have swept her aside. But you, my brother, how could you value my life so little? What will happen to the family if I am not here? Who will take my place? You, so weak in mind and heart? You were tricked by Amir's deliberate provocation, Darel. It is fortunate that the ritual was conducted by the Cadavercitan. I did not think he was so strong. A rare stroke of luck, without which we would all be dead and Miklosh Nachterret would be sitting here now. You are naïve and conceited,

Darel. And I . . . I have nothing more to say. Sisters, I await your decision."

"Darel Dahanavar, do you admit that you are guilty of a deliberate attempt on the lives of the elders of the House?"

"Yes. I admit it."

"Stephanie, your decision, my sister?"

"Expulsion."

"Constance?"

"I agree. Expulsion."

"Darel . . . you are dead for us."

Now I knew whom they were burying in that picture. It was me.

I lay on my back and looked at the sky.

It was turning lighter. Very, very slowly.

With a kind of morbid curiosity, I watched the pale light seeping into the courtyard that was like a well. My shadowy soul trembled and fluttered in fear, but I stayed there without moving.

I don't remember what happened after the council of the elders; it felt as if I had been filled with some cold, sticky emptiness and a repulsive numbness had paralyzed all my desires and thoughts. Pictures so vivid that they set my head spinning drifted past in front of my eyes: Chris's mutilated face; the terrible sadness in the Regenant's eyes; the beautiful, wise, icy Felicia; a boy I didn't know running along a dark street and casting a curious glance into my face, a boy who looked so much like Loraine in his carefree joy and naïveté; the terrible scenes from the night before.

I stood out in the rain in the middle of the street. A thunderstorm in November! Lightning flickered in the low clouds, the raindrops shattered into fine droplets as they struck the surface of the road, the thunder rumbled. The world trying to wash away the final remnants of the Darkness summoned by you, my Cadavercitan friend.

At home, there was another surprise waiting for me. The

apartment had been ransacked. All the furniture had been broken, the candlesticks and dishes were smashed, the books ripped to pieces, the refrigerator gutted and overturned, the floor was one big red sticky puddle—my entire store of blood had been poured out onto it. The bedroom had been totally wrecked, as if dozens of pairs of hands had torn the sheets to shreds and chopped up the bed with axes. The fresco was almost completely destroyed, with deep, ragged scratches running through the girls' slim bodies and beautiful faces.

My former brothers or enemies had tried to give me one final farewell kick, and it felt as if the blow had got through.

The sky turned white, and I could look at it only with my eyes screwed up almost shut. It was too bright, but my curiosity kept on insisting: "Just a little longer, watch it happen, see what it's like when the sun rises, remember!"

In this spare apartment I had only one little room, with a window that faced a blank wall. It was covered by an old dusty curtain that I had opened just a little bit, enough to see the sky. It was a convenient spot. The center of town, a strong door—just to be on the safe side—neighbors who took no interest in one another. I had never lived here, and I hadn't expected the room in this communal apartment to be useful . . . so soon. Yellow striped wallpaper, a table standing against the wall, a bed that creaked, and just enough space to stride backward and forward from one corner to the other.

I had to close the curtain. No, I was going to bear it for one more minute. Tears started pouring out from under my lowered eyelids. The blinding brightness was impossible to tolerate, and the sun hadn't even risen yet. One more second.

"Have you gone completely crazy?" a familiar voice said above my head, and the black blinds rattled down over the window. The gentle darkness felt cool on my blinded eyes. "Have you decided to commit suicide?"

"Chris! You! How did you—"

"I knew you'd come here sooner or later. I was waiting downstairs."

A greenish light ran across my eyelids, and the pain eased.

"I haven't told anyone about this apartment."

"Well done. I'm glad for you."

Chris. The same old sarcastic Chris with his green eyes and black hair, young Chris standing with his shoulder leaning against the upright of the door, looking at me lying on the bed, and laughing mockingly.

"You look great."

"And you look like a corpse, which is what you would have been if I'd got here any later."

"I wanted . . . I don't know what it was I wanted. Now . . . now I'm nobody, Chris."

"I know." His voice and the expression on his face were warmer now. He sat on the bed beside me. "I know, Darel."

"I didn't think . . . I never thought it would be that hard. I never gave a damn for any of them. I thought I didn't care. But now I have no name, no family, no friends. Nothing!"

"You still have your name, sooner or later everyone loses their family, and in your place I wouldn't be so categorical on the subject of friends. I think you have one of them sitting beside you right now."

"Chris, you . . . Thank you."

"Don't mention it. The punishment your Ladies came up with is too harsh altogether. You Dahanavar are very family-oriented. Your family ties are too important to you, far more important than they are for the others. Instead of excommunication, the Asiman would simply have slaughtered their brother and been happy with that. The Ligamentia would never even have noticed it, and the Upieschi would have set up an opposition group to harass the head of the corporation and got your rights restored.

I can only assume the Dahanavar have fallen into a state of depression."

"And what would you have done?"

"Me? I have no idea. But that's not the question. Do you regret going to the Regenant and demanding the ritual?"

"No. I suppose I'm stupid, as Felicia says. But if I had to choose again between the fate of my family and Loraine's fate, I'd choose her again. I suppose I'm just too egotistic."

Chris's reaction was completely unexpected. He started laughing. I think it was the first time I had seen him laugh so sincerely and lightheartedly.

"What?" I asked gloomily when he finally calmed down.

"You should just hear yourself," he said, still smiling. "Too egotistical! My boy, that is our fundamental, natural condition. We are all egotistical, mean, and devious. Your feelings for a mortal girl make you unique."

"Chris, I've decided that I shouldn't see her anymore."

"I see." The smile faded from his face, and his eyes turned angry. "What sort of news is this?"

"You were right. I shouldn't keep confusing her this way. Don't look at me like that! You can see I can't protect her anymore. I'm too weak and helpless myself. I couldn't protect her before, and now I don't know who to be more afraid of—my ex-friends or my enemies."

"You know, Darel," the Cadavercitan began, speaking slowly, and I could clearly hear the drawling Old French accent in his voice, "when I saw how attached you were to this girl, how concerned you were about her, when I realized that you were prepared to sacrifice yourself, me, your House, the whole world, for a human, I realized that everything was still not lost for you. If a deep human feeling like that can grow on all this pale, mildewed sickness . . . With all our centuries of infighting for power, plotting, and bloodlust, we are simply nothing compared with that.

If you're afraid for her and yourself, I'll give you both sanctuary."

"Loraine is afraid to go to your place," I said, feeling a lump rising in my throat. "It's too dark and gloomy."

"I'll redecorate a couple of rooms just for her," Chris replied with a smile. "I was going to rearrange things anyway."

"This is the third time you've saved me."

"The fourth. By the way, have you eaten today?"

"I don't remember."

"I knew it."

The sorcerer picked up a large cooler bag and put it on the table.

"This is for you from Vivian. Group one, your favorite."

"That's very kind of you. Why don't you have breakfast with me?"

Chris narrowed his eyes and looked me over coolly, then he chuckled again and shook his head.

"I only enjoy my food when I'm alone, so I never eat in company."

While I ate breakfast, the Cadavercitan stood facing the wall with his hands clasped behind his back, studying the inscriptions left on the wallpaper by the previous tenant. These included "Happy Birthday" wishes to someone called Boris, a couple of mottoes in Latin, several swear words, and a few phone numbers.

"You were going to tell me about the Vitdikta," I reminded him.

"Are you sure you still want to hear it?" he asked without turning around.

"Yes! Of course!"

"You must understand, Darel, that what I am about to tell you is not the same information that teachers usually give their pupils. You can regard it as my own thoughts on the origins of the blood brothers. I think it happened a very long time ago, before the rise of Rome, ancient Greece, Atlantis, Hyperborea, and Lemuria."

He paused, and when he started speaking again, his words sounded like musings on a completely different subject.

"People have been born, died, created empires, been reduced to savagery, attained the heights of civilization. And all the time, living beside them quietly and unnoticed there were other beings. What could separate these two different spaces? A subtle, invisible, insurmountable barrier. Imagine two worlds that are the opposite of each other. Like in a mirror. What do you know about your reflection? About what happens to it on the other side? Two worlds touching each other. Two opposites that cannot exist without each other. A reflecting surface with a layer of black amalgam under it. As time passes, the mirror darkens. Black spots appear on the reflecting layer from the inside. The boundary between worlds becomes thinner, and in places it tears."

Chris took three steps—the distance from wall to wall in that tiny room—and walked back to his place. Then he did the same thing three more times.

"I don't know why our forebear came here. Whether he was thrown into this space by some cataclysm or found his own way through the invisible barrier as it broke down. He almost certainly didn't resemble a human being. My House calls him the Founder. The Vitdikta was the concentrated focus of his power, a magical vortex, the power that transported him here. It possesses all the power of magic in pure form. Our power is a piece of the Vitdikta. We are its creations. The Founder knew that he couldn't survive, his body could not tolerate the energy of this world, it was deadly to him, and so he used human beings to create his heirs, his children. He divided his magic up between them. Some got more, some got less. And he died. When we turn a human, we appeal to the Vitdikta, draw a thread of power out of it, and add the magic dissolved in our own blood. That's why it is impossible to combine the powers of the different families. If all the energy is gathered together in a single being, that being will explode. It will be torn to pieces. This world"—Chris beat his fists on the wall with the scribbled inscriptions—"is not our world. We have adapted to it, but it remains hostile. You live in two realities. This one, and the one on the other side of the mirror."

I listened very carefully.

"That means the different magic of the Dahanavar, the Cadavercitan, the Upieschi, and so forth are just tiny fragments of some power that was once all one?"

"Yes, we are all tiny likenesses of each other. Reflections."

The sorcerer looked at his hand, at the ring in the shape of a cross that he wore only very rarely. He squeezed his fingers together, and the Cadavercitan relic glowed with green fire.

"The magic is leaving. I despise Miklosh, I can't stand him, but if he is killed, another small part of an irreplaceable substance will leak out of our world with him. The Mentor disappeared, Flora died, and the Vitdikta sucked half of the beauty, joy, and magic out of our world."

"She loved you," I said.

"How could you know," Chris replied in a hollow voice. "You were never able to read her."

He sat on a chair beside the bed, and neither of us spoke for a long time. Each of us was thinking his own thoughts. Chris about the woman he had loved and lost, I about the girl who meant more to me than anything in the world, the girl I had almost lost. I couldn't have cared less what the Vitdikta was and where our ancestors had come from.

Outside the door, we occasionally heard the neighbors' hurrying feet, whispering voices, the noise of water in the toilet, windows slamming shut. I lay on the bed, feeling myself bogged down in the human emotions of varying intensities that were flowing to me from all the floors in the building. Chris sat there, leaning against the hard wooden back of his chair with his eyes closed. He was sleeping or remembering Flora.

"A complicated plot," he said unexpectedly.

"What?" I realized I had been dozing, and his words had woken me.

"You were set up. Loraine was the bait. You became too attached to her. Apparently everybody knows about it now."

"Yes, Amir took revenge for his pupils. The ones you thrashed so thoroughly at the cemetery."

"No, it's far more complicated than that. More complicated than we can imagine. I don't know who's behind this, but I sense a malign plot in all this. I'm going to think about it."

He fell silent again, and his eyes suddenly flashed green behind his closed eyelids. A rather frightening sight. Evidently my friend had activated some special kind of Cadavercitan magic. They had a couple of spells that made it possible to extract every day in the past from their memories in great visual detail.

I let him get on with it. Got up, trying not to make the bed creak, walked over to the wall, and started amusing myself with the inscriptions on it. In response to my mental command, the scrawled letters quivered, stretched out into a line, started crawling across the wallpaper like caterpillars and curling up into different-colored shaggy balls. In a burst of inspiration, I shaped them into the Dahanavar arrow and had already drawn a circle around them when suddenly Chris interrupted my artistic efforts in a rather harsh tone of voice.

"What are you doing?" The sorcerer was looking at me hard, and the green glow had disappeared from his eyes.

"Why?"

"My friend, unless I am very much mistaken, you have just demonstrated the basics of the Faryartos magic. By using it, moreover, in the most stupid and idiotic fashion that could possibly be imagined. But I can't understand how it found its way into your none-too-bright head!"

"I would have to disagree with you about the none-too-bright head."

"I wouldn't if I were you. You should never fiddle with an energy that you know absolutely damn all about. Sit down and tell me about it."

Yes, I hadn't told him about my adventure. So I had to tell him now. At the end of my colorful story, Chris turned dark and gloomy.

"You shouldn't have got mixed up with Miklosh."

"I didn't get mixed up with him. All I did was—"

"You mustn't even go anywhere near him. Why are you always attracted to all sorts of garbage?"

"In the first place, don't shout at me! And in the second place, Hranya—"

"He'll gobble up Hranya and you, and a dozen more like you without batting an eyelid."

"Is he really that powerful? Even more powerful than you?"

"Darel, this is like a conversation between two pupils! 'Who's more powerful, my teacher or yours?' My magical potential is greater than Dona's, but she weaves her spells more elegantly and expends less energy on them. In terms of subtle professional skill, she stands above me."

"These are petty differences within the family. You're still more powerful."

"Yes. Because she's a mystic and I'm a warrior. Different psychologies." Chris paused and laughed as he remembered something. "And apart from that, I have green eyes."

"What's that got to do with anything?"

"Absolutely nothing. Cadavercitan prejudices. It used to be thought that someone with green eyes had greater potential for necromancy than anyone else. Evidently because our main spells are accompanied by a green glow."

"Nonsense—does that mean that those with the strongest smell of carrion make the best Nachterrets?"

Chris laughed. Then he took off his ring and tossed it to me. "Take it."

"What for?" I asked, weighing the item of jewelry on my open palm. It proved to be carved very skillfully out of a single piece of black stone: I could even see little ivy leaves decorated with tiny emeralds.

"I'm taking you under the protection of the House of Death. You are now a freelance Cadavercitan."

"Thank you, Chris."

"Don't mention it. If I were just a bit more rational, I would hire you to work for us. The official scanner of the House of Cadavercitan. It sounds good." He smiled, settled himself more comfortably on his chair, and closed his eyes again. This time intending to go to sleep.

I had never worn any of the identifying badges of my family—rings and medallions in the form of the Dahanavar arrow. And now it felt strange to see the symbol of a different House on my finger.

In late fall, the days are short. We woke up almost as soon as darkness fell. Chris stretched, holding on to his waist, and massaged the back of his neck.

"It's a long time since I last slept sitting in a chair. All right, I'm going home. I'll expect you at any time."

"Listen!" I exclaimed, jumping off the bed with a vague presentiment pricking at my chest. "Loraine's absolutely defenseless now. Won't they try to harm her?"

"Get a grip," the sorcerer said sarcastically, straightening the collar of his shirt in the greenish mirror that he had just created on the wall—yes, I had to admit that household magic was one of the Cadavercitan family's strong points, too. "It's all been taken care of without you."

"You've done something?"

"You'll be able to thank me later. Right. Time for me to be going."

He removed the mirror with his multipurpose wrist movement and walked out of the room. I wondered what it was I would have to thank him for.

I phoned Loraine from the communal telephone standing on the battered table in the corridor. The line was appallingly bad, but I managed to let her know that I was coming to her place. Told her to wait. She was glad to hear my voice.

She came rushing out of the entrance a minute after the Pontiac pulled up outside her building. She must have been waiting, looking out the window. She ran over, slipping on the thin crust of ice covering the asphalt. She halted beside me with an effort and gave me a tight hug. Then we examined each other for a few seconds. I tried to spot any signs of vampirism in her face, and she searched for something, too. She was concerned, upset. The Cadavercitan had told her.

"Chris called and said you had some problems. Very serious ones. What's happened?"

"Nothing. Everything's all right now."

How defenseless she was, how young and vulnerable. I was responsible for her. And if any bastard tried to hurt her again . . .

"Let's go. Get in the car."

She clambered obediently into the front seat, waited until I got in beside her, and said: "Vivian came to see me. Chris asked him to. And look . . ."

Loraine unbuttoned her jacket and unwound her scarf. She needn't have bothered, I'd already sensed it. There was a mark on her collarbone—the Cadavercitan cross. In shimmering green, just barely visible. The mark with which the sorcerers identified their human servants: "Property of the House of Death, do not touch."

"Vivian said that no one will touch me now. They won't want to face up to Chris."

I smiled grimly and showed her my ring. "Looks like he's taken care of both of us."

"You too?" Loraine frowned, and her delight at being involved with my friend's magic began to dissolve in a new wave of anxiety. "Why?"

"I've been expelled from my family. Now I need protection, too. Just like you."

"Expelled?" She swung round bodily toward me. "What for?"

"Profound internal differences." I turned the key in the ignition.

Loraine said nothing for a while, emitting a powerful aura of sympathy, and then touched my shoulder.

"Don't be upset. They'll come running to you and ask you to come back."

"Perhaps. But I'm not likely to want to go back."

At that moment, that was exactly how I felt. My confusion, weariness, and resentment were mingled with malicious gloating. I wondered how Felicia was going to manage without her irreplaceable telepath. Especially when Hranya came. Let Constance read her!

I laughed. And Loraine, who was watching me very closely, cheered up.

CHRIS was waiting for us in the sitting room. Looking very pleased with himself.

"Make yourselves at home. Loraine, sit down. Don't play the fool, it's an empty sarcophagus, there's nobody inside. No mummy's going to leap out of it. What terrible things the modern movie industry has done to young people's minds. Darel, how many times do I have to tell you, take your feet off the table. What is it, Vivian?"

The young Cadavercitan walked into the room, carrying a colorful gift box. He smiled at Loraine, nodded in greeting to me, and looked at his teacher.

"Look, I found it outside the door. There's no note or address. It's light, there doesn't seem to be anything in it."

He took hold of the lid and raised it slightly. My warning shout and Chris's exclamation came at the same instant.

"Stop!"

"Don't touch it!"

A faint cloud rose out of the box and settled on Vivian's hands and chest in fine gray dust. The sorcerer dashed toward him, knocking the "gift" out of his pupil's hand with a shaft of green flame from his open palm. The cardboard box was incinerated before it even reached the floor. I realized that I was standing at the other end of the room, holding Loraine tight against me.

For a few moments, Vivian looked down at his hands and his outstretched fingers, and then I was suddenly struck by such intense pain that I couldn't help groaning. But my groan was drowned out by the young Cadavercitan's scream. The skin on his palms started turning black, and the sweater on his chest started smoking. He started falling . . . he would have fallen, if Chris hadn't grabbed him.

"Chris!"

"Hang on! Hang in there! One moment! You'll feel better in a moment! Darel, get Loraine out of here! Immediately! Hang on, Viv! Hang on, my boy! Just a little longer."

He was lying. Viv wasn't going to feel any better. Chris's pupil was being killed by Grave Rot.

The wise, almost all-powerful Cadavercitan had no way to defend themselves against this spell that was entirely harmless to all the other families. Although I wasn't even sure it was a spell. It was the first time I'd ever seen its effect; previously I had only heard about this plague that could destroy the flesh of the

Masters of Death, causing them unbearable torment in the process. The Grave Rot hadn't been used for almost six hundred years. Since then, it was thought that the secret had been lost.

THE entire house was suffused with pain. From the basement to the roof. I could feel it every minute, even though I tried to cut myself off. Loraine sat on the sofa in the library, feeling scared, gazing at me in mingled hope and reproach. Her eyes were red and her nose was swollen from crying, she felt so sorry for Vivian.

"Isn't there anything at all that can be done?"

"Not a single thing."

"That can't be true! You can always think of something. Do you hear me?"

"Yes, I hear you."

"He helped save you! That time, from the Asiman. Why? Who did this? What for?"

"I don't know."

Vivian was lying on the bed in Chris's bedroom. Everything there was permeated with the smell of blood and the stench of corpses. Lying on the carpet beside the bed were empty plasma packets, with the remains of their contents slowly soaking into the thick woolen pile. The sheets and the bedcovers were covered in red smears. The bedside table was stacked with bottles.

The sorcerer was sitting in an armchair. His shirtsleeves were rolled up, and both wrists were covered with fresh bites and scratches. His white, empty face was almost expressionless; a streak of blood had dried on one cheek. Sam hovered beside the table like a pale ghost. And on the opposite wall, presiding over all this insanity with a serene smile, was Flora's portrait.

Vivian stirred, opened his eyes, and groaned. Then he shuddered and cried out in pain. Chris jumped to his feet, slashed his fangs across his own wrist, and pressed the bleeding wound to his pupil's lips. Vivian fastened his mouth on Chris's arm, took several swallows, and fell back onto the pillow, breathing jerkily. The sorcerer took another pack of plasma, tore it open, drank the donor blood, tossed the pack on the carpet with the others, and finally noticed me standing in the doorway. He wiped his mouth on his sleeve and sank back into the armchair.

"How is he?"

"Dying," my friend replied hoarsely. "I'm not letting him die, I'm keeping him going with my blood, but that can't go on forever."

He dropped his bitten wrists onto his knees and lowered his head.

"There's nothing I can do."

Vivian started tossing about in the bed again, and he groaned: "Chris, please . . ."

The sorcerer jumped to his feet and went over to him, rolling his sleeves up higher. "Hang on. You'll feel better soon."

"No! Don't. I can't go on like this. . . . No more."

"Hang on! I won't let you die!"

"Chris, you don't know . . . I've always been unlucky. Always. Only I could have . . . got caught . . . so stupidly."

He tried to sit up, and the smell of decomposition became stronger. The flesh on Vivian's hands and chest was falling apart, rotting alive; in places, the bones were visible through the blackened tissues. I felt like running as far away as possible, but I stood there and watched the sorcerer feeding his own blood to his pupil. Vivian couldn't regenerate, but at least the plague wasn't spreading deeper inside him.

Chris, I said in my mind. *Be careful. It might be infectious.*

Do you think I really care? he replied. He straightened up and took hold of the upright of the bed, to which the canopy was attached. His hand left a red print on the spiral of gilded wood.

"I don't care anymore," he said out loud, and sat down. Thrust his fingers into his black hair and squeezed his head tight, trying to remember, to think of a spell, a medicine, anything that could help.

"Chris . . ." The sound from the bed was something between a sigh and a groan.

"Yes, Viv?" The Cadavercitan raised his head, trying to conceal the despair in his face.

"Please . . . stop this. No more! I can't. I'm going to die anyway. Please, do it yourself. As long as it's quick."

"No," the sorcerer replied firmly. He hammered his fist down on the arm of his chair. "I won't let you die! Don't even think about it. You young idiot, why did you open that box?"

"You're only tormenting him," I said, walking over and sitting beside Chris.

"I can't lose Vivian. Not him, too." He looked at Flora's portrait. "If he dies, I'll have absolutely nothing left."

He glanced at me, and a strange expression appeared in his eyes.

"Darel, help me."

"How? What can I do?"

He grabbed hold of my hand with his bloody, sticky fingers and squeezed it until it hurt.

"You're a scanner. The best I've ever known. *Read* him." The Cadavercitan jumped up and dragged me across to the bed where his pupil was in the process of dying. "Read off all his feelings, memories, desires, everything that you can. Store them. Remember them."

"Chris! Wait! Stop! If only it was possible . . ."

"It is possible. I know. You'll read all his thoughts and knowledge, his emotions, his entire soul. Every day he has lived, every hour."

Now there was genuine insanity glittering in his eyes.

"You'll take his soul out and put it in a new body, and I'll bring it to life."

"Chris! Get a grip! It's impossible. Who are you going to transfer his soul into? A human? Or are you going to kill one of the brothers? If that is the crazy idea you have in your head—you won't even have time to do it."

The sorcerer clutched my hand even tighter. And now his face was glowing with insane joy and hope, his eyes filled with a magical green glow.

"I'll transfer him into Flora's body."

"What? You . . . you kept her?"

"Yes," he said with a proud, conceited smile.

"You crazy necromancer! You kept her body here all these years?"

"Yes!"

I sat on the edge of the bed, struggling to take it in, to imagine it.

"You're out of your mind."

"Darel!" He grabbed hold of my shoulders and shook me. "Help me! Help me to save Vivian."

"This is insanity. It's not possible! Flora and—"

"I know. I know! But a human body won't be able to hold a vampire's soul. And I don't have anyone else who would work. Although I suppose," he said with a crooked grin, "I could kill Sam. Do you want me to?"

There was the sound of breaking glass. Chris's second pupil, who was rearranging the bottles on the table, shuddered and turned to look at his teacher with an expression of horror on his face. But Chris had already forgotten about him.

"Can you imagine how painful it is when the Rot devours you alive? How terrifying it is for a young man to see his own body decomposing? Darel, he's so young! He's only just really started living. There are so many things he hasn't done yet. He was dreaming of learning the Dark Hunter spell. He was trying so hard. Darel, please, give him one last chance."

"Chris, I . . . I know all this. I haven't forgotten anything, I'll never forget what you have done for me. I'll try it. It's insane, but . . . I'll do my best."

"Thank you." He ran one hand over his forehead, sighed, and gradually changed back into the old imperturbable Chris.

"But a scan that deep will take a lot of time. A month, maybe two. And I'm still not sure that I can do it."

"You can."

"And Loraine . . ."

"I'll take care of her as if she were my own pupil."

Vivian started groaning. I put my hand on his forehead, trying to calm him down.

"Chris, will you be able to preserve his body until I'm finished?"

"Yes, I'll immerse it in . . . Never mind." He took a handkerchief out of his pocket, wiped his hands, and tossed the stained scrap of cotton into the armchair. "Sam, go to the hospital. Collect the entire stock of blood reserved for me. And tell them we'll need the same amount again next week. Take Loraine with you. There's nothing for her to do here at this stage. Darel, come with me."

He pushed me away from the bed, picked up the mutilated Vivian in his arms, and carried him out of the room. I followed him, and on the way I glanced into the library. Loraine jumped to her feet when she saw me.

"Well? What?"

I reached out a hand and pulled her toward me. She gazed into my face anxiously.

"I'm going to try to help him. It will take some time. You'll be staying with Chris. He'll look after you."

"And what about you?"

"I'll be out of circulation for a while. But don't worry, everything will be fine."

"I see." She nodded seriously and touched the shoulder on

which she had the mark of the Cadavercitan. "Only try not to take too long."

"I will."

"Good luck, then."

I bent down, kissed her hard, and let go of her.

Chris was waiting at the entrance to the basement. I was being allowed into the Cadavercitan's holy of holies—his laboratory.

"Come on."

The long stairway led into a spacious, bright hall. It was cold and sterilely clean in there. There were white lamps burning. The floor was covered with tiles, and one of the walls was covered with square hatches, as in a morgue. Several operating tables. Some medical appliances. In the far corner, the transparent glass cabin of an elevator. So there was another space below this one. A smell of disinfectant. The barely audible rustling of an air conditioner.

Vivian was lying on a table, in a transparent tank filled with a yellowish liquid, with only his face visible at the surface. Beside the tank was what looked at first glance like a perfectly comfortable folding chair.

I walked up and leaned down. The young Cadavercitan slowly raised his eyelids and moved slightly, and the oily fluid licked at the glass wall. His eyes were full of pain and entreaty.

"Darel," the black, cracked lips whispered.

"Don't be afraid, I'm going to help you."

Chris stood close by, calm and focused, waiting until I was ready to start working. Without hurrying me.

Now I would not exist for several months. I would become another being. I would feel his joys and suffer his sorrows together with him. Forget everything to do with my own life.

I lowered myself into the chair, made myself comfortable, and reached out to Vivian with my mind.